The Jiangxi Virus

a novel of bioterror

Steven Schlossstein

STRATFORD BOOKS

Library of Congress Control Number: 2002107795
ISBN 0-9627060-2-7

Published by Stratford Books
30 Amberwood Parkway
Ashland, OH 44805
Contact for Order Fulfillment & Distribution
Tel: 800.247.6553
www.atlasbooks.com

Printed in the United States by BookMasters, Inc.
1444 U. S. Route 42
Mansfield, OH 44903
All rights reserved
Tel: 800.537.6727
www.bookmasters.com
Jacket design by Ryan Feasel, Graphic Designer
First edition, first printing, July 2002

For author information, please contact
Mr. Andrew Berzanskis, Senior Publicist
Phenix & Phenix Literary Publicists
2525 West Anderson Lane, Suite 540
Austin, TX 78757
Tel: 512.478.2028, ext. 202
Fax: 512.478.2117
E-mail: Andrew@bookpros.com
www.bookpros.com

This book is dedicated to America's public health workers -- disease detectives, doctors, nurses, lab technicians, and paramedics all across the nation, both in the military and in mufti -- whose courage and selfless dedication will be called upon to defend us in the front lines of any infectious epidemic.

We hope and pray that such a horrible tragedy -- whether natural or man-made -- never darkens our land.

Nations do not have permanent friends,
Nor do they have permanent enemies.
They have only permanent interests.

William Evart Gladstone, 1809-1898
Former British Prime Minister

For a relatively long time, it will be absolutely
necessary that we quietly nurse our sense of
vengeance ... We must conceal our abilities
and bide our time.

Lieutenant General Mi Zhenyu
Vice Commandant, Academy of
Military Sciences, Beijing, 1996

I had a little bird,
Its name was Enza.
I opened up the window,
And in flew Enza.

Macabre skip-rope song,
United States of America, 1918

◦ Prologue ◦

February: mid-winter, on the East China Sea

Colonel Fu Barxu leaned forward against the ship's railing and steadied himself. He focused his heavy field glasses until he found the suspicious speck on the horizon.

A fierce winter wind whipped the East China Sea into angry froth as the massive aircraft carrier plowed effortlessly through the whitecaps. Fu winced as a sharp gust knifed across the broad deck.

Stiffening, Col. Fu adjusted his olive-green cap snugly around his short-cropped silver-white hair. He was tall, well over six feet, and hammer-hard. His eyes, black as coal and unblinking, scanned the cold gray distance like a hawk as the *Zhongguo* steamed south toward the Straits of Taiwan.

The Colonel knew from PLA intel reports that the *USS Nimitz* was illegally patrolling the East China Sea again. The People's Liberation Army was also sending its routine reconnaissance missions over the contested waters. Just months earlier, ships from America's imperialist Pacific Fleet had interfered with China's offshore missile tests by invading the target zone off the coast of its renegade province, Taiwan.

It was another arrogant attempt by the powerful to intimidate the weak. But the colonel knew that China was far from weak now and the *Zhongguo* proved it.

Zhongguo, China's first aircraft carrier and the world's largest, had been commissioned and launched on New Year's day.

Zhongguo.

The Central Kingdom.

Bright red pennants stood stiffly on giant stanchions in the harsh wind, flat against their guy wires as if pressed from steel. On its own recon maneuvers, the big carrier held steady off the coast of southern China, not far from the coastal city of Shanghai. To the northeast lay the peninsula of Korea; due east, Japan.

The ship was huge: five floating acres of sovereign Chinese territory, a massive displacement of 100,000 tons, four football fields from stem to stern. It was 10,000 tons heavier and fifty yards longer than the *USS Enterprise*, flagship of the American fleet. And it was home to a hundred of Beijing's most advanced *Julang* Great Wave JL-8-II twin-jet fighters, the greatest floating air force in the world.

Four state-of-the-art nuclear reactors powered the premier carrier, based on secret American technology covertly acquired from Los Alamos by Chinese spies. It boasted eight advanced Eagle missile launchers and a dozen Sparrow 20mm minigun mounts.

At the dawn of the new century, the *Zhongguo* had finally given China what it had always lacked: true power projection -- menacing, mobile, and fully armed.

Taiwan was China's internal affair, Fu muttered as he tracked the *Nimitz* in the distance. China would deal with the disloyal defectors in its own way, in its own time, on its own terms. Someday, like a petty trespasser, America would pay for its persistent meddling, for its uninvited interference in China's proprietary affairs.

Insensitive and hypocritical, the world's sole superpower continued to hammer China endlessly on American values and human rights. Washington was a tyrant, threatening to deny preferential treatment on trade, constantly harassing Beijing for more openness, more liberalism, more "democracy." To the Colonel, what America viewed as universalism was simply imperialism in disguise.

Zázhong!

Bastards!

It was obnoxious and it was demeaning and it made Fu sick.

His eyes narrowed as he glared at China's adversary across the water.

More than a century ago, drunk with missionary power, American religious zealots had tried to convert the Chinese to Christianity. When they met with only limited success, the Western imperialists then used superior military power to crush the central kingdom.

Like schoolyard bullies, America and Europe had brutally suppressed China, forcing it to become an impoverished prisoner in the West's new colonial empire. The once-proud and powerful central kingdom was carved into powerless pieces.

Enough!

Fu tried to ignore the pain in his fingertips as he refocused the binoculars.

But it was never enough and he knew it.

America's zealots were at it again, trying to subvert China to market forces, free speech and free elections. America flaunted its economic success like the *nouveau riche*, wore its status arrogantly on its sleeve, shoved its dogma in the faces of others with the hypocrisy that they were all inferior to its own narrow notion of grandeur and superiority.

Hushuo!

Nonsense!

Accumulation of wealth and power depended on a delicate balance of give and take. Now Washington had dangerously redefined the age-old equation. It had become a selfish one-way pattern: China has to give, so America can take.

Perched securely atop the peak of success, America kicked away the ladder just as reëmerging nations like China were clearing the bottom rungs. Using its obscene wealth and power to embarrass and weaken, America needed to keep China subservient, to suppress its authoritarian heritage and prevent the central kingdom from regaining its rightful place in the world.

The Colonel's eyes were glued to the hated object, tracking the *Nimitz* as it sailed steadily south on a parallel course. He glanced at the distance gauge and confirmed his hunch.

The Americans were also headed for Taiwan.

But not today.

Not if he could help it.

He reached down and slammed a large orange button.

A split second later there was a massive roar.

Fu spun around to watch a *Julang* Great Wave fighter leap out of its powerful catapult on the flight deck and soar into the flat winter sky. One by one, like clockwork, five sleek black jets blasted off the floating runway.

The squadron screamed overhead, wingtip-to-wingtip in tight formation behind the lead jet, 805. Then they rolled side-to-side and banked above the massive carrier.

Fu tugged on the left lapel of his dark green tunic and pulled it close to his chin.

He barked into the wireless closed-circuit transmitter.

"Engage the enemy."

He watched 805 peel away from the other four and roar toward the distant invader.

Raising his binoculars, Fu brought the *Nimitz* back into focus. Then he growled into his lapel mike again.

"Dash and smash."

In seconds, he saw 805 enter the airspace of the American carrier, its speed heightened through foreshortening.

His lips tightened into a thin smile as he watched the *Julang* jet descend sharply toward the *Nimitz's* command tower. Then it shot into a vertical climb and accelerated over the upper deck.

An instant later, Fu heard the thunder from the sonic boom and his smile broadened into a wide grin.

He couldn't see the direct damage but he knew the *Julang's* powerful twin-jet blast would shatter the glass on more than a few of the enemy carrier's reinforced tower windows and rattle their commander's nerves.

Maybe they'll think twice next time, Fu thought.

Stay the hell out of our territory. We control these waters now.

Above the *Nimitz*, 805 curled up in a sharp arc and accelerated toward home.

Suddenly Col. Fu's smile dissipated like his breath in the frozen air.

A gleaming silver F-18 Hornet had catapulted from the American carrier and was now in hot pursuit.

Fu pulled the lapel mike closer.

"Ready ... cross!" he shouted.

He refocused the binoculars and watched.

Two of the remaining four *Julang* jets reacted instantly and sped toward 805. One rose to an altitude above his returning companion, the other dropped below.

After passing 805, the two outbound fighters drew a bead on the encroaching Hornet.

The top Great Wave jet dropped into a steep dive while the bottom one entered a sharp climb. They crossed each other at Mach-II speed within a wingspan of the American, their timing as precise as a stopwatch.

The American had to pull up sharply and veer to the northwest to evade the Chinese cross, heading away from the *Zhongguo*.

Fu watched the dark tail from the American jet's exhaust as it roared back to its floating base. The two *Julang* fighters circled cautiously and then sped home.

They slowed as they waited for clearance to land. Down first, 805 caught the reinforced rubber and steel restraining device and bounced to a quick stop. The crew pushed it aside like a giant toy as the other four returned to deck in sequence.

Lieutenant General Min Taibao emerged from the control tower and clanked down the gray metal steps. His face was taut, his lips a thin line.

General Min was the second-highest ranking officer in the People's Liberation Army. Short and squat, like a Buddhist priest, his face was normally expressionless, an egg-shaped oval that belied emotion. Inside, he could be ecstatic. Outside, cold as stone.

But today was different.

Fu turned to greet his commanding officer.

"Very risky, Colonel," the general growled. "I know you want to show the barbarians a thing or two, but the next time they stick their damn noses in our business, let's get permission from Beijing first, just to be safe. I can't always arrange for the Admiral to be absent from his ship."

Fu returned his superior's stiff salute.

"I think we could have gotten even tougher today," he said crisply. "All we did was shatter a few panes of glass again. You think that's ever going to stop them?"

"Next time they might not be so lucky."

Col. Fu met the general's gaze head-on.

"Next time, *next time*. What song is that chorus line from? We need a new theme now, with new lyrics -- *this* time."

"You're still angry at the U. S. Navy for the way they humiliated you during the joint exercises last year. Let it go."

"This is no personal vendetta, General. You know I don't let personal feelings dictate my professional behavior. What their military did to me was unfortunate. But what their government is doing to our country is inexcusable."

General Min eyed the colonel carefully.

"We have a long history of success outside the chain of command, my friend, you and I. But sometimes I think you push the envelope too far, too fast."

"And sometimes it seems you don't want to push it much at all. Are we getting a little timid in our old age?"

The general stiffened.

"If I didn't know you better, Fu, I'd say you were after my job. You may be able to jump one rank, but not two. Don't forget, after all we've been through together, I'm still your superior officer."

"So stop whining about Beijing and give me a green light to go after the invaders. We can chase them out of these waters once and for all. Give them a real taste of what's about to come."

"Patience. Time is our ally."

Fu snorted in disgust.

"A convenient crutch. I thought you wanted to punish the Americans while we're still alive to enjoy it. Take down the pretenders in Beijing and teach the imperialists in Washington a lesson."

"I do. That's why I authorized your secret plan to create a covert laboratory in Jiangxi. Tell me the virus is still on schedule."

Fu shrugged.

"It's in Dr. Lukanov's hands."

After the collapse of Soviet communism, Russian scientists began defecting overseas, selling themselves and their dark secrets at high prices. To nations that sponsored terrorism, like Iran and Iraq. To splinters of their former empire, like Uzbekistan. To the growing Russian mafia at home, which thrived on chaos and corruption in Moscow.

Fu had a vision -- that China might be able to profit by investing in this new talent pool.

He knew the Soviets had run a well-disguised and heavily funded program to develop offensive biological weapons in their own hidden laboratories, despite having signed the multilateral agreement to control biological and chemical weapons in 1972.

By 1996, Moscow had successfully weaponized anthrax, tularemia, smallpox, Q fever, and plague, the Black Death of the Middle Ages. Soviet microbiologists had also created an aerosolized weapon that could spread a deadly African filovirus called ebola, a devastating microbe with a 90% kill rate.

After an extensive series of interviews in Moscow, Fu lured the famed Russian virologist Boris Lukanov to help China start its own bioweapons program. The Colonel ran it himself from a clandestine unit in the PLA called Technology Project/Millennium 21.

M/21 was not in the Army's routine-access database. It sat nestled snugly underground at the foot of the Jiulian Shan mountains in Jiangxi province across the border from Guangdong in southern China, well hidden from the intruding eyes of American inspectors and their prying satellite eyes.

Armed and closely guarded, the Jiangxi mission was to formulate a lethal pathogen unlike anything the Russians had ever developed before.

A killer virus that could masquerade as flu and cripple America. Get the barbarians off China's back once and for all.

Min eyed his protégé carefully.

"Time may be our ally, but it is not inexhaustible. I need hard proof that the Russian can do it."

"Like I've said before, General. By summer, not before."

"The Muslims upset our whole timetable," Min said. "We told them not to go through with the suicide attacks on September 11 but they ignored us. Target overseas assets, we said. Distract the Americans and let them believe they're invulnerable at home. *We* will show them just how vulnerable they can be."

A half-smile creased Fu's face.

"Well, the Muslims should really be suffocating now, after we cut off their weapons and their funding. Who do they think they are, disobeying an order from us?"

"They don't think, that's the problem. But they may have made our situation much more difficult because the Americans have tightened internal security far beyond what we imagined they could do."

The rebellious Colonel shook his head.

"I still say the situation works to our advantage. Don't forget, Washington has the Middle East as its prime target now. As a result, we're no longer on their radar screen."

"The American cowards live in constant fear of another attack from those who wear beards, hate life and preach death."

"So let them. This distraction provides precisely the temporary cover we need."

The two renegade officers stood on the upper deck, silhouetted against the dull gray sky and alone as sentries, hands clasped behind their backs. They leaned into the cold wind.

"*Ni chifanle meiyo?*" Min asked, blowing on his hands.

He used the intimate greeting common among friends and relatives, rather than the more conventional *ni hau ma?*

"What's the delay in Jiangxi?"

"You know me," Col. Fu said, still gazing out across the choppy sea. "Results are what matter. Lukanov is brilliant but slow. I need to squeeze him a little."

"So squeeze him. He's expendable, isn't he?"

Fu shrugged again.

"Only after he clones the deadly microbe. None of our people have that expertise."

"Well, keep the pressure on. August will be here before you know it."

"I realize that," Fu said. "But remember, time is not nearly as important as flawless execution."

His voice rose and then died, carried off by the harsh wind.

"Deng Xiaoping is dead," he went on. "President Jiang has become nothing but a puppet of his handlers. Hu Jintao, his anointed successor, is no better. China needs a strong leader now, a man with guts and backbone, someone who can stand up to the meddlesome Americans. Washington has become intolerable after September 11, using freedom and democracy as ill-conceived proxies for their imperialist arrogance."

Jiang Zemin, the President of China and current General Secretary of the Communist Party, had risen to power in the Politburo after Deng died. A former mayor of Shanghai, Jiang inherited Deng's delicate balancing act of keeping China's economy strong while blocking the frustrated throng of unhappy students, intellectuals, and entrepreneurs who agitated the government ceaselessly from within.

The general shook his head.

"But the domestic situation also works in our favor. Like undisciplined children, China's spoiled students and the new rich taunt and needle Beijing to allow more freedom and openness. And just like the Americans they praise, they're impatient and narrow-minded. They've given us a window, a domestic distraction."

Col. Fu turned to spit into the trailing wind.

"The President is completely rudderless," he said. "He's nothing but a fawning member of the *fengpai*, the moronic wind faction. Their principles are weightless and without direction, always changing like the weather. He must go."

"First things first," Min insisted.

He turned to look his trusted confidant in the eye.

"Your virus is critical. To get the Americans off our back, we need a breakthrough from Jiangxi. Otherwise, the barbarians will only get bolder. We can't do anything about the *fengpai* until that virus is ready."

Fu flipped up the collar of his tunic and tightened his wool scarf to shut out the cold.

The hated Americans weren't enough. He had to put up with the General's constant vacillation between too much pressure on his precious schedule and too little pressure on Beijing.

Suddenly a powerful explosion shattered his thoughts.

A shower of seawater sprayed the starboard side of the giant carrier. Colonel Fu tried to shield the general but the spray caught them both.

The *Zhongguo's* automatic alarm system pierced the air with a steady *whoop*.

Fu barked a series of brusque commands into his lapel mike.

PLA cadets streamed onto the upper deck and strapped themselves into their 20mm Sparrow minigun mounts. Orange-helmeted flight crews surged into action below and readied a half-dozen *Julang* fighters for takeoff. Every eye was on the feared Colonel.

Fu pulled a crimson handkerchief from his rear pocket and calmly wiped his field glasses. Then he dried his face, which stung from the cold, turned his skin numb, deadened his cheeks like novocain.

Lifting the binoculars to his eyes, he brought the distant *Nimitz* back into focus.

Lt. Gen. Min trained his own glasses on the enemy ship now.

"If I call Beijing," he said, "General Li may authorize full pursuit."

The noise of the alarm system was piercing.

"With clearance, we can steam forward and you can provoke them."

"No," the rogue Colonel said. "Let's keep this outside the chain of command. They weren't aiming to hit us. That was a dummy warhead. Look at their signal lights."

They watched a blinking comm pulse from the *Nimitz* tower.

Fu's lips moved as he converted the yellow flashes into recognizable words.

"What are they saying?" Min asked.

Proud of his English, Fu translated the cryptic code straight into Mandarin for the general.

"*Buzz... us... again... and... you're... toast...*"

General Min was furious now.

"This is humiliating. They can't even taunt us in our own language. Get another *Julang* squadron ready to jump."

"No, again I say wait," Fu said, pulling his glasses down. "That's what they want us to do. I have a better idea. In all our years of clandestine operations together, have I ever let you down? Watch."

He growled into the closed-circuit wireless lapel mike.

"Blinkers!"

A communications team scrambled quickly onto the upper deck with a portable signal light. They snapped it into place.

Fu scribbled a note and handed it to the comm team.

"Send this response to the American intruders."

They flashed his message back at the *Nimitz*.

"Get... out... of... our... waters... and... take... your... toys... with... you..."

Then Fu barked another command.

"Fire one."

Seconds later, a powerful Eagle surface-to-surface cruise missile exploded from its tunnel mount in the hull below and shot toward the enemy carrier.

Fu and Min watched it speed across the wide gray sea, hovering just yards above the surface. As it neared the *Nimitz*, they saw a flash from the enemy carrier as another missile was launched from the American carrier.

Then a sonic pop.

The two projectiles collided with an enormous blast and a blinding flash of light.

The two senior officers watched a cloud of black exhaust plume from the aft deck of the *Nimitz*.

Its engines had powered up. It was turning east, away from China, steaming back toward its base at Sasebo, in Japan.

General Min lowered his binoculars. He scowled at his protégé.

"That was a really high-risk tactic, my friend. Beijing's going to demand an immediate explanation."

"Well, you can tell Beijing that our missile was also equipped with a dummy warhead, programmed to splash harmlessly short of the target," Fu said, his eyes still glued on the American ship. "To return the insult. The barbarians aren't used to our floating power yet, so they're turning tail now. Be sure to tell that to Beijing, too."

The general was not amused.

"President Jiang will have me on the carpet as soon as Washington expresses its belligerent outrage through their Embassy."

Fu watched the Nimitz grow smaller in the distance. Then he released his binoculars and let them hang from his neck.

The colonel turned to face his mentor.

"President Jiang is on a very short leash now," he said. "His days of fawning are about to end."

He took a deep breath as he gazed out across the choppy ocean. Then he exhaled and stamped his wet feet, stretching his gloved fingers for warmth.

"Remember his prophetic words? *Open the windows, breathe the fresh air and fight the insects!*"

He coughed up a wad of phlegm and turned to spit again into the trailing wind. He shook his head.

"That's when our real problems began," he went on. "As if a great culture like China could ever tolerate Western ideas. That weak and pandering pretender is single-handedly responsible for infecting us with poison from the West."

He cracked a command into his lapel mike and felt the great carrier shudder almost instantly as it picked up speed, accelerating toward Taiwan.

"The *Julang* jets are ready for another flyover," Fu said with a thin smile. "This time we'll shake a few skyscrapers and rattle some windows in downtown Taipei."

The scheming officers watched the powerful aircraft queue for takeoff.

"Taipei turnaround," the Colonel barked into his transmitter.

One after another, the shiny black Great Wave fighters sprang from the flight deck catapult and shot south. Fu knew the squadron would be gone only long enough to break the sound barrier over the renegade island and remind the Taipei traitors who's in charge.

As the last fighter disappeared from view, Fu's thoughts turned to President Jiang and the obsequious *fengpai* in Beijing. He gripped the railing and grimaced as he thought about how weak and impoverished China's political leadership had become.

To Col. Fu, this was the deadliest fate of all: that Western insects would infect China with unrealistic ideas, letting loose a Pandora's box of illogical and unattainable demands for openness and democracy and freedom.

Before he knew it, two shrill blasts from the *Zhongguo's* powerful horn broke the silence.

Fu and Min spun and watched as the small squadron of black jets returned home.

They screeched to a halt on the broad foredeck, mission accomplished.

The general frowned.

"Well, my friend, I expect the corrupt Nationalists on Taiwan will also lodge a loud protest through their liaison office in Beijing."

"So let them, Fu said. "Their days are numbered, too."

"Was that really necessary, on the heels of the Americans' retreat?"

Col. Fu held his thumb and forefinger a half-inch apart.

"We are this close to having the virus," he said. "So yes, it was necessary. We've got to keep the pressure on. Soon neither Taiwan nor the United States will ever be able to challenge us again."

He took a deep breath. Then he commanded the engine room to reverse course and turn the giant ship north. Back to its home port of Pudong in Shanghai.

Turning to face his mentor, Fu crossed his arms.

"The new century is here," he said. "China's wealth and power are being redefined. Our economy is already being called the Next Japan and will be the second largest in the world by 2010. Nearly twenty of our DF-5 nuclear missiles now target continental America, along with more than 100 ABM interceptors."

He ticked the points off on his fingertips.

"Our regional position is secure. We recovered the Spratly Islands because Vietnam was too weak to challenge us. Then when America abandoned its bases at Subic Bay and Clark Field, we took Mischief Island and dared Manila to stop us. Now we have limitless oil deposits in the South China Sea."

Col. Fu rolled his fingers into a fist.

"But the best is still to come," he went on excitedly. "Hong Kong has returned to the motherland and the Portuguese colony of Macau is again ours. We have erased these two cruel blemishes on our past and can greet the new millennium with confidence. Taiwan will fall into our hands like a ripe fruit once we weaken the United States and eliminate the arrogant hypocrites as a hostile adversary."

They clanked up the metal stairs toward the conning tower.

"All the more reason the Jiangxi virus must not fail," Min cautioned. "America must be taught that interference in China's internal affairs cannot be tolerated. The Muslim extremists think they have a case against the United States, but they're only meaningless shadows. We control an entire population more powerful than all the Muslims in all of their corrupt desert kingdoms put together. Mark my words: China and America will fight the real war in this century."

The Colonel stopped and pulled himself erect.

"The pathetic Americans dare to challenge us. Guns and violence rule their people. Drugs control their cities. Children kill children in their schools. Fueled by greed, shameless artificial wealth props up one extreme of their society while homelessness and poverty ravage the other. Racial prejudice festers in their soil. *Imagine!* A decadent nation in decline telling an ascendant China how to behave."

"*Lu fen dan, biaomian guang!*" Min said.

Then he roared with laughter.

On the outside, even donkey shit shines.

Fu's dark eyes burned with fury. He clenched his fist and hammered the railing.

"President Jiang and the *fengpai* tolerate this disgusting nonsense. Fawning to foreigners, they kowtow to the West. But it's they who will soon kowtow to us. America is the only remaining obstacle to China's rightful place in the world. Vengeance is long overdue."

The general nodded, his face sober.

"Rulers lose the mandate of heaven because they fail the virtue of their ancestors. Our time is coming."

Fu composed himself, took a deep breath and eyed his mentor.

"I assure you, the Jiangxi virus is on course," he said. "But I'll turn up the heat on Lukanov."

The general frowned again.

"I'm giving you six months," he said. "No more."

The rogue Colonel crossed his arms.

"If you're so worried, why don't you come down to Jiangxi and see for yourself? August is cool and beautiful in the mountains."

Min's eyes grew wide.

"That's an excellent idea," he said without hesitation. "Count on it."

∘ **1** ∘

Late August: summer in New Mexico

A lean, dark-haired woman barely five feet tall led a team of CDC investigators off the small plane and onto the baking tarmac of Albuquerque airport.

Waves of late summer heat shimmered off the soft black tar and hung in the air like an invisible curtain. Breath came in short gasps. Albuquerque is a mile-high desert.

The Centers for Disease Control and Prevention was like the FBI for disease. Whenever unexplained deaths happened, CDC got the call.

Unexplained deaths were just what had hit Taos, New Mexico. Young Navajo Indians were fit and healthy one day, dead the next. Nobody had a hint of a reason yet.

The mortality rate -- the number dying among those with symptoms -- was nearly 50%. Fifty-three sick, twenty-seven dead. One out of two.

This was too much for Jimmy Arroyo, the director of Indian Health Services on the reservation, too mysterious for New Mexico's Department of Health, too spooky even for the state Medical Examiner.

This was a case for the disease detectives.

Ellen Chou saw the DOH/CDC card on the windshield and walked briskly to the waiting car.

She lugged a brown leather briefcase full of memos, faxes, and e-mails in one hand, a navy canvas overnight bag with her initials in block letters in the other. She'd read the reports from Taos on the flight down and she was deeply worried.

She'd seen nothing like it in nearly two decades of tracking down death. They needed more details on the index case -- the first person to be ID'd with symptoms -- but that would have to wait until they got north.

Ellen Chou was first Asian-American ever to head the CDC's Department of Emerging Infectious Diseases. She was a crack epidemiologist. An epi. The best disease detective on the force.

She was on the case when the lab pros at CDC headquarters in Atlanta couldn't decipher the evidence with enough confidence to know whether the cause of a mysterious disease was a toxic substance, a new bacterium, or an unknown virus.

Ellen had a sixth sense, a unique ability to cut through the CDC's turf wars, the interdisciplinary bickering, the bureaucratic backpedaling. Orphaned at an early age, she had learned the hard way to get results. People routinely tried to dominate her but they rarely made that mistake twice. They thought size mattered, but she taught them otherwise. Skepticism and stubbornness were her twin pillars of faith.

There was a popular perception that infectious diseases were finally under control at the dawn of the new century in America.

Smallpox was gone. Polio and tuberculosis were rare. Diphtheria, chicken pox, measles, mumps, all had been brought under control by new childhood vaccines. Even the pesky flu, the most mutant of viruses that caused epidemics every winter, had been tamed by a trivalent vaccine.

But Ellen and her CDC teammates knew better.

Changes in the environment caused pathogens to mutate. New viruses came out of nowhere to strike without warning. Old bacteria adapted to popular antibiotics and emerged stronger and even more deadly, like microbial Frankensteins, resistant to antibiotic treatment.

Legionnaires' disease, Philadelphia, 1976. New methods of genetic detection based on DNA sequencing had uncovered previously unknown viruses.

Ebola Reston, Virginia, 1990. Advanced technologies had revealed otherwise invisible adversaries like ebola, an hemorrhagic African filovirus, long thought to be dormant or dead.

West Nile virus, New York, 1999. Encephalitis-bearing mosquitoes seen before only in Africa had invaded the East Coast after hatching in stale water in shiploads of old tires from the Mediterranean.

Anthrax-by-mail, Washington, 2001. In the aftermath of the audacious attacks by suicide bombers on 9/11, militant extremists from the Middle East leapt to the top of the FBI's list of prime suspects.

Life was a constant battle between man and microbe, a zero-sum game of survival. In Ellen's world, there were only winners and losers.

She squeezed into the back seat of a late-model dust-covered lemon-yellow Taurus between Rakesh Gupta, a bacteriologist, and

Antonio Higueras, a toxicologist. Jonathan Feldman, a virologist from
her own division, sat up front. Disease was still predominantly a
man's world.

The driver nosed out the airport exit and wove through the
late afternoon traffic, speeding up as he turned onto I-25. It would
take them north to Santa Fe and beyond, to the village of Taos.

Ellen dragged a sleeve of her maroon reverse terry sweatshirt
across her forehead and then wiped her sweaty palms on the thighs of
her stonewashed jeans that were already damp from the oppressive
heat.

Unexplained deaths always made her hands sweat. Clusters
of unexplained deaths made her worry, invoking the epi's mantra.

If you hear hoofbeats, think zebras, not horses.

"So what are you guys thinking?" she asked. She crammed
her leather briefcase between her legs. "You were stone silent the
whole flight down."

Higueras leaned his slight frame forward.

He had thick, dark hair slicked back with gel in a single wave.
Small, deep-set eyes, like olive pits, framed his smooth face. A San
Antonio *barrio* survivor, Higueras had death as a constant
neighborhood companion. When he left Texas for Harvard, he never
once looked back.

"There's not enough evidence from the Indian Health Service,"
he said with a shrug. "I haven't seen any biopsy samples yet, so how
can I say?"

To Ellen's left, Gupta stared out his window and smiled.

"Tony, you always say you never have enough evidence. You
think your damn Harvard degree makes you so special, turns you into
a licensed no-comment fence-sitter."

Bright and contentious, from Bombay by way of Columbia
Med School, Rakesh loved big cities. He hated anyplace that wasn't
either paved or open 24/7. He had perfect teeth and a natural smile,
the kind that could make millions in chewing gum ads. It lit up his
chocolate complexion but masked an iron will.

"Besides," he said, tossing his head at the dusty landscape, "it
wouldn't surprise me if we find some totally new bugs under those
rocks. From the reports, this thing's got virus written all over it.
Bacteria hate dry heat."

"Yeah, right," Feldman broke in.

Whirling from the front seat, he leaned across Ellen and jabbed a finger at the Indian's chest.

"You guys with your coke-bottle lenses just *love* to pick on us virologists. We've got the sexy sub-micron organisms for sure, and with your dipshit high-school microscopes you can't see anything but big ugly bacteria so you just toss the unknowns in our laps. Do you have *any* idea how tedious that gets?"

Thick biceps rippled beneath Feldman's frayed cardinal-red T-shirt. Brooklyn-born and street-smart, he had done his medical work at Stanford and had a post-doc from Carnegie-Mellon. Stringy salt-and-pepper hair swept back from a receding hairline that disguised his youthful looks.

His mantra was, stay cool unless provoked. And Rakesh Gupta always managed to provoke him.

The Indian took Feldman's strong arm and tried to twist it back. Higueras reached in to pull them apart.

"That's enough," Ellen broke in.

"Go back to basics," Higueras hissed.

"Go back to med school!" Gupta fired back.

"Go back to India," snorted Feldman.

"*Idiot.*"

"*Moron.*"

"*Retard.*"

"I said, that's enough!" Ellen barked.

Her voice was stern now. Zero tolerance.

The three technical rivals pulled away and sat mute, staring out their own windows.

"Look," she said. "I thought we settled this on the plane. You can hang out all the dirty laundry you want when you're alone, but once we hit Taos you better all be on the same page."

"He started it."

It was Higueras, angling his head at Gupta.

"Yeah, well, Tony's always on the fence, won't ever make the call," the Indian countered. "And Feldman's so damned defensive, he thinks he's never wrong."

"You're both so full of hot air," Feldman said with disgust.

He crossed his arms and slumped down in his seat.

Ellen cut the diatribe by slicing the air with both hands.

"*Enough!* Keep it up and all three of you will be on the next plane back to Atlanta. Period, full stop."

The car was suddenly quiet again.

She hated this petty bickering, the constant catfights, the never-ending tension and stress that came uninvited whenever mysterious diseases caused sudden epidemics to break out.

They had no idea what they were heading into.

Disease detectives never did.

○ **2** ○

Wang Wei double-clutched the small Army truck as he accelerated up a steep hill outside Wuhua in eastern Guangdong province, just across the border from Jiangxi.

He was ecstatic.

The tireless Colonel had chosen *him* to take his load of prize birds to Hong Kong!

He had served Col. Fu with loyalty and dedication, looked after his flock, tended his livestock, fetched his supplies like clockwork. Now he was sitting behind the wheel of an official PLA pickup with a load of ducks and chickens for the wet market in the old Colony.

What an honor!

He rolled down the window halfway and spit. Half the glob caught on the glass. Wang rubbed it off with his jacket sleeve, then dragged the sleeve across his forehead to mop off the summer sweat.

He sneezed twice, rapid-fire, straight ahead. Millions of microdroplets covered the steering wheel, the dashboard, the windshield. The hell with this dust, he thought. Late August in Guangdong was hot and dry, not like the cool damp foothills of his beloved Jiangxi.

Col. Fu told him to take the back roads, stay off the main highway and stick to the one-lane laterite. Wang bounced ahead as fast as he could on the washboard surface, enveloped in a cloud of red grit.

Then he heard the mesh gate banging against the back bumper again.

Damn! Another nuisance.

He stopped, adjusted the wooden cages, checked the latches, refastened the gate. They were all flecked with bird dung from the rough ride. He wiped his hands on a clump of broadleaf weeds nearby and then on the seat of his frayed cotton pants to dry them.

Col. Fu had selected him just the day before to drive the first birds to market from the Army's special Technology Project. He was beside himself with joy.

Sure, he had a birth defect; he'd been born with only one ear and had paid for it big-time in school. Crazy lop-ear, they called him. Earless. *Dumb.*

Well, he wasn't dumb, he was just handicapped. That's why he worked extra hard to prove how good he could be. And that's why Col. Fu chose him over the others.

Even over Lo Fengbu, the Colonel's quiet assistant.

Everybody knew that Lo was a famous dissident, incarcerated in Fu's laboratory now instead of the *laogai* labor camp. So the Colonel couldn't send him anywhere. Too risky.

And nobody else took the care or paid the close attention to detail that Wang Wei did. When the M/21 Technology Project opened and he'd passed the Colonel's strict security clearance flawlessly, he knew he finally had the job of his life.

Wang shifted again as the truck careened down the hillside and onto a stretch of flat road. He sped up.

He'd show the Colonel another thing or two. He'd get his damn birds to the Fo Tan market in Sha Tin well ahead of time and have the proprietor's time-stamp on the receipt to prove it.

He was capable of a lot more than driving a dilapidated *changpeng* through the lifeless backcountry of Guangdong. This province was so cursed it had a language nobody else could understand.

Wang Wei coughed into a fist and pulled a pack of Red Star cigarettes from his jacket pocket. He squeezed it. Only one smoke left. Have to puff this one long and slow, he thought, suck it gently like a young breast.

He looked at his watch.

Well, if he kept moving, maybe he'd have time for that too. Col. Fu had given him a little extra cash for food and fuel. He could make do with a bowl of noodles, fill the tank halfway and have just enough left for a body massage.

He pressed the accelerator, hard.

If he wanted to make the border crossing at Shenzhen by mid-afternoon, he'd have to fly like the wind.

○ **3** ○

Ellen gazed forward through the windshield between Feldman and the driver, stared at the flat, arid landscape, pockmarked with cactus and wilting Mesquite.

In the distance she saw the soft, pastel hues of distant mesas against the horizon. Their angular shapes disappeared into the oven-hot azure sky.

She was no stranger to the desert. It was a familiar landscape that brought back so many painful memories.

Ellen Chou was born in Chengdu, capital of the arid province of Sichuan, known for its hot peppers and spirited people. Her given name was Chou Ei-lin: Eternal Brightness of the Chou family. Her father was a merchant from a long line of merchants who ran a small store in Chengdu that sold canned goods when he could get them.

She'd been the family's first-born, which meant trouble.

China had a one-family, one-child policy set by Beijing and strictly enforced. After Mao's Great Leap Forward, China's population had exploded far beyond the State's ability to cope. Drastic times called for drastic measures, so the government mandated family planning and rationed children like fuel.

Ellen's parents loved their first-born. But she was a girl, so they had to keep her secret and hidden. Because families with girls were scorned.

Everybody wanted a boy first. Boys inherited everything, girls got nothing. Even Mao's revolution couldn't stop this age-old tradition. The Mandarins were all men, so it was natural for Confucius to mandate male primogeniture.

But proud parents talk, and even when swearing secrecy, friends talk too.

Ellen was barely six when her little brother was born. His birth was registered with the Chengdu office of central records as the Chou's first child. Before long, two rock-hard thugs from the Public Security Bureau paid the Chous a visit.

They wanted to see the new baby. They had to chop his birth record.

And they demanded to see the girl.

At first the Chous denied her existence. Perhaps the PSB had them confused with another family, they said. Maybe the rice miller. Or the blacksmith. The new baby screamed in his mother's arms while the two thugs searched their tiny house in vain.

We'll be back, they said. And next time, you better give up the girl.

The mere mention of the notorious Public Security Bureau was enough to bring tears to their eyes. PSB goons routinely trashed human rights, bullies who knew they were exempt from the law. They dragged suspects away without warrants to be sentenced without trial. They jailed innocent detainees with hardened criminals and let the convicts beat them so the police could truthfully say they kept hands off.

Adults feared them like children feared the dark.

Ellen's parents were heartsick.

Chairman Mao's Cultural Revolution was in high gear at the time and the Red Brigades were on a rampage. Someone in the neighborhood had been pressured into giving her up, if only to save their own.

The State police goons were right. They would come back for her next time and when they found her, they would take her to a distant orphanage, find a foster mother for the new baby, and punish both parents by sending them to a *laogai* for reeducation.

China's answer to the Soviet gulag, the *laogai* were harsh, repressive labor camps that few survived. Physical torture was never necessary. The conditions alone were torture enough.

Despite her mother's desperate pleas, her father took her south to a cousin in Guangzhou and paid a small fortune in *yuan* to smuggle her through the underground network to Hong Kong.

The cousin had a sister in Kowloon; she would take Ellen to a brother in San Francisco; he would see that she could be legally adopted into a new family. Tears streamed down her father's face when he said goodbye for the last time and disappeared, never to see her again.

Ei-lin had been scared to death, her tiny, dark eyes wide with fear. She was told that she would stay with relatives while her mother recovered from the baby's birth. But instinct told her something was very wrong.

Her mother wasn't sick. Neither was the baby.

It was she. *She* was the problem. Something was going to happen to *her*.

Ellen closed her eyes now and leaned back as the underpowered Taurus began its slow climb toward the old capital city of Santa Fe. The tires hummed with a sonorous pitch on the smooth pavement. The air became thinner and drier.

She swallowed. Her throat felt like sandpaper.

Ellen remembered the day she escaped from China as if it were yesterday.

Late at night in a cold autumn drizzle, her cousin took her to the isolated coastal village of Pinghai on the South China Sea. They hid in a field of wet reeds, and while they waited he explained the plan. She didn't believe a word of it. She was tired and wet and hungry and thirsty and afraid.

He pressed a lump of sticky *bao* into her left hand but she was too frightened to eat. She stared at the little bun and clutched it in her palm like a good-luck charm.

Minutes dissolved into hours. Her little hands went numb. Shivering, she tried to revive them by clapping but her cousin had to stop her because of the noise. Finally, when she was about to collapse from exhaustion, she saw a blinking blue light in the distance, bobbing on the surface of the sea.

Without a word, her cousin tucked her under his arm and swam straight to the signal. She was trembling, soaked through and blue with cold, but made no noise when strong hands swept her aboard and wrapped her in a warm blanket.

Then her cousin was gone, the light was gone, and they were speeding toward Kowloon in a powerful boat with a muffled engine. The *bao* was still a charmed lump in her hand.

After a few days' rest, she flew to America with her aunt.

The yelling and shouting at San Francisco airport terrified her. Everyone was screaming in a cacophonous, sing-song Cantonese dialect, not in her native Mandarin. That night she was alone in a house with other small children as scared and clueless as she. But it wasn't long before a tall, sandy-haired man named William Evert Hartley came to claim her as his daughter and he took her to Dallas to start a new life.

And Ei-lin became Ellen.

The ensuing years went by in a flash. Her adoptive father had been a doctor, a brilliant heart specialist, and she knew by the time she was twelve or thirteen that she wanted to be a doctor too. Her new father's wife had died of cancer early in their marriage and he had not remarried; medicine became his sole passion. She saw the pride he took in his work and the magic he brought to his patients' lives.

But Bill Hartley complained constantly about his stubborn patients. They continued to smoke and drink to excess, they always overate, they never exercised. They wouldn't *listen*, he said, and as a result they were ruining their lives. What good was a doctor if his patients didn't take his advice?

So Ellen dedicated her professional life to public health. She studied microbiology at the University of Texas and earned her medical degree at Johns Hopkins, specializing in virology. After an internship at Columbia Presbyterian in Manhattan, she took a Ph.D. in epidemiology and public health at the University of California in Berkeley.

Every month she received a letter from Sichuan with news of her birthparents and her little brother. Every month she replied with news of her own.

The letters went from Dallas to San Francisco to Hong Kong to Guangzhou to Chengdu and back again, in anonymous, hand-printed envelopes each step of the way to shield them from the PSB.

Ellen often said she had the best of both worlds: an unflagging attention to detail from the patience and persistence of Confucius fused with the assertive individualism of her adopted country. She decided to retain her given family name when she buried her father in Dallas and had to face the future alone.

Ellen sat up and blinked away the memories as she felt the car bounce into a parking lot at the Department of Health in Santa Fe.

She glanced at her watch. It was already late afternoon.

∘ 4 ∘

Col. Fu Barxu stood at the high, wide window, his arms crossed, his back to the rows of beakers, pipettes, and microwells that covered the two large workbenches in his lab.

His thoughts shot back to the day nearly three decades before when Captain Min Taibao came to his isolated village of Puqi in Hubei province, soliciting young recruits for the People's Liberation Army.

It was a time of chaos in China. The Cultural Revolution had unleashed a torrent of anger as the Red Guards flooded the country, waving their little Red Books, mindlessly quoting Chairman Mao, thoughtlessly loyal to the Great Helmsman.

Few escaped their wrath. They judged by fiat, dragging suspected counter-revolutionaries from their homes. They sent others to the *laogai* camps without trial. They tortured and brutally murdered scores of political opponents.

But the PLA escaped the Red Guards because trusted survivors of Mao's Long March ran the Army with drum-tight discipline and their officers obeyed orders with unflinching dedication. They were loyal leaders and above suspicion.

So when Captain Min gave his fiery speech to Fu Barxu's tiny high school class, Fu was hooked. For the first time in his short life he saw a way out.

His parents were vegetable farmers who barely eked a living from the hard, rocky Hubei soil. They were too poor to afford the meager tuition required by the top prep school in Wuhan, which groomed Hubei's best students for China's best universities. Fu was stuck in a dusty, nowhere village, his life a permanent dead-end.

He lived in a tiny, one-room hut with a dirt floor and a leaky cracked-tile roof. A single incandescent bulb was their sole claim to modernization. The cabin was drafty in winter, suffocating in summer, and under the constant threat of typhus, cholera, or tuberculosis. Fu was more likely to be ravaged by dysentery, malaria, or rotting teeth than he was to survive and work the parched farms.

Fu Barxu grasped the opportunity of a lifetime and never looked back.

The PLA brought him to Beijing with thousands of other young recruits to be tested, evaluated, and stretched. Some failed.

Many dropped out. Fu flourished. There was something about this young man, something more than a high IQ. Something dedicated, something *hard*.

Min took Fu under his wing and mentored him throughout training. When Fu graduated at the head of his class from the prestigious Dengshen Military Academy, China's West Point, few were surprised. Over the years their relationship grew as close as father and son.

And their covert collaboration grew, too, year by year.

The encrypted satellite phone buzzed and broke his thoughts.

Fu picked up.

It was General Min.

The Colonel listened for a long minute. Then he gave his commanding officer a status update.

"Wang Wei is on his way to the Special Administrative Region as we speak. We'll know within the next few days if our Hong Kong experiment will succeed. If it does, then we can finally put the endgame in play."

The Colonel listened to the same questions again, heard the same refrain.

"So *what* if a few people die in Hong Kong? You know yourself they aren't true Chinese. They're aliens, products of British colonialism, descendants of more than a century and a half of corrupt decadence and oppressive Western imperialism! This is not the time to be humanitarian, General."

Still, his commanding officer reminded him of their tight schedule.

"I know time is critical," Col. Fu said. "But we're on *track*, I tell you. You've seen all the reports from the countless experiments we've done on these birds. And they all confirm the potency of the Jiangxi virus. We'll soon know if it can infect humans."

He listened for another long moment. Then he shook his head.

"That's absurd. Push the *fengpai* to lean on the China Lobby!"

Through its extensive network of covert overseas affiliates, the PLA funded Washington lobbyists for America's largest and most powerful corporations: General Electric, AT&T, Boeing, Microsoft, IBM. Companies that needed approvals from Beijing for new projects to expand their investments in China. Companies that needed official pink slips to buy dollars. Companies that readily complied when

Beijing threatened to withhold its approvals unless they made their political influence felt in Washington.

Fu frowned.

"Well, why not? The PLA has the best Congress money can buy."

His grip on the receiver tightened as he listened to the General's response. His lips straightened into a thin line and his eyes narrowed.

"Yes, sir. I understand. You'll hear from me as soon as I confirm with the adjutant on Stonecutter's Island. A full briefing will be ready for your visit."

Fu slammed the receiver into its cradle.

Instead of using the powerful China Lobby, the *fengpai* in Beijing had chosen to coddle Washington again. President Jiang Zemin had collapsed like an airless balloon, agreeing to still more human rights demands and granting America special economic incentives in exchange for trade concessions.

This would simply weaken China's internal security even further. It was not a good sign.

The President had agreed to lead a high-level State delegation from Beijing to San Francisco in a month to sign a new agreement with the hated Americans. This meant that another high-profile dissident would have to be released from the *laogai* as a gesture to the West.

And China would be humiliated again.

Fu was furious.

He knew President Jiang was hopeless. What's worse, General Min was getting even more impatient. But they had to stick with the Jiangxi plan and not be rushed, not panic, even if the decrepit politicians *were* wetting their pants like babies.

Fu turned to the Russian scientist and asked him again.

"You're *sure* you can guarantee the results?"

"*Da*," he said with a shrug. "Unquestionably. I stake my reputation on it. Is why you pay me."

The burly virologist looked up from his microscope and pushed a pair of clear goggles onto his head.

Thick black hair framed a long oval face and merged with an unkempt beard streaked in gray. The beard joined more hair down his wide neck and disappeared beneath the starched white collar of his lab coat. His dark eyes were pits of coal sunk deep in purple sockets, unmistakable signs of pressure and fatigue.

Boris Lukanov was Fu's prize catch. After Moscow and Washington signed the Biological and Chemical Weapons Convention in 1972, the Americans predictably stopped work on offensive bioweapons development. But the Russians kept working in secret.

By the mid-1990s, after Soviet Communism had collapsed and the Russian economy was on life-support, Moscow had no choice but to shut down its two-dozen hidden biowarfare installations, including Smutninsk, Sverdlovsk, and Stepnogorsk. These secret facilities had developed advanced bioweapons research and production capabilities for a wide range of lethal pathogens: smallpox, ebola, Q fever, Lassa, anthrax, plague.

Russian scientists who had developed the Soviet bioweapons program were now out of work. They started accepting attractive offers for their skills from countries that were covertly (or overtly) sponsors of terrorism against the Western capitalist devils -- Iraq, Iran, Syria, North Korea, Sudan. Slowly and methodically they sold their talents, their hardware, and their black-box know-how to the highest bidders.

Iraq had acquired the largest number of jobless Russian biospecialists. They helped Baghdad arm a half-dozen Scud missiles with warheads containing aerosolized anthrax by the onset of the Gulf War, prompting an aggressive UN inspection program in retaliation.

But Washington had made it patently clear to Saddam Hussein: you even *think* about using one of your bio-Scuds against our troops and Baghdad is toast.

Col. Fu had been a lot smarter.

He knew the West would be watching these countries like hawks. He also knew they would target known pathogens like smallpox and anthrax because they had strong defensive countermeasures against them.

Fu's vision was a new and previously undeveloped bioweapon, one that hinged on the fabrication of a totally new virus. A fatal microbe that had its natural host in birds but no previous history of infection in humans. One that would never even cause a blip on Washington's radar screen.

Fu wanted something new, something special.

He needed a virus that could be easily disguised, a lethal pathogen that would at first blush look like nothing more than the common cold or innocent influenza but would covertly and savagely decimate its human victims.

He wanted nothing less than a killer flu.

∘ 5 ∘

When Ellen glanced to her left, she saw a small media army camped near the Department of Health.

The reporters looked ready to attack, mikes held shoulder-high like potato grenades. Empty Styrofoam cups were scattered at their feet as they stood in a cloud of cigarette smoke. Saucer-like antennas rotated slowly atop their vans, satellite dishes poised to transmit.

Ellen's small, mahogany eyes narrowed as Jonathan Feldman spun around in his seat.

"Are you thinking what I'm thinking?" he asked.

She nodded.

"The last thing we need this early in the game is a media circus. The press is always ready to stir the pot with rumors and uninformed hypothesis. Facts turn into road kill at the altar of the sound bite."

"You got that right."

Then she grimaced.

"Uh-oh, there's Mitch Webster of CBS. Lord help us."

"Didn't you tangle with him on that case up in Montana?"

She nodded again.

"There was a vicious outbreak of *e.coli* that had paralyzed a little town called Dry Gulch. I spoke to Webster off the record and not for attribution. But he went live with my data and left me hanging in the wind. He doesn't know it yet, but he's getting dick from us today. You guys hustle on inside, I'll take care of Webster."

She smiled as she recognized his immaculately coiffed blond hair, his custom-made midnight-blue silk blazer with the ubiquitous CBS eye on the breast pocket, the stiffly starched Egyptian cotton powder-blue spread-collar shirt with French cuffs and logo cufflinks, his wrinkle-free ivory linen slacks with a crease that would make a military man proud, his hand-sewn Ferragamo calfskin loafers with the unique microfiber tassels that told everybody this dude bought nothing off the shelf.

Ellen had the driver pull up so her three colleagues could bolt inside. As the car slowed to a stop, the throng of reporters, photographers, and newscasters rushed toward her as soon as they saw the DOH/CDC placard in the windshield.

Klieg lights burst on and bathed the yellow Taurus in a wash of blinding light. Photographers snapped at everything. The saucer antennas rose high above their transmit vans and started spinning like toy tops.

There was a crush as the small army jostled and elbowed its way toward the car, Webster in front, picking his way forward carefully to preserve his crisp look. He trailed a crew of assistants in his wake like dust kittens.

Ellen raised both hands above her head, palms out, to stop them.

"There's only one person who's going to comment on this investigation," she said. "That's Dr. Jimmy Arroyo, director of the Indian Health Service in Taos. He -- "

They peppered her immediately with questions like machine-gun fire.

"How many more victims today, Dr. Chou?"

"When will you have a positive ID on the disease?"

"Why can't the medical staff make faster progress?"

Ellen cut them all off with a wave and a glare.

"We're seeing Dr. Arroyo and his staff right away. The CDC will be working around the clock on this problem. When a statement's ready, Arroyo will give it to you."

With that, she knifed through the crowd toward the squat, single-story, adobe brick building. The press pirates eased back to let her through. They continued to lob questions over her head in a desperate attempt to get something, anything, for the nightly news.

But Ellen knew from experience that medical mysteries always took longer to solve when there wasn't a single person with sole responsibility for the media. In an age of suburban smugness, she also knew Americans liked their news cut and dried. It was about the only way they paid attention.

She was almost to the door when the midnight-blue arm dropped like a barrier gate and blocked her way. More lights exploded above them as Webster's CBS crew jockeyed into position.

"Not so fast, Ellen. You owe us more than that. We can't go back with nothing."

Ellen turned and stared straight into the cosmetically correct face. Behind his shoulder she saw the blinking red lights. Cameras were rolling, mikes were live.

She shook her head.

"Yeah, right. Give us a break, Webster. You want to talk, cut the feed first."

Mitch Webster didn't move.

"I said, cut it. We don't owe you, you owe us. You want to talk, we'll talk, but not on tape."

He angled his head and sliced a finger across his throat.

Cameras dropped, mikes clicked off, lights went dark.

Ellen stood facing him, hands on hips.

"So what's your beef, Webster?" she asked. "How is it you guys with the national news always make us feel like wimps, like -- like we work for you instead of the other way around?"

"We have an obligation -- "

"To report the facts," Ellen interrupted. "Let's see, how long has it been since Edward R. Murrow set the broadcast standard? Fifty years? Sixty? It's been straight downhill for your network ever since."

"You want us to make something up tonight?" Webster asked, his tone heavy with sarcasm.

The CBS crew pressed forward again. They smelled a fight.

"You'll do that anyway," Ellen said with a shrug, "regardless of what we tell you. I'm talking about trust here, Mitch. It's just not in your vocabulary."

"Look, I know Montana was unfair. But sometimes we have to bend the rules."

"Yeah, right. Like the hatchet job your *60 Minutes* crew did on CDC after the anthrax cases broke in New Jersey. Well, if you want to play with fire, fine, but if you do, you're going to get burned."

"That was a public health hazard," Webster squawked, "and your people were dragging their heels. Colorado ID'd the virus first."

"*After* we put a specialist in their lab," Ellen said, jabbing a thumb and forefinger at his chest. "You know we can't go public with half-truths. I saw your segment and it sucked big-time. Pieces of B-roll taped earlier and spliced into the final version to look continuous. Taped interviews chopped up to take our comments out of context. Responses to specific questions spliced after other questions totally unrelated. All to give CBS the proper tone of arrogance that attracts big bucks from your advertisers to keep your ratings up. It's sick, Webster, and you're just a symptom of the damn disease."

There was a stunned silence in the small crowd. Other newscasters, sensing a coup, pressed up against the CBS crew now, edging in to listen.

"You know I don't work for Mike Wallace," Webster said.

His voice was softer and less pushy now, more compliant.

"You can't hold me personally responsible for what they did."

Ellen shook her head and stood her ground.

"That's nonsense, Webster, and you know it. It's the same corrupt news division, so don't try to put your personal spin on it. Like I said, you'll get something as soon as we have it. But it won't be me, it'll be Arroyo, because you've got zero credibility in Atlanta now so you might as well go pound sand."

Mitch Webster looked down at Ellen Chou for a long minute.

He realized he'd have to go away empty-handed and make do with filler tonight. No amount of special pleading was going to save his ass now.

He dropped his arm and stepped back. Ellen disappeared into the building.

That night the *Albuquerque News* hawked the local outbreak with a bold, 72-point banner headline on its front page.

Navajo Plague Attacks New Mexico.

∘ **6** ∘

Wang Wei sat in his pickup truck at the border crossing in Shenzhen, drumming his fingers on the wheel, gunning the engine, alternately inching forward and idling, breathing exhaust fumes from the long line of vans, trucks, and buses waiting for clearance into Hong Kong.

He sneezed again. If it wasn't the dust, he thought, it was the filthy exhaust gases. He dragged a sleeve across his mouth and wiped his nose.

Wang shot a glance at his watch.

Good. He'd made excellent time across the flat basin of central Guangdong, so he was still okay. But he couldn't waste any more time sitting in line, he thought.

He stuck his head out the window, cleared his throat and spit.

Glancing ahead, he saw the red-and-white striped guardrail rise and watched another truck roll through. Shouldn't be too long now.

He leaned on his horn and yelled at the container load in front of him. A dark, thick cloud of diesel exhaust plumed from its tailpipe and billowed over Wang's truck. Coughing, he pulled ahead.

Maybe it was the mid-afternoon break or maybe some of the commercial drivers were bribing customs again, but suddenly the line began to move faster and he was the next to go.

Wang handed Col. Fu's special pass to a uniformed border guard and glanced in his rear-view mirror at another guard inspecting the birds in back. A little too closely, he thought.

"What's so special about this load?" the uniform asked with a frown.

He eyed the barnyard fowl in back.

"Quite unusual to have senior Army clearance for such ordinary cargo, wouldn't you say?"

Wang Wei shrugged his shoulders and pointed to his earless side. He replied in Mandarin, China's national language, not the singsong, backwater Cantonese prevalent in Hong Kong.

The inspector had no answer and shrugged in return. He initialed the pass, handed it back, and waved him through. The documents were in order, approved at high levels; that's all that mattered.

As he shot forward, Wang wondered what could possibly be wrong with a small load of chickens and ducks? Countless truckloads of fresh birds crossed the border every day, supplying scores of live bird markets in Hong Kong with fresh fowl.

No Chinese ever bought a dead bird for cooking, let alone frozen, packaged, or processed, whether for restaurant kitchens or home woks either one. They had to be young, alive and *fresh*. Besides, this was an Army truck. No inferior border guard would ever question the PLA's authority.

Now the road was paved, with two-lanes in each direction but reversed right-to-left, British-style. Now he could accelerate and pass the slower commercial traffic. Ought to make even better time, he thought.

In his mind, he visualized the lithe form of a young masseuse, nude and lathered, sliding across his body. He shifted in his seat, adjusting his pants for the stiff bulge he felt in his groin.

At the sign for Fan Ling, he saw the famous golf course that had been created exclusively for the Western barbarians at Luen Wo. He downshifted and pulled into the left lane toward Tai Po. Getting closer.

It was still well before rush hour in the New Territories and Wang Wei was way ahead of schedule. But his heart sank when he saw a long string of taillights flashing ahead at Ma Liu Shui.

Not now, he thought. Not another inspection point. And so close to Fo Tan! He couldn't sit in traffic again, idle, waiting.

Suddenly he felt hot and rolled down the window. That made it even worse. Hong Kong's thick humidity forced rivulets of sweat down his face. He wiped his cheek with his other sleeve and coughed into an armpit. Fuming, he sat quietly and picked his nose.

He was out of cigarettes and getting low on gas. He had to get out of this heat, make the air move at least, take the back streets. This was his fifth or sixth run into Hong Kong. All the previous trips had been for supplies so he was getting to know the side roads pretty well now.

Glancing behind him, he stuck his arm out the window and cut in front of a stopped trailer-truck. Then he was free of the traffic and followed the small powder-blue signs with the characters for Fo Tan. At least the ideographs were the same.

Several intersections ahead, he saw the familiar canary-yellow Shell oil sign above the gas pumps. He could stop, refuel, and buy some smokes.

In sign language, he told the young attendant precisely how much leaded gas he wanted in the old truck and stepped into the kiosk for a pack of Red Stars. When he had them in his hand, he thanked the cashier, plucked out a cigarette, lit up, and exhaled, wrapping them both in a shroud of smoke.

Gesturing, the old lady made a comment about his ear in Cantonese and laughed.

He couldn't understand a single word she said, of course, so he laughed right back. Then he sneezed again, which surprised them both. Together, they laughed even louder, and then he went back outside.

As the attendant replaced the fuel cap, Wang reached into his pocket for a wad of bills. At least China's national currency, the *renminbi*, was legal tender in Hong Kong now so he didn't have to worry about changing money.

Coughing, Wang Wei peeled off a few notes. As he gave them to the boy, he sneezed on the lapels of the attendant's overalls. Apologizing in a stream of Mandarin that confused the kid even more, Wang tried to wipe the damp lapels with the back of his hand.

Then he rechecked the latches. As he got in to start the engine, he peered through the windshield and saw the unmistakable neon curl of a bright pink Turkish bath sign winking at him from across the street.

Finally, and for the first time, he smiled.

○ **7** ○

Ellen was still fuming from her altercation with Mitch Webster of CBS. He'd be on the phone whining to New York tonight, she thought, and New York will try to sweet talk Atlanta. But she felt confident about this one. With their botch-up on *60 Minutes*, CBS had made enemies of just about everybody at CDC.

She found the office of the Indian Health Service and went in.

"Jimmy?"

"Ellen!"

The director introduced her to his team and to two staff from the New Mexico DOH. Feldman, Gupta, and Higueras had already made the rounds and were helping themselves to coffee.

A state flag stood in one corner, the crimson and turquoise Navajo tribal colors in another, flanking the Great Seal of the Navajo Nation. Double-paned windows insulated them from the heat and dust outside. An air-conditioner whined from a third corner of the room.

"The press hounds are hungry," she said. "I sent them to you, as agreed."

"Thanks."

Arroyo frowned.

"We've got a lot of bones here, but no meat. Let me show you what we have so far."

Arroyo had sharply-angled features and leathery skin, textured and rough from over-exposure to the desert sun. He wore an old pair of khakis with a faded cotton shirt in cool Navajo salmon-and-blue pastels. His hair was clipped in a crew-cut and his eye sockets were rimmed with purple. The lids sagged from serious lack of sleep.

He handed Ellen a stack of glossy black-and-white photographs. They were recent victims, dead from the mysterious disease. Stats on each death were handwritten on the back of each photo.

Ellen examined them one by one and passed them around the table to her crew.

"Did you do a post on the index case?" she asked without looking up.

She examined a photograph of the first person to die.

Arroyo shook his head.

"Her family wouldn't let us do a full post-mortem. Since she was the first to come down with the symptoms and die from the disease, tribal tradition stood in our way. We were lucky to get a few blood and fluid samples but we were unable to autopsy her organs."

Ellen pulled out a sheaf of faxes she had received just the day before.

"Your cases still showing the same symptoms?"

Arroyo nodded.

"Fever at onset, then myalgias, pharyngitis, lingering malaise. Most patients had difficulty breathing. We dosed them with Relenza and sent them home. Not much else we could do. They were all dead within 24 hours."

"The early patients?"

"All of them. As a result, the tribe calls our clinic the dispenser of death. The sick have stopped coming so we have to go right out as soon as we get word somebody else has the symptoms. We're doing triple the number of daily visits."

"You think ARDS, maybe?" Gupta asked.

He drained a large terracotta mug.

"Symptoms sound the same."

Ellen frowned. Adult Respiratory Disease Syndrome was a catch-all category, a convenient recycling bin for diseases whose cause or effect were still unknown.

"We cited ARDS as primary on the death certificates, " Arroyo said. "But we have no idea, really. You guys are the experts, you tell us."

Ellen's frown deepened.

"So with the common symptoms, why do you figure some have survived, some not?"

Arroyo shrugged.

"No idea. We suspect the survivors may simply have a less virulent case."

"Barrier nursing, standard precautions?"

"For the staff, yes. Cap, gauze mask, latex gloves. We don't know if it's contagious person-to-person yet but we're treating it like it is and taking no chances."

"Very good. Have you quarantined the sick?"

Arroyo shook his head again.

"Even if we wanted to, the reservation's too big. It's spread across the whole northern half of the state. Plus there's widespread distrust in mandated grouping. Brings back bitter memories of the past, when the Federal government consistently over-promised and failed to deliver. Even now, our Tribal Council thinks the mystery disease is just another curse from Washington."

Ellen grimaced. She'd heard that before, in a lot of different ways.

"Well, if you can't quarantine, you need to ask people to minimize their social interaction. Tell them to stay home the rest of this week. Close your schools, shut all your theaters and community centers -- all the places people normally congregate. Give out face masks at grocery stores and gas stations, whatever you can do to eliminate contagion until we can pin this thing down."

Arroyo nodded as he scribbled on a pad.

"You've analyzed the subjects for commonality?" Ellen asked. "What they did, where they were, who they came into contact with?"

She knew there had to be a uniform link to the outbreak, somehow, somewhere. Something that connected all of them. Sooner or later it would materialize. It always did.

"Absolutely. We've interviewed every patient and cross-checked the responses. So far, there's no known behavior or common contact leading to a specific source."

He sighed and shrugged his shoulders.

"Absolutely nothing."

Ellen bored down. She wasn't about to give up so easily.

"Any clusters?"

When cases tend to "cluster" around a specific location, event, or individual, they stand out like bees around a hive. Clusters give disease detectives a critical clue.

"None. It's just random, all over the reservation. Only a couple of outsiders."

"What about environmental factors? Any unexpected or unusual occurrences lately -- more rain than normal, flash floods, windstorms?"

Frowning, Arroyo shook his head again.

"Pretty much normal up to now. We had good rains in the spring so we could irrigate the corn plantings for a big harvest. The *piñon* nuts were bountiful this year, too; good for the prairie dogs who burrow and aerate the soil."

Ellen asked permission for her team to collect physical samples from the homes and offices of the diseased: soil, dust, hair, surface scrapings, plates, pens, pencils -- obvious objects that might contain traces of the target substance. Plus fluid samples from patients still in the clinic as well as those who had been discharged: blood sera, throat swabs, sputum.

She wanted every sample bagged and sent overnight by courier to the lab in Atlanta so Sandy McDermott, the CDC's chief technician, could analyze them.

Arroyo gave Feldman, Gupta, and Higueras a computer printout summarizing the fifty-three sickness reports that contained relevant statistical data along with names and addresses of the patients. He assigned three members of his staff to accompany them.

"Masks and gloves," Ellen reminded them as they headed out. "No exceptions."

"Yes, mother," Feldman said. "When do you want us back?"

She glanced at a big wall clock on the other side of the room.

"Let's reconvene at seven-thirty. Then we can courier the samples to FedEx in Albuquerque and if we're lucky, Jimmy can feed the piranhas."

After they left, Ellen asked if they could exhume the index case and interview her family. The first victim to die had been a young Indian woman in her early twenties named Aalyah Constant who was fit and trim and teaching in the tribal schools a week before.

Arroyo hesitated.

"They just buried her last weekend, Ellen. Let her rest."

She leaned in closer and dropped her voice.

"Jimmy, without those tissue samples we can't begin to track down this killer disease. I'm sure the family would like to know why their daughter died the way she did, and we all want Navajos to stop dying, don't we? Every minute we lose means more bodies stacking up on your doorstep."

His head dropped.

"You sure we have to do this?"

"Yes. Come on, let's go see them."

○ 8 ○

Col. Fu turned to the Russian virologist and pressed him again.

"You're positive?" he asked.

He had to be certain. For the success of his project.

For China.

The scientist nodded unambiguously.

"Absolutely," he said. "Watch the situation reports from Hong Kong closely. You'll see."

What *was* it about the Chinese? Lukanov wondered.

Constant doubt, no confidence, always worrying about details. They paid him a small fortune for his expertise and he knew exactly what he was doing. So why couldn't they let up? He'd developed the deadly mutant virus Fu wanted. Why was he so bent?

Boris Lukanov had been director of the Moscow Viral Institute when he'd been approached by Colonel Fu for this job. China needed a special pathogen so they could keep pace with the bioweapons race, Fu told him. Lukanov thought they wanted to be ready to repulse a surprise attack, but Fu said no. They wanted offensive and defensive weapons both.

After subjecting the Russian to extensive security clearance procedures, Col. Fu invited him to Beijing. He rolled out the red carpet. Lukanov was impressed.

The Chinese were serious and offered him some serious money. As a world-class virologist, he faced a bleak future in a Russia ravaged by chaos, corruption and crime after the collapse of Communism. So he agreed to help.

Lukanov had also been surprised at the secluded location of Fu's facility.

It was an isolated farm outside Zhao'an at the base of the Jiulian Shan mountains in southwestern Jiangxi province. To the casual observer, it was nothing more than a typical Chinese animal farm. But unlike Soviet farms, barnyard birds in China were not segregated. They lived openly inside fenced areas, cheek-by-jowl with swine.

The Russian virologist had been shocked. This was highly unsanitary if not downright uncivilized. Poultry and pig feces invariably intermingled, producing unhealthy and unpredictable parasites that would infect their own food.

Fu dismissed his worries with a wave of his hand, saying this had been common practice in southern China for centuries. Besides, the arrangement was an integral part of his plan.

Through his background research prior to hiring the Russian, Fu knew that the intestines of migratory birds and waterfowl were a natural reservoir for the avian strain of flu. He also knew that pigs were a natural host for the human flu virus. People couldn't catch the flu directly from birds; they caught it from swine. Southern China was well known to microbiologists as a natural "mixing bowl" for the flu virus because birds, pigs, and humans lived in dangerously close proximity on Chinese farms.

Farmers caught the flu from their livestock. Because the flu virus is highly contagious, the farmers quickly passed it to their customers and suppliers. Before long, it made its way to nearby Hong Kong.

Commercial aviation did the rest, speeding the flu to Europe and America within 48 hours, hitching a ride on the jet stream on its way to infect the rest of the world. Hence the Chinese origins for names given to the common influenza virus.

Hong Kong flu.

Asian flu.

Beijing, Wuhan, Harbin.

But the common flu never killed its victims. It only made them sick.

So the very conditions that Lukanov at first thought unsanitary were the perfect conditions for creating a mutant virus. What if the avian virus could be manipulated in the laboratory? What if they could find a way for birds to infect humans? Could the brilliant Russian figure out how to combine the avian and swine viruses and thus clone a mutant killer flu?

Lukanov was more impressed than surprised when he walked into Fu's hidden laboratory for the first time.

From the rear of a dilapidated shed, he descended a concealed stairway that took him underground into a subterranean room equipped with the finest and most up-to-date collection of laboratory equipment he'd ever seen.

A pair of spacious workbenches, shielded by hoods with advanced laminar flow vents, separated abundant storage cabinets for glass beakers, pipettes, and microwells. The entire room was kept under negative air pressure by advanced vacuum equipment obtained through one of the PLA's covert holding companies overseas.

There was a centrifuge for liquid separation. A scanning electron microscope. Two floor-to-ceiling refrigerators and a matching freezer for storing lab samples. Volume after volume of reference texts on microbiology, genetics, and gene sequencing, both in Russian and in English, lined a bookshelf against one wall.

Fu had assembled a small but competent staff of laboratory assistants who lived in captive and strictly controlled conditions on-site. Lukanov liked the reticent Lo Fengbu the best. He did precisely what he was told, kept strictly to himself and never talked back.

Armed guards in mufti manned the front gate around the clock; it was connected by a series of electronic sensors to an electrified perimeter fence. Uninvited visitors were politely but firmly told that it was a government agricultural site and off-limits. When they left, they were tracked by the PSB who made sure they stayed away.

Lukanov had taken an instant liking to Col. Fu. He was a no-nonsense leader, totally consumed. As they talked now, he noticed again the portraits of heroes Fu had assembled on his laboratory walls, starting with Chairman Mao Zedong. Fu called him the Great Helmsman and seemed to worship his image. But Lukanov still got chill bumps when he saw the others.

There was Dr. Dmitri Ivanovski, the Russian botanist who first discovered microorganisms smaller than bacteria through his work on tobacco mosaic disease in 1892.

Ivanovski had squeezed juice from infected tobacco leaves through special sieve-like porcelain screens called Chamberland filters. He believed, as did everyone else at the time, that nothing pathogenic could possibly pass through them. But he discovered he was wrong when he coated the leaves of healthy tobacco plants with the filtrate and saw to his chagrin that they had become infected as well.

Then there was Martinus Willem Beijerinck, the Dutch chemist who confirmed Ivanovski's results in 1898 and became the first to call the invisible microbe a *virus*. From the Latin word for poison.

And Prof. Ilya Medhnikov, the Russian microbiologist who discovered cellular immunity at the turn of the century.

And Dr. Albrecht Kossel, the German who won a Nobel Prize in 1910 for his advances in cell chemistry that led to a new understanding of proteins and nucleic acids.

Lukanov respected Col. Fu because he understood his nation's own weaknesses and tried to compensate for them by acquiring world-class talent. He still had no idea what Fu was going to do with the lethal mutant the Russian was creating, but the Chinese compensated him with generous payments to an offshore account in hard currency, so he didn't press it.

The Colonel clammed up tight every time the Russian raised the subject. Once a month they flew him to a PLA resort at Haikou on the nearby island of Hainan for a little decadent R&R.

Providing he kept to the schedule.

The same schedule Wang Wei was hurrying to meet in Hong Kong.

∘ **9** ∘

Arroyo led Ellen quickly out the back exit, away from the press to his open jeep.

They both wore gauze facemasks against the dust as he drove across the pancake terrain. Rows of young, mint-green Mesquite lined the gritty road, fed by runoff from the recent rains. Broad, angular mesas dominated the distant horizon.

Before long they were bouncing along the narrow stucco streets of the ancient Navajo village of Taos.

Ellen saw the familiar square-roofed adobe-block Pueblo houses with the distinctive pine logs jutting out from their flat rooflines like half-forgotten scaffolding. Quilts and blankets hung from the logs, limp in the hot air, with faded turquoise and crimson pastels of the tribal colors.

They drove by the clinic and saw a line of patients waiting to enter. They were being interviewed by a Navajo nurse holding a clipboard and dispensing gauze masks. Fearful eyes followed the jeep suspiciously as it rolled by in the dust. A big yellow flag had been hoisted on the flagpost out front, signifying contagion and local quarantine.

God, Ellen thought, don't let this turn into a huge epidemic. But if it does, please let it be on my watch.

Just past the village they pulled up to an isolated ramshackle hut. A yellow card was tacked to the front door.

Jimmy Arroyo introduced Ellen to the dead girl's parents and explained in Navajo dialect why they were there. At first they opposed exhuming the body so soon after her burial. But when Jimmy explained the reasons, they reluctantly relented. But they insisted the Tribal Elders do it.

Arroyo quickly called the tribal chief on his cell phone as they bounced toward the tribal cemetery along another dirt road.

When they got there, a tall white-haired Navajo stood blocking the grave with his arms crossed. He wore a feathered headdress and a full-length black-and-white horsehair robe. Off to one side, a pair of gravediggers leaned on their shovels, chewing tobacco and spitting unceremoniously in the sand at their feet.

The chief extended an arm.

They stopped. Arroyo shut off his engine.

"The holy people of the *diné* believe human suffering is caused by disharmony," the chief said.

His voice was stern but not hostile, like a scolding father.

"Disharmony results when one disobeys the laws of nature, just as your government did when it caused the tragic event we call the Long Walk. Pain and death continue to this day."

Ellen approached him slowly.

"These deaths are not Washington's fault," she said softly.

She gestured toward Arroyo.

"My team is here to work with your people. We can never undo what was done in error before. But I know we can prevent more pain and death from coming."

There was a long period of silence.

Finally, the big man raised his feathered arms.

"The skies must brighten," he said. "Let the black clouds part."

They walked to the gravesite and stood back as the chief presided over the disinterment, chanting to the sky while waving azure and crimson feathers across the mound. The sandy soil was soft as sponge from the recent burial.

When they had exposed the shawl-wrapped corpse, Ellen kneeled down and opened a small bag of instruments. She pulled on a pair of latex gloves and took a biopsy tool, like a stainless steel corkscrew with a reservoir at one end, from her bag.

Ellen pulled the shawl aside and felt the ice-cold, stone-hard surface of skin. She twisted the miniature drill into the dead woman's flesh and extracted a tissue sample from her lungs.

Suddenly, she gasped.

Something wasn't right.

Frowning, Ellen repeated the procedure, removing additional tissue samples from her throat, her liver, her kidney, her spleen. She put the samples in separate color-coded Ziploc bags, labeled each one, and tossed them into a Styrofoam cooler in Arroyo's jeep.

She nodded to the chief. Removing her gloves and gauze mask, she stepped back and stood silently as they ceremonially reburied the body. She put the used instrument in another Ziploc to be disinfected later. She did the same with her gloves and mask and tagged them as medical waste.

But she worried about that first sample.

The lung tissue was much thicker and heavier than normal. Something was terribly wrong.

○ **10** ○

Wang Wei started to worry a little about his precious truckload of ducks and chickens as he pulled behind the flashing pink neon sign and parked in back.

What if someone stole a cage while he was cavorting in the bath, or even made off with a single bird? That was the downside of stopping before he delivered the load to Fo Tan.

Besides, the constant squawking made so much noise it would surely attract unwanted attention. Col. Fu would have his hide if anything happened to just one of his birds. Everything Wang Wei had worked so hard to achieve would be lost, like hard-earned money at a crooked casino.

No, he could never risk that.

Wang glanced up from the parking lot and saw a cluster of semi-nude women behind the wide panes of glass. They waved at him in the pink light. He smiled and waved back. They wouldn't be busy until later anyway, he figured. Plenty of time.

He'd still have easy access in late afternoon, before the night crowd of addicted gamblers, itinerant day workers and drunks descended on the bath. And he knew he could make better time with an empty truck once he'd unloaded the cages. Even more important for Col. Fu, he'd have an earlier time-stamp from the market.

Wang looked at his watch.

It was barely four o'clock. He'd stop for some *gyoza* and a bowl of *lo mein*, offload the birds in Fo Tan and slip back by the side streets. As he stood and watched the girls, he felt the familiar throbbing in his groin and grabbed his crotch.

He couldn't wait.

One of the girls saw him and laughed, covering her mouth.

He grinned back, pointing at his watch.

She nodded. Then she gestured to her ear.

He laughed again, cupping his hand over his earless side as if to say he couldn't hear.

She laughed again.

She was cute. She'd be fun. He wondered if he'd remember her when he returned.

Just then he saw the bright red ribbon in her hair. He'd remember that for sure. A prize, a gift-wrapped present, a little reward just for him.

He climbed back into the cab and restarted the engine.

As he wove back into traffic, he glanced at the street marker -- Tolo Harbor Road -- and looked up at the blinking characters on the neon sign.

Tu'erqi Daishiguan, it read.

The Turkish Embassy.

That'll be really easy, he thought.

∘ **11** ∘

When they got back to the clinic, the other CDC specialists had already returned with their samples, bagged and tagged. Feldman packed them all in dry ice and labeled the box for next-day air to Atlanta while Ellen disinfected her biopsy tool.

She asked to examine the patients who had recently arrived. Masked and gloved and wrapped in full-body paper gowns, they disappeared into a hastily-built intensive care facility that had about a dozen beds.

Ellen went from patient to patient, listened to their faint breathing, felt their weak pulses, peered into runny noses and throats, read the charts.

"On the surface, these symptoms certainly suggest flu," she said. "But it's way too early in the season."

"Could it possibly be remnants of toxic gas the Federal government used decades ago?"

Ellen shook her head.

"I read about the dangerous weapons testing in Utah, but that was a thousand miles away and thirty years removed in time."

"You think maybe the tribe has unearthed a dormant bacterium by over-plowing the soil for corn?"

"There's clear evidence of URI, Jimmy," Ellen said. "Every patient is suffering from upper respiratory infection and they're all mildly febrile, with elevated temperatures over 100°. But you told me that antibiotics have had no effect so I'd tend to rule out bacteria for now. Pharyngitis is indicated, their lymph glands are adenopathic, and everyone's complaining of neuralgia."

"I know," he said. "That's the frustrating thing. We isolated a pair of moribund patients like lepers behind a makeshift curtain and intubated them. I don't think they're going to survive."

Ellen heard the hoofbeats again.

Think zebras, she said under her breath.

She drew some additional blood from each patient. Then she took throat swabs and had them spit into sputum-capture vessels. Feldman labeled and wrapped the new samples and packed them in dry ice with the others. Arroyo boxed the finished packets and dispatched a staff member straight to FedEx at the Albuquerque airport.

Ellen e-mailed Sandy McDermott a brief summary of their observations and a description of the samples Atlanta would receive in the morning. Ellen asked her to call the next afternoon at four o'clock Mountain time. That would give Sandy virtually the whole day to run a sequence of tests with her sophisticated equipment. She also said she'd try to call mid-day from the field for an interim report.

When they were ready to break, Arroyo invited the CDC team to dinner. Ellen declined and sent him home to be with his family and catch up on sleep. The next day would be hectic. They had to review their statistical data with the DOH, corral more patients for interviews, prep for the telecon with Atlanta.

So the DOH car took them back to Santa Fe. As jet lag kicked in, the trio of combative specialists dozed during the ride. Ellen was still worried about the lung sample she had extracted from the index case, tormented by the symptoms she'd seen in the clinic.

Something wasn't right.

She stared out the windshield of the car, impervious to the historic buildings in the old capital as they approached the town square. Toney restaurants and upscale fashion boutiques had replaced the indigenous shops and agricultural supply stores. They were all ominously dark and empty.

The lobby of the La Posada hotel, normally brisk with business every season of the year, was dead. Tourists and commercial travelers alike were avoiding Santa Fe in droves because of the mystery sickness. The desk clerk wore a gauze facemask and his eyes were wide with fear. He looked as if he had just been mugged.

Uninvited, the Navajo plague had created a ghost town.

○ **12** ○

Col. Fu shot a cuff and glanced at his watch.

He figured Wang Wei ought to be at the wet market in Fo Tan by now. He paced back and forth in front of Lukanov's workbench. The plan for the Jiangxi virus had to stay on schedule. They shouldn't have to wait much longer, just a day or two at most. Then he hoped to have some good news for General Min that would put them a step closer to their goal.

Fu and Lukanov reviewed the delicate process the Russian had developed during the past few months. It had not been easy to clone an avian viral mutant that would be lethal to humans.

At first, Lukanov worked on derivatives of known pathogens that the Russians had perfected in their own covert labs. He'd personally supervised the development of a new hybrid virus that combined the airborne contagion of smallpox with the hemorrhagic destructiveness of ebola, an especially nasty filovirus from Africa.

The mutant was a killer and virtually impossible to defend. It had no known antidotes.

Smallpox had been a dread disease throughout human history. The Athenians were devastated by it in their war with Sparta. Roman and Carthaginian armies spread it like the plague throughout the Middle East, where it infected Muslim pilgrims on their *hajj* to Mecca. Merchant ships in turn took it to Europe, whose ports spread it rapidly to the rest of the world. Smallpox ravages with ugly red pustules that scar for life, killing a third of those it infects.

Smallpox was a perfect bioweapon because it had already been eradicated from the world. By 1980, the World Health Organization had created a global system of smallpox surveillance. It treated only new cases by vaccination, so there was a whole generation of unprotected people now. Everyone inoculated before 1980 was a perfect candidate for infection because the vaccination had a limited efficacy of only seven years.

After its eradication, two official reservoirs of the frozen pox virus had been retained. One was at the CDC in Atlanta, the other at Lukanov's institute in Moscow. But Fu knew that America could ramp up vaccine production in no time, and did so dramatically after 9/11.

Its armed forces and public health staff were already routinely vaccinated. So a smallpox clone was not the answer.

The same held true for anthrax.

It was first discovered in the early 19th century when the lungs of textile workers were first exposed to its sub-micron spores. Called wool sorter's disease, it was even more lethal than smallpox; it killed about half its victims. Anthrax bacteria produce poisonous toxins that attach themselves to the protective membranes of white blood cells, crippling their ability to fight disease. It's the toxins, not the bacteria, that cause death.

By freeze-drying and aerosolizing anthrax microparticles, Lukanov had previously created a battle strain of the microbe in Moscow that was stable, easily reproducible and highly virulent. But Fu knew that the Americans had targeted this bioweapon too, after the lethal envelopes started arriving by mail at random in the fall of '01, right after the suicide bombers. As a result, they were stockpiling Cipro and similar antibiotics in bulk as a defense against future attacks.

So Fu said no to both smallpox and anthrax.

He'd been very clear with Lukanov: he wanted no cloned viral pathogens, mutant or otherwise, that were even *remotely* related to known bioweapons. He knew the Americans were working aggressively on defensive countermeasures against every conceivable biological threat in the book.

The rogue Colonel was adamant.

He wanted a lethal mutant of an avian virus that could masquerade as flu and be transmitted directly from bird to man.

He needed a killer flu.

A virus they'd never be able to identify, let alone stop.

○ **13** ○

Ellen slept fitfully that first night in Santa Fe. The Navajo plague swirled around her like a fog.

Two fears gnawed constantly at her subconscious, made her toss and turn, gave her nightmares every time she confronted a mysterious new disease.

One was the Black Death, a.k.a. Spanish Flu, the global pandemic that exploded in 1918. Attacking at the end of World War I, the influenza virus type A/subtype H1N1 killed more than half a million Americans in a matter of months -- more Americans than died in that war or in all the wars of the 20th century combined.

In Pittsburgh, in 1918, nearly 50,000 people caught the flu and more than 5,000 died.   In Philadelphia, 20,000 died *in two weeks.* Lincoln, Nebraska, had been flu-free until the postman brought it, innocently stuck to envelopes mailed from the east coast where returning GIs had carried it from Europe.   From there, it swept overnight to the west coast in a wild dust storm.

H1N1 was a relentless killer in its time. It murdered people in the prime of life. Sick Americans begged for medicine, but there wasn't any because microscopes didn't yet exist that could identify a bug that small.

Public events were cancelled.   Masks became mandatory. Funerals were banned because of the health risk, gravediggers went on strike and bodies piled up like logs on streets all across America.

In all, more than twenty million people died from H1N1 in this global flu pandemic, the world's worst disease disaster since the black plague of the Middle Ages.

What if another vicious flu virus was loose in New Mexico?

Ellen rolled over in a cold sweat and squinted at the desk alarm.

The red diode glowed 2:39am.

She groaned and pulled the covers over her head, trying to block the deadly images out of her mind. But they were uninvited invaders, like the germs that caused them.

Her other haunting fear was bioterrorism, known by its simple acronym BT.

When the Soviet Union collapsed and communism had become discredited, the Cold War evaporated and the threat of thermonuclear war had become remote. Absent the two hostile superpowers, the world was now suddenly and totally fragmented.

More and more rogue states run by madmen were destabilizing their regions and thumbing their noses at the United States. Iran, Iraq, Serbia, North Korea, Syria, Somalia, Sudan. Civilizational conflict was now the new world order.

Scientists from the former Soviet Union auctioned their black-market skills and former Soviet military officers sold lethal weapons to the highest bidder. The al Qaeda terrorist network run by the elusive Saudi Osama bin Laden had become America's new enemy, spawning the horrible suicide attacks in New York and Washington on 9/11 and fanning the flames of hatred in the Middle East.

Biological agents were lethal because they were invisible to the human eye and produced symptoms resembling conventional disease. They posed a deadly inhalation threat, with microparticles tiny enough to escape a front line of defense in the human nose and throat. They remained undetected until it was too late and casualties soared.

BT, not to mention random acts of terror, had changed the rules of engagement.

In 1993, militant Islamic extremists from the Middle East attacked the World Trade Center in New York with a chemical bomb, killing a dozen innocent Americans and wounding more than a thousand. In 1995, domestic American terrorists blew up the Federal building in Oklahoma City with a fertilizer bomb, killing nearly 200 innocent civilians and injuring a thousand more. In 1996, the Japanese cult Aum Shinrikyo planted deadly sarin gas in the Tokyo subway. A dozen people died, nearly 6,000 seriously injured.

Then came 9/11, and shortly thereafter the postman delivered anthrax in innocent envelopes sent by other terrorists. These were not just nut cases or disaffected postal workers or the mentally deranged. They were smart, highly motivated, disciplined fanatics dedicated to passionate causes, political and religious alike, forging ultimate fanaticism with ultimate weapons.

What if this otherwise mysterious Navajo plague was the result of a deliberate, unprovoked bioterror attack by Saddam Hussein or another Muslim madman, picking a totally remote BT launch site in the arid Southwest, far from Washington or New York?

What if?

The phone rang and the demons scattered.

Ellen blinked herself awake and dragged the receiver across the night stand. She brushed strands of damp hair from her sweaty face as she picked up the phone.

"Ellen?"

A familiar voice echoed in her ear.

"Who wants to know?" she mumbled.

She tried to rub the sleep out of her eyes.

"Come on Ellie, it's me. I just got in on the red-eye. I told you I'd be coming down, remember?"

She sat up and stared at the glowing red digits on her alarm.

"*Paul!* Jesus, it's barely five o'clock."

"O'Hare was a zoo, as usual," he said, full of energy. "It looks like airports have finally replaced bus terminals as magnets for the masses."

His voice was warm and friendly and fresh. He was either working off surplus deposits in his sleep bank or chalking up a new deficit fueled by adrenalin.

"Breakfast at six?"

Ellen's demons were completely gone now. They never liked company.

"Absolutely. Give me a half-hour. I'll be right down."

∘ **14** ∘

Wang Wei was starting to feel giddy.

He was in an anticipatory mood now, relishing the treat he had in store for himself after offloading the birds. With one hand, he reached up to the sun visor and pulled down the papers that Chow Fat, the old market proprietor, would chop when he got there.

He glanced at his watch. Won't be long now at all, he thought.

Wang Wei saw the sign for Fo Tan and downshifted as he slowed to make the turn.

Fo Tan was characteristic of Hong Kong's unzoned and open live-bird bazaars. It sat nestled between a thriving Burger King and the popular Wing Lung Department Store. Across the street was a typical Hong Kong Government housing project, Estate #207, an 8-story concrete high-rise.

Wang Wei slowed as he passed the public housing project.

Project 207 was home to more than a thousand residents, blue-collar workers who had toiled long hours every day and waited many years for these cramped one-room apartments. Hundreds of bamboo poles poked through rusting iron guardrails of narrow balconies like scaffolding. Wet laundry hung from the poles, limp and still in the thick humid air. The Fo Tan Middle School was next door, packed to overcrowding with the children of 207.

Wang Wei turned the corner and nosed the pickup into an empty stall.

Inside the market, a throng of chefs and housewives prodded and poked through cage after cage of clucking, squawking fowl. The cages were stacked floor-to-ceiling.

There was poultry for ordinary stir fry or sautéed cooking. Plump, colorful wild game for baking as Peking duck. Geese, teal, and tern as delicacies for special occasions like birthdays and weddings.

Wang Wei saw Chow Fat stomping around in knee-high rubber boots, hosing down the slick concrete along a row of roped-off cages.

Chow was short, squat, and bald as a bowling ball. He wore a pair of plastic goggles over his eyes. An unlighted Red Star hung from his lips.

The foul mixture of bird excrement and urine was everywhere. Wang slipped on the slimy surface, steadying himself by grabbing a cage. A frightened hen pecked at his knuckles. He snatched his fingers out and then turned and blinked as spray from Chow's hose ricocheted off the hard floor.

The tight space gave the market air a tartness that smacked Wang Wei's nostrils and forced him to breathe through his mouth. He coughed and spit, then tried to swallow.

For the first time, he felt a lump in his throat. Probably the damp market air, he thought. That and all the red laterite dust he'd inhaled on the drive down.

Chow saw Wang and nodded.

He walked to the wall cock and shut off his hose. When he removed the gauze mask covering his mouth, he laughed.

"What's the matter?" he asked. "Still not used to the live market?"

Wang shrugged at his ridiculous sing-song accent as he shoved the papers at him.

"I never know which is more disgusting," Wang Wei coughed, "the air or your floor."

Chow laughed harder. He couldn't understand a word of Mandarin himself, but he knew Wang was always watching the clock.

The old man checked the papers over and nodded again. The numbers checked. They went out together to unload the truck.

When the last cages were inside, Chow signed the invoices and chopped them with his red wooden stamp. At Wang's gestured insistence, he wrote down the precise time. He kept one copy and gave Wang two.

For the first time, Wang Wei noticed that the papers bore an unfamiliar Guangdong address. But he had learned long ago not to question why the Colonel used multiple addresses for his Army project. This was the Chinese government. Low-level workers like Wang Wei never questioned the State.

Old man Chow counted out a thick wad of bills. Wang stuffed them in a zippered vinyl case which he sealed and locked in the glove box of the truck.

Wang smiled, fired up the engine, and waved goodbye.

He threw the empty truck into first gear and laid rubber.

He was ready to unwrap that pretty red ribbon back at the Turkish Embassy.

∘ **15** ∘

Ellen sprang out of bed and flicked the master switch, shielding her eyes momentarily when the room flooded with light.

Within minutes, she was in and out of the shower. Her dark hair was short, barely neck-length, which she could blow-dry and fluff out in no time.

Downstairs, a tall, auburn-haired guy in a black windbreaker whispered into a landline handset, hunched over the instrument with his back to the lobby.

She tiptoed up behind him and covered his eyes with her hands.

Paul Cerrutti spun around and eyed her with a wide grin.

At six-two, he was a full foot taller than she, with firm upper-body strength and broad shoulders. Hazel eyes framed a classic Leonardo nose and sparkled at the sight of her. Paul and Ellen had been an item, off and on, for the past several months.

"So how's the Navajo plague?" he asked quietly, replacing the receiver.

"Terrible name, isn't it? After a day of collecting samples, we're still in the dark."

She stifled a yawn.

"What's up on your end?"

He frowned.

"Our knuckle-draggers think they're onto something over the border. I'm here to work undercover with the state police."

"Drugs?"

"Bugs."

"Excuse me?"

He looked right, then left.

"Let's find an isolated booth in the coffee shop."

She glanced at her watch.

"We haven't got much time. My crew will be here and ready to go by seven."

Paul Cerrutti grabbed Ellen's briefcase with one hand and took her elbow with the other. She wore a fresh pair of well-worn stonewashed jeans and a short-sleeved sky-blue mock-turtle tee.

They settled in a quiet corner, which at daybreak was not hard to do.

The menu offered typical hotel food that comes with captive markets: mediocre quality at exorbitant prices. Speakers in the ceiling pumped a local FM station playing undecipherable hip-hop lyrics over a thumping base with a electric guitar twang in the background.

"What's this business about bugs?" she asked. "The FBI treading on my turf now? I thought it was bad enough with the Office of Homeland Security making things tough for us."

Cerrutti shook his head.

"Electronic eavesdropping," he said softly. "Different breed of bug. One of our birds in the sky has been keeping an eye on illegal traffic across the flats from Chihuahua. When our border agents made the target, we saw we could get good infra red images of the van by satellite, so we've been tracking it back and forth."

"But why you?" she asked. "I thought they had you working around the clock as a special agent in charge of counter-terrorism."

Cerrutti smiled.

"They do. One of our Mexican assets captured a dialogue via wiretap. Someone's putting the squeeze on a big oilman in Arroyo Seco, north of Taos. Seems they want to pick up his land cheap by forcing the market price down."

"And how do they plan to do this, exactly?"

She sipped hot coffee from a large brown stoneware mug.

"Sounds relatively innocent, but it's malicious. We think they've been trucking over vanloads of desert rats. So the state will have to condemn the guy's land and declare it off-limits."

She couldn't help shaking her head.

"Nothing works better than Hollywood to get my mind off the horror of a new disease," she said. "This is pretty tame stuff for the FBI, isn't it?"

"I wish. But listen to this. Our remote sensors have picked up both weight and content readings that are inconsistent with truckloads of little four-legged critters. All the data suggests explosives. We suspect these guys could be a front for militant Islamic extremists from the Middle East who may have other American bombing targets in sight."

"Terrorists? From Mexico?"

"Sounds bizarre, I know. But these guys are getting smarter. You remember when I tracked that Algerian to Windsor late last year and arrested him in Detroit with a trunkful of potassium cyanide in his car? Well, now that we've got the Canadian border practically sealed shut, the terrorists are starting to infiltrate from the south. But instead of recruiting Muslims, it looks like they're bribing Mexicans and sending them over here as a means of disguising their intentions."

"But why New Mexico, Paul?" Ellen asked, frowning. "So far the terrorist targets have been in big urban areas -- Federal buildings, skyscrapers, obvious symbols of American power."

"After 9/11, nothing's safe anymore. They could be setting up a base north of the Navajo reservation, maybe use the desert as a staging camp for future attacks or just create diversions and instill fear. The unexplained explosions in Arroyo Seco could be a rehearsal for something a lot bigger and a lot uglier than just scaring an absentee landowner. These guys are bright, highly motivated and resourceful."

Ellen's face grew serious. Her twin demons suddenly resurfaced.

"It never stops, does it?"

"No," Paul said. "The rules of the game have changed for good."

Their eyes met and locked.

"The more successful this country gets," he went on, "the more it sticks out like a sore thumb. The militant Muslims want to bring us down a notch or two. Okay, so they don't realize it's a not a zero-sum game, but what the hell do they care? Their economics only addresses how you slice a shrinking pie, not how you can make it grow, because Islam has produced a huge bulge in unemployed teenagers without the economic growth to absorb them. So they become ripe recruits. Envy and jealousy lead to resentment, which in turn leads to hatred and rage. And it's not going away anytime soon."

Ellen thought back to her own origins, to her small family, to the Catholic missions in her home province of Sichuan.

"It's pretty predictable, Paul. First, American missionaries try to convert them from Islam to Christianity. So you have a religious war underway. Then the religious extremists think Washington's trying to subvert their Islamic economies to capitalism. Rage is the inevitable next step because paranoia is such a powerful drug."

"It is. And when we trumpet commercialism without the restraining influence of deferred gratification or any of our broader traditional values, we provoke this deep resentment. Ever since the art of making money seems to have replaced the sport of baseball as our national pastime, we get richer and fatter and use more and more of the earth's non-renewable resources. We're such an obvious target, it's no wonder they hate us. What we see as universalism -- freedom, democracy, the fight for human rights -- they see as cultural imperialism."

She took another sip of coffee and smiled.

"You've turned into quite the philosopher. Is it the coffee or just sleep deprivation?"

Cerrutti frowned.

"When poor countries fear they can't compete," he said, "they lash out against their perceived enemies any way they can. That's the dark side of their authoritarian politics. So Israel and Palestine fight it out as proxies for America vs. the Arab world. Unfortunately, 9/11 may have been just the beginning."

"It scares me because this has become the nature of conflict in the new century," she said. "The cold war ended with an illusion of harmony, but reality is totally different. Just read the headlines every day: religion against religion, culture against culture, civilization vs. civilization. You see it in the war between Arabs and Jews, or Russia and Chechnya, or India and Pakistan. Or in the wider war between authoritarianism and democracy -- all ignited by random acts of terror and made worse by the proliferation of weapons of mass destruction. But what I really fear is what we can't see -- bacteria and viruses -- and God help us if these deadly weapons become part of the mix."

Suddenly, her eyes grew wide.

"Paul, here's a terrible thought. What if our two cases were somehow related?"

He hesitated for a moment, then shook his head again.

"Not very likely," he said. "This looks and feels like munitions, not medicine."

"Enough to stock a weapons cache?"

"Don't know. That's still a bit of a mystery because they haven't put anything in play yet."

"Then it sounds to me like you guys may be skating on pretty thin ice."

"Yeah, but it gets still weirder. Listen to this. Something happens to their driver one night. He disappears and the van never comes back to Mexico. So the Mexicans send a second courier over the border by bus to find the first guy and *he* doesn't come back either."

"So you think the landowner could be fighting back?"

"At 72 and certifiable? I doubt it. We think the van is somewhere north of here, so I'm heading up with the state cops to look for it today."

Ellen frowned.

"Well, be careful. We're all in the dark on this horrible outbreak. It's killing nearly half the Navajos it infects."

He drained his cup.

"I've seen the press," Paul said. "Still no clues?"

She shook her head.

"Not yet. We FedEx'd a boxful of tissue samples back to Atlanta last night for biopsy work in the lab. I hope we know more by this afternoon."

"You'll nail it, whatever it is. You always do."

Ellen chuckled as a flood of memories submerged her twin demons.

"Remember the Big Sky case last year?"

"How could I forget?" he said. "Montana was a trademark case for you."

She grinned.

"Everybody at the Dry Gulch Motel was coming down with dysentery and it took me forever to find the answer."

He laughed.

"So the motel owner gets pissed and calls the FBI because you scraped evidence samples from every room, tested his water, shut down his whole kitchen, even threatened to quarantine his customers for Christ's sake."

"Come on, it was a public health menace, remember?"

"Yeah, right," he said, shaking his head. "Fifty people leaking with diarrhea and he rings the FBI. I never lived that case down. But you hung in there and went after it like a terrier. I've never seen such perseverance."

She started to laugh now too.

"There I was, one hot-shot disease detective coming up empty-handed every time I turn around, when it hit me like a bolt out of the blue. We never checked the water in their damn hot tub. Why is the answer always where you least expect it?"

Paul reached across the table and blanketed her hand.

"But that's you, Ellie," he said softly. "You've got this incredible imagination and persistence -- you never give up until you either piss somebody off or solve the case. Usually both."

She blushed.

"God gave me some brains but no breasts," she said with a sigh. "That's my only excuse."

Paul smiled.

"What he didn't put up front, he put up top."

She squeezed his hand and cupped it in hers.

"Well, he more than made up for that with you."

Cerrutti rolled his eyes and let out a slow sigh.

"Come on, Ellie. We've been through all that. I know I used to be a bit of a wild horse, but you've tamed me. Can't you accept that?"

Her eyes met his, and Ellen thought about their relationship.

Commitment had been difficult for her. She shied away from emotional involvements because she saw how her colleagues always seemed caught in a constant jigsaw puzzle of affairs, divorces, and burnout. It was the inevitable outcome of high-bandwidth professionals working on high-profile cases with deadly microbes under high-pressure deadlines.

But Paul had been different. For the first time, as their relationship evolved, she felt compatible.

"I know you've got this fear of abandonment," he said. "But I'm telling you, I'm not going to let you get away."

Her eyes dropped.

"Yeah, well. That's what they all say."

"I'm serious, Ellie. Look at me."

She glanced back up.

"Just because you were abandoned as a kid doesn't mean it's going to keep happening."

"Don't go there, Paul. Please."

He shook his head.

"You've got to shake this fear you have and put the past behind you. Please. Let it go."

"Right, just like you turned your back on your family when you said you'd have nothing to do with your father if he insisted you follow his career path in accounting."

"Well?"

"Well, he did, and you did, because both of you were so stubborn you wouldn't compromise. Is that the kind of a future you have in store for me, too?"

"Touché," he said softly. "Let's leave my dad out of this."

"Paul, I had a family once. Twice, in fact, with Dallas. I want one again."

"Then don't keep comparing me with my father because I'll never be able to match his accomplishments, either in his eyes or in anyone else's. We've got to give ourselves a chance, you and I."

She looked at her watch.

"It's almost seven. I've got to go. My team will be waiting for me in the lobby."

"Look," Paul said.

He stood up to sign the breakfast chit to his room.

"Just remember one thing: I'm going to chase you every bit as hard as you run after these goddam diseases, so you better get used to it because you and I have a bright future. Together."

After reaching down for her briefcase, Ellen stood on tiptoe and kissed him softly on the cheek.

"Not too shabby," she said. "And a whole lot better than last time. Keep working on it."

○ **16** ○

In the sequestered silence of Jiangxi, Boris Lukanov reviewed his experiments with the rogue Colonel. It was another late night and the laboratory staff had returned to quarters. The two of them were alone in the lab, impervious to the steady rain that drummed sonorously on the louvered windows outside.

Step by critical step, Lukanov documented the process he used to clone the viral pathogen. Fu needed every detail for his briefing to General Min, who would arrive by helicopter from Beijing once they had firm results from Hong Kong.

"You understand there are more than a dozen different subtypes of the influenza virus, type-A," Lukanov said. "Hogs and pigs are natural breeding grounds for those that infect humans with the common flu. The intestines of barnyard and waterborne fowl are natural hosts for the rest."

He handed the Colonel a computer printout.

"These flu subtypes are classified according to the location and type of their Hemagglutinin and Neuraminidase glycoproteins -- microscopic spikes that cling to the surface of the virus. The glycoproteins are special markers that identify the viral strains; there are fifteen known varieties of Hemagglutinin and nine of Neuraminidase. Any one 'H' can combine with any other 'N' to create a completely different strain of flu."

Lukanov paused and sipped tea from a small ceramic bowl as he watched Fu scan the readout. Then he handed the Colonel a pair of electron microscope scans.

"Look at these EM photos. The flu virus looks round, like a microscopic golf ball," the Russian went on. "It has a sticky envelope composed of a lipid bilayer that surrounds a single-strand 8-gene RNA genome. At the core of the virus is a matrix -- the gene that's involved in assembly and budding -- together with a nucleoprotein that encapsulates and protects it. Three polymerase proteins and a single nonstructural protein of unknown function complete the genome."

As Fu studied the scans.

"This was the first virus identified by the electron microscope in -- when was it, the early 1930s?"

"Correct," the Russian said with a nod.

He reached across and circled two magnifications.

"This is hemagglutinin, the 'H' spike. It looks like a tiny rod and acts like radar. It finds a site where the virus can attach to its host so it can initiate infection in red cell membranes. This gets the virus straight into a cell so it can hijack the reproductive machinery and start multiplying. Neuraminidase, the 'N' spike, resembles a tiny sledgehammer. It coats a slimy substance on the external surface of the host cell to facilitate the release of millions of mature viruses after reproduction. They have only one job -- to move on and find more cells to infect."

Fu looked up from the EM scans.

"And that's all the virus can do."

"Precisely. It's the limit of viral intelligence: attack, infect, and multiply."

Fu smiled.

"But it's so powerful, it ought to be capable of more. "

"It can't, because the influenza virus is only a single-strand 8-gene RNA genome, not the more robust double-helix DNA," Lukanov replied. "So it's notoriously unstable, subject to frequent change in antigenicity through a random process called genetic mutation, or reassortment. This occurs annually, which is why nobody can create a dependable flu vaccine. Serum that's used this year is useless against a new strain of type-A that may emerge next year."

Fu kept writing as the Russian spoke.

"I take it this is where drift and shift come in?"

"Precisely. The annual flu that humans get each winter is a result of this never-ending viral mutation, called antigenic *drift*. For example, subtype A/H1N1 attacks, infects, and multiplies. Until human host cells develop H1N1-specific antibodies, they'll be weak until they eventually grow strong enough to defeat and kill the invading virus."

Lukanov stood up and stretched.

He walked over to a portable whiteboard where he sketched a pair of drawings to illustrate the concepts.

"When a more dramatic reassortment of the 'H' and 'N' proteins occurs," he went on, "you get antigenic *shift*, which produces a completely different subtype like A/H3N2. So despite having antibodies for H1N1 now, which protect you only against that particular subtype, you'll get sick again until your body can produce enough H3N2 antibodies to kill the new invader."

Fu rearranged the order of his note cards so General Min could follow the flow.

Lukanov drained his cup of lukewarm tea. Outside, the patter of rain grew louder.

"So in the lab, I isolated subtype H5N3 from the fecal matter of your ducks. I knew it would be easy to find H3N2 and H1N1 in swine -- they're the two principal subtypes that attack human cells. The trick was to genetically engineer a specific reassortment by cross-breeding avian cells with swine. I cultured the laboratory samples in mammalian cells obtained through your Institute for Viral Biology in Beijing. I still don't understand all the connections in your personal network -- what did you call it, *guanxi*? But you got me everything I needed for my experiments."

"Just worry about the results," Fu said abruptly. "Forget the network. Go on."

"My target was a mutant virus, H5N1. It incubates in birds as a natural host without infecting them. Birds don't normally transmit H5N1 directly to humans. But I knew if I could engineer a cloned virus that can be transmitted, then it wouldn't just make people sick. It would probably kill them by causing fatal respiratory congestion and internal hemorrhaging."

Tracing his finger over a genetic diagram, Lukanov showed Fu the critical path.

"I started by mapping the RNA genome of the source viruses, here," he said. "And here."

He pinpointed the specific locations of each of the two key genes.

"You will appreciate the difficulty of this technique. I had to be gloved and masked at all times and work directly under the laminar flow hoods. But after I mapped the precise genetic location of H1 in the H1N1 swine subtype, I did the same for H5 in avian H5N3. Next, I stripped H5 out of H5N3 by means of RNA gel electrophoresis."

"You make it sound so simple," Fu said, glancing up from his notes.

"Mapping is the easy part," Lukanov said with a smile. "But I am one of very few people who have mastered the delicate process called site-specific mutagenesis. That's how I was able to swap the H5 gene with H1 and cleave it at H1's precise position 523~637 on the genetic map of the H1N1 genome, to create a cloned H5N1. Only then could I replicate the new strain in the lab using reverse transcriptase, a kind of genetic Xerox. So I grew the new H5N1 subtype using avian cell cultures from your birds and collected an H5N1 concentrate called a supernatant. Then I could confirm the presence of the target subtype in the scanning electron microscope."

Lukanov refilled his teacup and continued.

"Diluting the supernatant with distilled water at a ratio of 50:1, I loaded a mister to create a fine spray of H5N1 microdroplets. I sprayed those birds every day for three days, coating their heads and feathers. I then collected sample swabs of their fecal matter and analyzed them via EM scan. If the H5N1 clone had adapted successfully in their intestines, its presence would be confirmed in the microphotos."

Lukanov said that it took less than three months to create a lab strain but nearly three times as long until it replicated in the birds. Jiangxi weather was an impediment -- a constant drizzle, cool and damp in summer but hand-numbing cold in winter -- a far cry from Moscow's dry snow-packed winters and endless summer days.

"But I knew I finally had it this month when I tested the cloned H5N1 strain from the ducks with an H5N1-specific enzyme derived from special monoclonal antibodies. Watch, we'll replicate this process when the General comes. It's impressive, and very colorful."

He shared his excitement as he held the pipette and methodically dripped the enzyme into microwells containing the H5N1 clones.

Col. Fu beamed when he saw the wells glow a deep midnight blue, confirming the precise genetic reassortment.

"So it works, my friend," Fu said excitedly. "It works!"

"In the laboratory, Colonel. So far, only in the lab."

Fu's smile was tight and thin as he stacked his note cards for General Min. They had flawless clinical proof that the engineered viral mutant was alive and well in the birds.

Now he needed an answer from Hong Kong.

Could the man-made H5N1 clone infect humans -- and kill them?

∘ **17** ∘

By the time Ellen and her CDC crew roared into Taos trailing clouds of dust from the dry road, they had reviewed their assignments for the day and agreed on a plan until Sandy called from Atlanta that afternoon.

Because he spoke fluent Spanish, Higueras went out to conduct more background interviews with sick patients and run some basic elimination tests at the DOH lab in Santa Fe in parallel with the analysis in Atlanta.

Ellen figured he could do a serological workup, test for known toxins, and try to culture some bacteria. He could also eliminate cross-contamination from medical instruments and local lab gear, a common problem in the investigation of any new disease.

Gupta agreed to go back into the field with Arroyo's staff. They would capture environmental evidence for lab workup later: small animals, insects, rocks, soil samples, clothing, tools. Though they all agreed that bacteria was a doubtful suspect, they knew they had to eliminate it as a probable cause.

Feldman agreed to collect additional tissue samples and work on common threads.

He knew there had to be one event or a single substance -- some contaminated food, perhaps, or unexplained behavior or even an unidentified person -- that might link the index case to all the others. Without this common thread, Atlanta might be able to say what the mysterious pathogen *was*, but they'd be helpless in trying to eradicate it if they couldn't trace it.

When the trio had gone, Ellen went into Jimmy Arroyo's office to collect her files before heading back to the clinic.

"We're going to be somewhat limited here in Santa Fe," she said, "because the only BL-3 and BL-4 labs in the country are either at CDC in Atlanta or at the Army's Medical Research Institute for Infectious Diseases at Ft. Detrick in Frederick, Maryland."

Arroyo gave her a quizzical look.

"Why is that?"

"They're the only two domestic sites authorized to work on lethal pathogens, known or unknown, because of the higher security they provide."

"I've heard about these special labs," he said, "but I've never seen one."

Ellen flipped open a file folder and showed him a glossy 8x10 photo.

"Here's your basic Biosafety Level-3. Specialists work in canary yellow Tyvac moon suits. As you can see, they're head-to-toe nylon coveralls with a clear, built-in hood that provide both filtered respiration and eye protection."

She turned the page.

"Clinicians dissect tissue samples on workbenches covered by laminar flow hoods, which prevent airborne microparticles from escaping into the open lab. The lab itself is further protected by a dedicated negative pressure system that forces air into the room all the time. All tools, beakers, and lab instruments are autoclaved afterward -- vacuum-steamed at high temperatures in an industrial-strength dishwasher to kill any deadly microbes."

"So what's the fundamental difference between that and what you call BL-4?"

"Biosafety Level-4 goes a step further, creating containment within containment," she said, flipping to another glossy. It has all the protection of BL-3 but technicians wear thicker Tyvac suits with very sensitive Racal respirators connected to an independent air supply triple-filtered through high-efficiency particle-assort HEPA filters that trap microbes as small as a tenth of a micron. In addition, technicians go through decontamination buffer-showers both before and after their work."

"So where do you figure your colleague McDermott will be working on our samples?"

"Since the BL-4 labs at CDC and USAMRIID hold the hottest agents -- nasty filoviruses like Ebola or Marburg and lethal pathogens like Lassa fever -- I assume Sandy will work your samples at BL-3 and not run the risk of cross-contamination with the deadly bugs in BL-4."

Ellen shut the folders and stuffed them into her briefcase.

When she and Arroyo stepped out the front door, an ugly crowd had gathered in the street outside. A mob of angry Indian teenagers was blocking the entrance, guarding the small building with shotguns.

A squad of New Mexico state troopers stood off to one side, watching nervously as they squawked to headquarters for backup on a 2-way radio. They had no jurisdiction on the reservation and they

knew it. Ironic as it was, the Navajo nation was Federal property, so
the doctors from Atlanta were legally in charge of the cops from Santa
Fe.

"What in the world's going on, Jimmy?" she asked. "We're
not dealing with a damned casino license here. This is a deadly
disease that's infectious as all get-out."

"I know, Ellen, I know. Calm down. I reminded these guys
again last night but they say they want action and they're armed. They
think the Tribal Council is not sticking up for their generation.
Unemployment is up, jobs are evaporating, and they see their future
going down the drain."

Ellen was really angry now.

"Jesus, Jimmy. These hotheaded kids could stand in the way
of a solution. Worse, they could trigger an even more explosive
outbreak of this terrible disease."

"Yeah, well they're focused on the next generation, not the
here-and-now."

"There won't *be* a next generation if they keep this up," she
said. "Who's the leader, the fat guy in the jeans jacket or the dude with
the buzz cut?"

"The buzz, but he won't give you the time of day. He thinks
you're the problem. And you're a woman to boot."

"That's nuts and you know it. I'm a medical doctor, for
Christ's sake. You get him out of that mob right now so he and I can
have a little talk in private."

○ **18** ○

Wang Wei parked his empty truck behind the Turkish Embassy, locked the cab, and glanced up.

It was turning darker now and the sky burned a deep orange through the thick industrial smog. He saw the red ribbon again and smiled.

He waved and she waved back.

He hurried around to the entrance, stopping only to blow his nose onto the sidewalk, first emptying one nostril and then the other, just like he did on the farm. He dragged a sleeve across his nose to dry it.

Inside, he paid the old lady at the front counter. She took his money and stuffed it in a small drawer without looking up. She motioned him upstairs. He scribbled the two characters for red ribbon on a scrap of paper since there was no way she would ever understand his Mandarin.

She glumly picked up a phone and punched in a number.

"Ah Kwong," she said.

The name had a nice ring to it.

She motioned absently for him to sit.

He waited in a dusty, threadbare chair and picked up a local newspaper, thumbing through the pages without reading, thinking about Ah Kwong and her bright red ribbon.

He felt hot and wiped a jacket sleeve across his forehead. He could feel his pulse quicken.

A circular fluorescent light, faded and brown, flickered overhead. A curling strip of flypaper doubled as the light cord, pockmarked with dead flies and mosquitoes.

When he heard her slippers slap against the bottom steps, he looked up.

Ah Kwong wore a faded blue halter-top and skimpy shorts that exposed the underside of young, firm buttocks. She approached him and smiled. Standing, he coughed nervously and took her hand as she led him up the empty flight of stairs.

Ah Kwong escorted him into a vacant room on the third floor and flipped on the hot water in an empty soaking tub. As it filled, tiny spirals of steam leapt from the surface.

She helped him off with his jacket, brushing a hand along the smooth cloth. She rubbed his crotch lightly and smiled as she felt his firmness. She pulled his head down and kissed him, hard, as their tongues met and danced.

She splashed water onto a rubber mat, squirted a stream of liquid soap across it and brought it to lather. Wang Wei tore off the rest of his clothes and tossed them in a corner. As she slipped out of her shorts, he unfastened the two buttons on her halter. Her nipples were erect and firm.

As they writhed on the slick mat, their lips met again and their tongues touched. In an instant, he was inside her and came quickly. Her smooth body glided underneath him as their motions became slower and more rhythmic. He felt her shudder as she climaxed and he kept on pumping until he came again.

And Ah Kwong never once made fun of his ear.

∘ **19** ∘

Ten minutes after Ellen had disappeared with the young Navajo kid, a single shotgun blast ripped through the air.

Ellen and the buzz cut came running around a corner. Her lips formed a tight line and he looked damn scared. His face was white and his hands were empty. The disease detective now had the gun.

The kid approached the assembled gang and said a few nervous words in Navajo. They grumbled but began slowly to disperse.

She uncocked the shotgun, extracted the remaining cartridge, and handed the empty gun back to him. The two eyed each other warily for a moment until he grabbed the gun and took off.

"So what the hell happened?" Arroyo asked. "You threaten him?"

She laughed.

"Look at me, Jimmy. I'm barely five feet tall. Do I look like a threat?"

She tossed him the remaining shell.

"I asked him if he wanted to do this the easy way or the hard way."

Arroyo frowned.

"And?"

"And he wanted to know the difference. So I told him we have an old saying in China: people who talk by the yard and think by the inch will be moved by the foot. The easy way was to let us keep working. The hard way was for me to disarm him because I used to be certified in martial arts and wouldn't hesitate to use it if he and his gang persisted in obstructing our investigation of this disease."

Arroyo swallowed hard.

"You bluffed him like that?"

"It's no bluff, Jimmy. The explosion you heard was the gun discharging when I kicked it out of his hands. He chose the hard way. Can't reason with teenagers any more, anywhere."

After the entrance had cleared, Feldman came running out of Arroyo's office.

"What was all the commotion?" he asked.

She told him. He tried hard to suppress a smile.

"I guess we're lucky you never use that stuff on us."

"Yeah, well, it's still an option. Now get back out and finish collecting those samples."

As they prepared to leave a second time, she pulled Arroyo aside and told him about her private conversation with Paul Cerrutti that morning.

"So what do you think?" he asked.

"I'm not sure. Did you say you had a list of the diseased and dead patients?"

Arroyo led her back into his office. He leafed through some files on his desk and pulled out a manila folder. He handed it to her.

She extracted a single sheet of paper and began scanning the names. She wasn't sure what she was looking for but she knew a non-Navajo name would stand out.

The dry air began to warm as the late morning sun rose in the flat sky outside. Shafts of sunlight filtered through half-open Venetian blinds on the clinic's floor-to-ceiling single-pane windows.

Ellen filled a glass and took a long draw of water. She thought back to Paul's comments about the two Mexicans who had disappeared from the FBI's surveillance reports.

"Didn't you say there were a couple of deaths from outside the reservation?" she asked without looking up.

He came around and stood behind her.

"This is one," he said, ticking the name off with a pencil.

Miguel Jimenez.

"And here's the other."

Ramon Cortez.

"Know anything about these guys?" she asked.

He shrugged.

"Not really. We assumed they were both drifters. The only IDs they had were drivers' licenses from the state of Chihuahua in Mexico. No cash, no personal jewelry, nothing much of value in their pockets. One was a treat-and-release here at the clinic; we found the other collapsed by the road up at Arroyo Seco. They're both dead and buried now. We get a lot of homeless and drunks out here. Why?"

"Let's go check their graves."

She grabbed her instrument bag.

"I want their tissue samples."

As they drove back to the graveyard in his jeep, Ellen gave Arroyo more details about the suspicious van traffic from Mexico and Cerrutti's undercover role tracking the Islamic militants.

"If these two died from this mysterious disease," she said, "then their van could be contaminated, and if it is, Paul might be at serious risk when he finds it."

Ellen held onto the windshield frame as they bounced over the rough surface. She was glad she had digested her breakfast.

"You think the FBI may be onto something?" Arroyo asked.

"I don't know. But we'll never know without these samples."

Once she had collected, bagged, and labeled the tissue samples, she punched Paul's number into the keypad of her cell phone as they headed back toward Taos.

After three chirps, he picked up.

"Paul? Ellen. Listen, there's a pair of unknowns on Arroyo's dead list, both Mexicans. They could be your two couriers who disappeared, so be careful. Stay away from that van if you find it. It may have traces of this awful bug."

Her voice was thin, shredded by static caused by the long distances between transponders in the dry desert air.

"Where are you now?" she asked.

"East of Arroyo Seco, near Cimarron. Running a damn tag-and-match on suspect vehicles. Since we can't go by number plates, we're tracking their vehicle identification numbers. Once we hit a VIN that's not state-registered, I figure that may be it. The Santa Fe cops can call Chihuahua for a match."

"Paul, I'm telling you, keep away from the van. Find a hardware store, stock up on some gauze masks and latex gloves. Wrap cheesecloth around your nose and mouth if you can't find masks. And bag everything you use, after."

"Ellie, this is nuts. How can one van infect fifty people?"

"It can't. All it has to do is infect one. If it was the driver and he somehow contaminated a common object that the index case contacted, or vice-versa, that's all it takes. People will do the rest. They're the ultimate vector for infectious diseases."

"So where are you?" he asked.

He had to shout when the signal faltered again.

"In Taos, with Dr. Arroyo. We're heading back to the clinic."

"All right. I'll call if I find anything. And chill, Ellie. We'll get all that protective stuff first."

○ **20** ○

Col. Fu had not become a rising star in the PLA without staying consistently a step or two ahead.

By the mid-1970s, when China and the Soviet Union were on a collision course, the two countries heatedly contested a traditional border in China's northeast. The Soviets claimed territory that included the Emur Shan mountains. China insisted on the Amur River as the natural boundary.

The PLA quickly sent two clandestine divisions to block the Russians at the border. When the Soviets attacked, Sergeant Fu demonstrated the kind of fearlessness that builds leaders and inspires subordinates.

He led a stealth patrol under cover of darkness, invisible and silent as the wind. Armed with razor-sharp bayonets, he and his platoon slit the throats of countless Russian soldiers in their sleep to send Moscow a more ominous message.

Foreigners would *never* dictate demands to China.

Lieutenant Fu returned to Beijing destined for greater things.

In 1980, the Vietnamese Army pushed up the Yuan Hong river into Yunnan, China's southernmost province, in a bold attempt to link a northern village, Phong Tho, to Hanoi by water.

Lt. Fu commanded one of three battalions sent to repulse the Viets. The other two took a licking from the Vietnamese that shocked the PLA. Using a surprise maneuver, Fu divided his troops, sending half west to distract the invaders while he led the others east in a circular movement. Then he attacked from the rear with powerful Xin-81 automatic assault rifles and annihilated the enemy. He executed their commander with a single bullet to the base of his skull.

As Fu would say later, foreigners owed fealty to China,.

Always.

In Shanghai, Captain Fu created the first of several business plans that would cement his brilliant military reputation. He vowed not to marry; the Army became his heart and soul. He dedicated himself to the study of English so he could read foreign press accounts and external intelligence reports.

With a carefully selected covert cadre, Fu created a secret account funded by proceeds from the PLA's undercover sales of *East*

Wind missiles to sponsors of terrorism in the Middle East like Iran, Iraq, and Pakistan. At the time, in 1989, many of his classmates had been dispatched to Beijing to put down the Tiananmen riots. As he tried to craft a web of covert commercial enterprises for the PLA overseas, he was left ashen-faced when he read reports of the Beijing Massacre.

Grizzly images of Army troops shooting and killing their own brothers and sisters haunted Fu like a nightmare.

He knew the real enemy was always outside. Never at home.

By 1990, China's traditional nemesis, Japan, had developed a cocky attitude of arrogant superiority. As a result of their artificial bull market, Tokyo stocks defied gravity. Investing $150 billion from one of his secret PLA accounts, Fu ran up the share prices of Japanese companies with hidden assets that he planned to dump when the market peaked.

Barely a year after he launched his attack, the Nikkei Index soared to ¥37,000. When the Bank of Japan began raising its discount rate, Fu started to sell his holdings. Like tulip bulbs in Holland three centuries before, Japanese share prices collapsed and never stopped sinking until the Tokyo market had lost more than half its value. Japan's economy would languish in recession for years to come.

On his return to Beijing to brief his superiors at his promotion, Colonel Fu made it patently clear that he would never allow China to be intimidated by a foreign power.

Ever.

So the rogue Colonel knew it wasn't sufficient just to have a laboratory mist that simply sprayed H5N1 supernatant onto live birds. He had to have a battle strain of the aerosol that was robust and durable, with microdroplets tiny enough to penetrate the human nose and throat. Even before the Russian had perfected the deadly viral mutant itself, Fu had him working on an aerosolized version.

Lukanov experimented with portable hosts like desiccated canine cell cultures to see if they could keep the H5N1 virus alive for extended periods without a natural human host to culture them. This was tricky.

He found some stable hosts but they wouldn't culture the virus. Then he found he could culture the virus but the hosts proved to be unstable. When he couldn't get the necessary cell samples from Beijing, Fu bought them from the United States through a covert PLA affiliate overseas.

At the right price, he said, Americans will sell anything to anybody, even after 9/11.

For the first time, Lukanov began to get seriously discouraged until he stumbled onto a solution that was both accidental and promising: wheat germ dust. It was commercially available, easy to culture, and surprisingly stable.

When he freeze-dried it with H5N1 samples, the Russian found he could keep the cloned virus alive for more than a week. But the microparticles had to be smaller than 5 microns in order to be "breathable" and captured by the alveoli. They were tiny air sacs in the human lung where respiratory infection sets in.

The EM photos confirmed it. Lukanov's H5N1 particles measured a perfect 3.1 microns.

Lukanov wanted to wait until after the Hong Kong results were in to tell Fu about his stable aerosol. If Wang Wei's birds could infect humans with the mutant virus and kill them, could the lethal virus then be transmitted by spray through the air?

If Col. Fu could broadcast the microparticles just once by means of an aerosol, he would have the most powerful, efficient, and undetectable biological weapon of all: ordinary people doing ordinary things -- breathing, talking, laughing, sneezing, coughing, kissing, embracing.

Even that disgusting, decadent habit so prominent in the West: the simple, unconscious act of shaking hands.

∘ **21** ∘

After they returned to the clinic, Ellen sorted the new tissue samples, tagged them and packed them in dry ice. Arroyo arranged for someone from DOH to drive them down to Santa Fe.

It was nearly mid-day. There was nothing new from Higueras or Gupta and Feldman was still out collecting his samples.

Ellen decided to call Atlanta, try to catch Sandy McDermott in the lab.

She used Arroyo's speakerphone. Since she assumed Sandy would be working in a BL-3 lab without the noisy Racal respirators, she should be able to talk over a hands-free wall phone.

When she picked up, Ellen recognized her crisp brogue instantly. McDermott was a fiery redhead, an excitable Scot who had gone from Edinburgh to Cambridge to MIT and never returned.

"Ellie, you sure you want to stay in the field rather than advance the cause of medical science here in the lab? This could be your last chance."

"Be cool, Sandy, you've got an audience here. Dr. Arroyo's with me."

She introduced them.

"Well, you'll be happy to know I've confirmed this bug -- whatever it is -- is definitely some kind of virus, not a bacteria or toxin," McDermott said. "You can tell Higueras and Gupta they can pack up and come home."

"Feldman will love you for that," she said. "You sure?"

"Damn sure," she said. "We tried the tissue samples on a dozen different bacteria cultures all morning and got zip. We made homogenates, ground them with mortar and pestle the old-fashioned way and centrifuged them in test tubes. They all passed through the sub-micron filters, so we know from their particle size that it has to be a virus. But nothing specific yet, and it's what -- two o'clock here now."

"Nothing positive for toxins, either?"

"Nope. We tested the evidence samples -- dirt, hairs, surface scrapings -- across a range of wavelengths, checking for known chemicals and gases. Zilch."

"What about phosphene or phosgene?" Arroyo asked.

He leaned in closer to the speakerphone.

"Phosgene is normally banned but that hasn't stopped people from using it as fertilizer. It was implicated in the Oklahoma City bombings, remember. And the Navaho tribe buys canisters of phosphene gas from the state to use as a pesticide."

"Negative for both," McDermott replied crisply. "Toxins are out of the question."

"Sandy," Ellen broke in, "what can you tell us about the virus? We need to start thinking about anti-virals and treatment."

"Nothing yet," she said. "Could be an arena virus, a retrovirus, or even just a damned flu bug that's drifted into a new mutation. We haven't had time to do EM scans or run ELISAs on them yet, let alone try PCR. I need the rest of the afternoon for those and if you don't get off the phone pretty soon we may not have time."

"Okay, okay. When you run the tests, you'll double-check the results with USAMRIID?"

"I love you too, Ellie. Of course we will."

As soon as they rang off, Arroyo eyed his notes and asked her about the cryptic buzzwords.

"The hell is EM, and ELISA, and PCR?"

Ellen nodded.

"Sorry about that. EM is standard shorthand for electron microscope scans, a standard entry-stage process of pathogen identification. That's what we use to get a first pass."

"ELISA?"

"That's an anacronym for Enzyme-Linked Immuno-Sorbent Assay, a blood test to confirm the presence or absence of pathogen-specific antibodies."

She took a sheet of note paper and sketched a diagram.

"Tiny droplets of blood samples are dripped into a grid of microwells by pipette, followed by droplets of specific viral antibodies and finally by tiny quantities of a marker enzyme. If the target antibodies are present, the wells will emit a nice blue neon glow called viral blue. ELISA can confirm the presence of a category of a virus but PCR is needed to determine the precise genetic structure.

"Jesus, you guys really go in for a lot of shorthand, don't you?"

She smiled.

"Yeah, well, it's like anything else. Use it often enough, it takes on a life all its own."

"And PCR?"

"Right. PCR stands for Polymerase Chain Reaction. It's a gene-sequencing technique that was developed by microbiologists in the early 1990s. PCR amplifies microscopic quantities of genetic code so it can be analyzed in detail. We can make a DNA copy of the virus utilizing a process called reverse transcriptase that 'Xeroxes' the RNA building blocks of the genome to create an exact DNA copy. Then we add gene-specific primers to generate multiple quantities of the target virus so its exact genetic sequence can be determined, mapped, and matched to file copies of known viruses. That's how the lab can ID a mystery virus for sure."

Arroyo frowned.

"So fulminant tissue in the lungs was not triggered by bacteria?" he asked. "If I hadn't seen the antibiotic resistance in all these patients, my guess would have been staphylococcal enterotoxins."

Ellen shook her head.

"Remember the tissue samples we collected from Aalyah? I was very worried about the weight and color of her lung tissue. Supernatant in the lungs could be the result of a rare flu virus, despite the off-season timing. But it's definitely not a bacteria. We should know more when Sandy calls back."

"Now I've finally got something for the press," Arroyo said. "Thank you."

He picked up the phone.

Ellen reached across and took the receiver from his hand.

"I wouldn't do that just yet," she said. "We're not infallible and we've been proven wrong before. The last thing you want is a retraction tomorrow from erroneous data today, which will damage your credibility with the Navajo people, not to mention the outside world. You have nothing to lose by waiting."

She slowly cradled the receiver.

"But I've got to give them something," he said. "Something's better than nothing, isn't it?"

"No. Let them wait. If Sandy can isolate and ID the virus, then you'll be good to go this evening in time for the nightly news. If not, well, we're probably in for the long haul anyway. All of us."

An hour later, when Jonathan Feldman returned with his field samples, Ellen gave him a brief recap from Atlanta.

He danced a little jig, Navajo style, to celebrate McDermott's confirmation of the virus, until Ellen reminded him not to gloat. She sent him with his collected samples back to Santa Fe to help Higueras at DOH.

She spent the rest of the afternoon reviewing data with Arroyo, worrying about Paul and the van, still concerned about the dead Mexicans and the mystery virus.

At a quarter past four, Sandy McDermott rang back. It was early evening in Atlanta.

"We found very low blood platelet counts," she said in her familiar brogue, "which is consistent with arena virus. But we also found something really strange, something that doesn't quite fit. The samples all show a huge number of white blood cells -- more than 50,000 in most cases. We've seen white cell counts that high in the presence of bacterial infections but viruses don't normally affect the whites. Or if they do, they should lower the count, not raise it."

Ellen tested her.

"Sandy, a flu virus could raise the white cell count."

"True," she agreed, "but both the EM and ELISA rule out flu as a suspect. We got no viral glow from any of the flu antibodies. ELISA for arena turned a cool blue."

Ellen frowned.

"But arena viruses cause kidney breakdown and internal hemorrhaging," she said. "Not respiratory failure. And its natural host is the bat, for God's sake. No bats out here in the desert, Sandy, so how can arena be a suspect? Its mortality rate is nowhere near the 50% we've got here."

They knew arena virus was prevalent primarily in Africa and Latin America. It was called Lassa fever after its discovery in Nigeria in 1969 and Machupo in Bolivia a decade later. The arena family had been isolated in St. Louis in 1933, when it was thought to cause a mild form of encephalitis. It was named after the Latin word for sand because of its unique granular shape on EM scans.

"I know," McDermott went on. "So we didn't stop there. We also know that hanta is another virus that raises white cell counts. But since hanta attacks and infects the victim's kidneys, your patients ought to be dying of renal failure, not respiratory failure. And your tissue samples should show signs of hemorrhaging and be flooded with blood. But they're not."

Ellen was stumped.

Hantavirus had been isolated in Korea in 1976 after it had infected several thousand American soldiers along the DMZ. It causes internal bleeding and was named after the Han River. Hanta provoked a huge controversy at the time because the Allies worried that North Korea might have launched the virus as a terrible new bioweapon.

"So what did you do next?" she asked.

"I got Pete to run a PCR, to test the fluorescent antibody results of your blood sera. See if we could find an antibody that might cross-react with the assortment of viral antigens we had here. They were all negative, every one. So I ran an isolated test using nested PCR on a second amplification against a batch of hanta virus-specific antigens alone. This gave me a monoclonal hanta primer, which I ran through our automated gene sequencer to compare the results. Bingo, they were all positive, every single one of them. Your culprit is hanta, Ellie. Believe it or not."

Ellen was speechless.

Her mind was racing in three different directions at once.

"But this is nuts," she said. "You know as well as I do that there's no hanta virus in this country anywhere at all. None! This can mean only one thing."

"You got it, Ellie."

"It's a newbie. A new strain of hanta that causes pulmonary infection instead of renal failure."

"Not so fast," McDermott cautioned her. "Don't forget, hanta is spread by rats and mice. The virus is transmitted through the air, contaminated with microdroplets from their crap or piss. There's no other known vector."

"Rats?" she asked. "Did you say *rats?*"

Ellen suddenly heard hoofbeats and saw a thundering herd of zebras racing at her. The pieces of the puzzle suddenly started coming together.

It was something Paul had said about the mysterious van traffic from Mexico.

The couriers had smuggled explosives and ... *desert rats* ... into Arroyo Seco to get the old man's land condemned.

They got their condemnation, all right. But not by inundating the real estate with pests. By accidentally -- or on purpose -- infecting it with a virus.

"Sandy, as usual, you're brilliant," Ellen said. "FedEx us five thousand doses of ribavirin and a couple dozen moon suits overnight. We've got to start killing some rodents."

"I thought all they had out there was prairie dogs," McDermott said.

"Long story. Just hurry up and FedEx us that stuff."

Ellen hung up and turned to Arroyo.

"*Now* you got something for the press."

Then she remembered an old Chinese proverb: never neglect an opportunity to turn an enemy into a friend.

"Call Mitch Webster at CBS first," she said. "Give him a ten-minute head start and make sure he knows this came straight from Atlanta."

After he spoke to the media, they had to get the word out to the Navajo community to avoid all contact with rodents. Regardless of species.

Arroyo's staff quickly sent sound trucks into the rural areas, flooded the village with posters, broadcast the message over TV and radio, posted the news on the Navajo website at www.navajo.org.

They devised a plan for eradication that would start the next day when the CDC gear arrived. Arroyo called the New Mexico Department of Health and gave the chief of infectious diseases an update. Then he arranged for a team to help the Navajos set traps and stretch nets over known nesting areas where they could scatter poisoned *piñon* nuts for the rats to eat.

"And I'll supervise the distribution of ribavirin to sick patients as soon as it arrives," he said.

Ellen called Paul.

"Call off your search for that van until we can decontaminate the area," she said. "And steer clear of any contact with rodents."

"Ellie, we're wearing shit-kickers, for Christ's sake. Why can't we just ignore them?"

She told him.

"Jesus."

"Yeah. So stay masked, wear gloves, and destroy all your clothes when you're done."

He chuckled.

"All of them?"

"Right down to your Agency-issue briefs."

"So what do I wear back to Santa Fe?"

"You'll think of something. I'll see you back at the hotel later tonight."

Turning to Arroyo, she said, "There's one more thing we need to do."

"What's that?"

"You've got to name this disease," she said. "Whenever a new microbe is discovered, it takes its name from the area in which it was found. As the top Navajo medical officer, you deserve that honor."

"I'm flattered," he said. "But I couldn't. The Tribal Council has to do it."

"How fast can you convene them?" Ellen asked.

"I think they'll want to do this right away."

○ **22** ○

Wang Wei unlocked his truck and climbed back in the cab.

He saw Ah Kwong at the upper window again and waved goodbye. She waved back, with a smile.

But as he fired up the engine, he suddenly felt queasy. A chill coursed through his body. He shivered. Probably just the hot bath, he thought. It will pass.

When he sneezed onto the windshield, however, he noticed the pink mist for the first time.

He spit quickly into the palm of one hand. When he saw the blood now, he got really scared.

He slammed the door and shot forward.

His tires squealed as he surged around a corner into the early evening traffic. His nose began to run, and when he wiped it with the back of one hand he noticed that his phlegm was pink too.

His pulse raced. He sneezed again and suddenly his vision began to blur.

Wang knew he needed help, fast. He thought the body massage would make him feel better, and it did. But now his head throbbed with a piercing pain and he couldn't stop coughing.

He careened around a corner and saw the familiar blue sign with a white "H."

He followed the arrows until he pulled into the Fo Tan hospital parking lot. Staggering, he pushed through the entrance and collapsed, face down, in the lobby.

A receptionist behind the desk flipped a switch.

The ear-piercing whine of an emergency alarm filled the entryway.

A gurney rolled out.

Within minutes, Wang Wei was intubated and on his way to the ER.

○ **23** ○

Sometime later, after a traditional Navajo dinner of corn and *salsa* cooked over hot coals in the cool desert air, Ellen listened carefully as the Tribal Council debated the new virus.

Jimmy Arroyo suggested calling it *arroyo muerto* -- the canyon of death -- despite the dubious distinction of having his name, a common Indian word, linked to it.

The Tribal Council demurred.

They argued that no disease should associate the Navajos with death. Like the Long Walk, it could only bring them more pain and suffering. The name had to be neutral, invoking no reference to the past.

After heated discussion, the old chief who met Ellen at graveside the day before raised his hand.

He stood and faced the assembled group as he cleared his throat.

"This evil creature deserves no name," he said hoarsely. "We will simply call it *sin nombre*."

The virus with no name.

There were no objections.

It was done.

"You're not giving us a chance to thank you properly," Arroyo said as he drove Ellen back to Santa Fe. "I wish you could stay and help us wrap up."

"Feldman will," she said. "Virus is his big thing, his passion. He'll help you handle the drill tomorrow. He can also collect samples from the captured rats before they're killed so we can add the live virus to our inventory of antigens and store the genome in our gene bank. Higueras and Gupta will also stay to help the DOH catalogue its lab samples. But I've got to get back."

He stopped to let her out in front of the La Posada hotel.

"Good luck."

"You, too, Jimmy. Thanks for everything."

They shook hands warmly as she got out.

She watched his jeep disappear around the square and looked at her watch. She suddenly felt drained, bone-tired with fatigue. She knew it was too late for the red-eye back East so she'd have to take the first flight out at dawn.

Paul caught her eye as she entered the lobby. Despite the fatigue, or perhaps because of it, she doubled over with laughter.

He was wearing a traditional Navajo woman's tribal dress, fashioned out of rough burlap and held together with a string of polished turquoise beads.

"That the best you could do?" she asked. She was feeling giddy now, having nailed the bug.

"Don't knock it," he said, blushing. "Three guys started hitting on me as soon as I got back."

"Come on, let's go upstairs and you can change."

They walked toward the elevators through a chorus of catcalls from the bar.

"You find the van?" Ellen asked as they walked toward her room.

"Yeah. Abandoned just outside Taos. The poor bastards never made it to Arroyo Seco."

Ellen pulled out her cell phone and gave Feldman the plate number and location.

"That's it," he said. "You've got to stop now."

He reached over and flipped her phone shut.

"Bedtime."

"Wait," she said groggily. "There's something I want to show you."

She reached across the bed for her briefcase and pulled out a small object no larger than a pillbox.

"What the hell's that?" he asked.

"A new prototype from Hewlett-Packard," she said. "A chip-based genetic sequencer made from ceramic on metal. All the sensors are buried in the substrate so it can't be reverse-engineered. We call it the HP/UP because it's ultra-portable."

She flipped open the lid and extended a small surface.

"You put a droplet of fluid sample here," she said, pointing to a tiny crevice, "and the microprocessor analyzes it against digitized genetic sequences. It measures changes in the optical properties of the virus when it binds to antibody complexes and then compares the results with direct immuno-fluorescence assays stored on-chip."

"And it works?"

"So far. It's programmed only for a range of known flu viruses but it's 98% accurate. Once the device is fully functional across a complete range of microbes, we can take it into the field and sequence an unidentified microbe in a matter of minutes. It took Atlanta the whole day to do this today."

"How long before it's operational?"

He took the slim, compact unit and held it in his fingertips.

"Don't know," she said with a shrug. "We've got a team of programmers working full-time on it with HP. But since viruses are so unstable, they tend to mutate faster than our computer guys can get the sequenced assays digitized on chip. At least they've coded all the known flu strains so we can keep testing it. When I get back, they're supposed to have a new version ready with a mouth-activated breath analyzer that's even quicker and more accurate. It will do instant analysis in an emergency."

Emergencies were what Ellen trained for, two weekends a month. With specialists from 40 Federal agencies and Early Responder teams -- local police, fire, and emergency rescue squads -- she traveled to different locations around the country, simulating public health drills for bioterrorism preparedness. She told Paul she worried constantly about the unwieldy collection of competing state and federal teams, which was why she of all people felt qualified to call them Chinese fire drills.

"But we need that breath analyzer for the Big One, Paul. My friends say I'm paranoid, my superiors tell me I'm too careful, and my colleagues say I'm over the top. But I know it's coming. It's only a matter of time."

He leaned down and kissed her on the forehead.

"That could be anywhere, anytime," he said.

"I know, and probably when we least expect it. That's the tricky thing about a virus. All it knows how to do is hunt for a host cell and hijack its reproductive machinery to make countless copies. I'm worried that this hanta outbreak may not have been inadvertent or accidental. An unidentified virus killed those two couriers from Mexico and scores of Navajos here. It could have been a whole lot worse."

Paul stood and stretched.

"I think I'll stick around a while," he said. "See if can we dig up anything more on this network of Islamic militants south of the border. After your people clear and disinfect Arroyo Seco, I want to do a separate search up there for any explosives."

"I'll mention that to Atlanta. If those desert rats were infected coming up from Chihuahua, we'll need to send a decontamination team down to Mexico too. This may not have been an accident."

Just then, the phone rang.

Paul stretched across the bed and picked up the receiver.

"It's for you," he said. "Atlanta."

Frowning, she took the handset.

"Ellen? It's Sandy. Thank God we found you."

"Sandy, what's up?"

She glanced at her watch.

"Christ, it's way after midnight in Atlanta. Don't tell me you're backing off."

"This is not about hanta, Ellie. I've got Hong Kong on the line and they're frantic. They think they may have a flu epidemic on the loose and they don't know what to do. They can't identify the subtype and need a flu expert from here desperately. The Director wants you out there on the next available flight. How soon do you think you can leave?"

"Put them through. I'll talk to them directly."

She cupped the receiver and turned to Paul.

"It's China," she said, her eyes wide. "Sounds pretty bad. I may be gone for a while."

○ **24** ○

The Cathay Pacific twin-jet Airbus began its long descent toward Chek Lap Kok. Ellen's flight had been delayed by Hong Kong air traffic control, a persistent problem after the new airport had replaced Kai Tak.

Despite its precarious location in the virtual backyard of a notoriously congested housing project near Hong Kong Harbor, Kai Tak had attained a consistent reputation for safety and forced efficiency. Chek Lap Kok was like a new theme park on Lantau Island, far to the west. Stricter security protocols were in place both in the air and on the ground.

Ellen snapped awake.

She felt the landing gear vibrate and glanced at her watch.

It was midnight local time, nearly two days after Albuquerque. Unable to make a Dragon Air non-stop from LA, her only option was the Cathay connection through Tokyo. Asia-bound flights always lost a full day when they crossed the international dateline flying west across the Pacific.

Ellen gazed out the small window through the thick September air. She could see illuminated container ships in the Harbor, their cargo cranes silent and still. A Star Ferry inched between Hong Kong Island and Tsim Sha Tsui in Kowloon. The silhouettes of Hong Kong's gaudy office towers reflected in the water. Their enormous windows glowed with ostentatious wealth, halos of immense power.

Past Kowloon were the New Territories, darker and with fewer lights. Beyond the farms and food plots was Lok Ma Chau, the old border crossing into China, not far from where her aunt used to live. The Shenzhen special economic zone stretched across lower Guangdong province, home to Hong Kong's ramshackle factories and rickety textile mills that took constant advantage of China's low-priced labor. They churned out cheap toys and designer dresses for the West's insatiable consumers.

Shenzhen was home to China's emerging "red chip" companies, local listings on a loopy stock exchange that was operated like a lottery by corrupt bureaucrats in the Finance Ministry, manipulated by swindlers and speculators. Shenzhen sweatshops routinely sewed fraudulent European and Japanese labels into their knitwear to skirt the tight U. S. textile quotas.

From the outside looking in, China was an entrepreneur's paradise. But from the inside looking out, Ellen knew it was a different story.

She smiled as she remembered the popular if pejorative phrase her family had often written in their letters.

Lu fen dan, biaomian guang.

On the outside, even donkey shit shines.

Ellen routinely saw visiting delegations of Chinese public health officials when they visited Atlanta and she met periodically with political dissidents when they won asylum in America. She knew President Jiang was reviled as a member of the *fengpai* political faction in Beijing and that Hong Kong and Macau were finally back under Chinese control.

Real estate drove everything in the former Colony -- the stock market, the housing estates, the huge corporate towers. Property was the only god, worshipped by working-class gambler and rich tycoon alike.

Her last visit to Hong Kong had been a decade earlier, on a trip with her father after he retired. She'd wanted to visit China after such a long absence, too, to see her younger brother. But it was too soon after the horrible Tiananmen Incident called the Beijing Massacre. She knew she couldn't risk it because the PSB would try to track her down and arrest her if she ever did.

So Hong Kong was as close as she got.

Her working knowledge of China came through regular reports she received from Stanley Novak. He headed the CDC's Institute for Viral Diseases that tracked seasonal migration of the flu like a bloodhound. His worldwide network of influenza sentinels included six regional centers in China that fed statistical data on local cases to the Institute of Viral Biology in Beijing.

According to his most recent reports, there was nothing out of the ordinary in China. Situation normal.

The big jet touched down softly and taxied to the gate.

Ellen stepped crisply out of the jetway, wearing pearl gray gabardine slacks with a cotton piqué peasant's blouse in navy blue. A light, bright red waterproof jacket was draped across her shoulders.

Hong Kong's Deputy Commissioner of Health, Dr. Amy Wu, greeted her immediately. Her dark hair was swept back in a short ponytail. She wore a starched white lab coat over khaki slacks with a maroon polo shirt. She had come straight from the hospital, her eyes ringed with fatigue.

"It's an honor to meet you, Dr. Chou."

She took Ellen's arm as they walked quickly ahead.

"The Big Sky case you solved in Montana is a kind of legend here."

"We were lucky," Ellen said. "That was just a common bacteria, but it sounds like Hong Kong's been hit by something far more serious. Tell me what you've got so far."

Dr. Wu escorted them swiftly through customs and immigration. Two uniformed policemen led them to a waiting car.

On the drive across the Harbor Expressway, she handed Ellen a sheaf of medical reports on their most recent cases.

"We've run all the lab tests we know," she said. "But we can't confirm the microbe so we can't sub-type the virus. We iced down another packet of blood and fluid samples and FedEx'd them to Dr. McDermott's lab in Atlanta today."

Ellen scanned the test results.

"We may be able to learn something in short order," she said.

She reached into her briefcase and pulled out the HP/UP chip-scanner. She handed it to Amy Wu and explained what it did.

"This can't be real," Wu said.

She frowned, looking at the tiny apparatus with skeptical eyes.

"It looks so … artificial."

"It's real, all right. We've tested it extensively on a range of known flu viruses with reliable specificity."

She took the device from Dr. Wu and put it back in her briefcase.

"If what you have is a bona fide flu strain, we'll know as soon as we get to the hospital and can test some lab samples."

Ellen looked up and noticed the bridge lights as they crossed the causeway. The heavy mist made them sparkle like tiny stars. Moments later they cut through Kowloon and headed for the dense sub-district of Sha Tin. The slick streets were dark and quiet.

"I'm worried about all this internal bleeding," Ellen said, breaking the silence.

She flipped through the Hong Kong DOH reports.

"It's not consistent with flu."

"We know," Dr. Wu said. "But the other symptoms -- fever, chills, upper respiratory infection, pharyngitis, myalgias -- all fit perfectly. We think it may be flu plus complications from something else, pneumonia maybe."

Ellen frowned.

"What's the current patient count?"

"Up to 105 now," Wu said. "Eight more admitted today. Two died last night, twenty-four total so far. The death rate's in excess of twenty percent and rising."

Ellen winced.

"How much do you know about the index case?"

Dr. Wu leafed through her papers.

"Male, 27, collapsed on arrival four days ago," she read in a monotone. "Rushed to ER, held in ICU. Febrile, URI, blood in sputum. No ID, no papers, just a set of keys and some loose change in one pocket. Only one ear, likely birth defect in the other. Died night before last."

She looked up.

"Strange," she said.

"How so?" Ellen asked. "The birth defect?"

"No, the floor nurse says he mumbled in Mandarin so we knew he wasn't from Hong Kong or Guangdong. We put him on continuous IV drip but he was weak and delirious. We called in a translator too late."

The car wove through another series of back streets and began to climb.

Ellen glanced out the window and saw block after block of large public housing estates, their horizontal bamboo staves bare, glistening wet and eerily empty in the darkness.

No wealth here, she thought; Hong Kong's power was all downtown, across the harbor, in the glass skyscrapers. But the big apartment buildings were perfect for an infectious epidemic: dense population, congested conditions, cramped confines. One contagious resident could infect the rest in a heartbeat.

"We've transferred all the known cases to University hospital," Amy Wu said.

She handed Ellen a folder marked '*Chinese University of Hong Kong -- Proprietary and Confidential.*'

"They're all from Sha Tin, in the New Territories. Every time the DOH confirms a similar case at other medical centers nearby, we bring them over here to Fo Tan."

"Very good," Ellen said. "Universal precautions, I assume. Barrier nursing?"

Dr. Wu hesitated.

"Not exactly. You see, the staff's been so busy."

"Ouch. Not good. What have you done about isolating the sick patients?"

"We have no confirmation yet that this bug, whatever it is, may be contagious. So Dr. Yee -- he's the hospital director -- hasn't mandated isolation procedures."

Ellen started to worry now.

Rising admissions with a budding mortality rate from an unknown disease were classic symptoms of an infectious epidemic.

"Then you may have a worse problem than you think," she said.

The car pulled into a semi-circular driveway in front of the University Hospital.

"I'll need a lab coat," Ellen said. "And a face mask and gloves."

"But you must be so tired from your long flight," Dr. Wu insisted. "We have a room ready for you next door."

Ellen got out of the car and shut the door.

"I can bunk later on a cot in the same room the interns use," Ellen said as they walked in. "We need to start testing your samples right away."

◦ **25** ◦

"Where's Wang Wei?"

Col. Fu shouted into the handset. He pounded a workbench as he paced nervously from bench to window.

The adjutant of the PLA garrison on Stonecutter's Island in Hong Kong was on the line.

When Hong Kong reverted to China in 1997, a garrison of the People's Liberation Army had replaced the Royal British Forces and their Gurkha troops on the nearby island. Their role was nominally ceremonial but the PLA used the troops covertly for other purposes.

Col. Fu was worried. His loyal assistant was late, hadn't called, had just ... disappeared. He had no reason to believe that Wang had pulled a fast one and tried to escape. That wouldn't be Wang Wei. He'd gone and come back reliably many times on routine supply trips before. Why would he do something stupid now?

Fu knew the answer. He wouldn't.

"What do you mean, you can't find him?" Fu screamed, his voice shrill. "It's been four days. The man has only one ear and speaks no Cantonese, can that be so damn hard? And the truck has a GPS sensor in the glove box, so get your troops out there with a tracking device and *find* it."

Fu slammed the receiver down.

He glanced again at the adjutant's report from his covert contact at the Hong Kong Department of Health. More than a hundred cases of a mysterious illness confirmed. All in the New Territories, all at University Hospital for treatment. Four days, 105 patients. So far, so good. But none of them had been typed yet, let alone subtyped, and there was no word on the death rate.

Were they all still alive?

Either the DOH knew something and weren't admitting it, or they knew nothing and were still waiting for confirmation. Had to be the latter, Fu thought. Hong Kong labs lacked the advanced technology needed to subtype viruses.

But the Colonel knew from the adjutant that the DOH had contacted the Centers for Disease Control in America and the CDC had dispatched an expert, a Chinese-American virologist, a woman doctor, who had just arrived. This meant they would start sending fluid samples by overnight courier to the U. S. for subtyping without delay. Then his contact at DOH would definitely know more.

But that still didn't explain Wang Wei.

"You are worried?"

It was the Russian.

Lukanov studied the Colonel's face, saw his usual expression of confidence replaced by a frown.

"You said it would be *simple*," Fu hissed.

He slammed his clipboard down on the workbench.

"Take a few chickens and ducks to the wet market in Hong Kong, you said. Wait a couple of days, you said. Watch the health reports. You'll see."

His tone mocked the Russian's deep voice and thick accent.

"When the adjutant calls his contact at the Department of Health, they'll confirm a mysterious disease," he went on. "And when you see the death rate, you'll know the cloned virus is lethal. But there's no corroboration of the illness yet and no confirmed deaths. Now Wang Wei has vanished. And you ask if I'm *worried*?"

Fu walked smartly to the windows along the wall. He stood with his arms crossed and stared out the narrow slits into the darkness.

Lukanov tried to calm the agitated rebel.

"Look, you know we've succeeded," he said. "There's no doubt those birds infected the people who bought them. For sure, they've in turn infected others. But maybe the airborne incubation period from human to human is longer than I thought. We don't know yet. Give it another day, you'll see."

Col. Fu thought for a long minute and turned back to face the Russian.

"And Wang Wei?" he asked. "What about my courier?"

Lukanov shrugged his shoulders.

"Think about it," he said. "Wang Wei is young. He's a virtual captive here, wants to enjoy a little freedom. Maybe he stops for a drink. Maybe he spends some time with a young woman. And maybe he's on the road right now, heading back to Jiangxi."

"Or maybe he's dead."

It was the voice of Lo Fengbu.

Fu spun around and eyed the young assistant who busied himself cleaning beakers and pipettes at the far workbench. A short lab coat covered his stocky frame. He had thick black hair combed neatly back from an oval face framed by large, outsized spectacles with thick lenses that turned his eyes into pinpoints.

Fu approached the workbench.

"Tell me again what you just said."

Lo kept his head down as he kept working.

"I'm serious," he said without looking up. "You probably created a more lethal mutant than you ever dreamed. If the birds were hot -- and you know they were -- then Wang was most likely your first case."

"Was he acting strangely before he left?" the Colonel asked, frowning again.

Lo wiped his hands calmly on the white lab coat and looked up.

"No, sir. Not at all. Not in my presence anyway. But knowing my background, he always kept his distance."

Fu approached the former dissident and looked him directly in the eye.

"If you're lying to me, Lo, you know what will happen."

Lo met Fu's stare head-on now without blinking.

"There was no strange behavior, Colonel. None whatsoever."

Fu turned back to the Russian scientist.

"Well?"

Lukanov shook his head.

"Look, General Min seemed quite pleased with your briefing," said the burly Russian. "He asked tough questions and pushed hard. You were well prepared with the data and handled his concerns skillfully. You never backed down, even when he pressed you time and again to accelerate the schedule."

Fu scowled.

"But he knows the live experiment is still unconfirmed," he said. "He calls me every day for news from Hong Kong and I have nothing to give him. *Nothing!*"

"You said yourself, many times ... how does it go?"

The Russian paused, looking down.

"Ah, yes – 'don't fear failure, be capable of successful execution.' So give it another day. What other option do you really have?"

The Colonel was silent for a moment.

He took a deep breath and exhaled slowly.

"One day," Fu said, holding up an index finger. "I'll give it one more day."

∘ **26** ∘

Despite the pre-dawn hour, the University hospital was busy and frantic.

Ellen stepped aside as yet another gurney rushed down the hallway. She hustled toward the lab. An orderly steadied an IV pack as another cart turned the corner. Interns ran from room to room, their deep-set eyes rimmed in purple with the telltale signs of fatigue.

The hospital intercom blared calls in a monotone. Cell phones chirped endlessly in shirt pockets and lab coats. At one end of a corridor, a solitary janitor mopped the floor.

Amy Wu took Ellen to the hospital lab on the second floor where they found a small refrigerator padlocked and crisscrossed with strips of bright orange Day-Glo tape. Dr. Wu spun the combination lock, opened it, and extracted a specially marked tray of fluid samples. She set it on top of a workbench.

"We'll still need results from the PCR and ELISA tests in Atlanta," Ellen said. "But this should give us a preliminary indication."

She pulled a facemask over her mouth and nose and snapped on a pair of latex gloves. She glanced at the workbench with the familiar hood overhead.

"Laminar flow?" Ellen asked.

Dr. Wu shook her head.

"No, just straight vertical exhaust," she replied. "Sorry, there's no BL-3 in Hong Kong."

Ellen paused, holding a gloved hand under the airflow.

"HEPA-filtered?" she asked, looking up.

"I really don't know," Dr. Wu said with a frown. "We don't analyze anything more dangerous than staph or nosocomial bacteria here."

"Then we need goggles."

Dr. Wu sent an orderly after two pairs of clear plastic safety glasses. She helped Ellen arrange the tray of marked samples on the workbench and pulled on her mask and gloves.

In minutes, the orderly was back.

Ellen adjusted the goggles over her eyes and sat in front of the bench. She took out the HP/UP sensor, flipped open the lid and set it under the hood. She could feel the upward tug of air on her hands.

Taking one of the sample vials, she inserted a hypodermic needle through the rubber vacuum cap and extracted a tiny sample of fluid. She returned the vial to its numbered cubicle in the tray and held the needle directly over the crevice on the miniature device. She placed two drops of fluid in the slot and waited.

"How does this thing work?" Dr. Wu asked.

Ellen explained it to her as she leaned in to look.

"Watch the LED display," Ellen said, pointing to a mini-readout at the tip of the lid.

It was blank now but a series of miniature lights blinked green as the processor started its routine, analyzing the fluid sample against genetic code in memory.

Suddenly the lights stopped blinking and the diode glowed red.

Ellen's eyes went wide.

"This is strange," she said. "Very strange."

"That can't be right," Dr. Wu said. "It says A/H5N1."

"Exactly," Ellen nodded. "Give me another sample. Specificity is 98% accurate so that one could have been in the 2% error range."

She went through the identical routine with a fresh hypodermic so as not to contaminate the samples. She swabbed the receptor crevice with a disinfectant and dripped in a new sample while Dr. Wu made a notation on the chart that listed the fluid samples, coded with their numbered positions in the tray.

Moments later the LED display blinked its response.

A/H5N1.

There was no mistake.

Ellen's heart began to pound. She heard the distant thunder of hoofbeats again. In her fatigue, she saw another herd of wild zebras galloping straight toward her.

"Get me some control samples," she said. "Fast."

"What kind?"

"I don't care. Anything previously confirmed as flu. *Quickly.*"

Dr. Wu hurried to another refrigerator, unlocked it and withdrew a similar tray of vials. Ellen prepped the receptor for a fresh sample.

"Don't tell me what they are," she said. "Just hand me the vials one by one so I can't read the labels."

Dr. Wu watched as Ellen took a new syringe. Extracting a small sample, she squeezed a droplet onto the scanning device. Within seconds, the LED glowed red.

"A/H3N2."

"Correct," she said, nodding. "Another?"

"Yes," said Ellen, gesturing for a vial.

She repeated the process step by step.

"A/H1N1."

Dr. Wu nodded.

"Right."

Ellen exhaled quietly.

"Well, it looks like accuracy is not the issue," she said. "The device appears to be functioning properly so let's go back to your new samples."

Ellen turned around, withdrew another test tube from the tray and tried again.

The response was no different from before.

A/H5N1.

They repeated the same process randomly for 27 samples.

All positive for H5N1.

Every single one.

Ellen turned back to face Dr. Wu, who saw the fear in her eyes.

"I'm not a virologist, Dr. Chou," she said. "What does this mean?"

"It means you may have lethal viral shift, Amy."

She disinfected the digital detector and put it back in her briefcase.

"H5N1 is an avian virus. It lives naturally in the intestines of birds. They don't normally infect humans and we don't know what might happen if they do. But it looks like we're starting to find out fast. The fact that all these samples came from humans means we're in some pretty serious trouble."

She shut her briefcase.

"Go back and interview every surviving patient. We're going to need a full background review -- where they were, what they ate, who or what they contacted, what they were doing prior to the onset of symptoms, environmental factors, everything. You have people who can get started on this?"

Dr. Wu swallowed and nodded nervously.

"Right away," she said. "You think it's really serious?"

"It could be deadly. Get those patients isolated in one wing. *Now.*"

∘ **27** ∘

Lo Fengbu stared at his workbench and continued his work.

Two short years before, at the age of 26, he'd been a dissident leader at Beidai -- Beijing University. Too young to join the demonstrators at Tiananmen Square in 1989, he missed the Beijing Massacre so he wrote volume after volume of poetry inspired by Western ideals -- long, rambling poems about freedom and democracy, individualism and responsibility, openness and transparency.

He courageously painted his verse on Beidai walls with a thick-bristled brush, and his black flowing characters stirred a post-Tiananmen generation into action. Soon he found himself heading a secret society that met at random in different dorm rooms to avoid detection by the hated Public Security Bureau goons who regularly shadowed them.

Lo's group included a pair of hacker friends who jerry-rigged a cellular hookup via satellite to a remote wireless server in Hong Kong. Lo downloaded countless manuscripts from the Internet, which he printed, copied, and distributed to hungry readers both inside and outside Beidai until the PSB eventually blocked access to all Websites abroad.

After that, no one inside China could log on overseas without a police permit. So Lo started an underground CD magazine called *Freedom*, which not only aroused eager readers in Beijing but also fell into the hands of ham-handed censors at the PSB.

As the leader of a dangerous new cult, Lo was arrested and arraigned for trial. The charges were threatening public security and undermining State control. He was randomly assigned a public defender.

When the young government-appointed attorney tried to defend Lo too aggressively, he was himself charged by the State with fabricating evidence and imprisoned without defense pending his own trial.

Left with no recourse, Lo was quickly tried and convicted. He was sentenced to ten years of labor and reeducation at the Shandung *laogai* by a Beijing judge with a reputation for harsh punishment.

Col. Fu was keenly interested in the *laogai* prisoners, especially young student leaders who were assigned to assemble cheap exports to America. He knew that if the State could break them while they were still young, they might remain loyal and no longer incite others to follow. There would always be followers but they could be dealt with simply enough by imprisonment, isolated from their leaders. Followers sooner or later become meek and enfeebled, no threat to the State.

But the leaders?

They had to be dealt with separately and severely. Taught a lesson. Broken.

The State had to destroy their souls, not just incarcerate their their bodies.

"Do you know the meaning of power, Lo Fengbu?" Col. Fu had asked on a routine visit to Shandung to investigate possible recruits for his new laboratory in Jiangxi. He held a clipboard with a list of young dissident leaders.

New to the *laogai*, Lo was proud and resistant.

"Power is decentralized among the people," he said. "Through freedom, each individual has the power to give his life unique meaning and shape."

Fu frowned.

"No, that is not the correct answer," the Colonel said. "Power is the ability to inflict fear and pain, to cause suffering and humiliation."

"I have no fear," Lo said, standing proudly. "I feel no pain."

"You will soon," Fu said, his voice steady. "The American barbarians call us brutal, repressive. They accuse us of terrorizing and beating our prisoners. They say we take away their rights, that we kill them. But that's not true."

Col. Fu gave Lo the litany of traditional treatment in the *laogai*.

"There will be no torture by forced drinking," he explained. "Otherwise, you might retain water in your legs. Water is evidence. Neither will we bake spun glass in stale buns; otherwise, your intestines will be shredded like sausage and you'll bleed to death internally. No electric prods or racks, either, because they leave burn marks and permanent scars."

Fu stopped and looked down at the young dissident.

"In China, prisoners die only from natural causes," he said. "Tuberculosis, a little subcutaneous infection, maybe dysentery. Incurable illnesses, certified by State doctors, unassailable in court."

"You mean manufactured by medical malpractice, fabricated by the PSB and upheld by corrupt judges in kangaroo courts," Lo hissed.

His sarcasm dripped with hate and slapped the Colonel in the face.

Fu stiffened. His dark eyes narrowed. But Lo's impertinence never tempted his anger.

"So," Fu said. "You prefer to play games? Fine. We'll start with the Black Chicken. Your right arm will be stretched tight behind your right leg and handcuffed to the front of your left knee while your left wrist is shackled to the wall at shoulder height. The entire weight of your body will eventually rest on your left leg when you're too tired to stand upright. Whenever your right foot touches the ground, the guards will -- how should I say this -- remind you to raise it. They won't beat you, you'll beat yourself. I'll come back and ask you the same question again tomorrow."

Lo stood painfully erect throughout the night. When his right leg started to sag, the guards poked him with a sharp bamboo pole, forcing him to stay awake with his entire body weight on his left leg.

By morning, the leg had cramped so severely that he had collapsed, unconscious, his body hanging entirely by the socket of one arm.

There was no bedding or blanket in Lo's cell, and no toilet.

A small square hole in one corner served the dual function of toilet and basin, with a dripping faucet directly above, turned on and off with a special key kept only by the guards. Worse than no food, Lo was given rotten bits of putrid sticky buns that went uneaten and added to the foul stench of his cell.

When Col. Fu returned the next morning, he prodded Lo awake from his cramped position. Forcing him to stand on his right leg, he repeated the question.

Lo drew himself stiffly erect and looked Fu in the eye.

"Power is unique to each individual," he said, meekly but with pride. "Some may choose to use it, others may not. Such is the gift of freedom."

Fu cursed.

"Imbecile!" he hissed. "You know that is incorrect. I shall return again tomorrow. Until then, we will put you in the Standing Pillar position, balanced on a small column with both of your hands cuffed to the wall behind your back. If you doze and fall off, your arms will come unhinged at the shoulders. Most prisoners prefer to commit suicide rather than endure the pillar, Lo. I think you're too smart for that."

For two days and nights, with no food, no water, and no sleep, Lo endured Fu's torturous tests.

Every morning, Fu asked the same question. Every morning, Lo gave the Colonel a different response: independent, provocative, unyielding, despite the searing pain.

On the third day, Lo was feverish and began coughing.

The prison doctor diagnosed TB. Fu ordered a maintenance level of antibiotics to prevent Lo's condition from worsening but not so that he could heal.

Lo was worthless to the PLA dead. Fu wanted him kept alive.

"You see, Lo," the Colonel said as he paced back and forth in his cell. "You can't possibly win. You may talk about your precious ideals of power and your so-called gift of freedom, but in reality you are suffering. You're in extreme pain. Only you have the power to change."

Too weak to stand, Lo lay naked and shivering on the cold stone floor, smeared with his own excrement, a whisper of life.

From the outside, he looked emaciated and drawn. Inside, he felt calm and strong, undefeated. But he knew he was dangerously sick and his sickness could result in death and death would only mean victory for Col. Fu and the State.

If Lo died, Fu would find another leader, and if not that one, then another, slicing through an endless sequence of others until he finally found one weak and pliable, one who could not endure.

Endurance was the key to resistance. The race against Communism and the corrupt power of the State -- the race to win *fazhi*, the rule of law -- was a marathon, not a sprint.

Whatever happens, Lo thought, the cause must not die. To win, he had to feign defeat. Any fool could die. To keep the flame burning brightly, Lo had to stay alive.

He mouthed several words, his voice but a whisper.

"What was that, Lo?" Fu asked. "You'll have to speak up."

"I said," Lo coughed, "power is the ability to inflict fear and humiliation, to cause pain and suffering."

Fu smiled.

"Could you repeat that? I seem to have a little trouble hearing you today."

The prisoner complied.

"Very good," Fu said.

He dangled three fingers in front of Lo's emaciated face.

"How many fingers am I holding up?" he asked.

Lo lifted his head weakly and opened an eye.

He blinked.

"How many would you like me to say?" he replied hoarsely.

"Very good, Lo," Fu said. "Very good indeed. I think we will be able to work well together."

With that, Fu gave two brisk commands.

The guards came, put Lo on a stretcher and moved him to the *laogai* infirmary, where he was fed intravenously with more powerful antibiotics. In a week, the tuberculosis had abated and he began to eat solid foods again. In two weeks, he was doing simple exercises in his room to regain strength.

Healthy again and fully alert, his mind began to function. Lo started thinking about what he had to do. And when.

"If you cooperate," Fu told him as they prepared to leave for Jiangxi, "your *hukou* will be returned. Without a national identity card, you know you cannot live, cannot work, cannot *exist* in China."

He glared at his new laboratory assistant.

"If you fail to cooperate," he hissed, "your death by disappearance will simply be another one of the many mysteries of modern life in the backward provinces."

Lo straightened, lifting his head.

"So when do we begin?" he asked with a weak smile.

His voice was flat and empty, like an echo, void of emotion.

"Very good, Lo," Fu said. "Your new spirit is impressive. We leave tonight."

∘ 28 ∘

While Amy Wu and the Fo Tan hospital staff hurried to isolate the sick patients into a common wing, Ellen Chou felt her eyes burn with the telltale signs of jet lag and exhaustion.

She found an empty cot in a corner of the interns' quarters and stretched out, setting her pocket alarm for six a.m. Three hours would have to do for now. As she lay down, she worried about the isolation wing. It was old and had no negative pressure. How were they going to keep the airborne germs from spreading?

It was gray and drizzly outside when she awoke. She rubbed her eyes. They felt hard and coarse, like emery boards.

Ellen threw some water on her face and found a fresh gauze mask.

She walked quickly down the hall to find the hospital cafeteria for a quick cup of coffee. As she passed the patient rooms, she saw the staff working exposed, still unmasked. She filled a Styrofoam cup and hurried upstairs to the lab.

Dr. Wu had dozed off at the workbench. Ellen nudged her awake.

"You've absolutely got to mask the staff," she said. "They're running a huge risk now."

Amy Wu nodded. She stretched and stifled a yawn.

"And I need to see the hospital director," Ellen said. "When will he be here?"

Dr. Wu looked at her watch.

"Dr. Yee's usually here around 7:30," she mumbled.

"Good. Let's take a look at the latest epidemiological reports on the patients."

Amy Wu yawned again. Part of her still hovered in sleep. She reached behind her.

"They're right here. Some patients are still being interviewed, and nobody was happy about being awakened so early, but …"

"Thanks ," Ellen said, taking the file.

She tore a sheet of blank paper from her yellow pad and started drafting an epi map based on evidence collected from the patients whose blood samples had tested positively for H5N1.

Across the bottom, she sketched a frequency polygon with the dates and times of the onset of symptoms; down the left side, she made a list of critical factors -- age, profession, home address, place of employment, patient contacts, recent activities, food eaten and where consumed, odd behavior -- to determine possible commonalities. Across the top, she wrote a sequence of numbers, one for each patient.

As she entered the data, she noticed the even distribution of age and gender immediately. Young children as well as adults, boys and girls, men and women.

A dozen patients, including the index case in intensive care, had been intubated. Ten required mechanical support, either cardiac or respiratory. All were on IV drips.

When she matched the list of addresses with recent activities, an obvious cluster in the Sha Tin neighborhood of Fo Tan struck her instantly.

Five poultry workers listed their place of employment as the Fo Tan market. Nearly 30 adults were residents of Housing Estate #207 across the road. More than a dozen had shopped at the Wing Lung Department Store next door. Twenty children were students at the Fo Tan School. And a dozen patients -- eight adults and four children -- had eaten at the local Burger King, all within the last three days.

It was obvious they had to get a team out there, fast, to collect swab samples. Analyze them, subtype them, try to screen for antidotes.

Before Ellen could scan the sections that detailed their contacts and recent activities, an orderly burst into the lab for Dr. Wu.

Five minutes later Amy Wu returned breathless, her lips forming a tight line.

"Admissions has just sent a dozen more patients to ER."

Ellen frowned.

"How soon can you get them up to isolation?" she asked.

"We're working on it," she said, "but we're running out of space."

"Ask the staff to finish collecting the patient data quickly. And remind them to mask up. They simply shouldn't work any longer without protection. I'm going down to find your director."

○ **29** ○

Col. Fu grabbed the lab phone on the first ring.

"*Hao*," he said brusquely.

Squinting, he listened for a minute. Then he nodded.

"*Hao, hao.*"

Cupping a palm over the receiver, he turned to face Lukanov, who was working at a lab bench with Lo Fengbu.

"Finally, something good," he said. "They found Wang Wei's truck parked behind the University hospital in Sha Tin."

Lukanov's eyes widened behind his clear goggles.

"Tell them not to touch it unless they're masked and gloved," he said through his mask. "Wang's probably sick and in the hospital. His truck will be full of bird excrement that's rich with our virus. It's a deadly weapon, maybe more deadly than we imagined. Order those men to wear rubber suits if they have them, plastic sheets if they don't."

Fu uncapped the phone and cautioned the adjutant.

"I don't care!" Fu screamed. "Tow it! Hook it to one of your jeeps and get it the hell out of there. Take it back to the Island and disinfect it."

He listened to more excuses.

"What? I don't *care*, spray it with bleach. Yes, inside and out, you idiot. Lock it up and don't let anybody near it. Then disinfect and torch your gear."

Fu cradled the receiver and spun around to face the Russian.

"Do you know what this means?"

Excited, the rogue Colonel ran a hand through his white hair, smiling broadly.

Lukanov nodded.

"Of course. It means you've gained a vital step in your plan," the Russian said.

"More than that," Fu said, his voice full of energy now, eyes bright.

He began to pace rapidly back and forth.

"It means we may have captured two stones with one move. Let's say Wang Wei was a little sloppy. He may have caught the bug himself and passed it to others. If not, the Fo Tan birds are surely infecting the market's customers and those people are transmitting it now themselves. I'll have a fresh report from the adjutant tonight. If the number of new cases keeps rising, we have conclusive proof that H5N1 can be passed from human to human."

He paused, glancing at the wall clock.

"Push ahead with the aerosol. The nose and throat are perfect targets for the spray."

Lukanov raised one hand in caution.

"But you still need confirmation of the mortality rate," he said. "Otherwise, you can't be sure you have -- "

"I know," Fu interrupted. "A killer virus."

He picked up the phone and punched in a special number to give General Min the good news.

∘ **30** ∘

Ellen felt helpless as the next couple of days flashed by, stuck on fast-forward and out of control. Her meeting with the Hospital Director was going a lot worse than she expected.

A bald, moon-faced bureaucrat, Dr. Youngston Yee was known for his institutional efficiency. He kept the hospital's occupancy rate low, its fees right at the Hong Kong government average, its name off the radar screen of prying auditors.

Dr. Yee hated surprises. In a crisis, he was like a cork on water.

He sat behind a large desk packed with file folders color-coded by DOH organizational hierarchy, rocking back and forth in a squeaky swivel chair covered in gray naugahyde. His telephone sat buried beneath a blizzard of message slips. He held a burning cigarette between the third and fourth fingers of his left hand the way some affected celebrities do, flicking ashes nervously onto the floor.

"I don't like the way you've taken over this outbreak," he said bluntly as Ellen sat across from him in his cramped office.

His voice rattled like gravel in a tin can.

"It's Hong Kong's responsibility, not yours. I hear you've already gone to isolation without my permission."

She hadn't expected hostility. Fatigue was eating her like acid, making her irritable and cranky. Her eyes flitted nervously across his cluttered desk. Her left eyelid twitched uncontrollably.

"I'm sorry, Dr. Yee. The staff is still working unprotected when you know they ought to be masked and gloved. Those patients need to be isolated and the crew in that wing definitely needs rebreather masks. We don't know how infectious this microbe is but based on the death rate so far, it looks deadly."

"We've had these incidents before, Dr. Chou," he said, pooh-poohing her concern. "It's probably nothing more than food poisoning or *e. coli* from poor sanitation in the housing projects, despite what your high-tech gadget says. You Americans always think you know everything, but we know technology never has all the answers."

"Tell me how you can justify ignoring basic precautions?"

"If and when your Atlanta lab subtypes the microbe and confirms its toxicity, then we'll take the necessary precautions. This is a Hong Kong hospital, don't forget. I call the shots here."

Ellen leaned forward in her chair.

"Look," she said firmly. "I know I'm an outsider. But I have a professional obligation to prevent this epidemic from spreading."

"Is that so?" he said.

He picked up a green file folder from his stack and waved it at her.

"I still have no confirmation from my government that you're even officially here. Our Commissioner of Health faxed your State Department but there's been no response. Therefore I must ask that you continue to defer to Dr. Wu."

Ellen thought ahead as he spoke.

"There's always a delay in formal channels," she said with a slight wave of her hand. "You know yourself how slowly the wheels of government turn. The CDC is used to acting on a phone call. We have to, in the interest of time. And you have a potential time bomb here, Dr. Yee."

"Perhaps," he said. "But where is the factual evidence to support your fears? Unsupported allegations lead to panic, and panic can only make things worse. Now are you going to follow Dr. Wu's orders or do I have to call the Commissioner?"

He glanced at the phone on the corner of his desk.

"Of course we can work together," she said, her voice softer now. "But I would appreciate some critical data from you first."

His chair creaked as he rocked back and eyed her warily. He took a long drag on his cigarette and stubbed it out in an ashtray that overflowed with stale butts.

"What kind of information?" he asked, exhaling.

"Surge capacity, for example. How many additional beds can you take in a real emergency?"

"Ten percent," he said without hesitation.

"That's all?" she frowned. "Twenty percent of average daily capacity is standard. That means you can accept only twenty-five extra patients."

Dr. Yee nodded.

"But a dozen more were admitted to ER this morning."

He shrugged his shoulders.

"Ten percent," he said. "That's the number. Set by DOH. We comply fully with all government regulations."

"Any rooms with negative pressure?"

"No, just the ICU suite."

"Then I need your authorization to convert the isolation wing into a real containment facility if the number of new cases keeps rising and we confirm the bug is airborne. May we have your permission to do this?"

"That's up to Dr. Wu. She may consider it."

She glanced at her notepad.

"Inventory of antiviral medications?"

He shook his head.

"None. We requisition what we need from the central government."

"What about the capacity of your morgue?"

"Six slots," he said. "Since this hospital was built 23 years ago, we've never needed more."

Ellen's face turned pale. She couldn't believe what she was hearing. She realized they may have to fight a raging fire with not much more than a limp garden hose.

She felt her heart skip a beat as she closed her notebook. Her voice went flat.

"I have no problem deferring to Dr. Wu. But for Hong Kong's sake, I hope this is nothing more than an isolated event."

"Please, Dr. Chou, spare us the melodrama. For your sake, I hope your visit here can be confirmed formally by your government, and soon."

"Yes, of course," she said nervously. "It will be."

○ **31** ○

"You're tight," she said. "Too tight. Relax. It's not good for your muscles to be this stiff. The brain is a muscle, too, and it mirrors your body."

Tian Ling pressed her fingers into the Colonel's neck and shoulders, kneading his hard flesh like dough. She gathered her long, black hair over her head and tied it in a loose knot, out of the way. Leaning forward, she sat on her knees for more leverage.

Col. Fu lay on his stomach on a mat in his laboratory office, his mind glued to Hong Kong.

He worried about Wang Wei, about the absence of data confirming the mortality rate, about the mountain of work that was on the verge of evaporation and his career along with it.

"There have been a few … delays," he said. "My project can never succeed without critical information reliably supplied by trusted subordinates. When they can't use their brains or don't give me what I need, I get impatient. Of *course* I'm tight."

He clenched his fists on the mat and punched it.

"I knew something was wrong when you couldn't be in Nanchang tonight but asked me to come here instead," she said softly.

The provincial capital of Jiangxi, where the Colonel maintained a modest villa, was a half-day's drive away.

"This is the first time you've ever let me be so close to your … work."

"If I had faith in my juniors the way I can trust you, I'd feel a lot better."

His voice rattled in syncopation with her pounding.

"This is the most important project I've ever run. It's not about the Army this time, not just another strategic maneuver. It's critical to the future of China. If we succeed, I go to Beijing a hero and you come with me. If I fail … "

Fu's voice trailed off to a hoarse whisper. He put the thought of failure aside.

Tian Ling unwound her knees and straddled the small of his back. She dug her strong fingers into his shoulder blades, massaging the hard fiber. It was tight as piano wire.

"Well, it was not easy getting past your guards," she said softly. "Not like Shanghai, where the Pudong operation was more accessible. Tell me why this strange place has more animals than people."

"I can't," he said. "It's a covert experiment. Classified."

That's all he would say.

She smiled at the back of his head, her eyes dancing.

"And that's the kind of faith you want from your subordinates?"

"This is different."

"Different? Like you can't trust Tian Ling?"

He twisted under her straddle onto his back, facing her.

"No, different like Shanghai was different," he said.

He reached up and stroked her smooth cheeks.

"You'd still be cruising the waterfront if it hadn't been for me."

She squeezed the tight tissue in his neck.

"And you might still be a bone-thin farm boy stuck in Puqi without me to help you be more patient in Shanghai. Don't forget, you could have lost Japan."

"Easy," he said. "Not so rough. If I were still in Puqi, China would still be a third-world backwater country. The *fengpai* in Beijing have no idea how lucky they are, and yet they piss away our nation's strength. They have no right to the mandate of heaven."

It wasn't just his body that felt tight. It was his mind too. He wanted to choke the adjutant, send Tian Ling down to Stonecutter's Island, get *results*.

"Every night, in my dreams, I see you and feel you," she said, caressing his chest lightly. "Wherever you are, whatever you do, I hear your heartbeat."

Fu closed his eyes and folded his arms behind his head.

"Every night, in my dreams, I see a resurgent China. Wherever I am, whatever I do, I hear the massive crowds at Tiananmen Square, cheering a new generation of leadership in Beijing. Leadership that ties us to the strong roots of our great history, that inspires our creative genius instead of stifling it, that controls the hated Americans instead of kowtowing to them."

Tian Ling scooted down to sit astride his thighs now and unbuckled his belt. With a gentle tug, she drew his trousers away from his hips and caressed his fullness.

"You are much too tight," she said. "I know exactly what you need."

And she took him in her mouth to soothe him as only she knew how.

∘ **32** ∘

Ellen left Youngston Yee's office fuming.

She had collided with bean counters before, but the CDC had such a squeaky-clean reputation for results that his rejection of her authority left her stunned. Well, the hell with him, she thought. Public health was the primary concern, now and always.

She raced back to find Amy Wu, who was neither in the hospital lab where Ellen had left her nor in the ER. Ellen pulled on her gauze mask and a fresh pair of latex gloves and ran to the temporary isolation wing.

They nearly bumped into each other as Dr. Wu backed out of a patient room with a tray of blood samples.

Ellen pulled her aside.

"You didn't tell me you had a damn accountant in charge here," she said.

Amy Wu frowned for an instant and then smiled.

"Oh, Dr. Yee," she said. "He thinks he's the Emperor of Fo Tan. Don't worry, he tries to make all of us feel uneasy."

"Well, I *have* to worry," she said. "He could queer this investigation with my seniors. You're now officially in charge."

"*Me?*" she squeaked. "But I know nothing about epidemiology."

Just then, the hospital intercom squawked, interrupting them.

"*Code Blue! Code Blue!*"

The monotonic message repeated at fixed intervals. Traffic in the hallway froze.

Ellen's heart skipped another beat.

"Don't tell me."

Amy Wu nodded.

"We've just hit capacity. Every bed is full."

"Let's go."

They hustled past stationary gurneys toward the ER. The warning echoed through the halls as the tape looped endlessly in the PA system. It was accompanied by a constant beep pitched an octave higher as a irritating reminder.

The chief of medicine barged through the ER doors as they approached.

"That's it," he said.

He shut the doors behind him.

"We're full and into surge. Start doubling up."

Ellen glanced at the report Dr. Wu had received. Nine new patients had just been admitted.

There was a young masseuse from a nearby bath called the Turkish Embassy, together with two co-workers. A gas pump attendant from Tai Po. An old woman who ran the kiosk there. Her daughter. The proprietor of the Fo Tan wet market. A poultry worker from the Lim Kang farm in Tsuen Wan and the first patient not specifically linked to Fo Tan. Tsuen Wan was one village closer to Kowloon and Hong Kong Central, the two most densely populated sectors of the Special Administrative Region.

The killer microbe was already playing leapfrog.

The hospital staff collected blood and fluid samples from every new patient and brought them to Dr. Wu. They hurried the epi studies based on Ellen's frequency polygon and her template of questions.

As the samples came up to the lab, Ellen checked each of them with her device.

All of them tested positive for H5N1. Not a single negative.

An intern burst into the lab from isolation to report two more patients dead. Ellen asked Dr. Wu to have the autopsies completed immediately so they could confirm the cause of death. Without saying a word, Ellen knew what they would find.

With two new cadavers, the hospital morgue was now full.

Dr. Wu called the DOH to request temporary cadaver storage.

"The government keeps a pair of refrigerated containers on standby for emergencies" she said.

Ellen was worried.

"Two won't be enough. You're going to need more. A lot more."

"If we need more, we'll just rent them. Hong Kong is the container capital of the world."

The cold monotone of the hospital intercom squawked again.

"Dr. Wu to isolation! Dr. Wu to isolation!"

They ran back downstairs, two steps at a time.

"Another pair of casualties," a young nurse said, breathless. "This time from inside the hospital. One from the second floor, one from the third."

Ellen's reaction was immediate.

"Were they originally diagnosed with flu symptoms?" she asked.

The nurse scanned the reports.

"No. The old man from two broke his left femur when he fell on the stairs of his housing unit," she read. "He was admitted for surgery. And the young secretary with carpal tunnel syndrome on three came in for prophylaxis and PT."

"Totally unrelated to the microbe," Ellen said, turning to Dr. Wu. "Get me -- sorry, could you find someone to collect their fluid samples right away?"

Amy Wu gave the order as Ellen pulled her aside. Her mind was racing and her eyes were wide.

"This bug is really hot," she said. "The only way those two could have gotten infected is through the hospital's ventilation system. Shut it down immediately. Push Dr. Yee to protect all the staff, *now!*"

Dr. Wu yanked the receiver from a wall phone and called the Director. When he understood the order came from the Department of Health and not CDC, he complied. Nobody could ever criticize him for not following protocol.

"Next we've got to close off the isolation wing," Ellen said as they hurried down the hall. "Call your office and try to get a power generator over here right away. We can suck the air into the basement, pull it through a series of HEPA filters and bypass the ventilation system. Does the DOH have any micro filters on hand?"

"I ... I don't know. I suppose so."

"Ask them to rush over whatever they've got. We need to HEPA the air in all your vents. They'll capture and kill any microbes circulating in the hospital air."

As they talked, a nurse brought fluid samples from the two internal patients. After handing them to Amy Wu, she staggered unsteadily and braced herself against a wall. Wasting no time, Ellen requested a pair of blankets and lay the nurse down in the hall. She swabbed her throat, put that sample with the others, and ran to the lab.

Ellen watched grim-faced as the HP/UP device glowed red for all three samples. H5N1 was loose and on the prowl.

She glanced up at a wall clock. McDermott better call pretty soon, or she'd have to butt in and call Atlanta. They needed official confirmation of the virus to countermand Youngston Yee. What in the world was taking them so long?

Dr. Wu entered the lab sandwiched by a pair of technicians wearing brown windbreakers with the initials "DAF" stitched on the front in bright red. She introduced them as the team from the Department of Agriculture and Fisheries.

They had worked Fo Tan all day, collecting swab samples from the poultry market, the Burger King, the Wing Lung department store, Housing Estate #207, the Fo Tan school nearby.

Ellen listened as they listed their findings.

The wet market proprietor said he regularly received birds from Guangdong province. Several days ago he noticed that a number of birds from one shipment seemed atypically quiet, almost motionless. Bird fatigue, he thought at the time, so he put it out of his mind. He'd never had problems from Guangdong before.

The proprietor had called the Lim Kang farm in Tsuen Wan and told them he had some new tern, so they came over and picked up two. A teacher from the Fo Tan school bought three petting chickens for the primary grades. And there had been constant demand from the housing estate residents for fresh birds. They had gotten upset when they saw the quality was not up to his usual standards. But they took them anyway, because nobody ever cooked with frozen or packaged poultry.

Ellen took their notes and flipped through them. It was worse than she thought.

At the Fo Tan wet market, she noticed, they'd seen a large number of sick and diseased birds. Chickens lay dead or dying in their cages, oozing bloody fluids from their eyes and blood-spattered mucous from their beaks. Ducks had yellow diarrhea. Tern and teal gasped for breath, the geese moribund and still.

The Jiangxi virus was killing the birds now. It had jumped from Fo Tan to Tsuen Wan.

Hong Kong was on the verge of a chicken plague.

Ellen knew what the swab samples would show but she tested a few at random anyway. They were all positive for H5N1.

Because the preliminary evidence was so overwhelming, there was no question but that Atlanta would confirm the results. She had to stay a step ahead, keep thinking about isolation, protecting others.

She slumped down in a corner chair and looked up at Amy Wu with the DAF team watching every move.

Her throat was dry as she whispered the critical word.

"Quarantine!"

∘ **33** ∘

Fu Barxu gripped the telephone tightly. His eyes were thin slits, his breath short.

The Colonel was ecstatic. He could hardly believe the latest report from his adjutant on Stonecutter's Island in Hong Kong.

The number of new patient admissions was exploding now, with a mortality rate in excess of 20%. Nearly one in four victims was dead or dying. Before he rang off, he ordered the adjutant to call with more frequent updates.

"At last!" he said excitedly. "Pushing twenty-five percent! Can you believe it?"

The Russian scientist nodded proudly.

"Of course. I *told* you it would work, Colonel. Now you can tell your superiors in Beijing to relax. They will all want to take credit for your success."

Fu shook his head.

"Not yet. This report is only for General Min," he said, tapping his notebook. "We still have work to do. You've got to aerosolize the microbe with an intermediate host and make sure it can survive vacuum packing. There's no time to spare."

Lo Fengbu was cleaning a lab bench nearby. As he listened to the exchange, he understood the end game clearly now. Horrified, he suddenly felt trapped.

He had to start thinking about getting out. When Fu finished his work, he would have no further use for the dissident leader, despite his empty promises. Based on past habit, Lo knew that Fu would send Lukanov on a final junket to Haikou for R&R after he successfully aerosolized the virus. The only question was when.

But escape? How? Fu kept the covert laboratory under strict surveillance. A high-voltage fence with electronic sensors trapped the compound in a tight net and the entrance was guarded around the clock. Fu reported daily to his superior in Beijing.

But Lo knew he had only two choices: stay and die, or get out.

As he autoclaved a pallet of glass beakers, he played through a series of possible scenarios in his mind.

He could try to smuggle himself out in one of the delivery trucks that came every day. Laundry. Food. Supplies. Slip into the back as the truck was being unloaded, cover up, and hope that the gate guards would overlook a random departure.

No. Fu would never be so careless, not now. It would never be that easy.

As he wiped down the workbench, his mind churned. What about *under* the truck, he thought. Fit and healthy now from his daily workouts, Lo had enough upper body strength to hide himself under the rear axle. If he could hold on long enough to pass through the main gate and into the clear.

But the guards checked under every vehicle with their little mirrors on wheels. If he wasn't discovered then, he might be when he released outside. The driver would surely stop to check the truck's sudden disparity in weight.

Still, Lo knew Lukanov's junket would come soon, so he focused on the Russian's departure. The more he thought, the harder he wiped. It was always the same pattern. He had seen it many times from the small slit in his cramped room.

A late-night pickup. An unmarked van with a driver and a personal guard. The driver waiting while the guard fetched Lukanov and escorted him back to the van.

Lukanov and the guard always sat in back, the driver alone in front. There was a sliver of hope, an instant in which Lo could make his move.

It was his only chance, he thought. He would become invisible as he refined the plan. Speak only when spoken to. Be totally deferential. Escape attention.

Yes.

It was his only chance.

∘ **34** ∘

The hospital pathologist had completed his analysis of tissue samples after his biopsy of the newly deceased patients. Ellen was glancing through the autopsy results when the lab extension rang.

Dr. Wu picked up, nodded, and turned.

"Dr. Chou, there's a Dr. McDermott calling for you. Line one."

Ellen sprang up and grabbed the receiver.

"Sandy? Finally! What've you got? All hell is breaking loose here."

"Bottom line? Get the coffins out. You've got a lethal avian virus on the loose."

Ellen's eyes darted back and forth as she listened to McDermott's report. She was relieved to know the chip scanner had performed flawlessly but she braced herself for what she knew would be bad news. They had to get past Murphy's Law first.

"We've been working around the clock once we got the damn samples," she said. "But they were delayed getting here. Turns out, a ring of local FedEx drivers was arrested smuggling drugs into Atlanta and a shitload of CDC packets got confiscated with their loads. We've been on the phone non-stop with Memphis for the past day. Then as luck would have it Hong Kong never tagged their parcels as urgent so they just sat buried in our normal queue. It took us forever to find them and dig them out before we could even start testing."

"Jesus," she said. "You guys are normally so quick."

She sat down at the lab bench.

"Tell me what you got. Did you run a full sequence?"

"Everything, soup to nuts. You haven't seen Atlanta this frantic since the ebola outbreak knocked off those monkeys in Virginia a few years back. I had to break up two other teams to get enough people analyzing your samples and make up for lost time. We ran PCR, nested PCR, ELISA. All H5N1, every single one. But this microbe was very odd."

"How so?"

"Well, listen to this -- at first we were shocked, didn't believe it ourselves. But the samples? It's like they're all the same. *Identical,* right down to the genetic map, as if they were Xerox copies of the same virus. Never seen anything like it before."

Ellen sat back in her chair, stunned. She stared vacantly into space.

"Sandy, are you sure?"

"No question about it. We ran nested PCRs repeatedly. The computer spit out the exact same site for each and every one, every sample, every time. To us, it looks like somebody has grafted the H5 gene *precisely* into the H1 position 523~637 on the H1N1 genome. Ellie, this is a man-made virus you're dealing with."

"From *China*?" Ellen sputtered. "That's impossible."

"Tell me about it," McDermott replied. "We're still scratching our heads back here, too"

"But who? How? Why?"

There was a rustle of paper on the other end.

"I just got off the phone with Stan Novak and he's as confused as the rest of us. You'd expect Saddam Hussein or al Qaeda to try some shit like this. But not China."

Ellen glanced down at the autopsy report.

"Sandy, something else is weird."

"Tell me."

"These patients are not dying of excess fluid in the lungs or secondary bacterial infections from pneumonia, as we would expect from type-A flu."

"Then what does the medical examiner confirm as cause of death?"

"Renal failure."

"*What*?"

"That's right. Massive internal hemorrhaging of the kidneys."

"That's absurd. From a subtype of the influenza A virus?"

"Now we know what the avian flu does to humans."

"So the situation's worse than we thought."

"Far worse. The mortality rate is just south of 30% and still rising. If this killer virus gets out of Hong Kong, it'll be a hell of a lot worse than 1918."

"You hit them with the big Q?"

"Absolutely. The hospital director's got his nose out of joint but that's another story. We're working on containment within containment right now. I need you to call LeRoy. Get the Director's clearance to FedEx us as much rimantadine as you can. We need to start massive doses of anti-virals to keep the others alive and give the hospital staff adequate protection. And send a carton of HEPA filters with a box of rebreathers."

She closed her eyes for a moment.

"And Sandy?"

"I'm here."

"Moon suits."

Ellen cradled the receiver and turned to face Dr. Wu, whose face was sheet-white.

"What do we do now?"

Ellen thought for an instant about Dr. Yee but just as quickly put politics out of her mind.

"You shut down the Fo Tan market, you close the Burger King, you rope off Wing Lung, you start disinfecting that housing estate and you shutter the school in Fo Tan. You're going to need blood samples from every patient's family, friend, relative, and cohort in their neighborhoods, including the *entire* population of 207."

"I'll call the Commissioner and request more teams immediately," she said. "What about the hospital?"

"Quarantine is your only answer," Ellen said. "This is plague central now. Call the Hong Kong police and order an armed squad to guard the entrance. Nobody gets in or out without DOH clearance. And raise the yellow flag on your flagpole."

"But more patients are still arriving."

"Take them to ER for fluid samples. If they're H5N1-positive, they stay here. If they test negative, give them a double-dose of rimantadine and get them to another hospital. We need every available inch of space. In the meantime, test samples from all the patients not in isolation. Same bifurcation. We're on straight triage now."

"What about the press?"

"Send the news hounds to Dr. Yee. I'll talk to him next."

∘ **35** ∘

Col. Fu watched carefully as Lukanov compressed the aerosolized virus into a small can and applied pressure to vacuum-seal it. In his laboratory experiments with the aerosol, Lukanov's wheat germ dust had behaved perfectly.

Wheat germ made an ideal intermediate culture to keep the virus alive prior to discharge, a state Lukanov confirmed could be consistently maintained for an average of 14 days. Despite the Russian's impressive statistical data, Fu discounted his number by a safe margin and assumed half the time. A week to ten days, max.

From his broad network of *guanxi* in Shanghai, Col. Fu had obtained a sample can of the aerosol disinfectant China Airlines routinely used to purify the cabin air prior to departure of their international flights. A practice no longer in use by all carriers, China Air used it to avoid the frequent criticism from the West that influenza originated every winter as an invisible, non-paying passenger in one of their eastbound widebody jets.

A flight attendant simply walked down the aisle and sprayed the cabin air with a fine mist. It was slightly perfumed and not offensive. A single pass was typically sufficient. The process was explained during the pre-departure security check and safety drill that provided routine instruction in the proper use of seat belts, oxygen masks, and life preservers.

Fu held the can of China Air's commercial disinfectant in one hand, stared at the label and smiled.

He had a junior officer in Beijing whose calligraphy was nearly letter-perfect. When Lieutenant Kang Zhiyen dipped his fine-tipped camelhair brush into a smooth blend of charcoal *mòshui* ink and water, the deep black characters he drew were practically indistinguishable from those on a printed page. He had a talent that few were given and even fewer could learn. Lt. Kang's skill also came in handy when the PLA needed forged travel documents such as foreign passports or identity cards for their numerous covert assignments overseas.

Fu grasped the legitimate can of disinfectant and held it carefully over the workbench but under the laminar flow hood. He pressed the button to release its contents into the double-filtered exhaust air.

When the can was totally empty, he set it next to a cylindrical container that was identical in all respects except for its missing bottom. That would be sealed into place when Lukanov packed it with the aerosolized H5N1 particles under pressure.

Col. Fu scribbled a brief memo to Lt. Kang with instructions to be followed when he counterfeited the new labels. He wrapped his note around the empty can to be used as a model, labeled the box, and set it aside for the chopper that would arrive later that afternoon.

It would be in Beijing that night, Kang could create the forged labels the next day, and Fu would have them back within 48 hours. As usual, a payment from one of the Colonel's secret accounts bought and paid for Kang's silence.

His package wrapped and ready, Fu walked to the horizontal window slits and gazed across the compound at the innocent barnyard creatures, all of them unwitting co-conspirators in his Jiangxi plan. In his mind, he rehearsed the steps he would take after Lukanov had the can of "atmospheric disinfectant" ready to go.

Transiting Hong Kong was too dangerous. The border would now be closely guarded, visitors carefully searched, imports restricted to essential goods only -- canned or frozen food and medical supplies.

No, he had to use Shanghai. Fly to Hongqiao airport himself. Find a friendly China Airlines employee and bribe him or her to spray the cabin of a non-stop flight from Shanghai to America with a new, experimental disinfectant from one of the PLA's many commercial enterprises.

Employees of the State were notoriously underpaid; all of them came to expect "gratuities" from time to time for "special favors" rendered on behalf of government officials. Two-way smuggling was frequent and popular, and crewmembers were never searched when they passed through foreign immigration or customs.

Col. Fu had a very special favor to ask this time and he had a generous fee in mind to make sure his request would not be rejected. He'd make the liaison himself, of course. An officer from the Shanghai corps wouldn't have the right authority. But the airline staff wouldn't know that. They would respect if not fear the Colonel's Army uniform and senior rank. Particularly the young women.

When the flight attendant made her pass down the aisle, the passengers would be impervious, distracted by their magazines or the in-flight entertainment guide. They rarely paid attention to pre-departure routines anyway. She could start at the back, hold the can behind her, and walk slowly to the front, a single step ahead of the spray.

It was perfect.

Fu pulled a China Airlines schedule off one of his laboratory shelves and leafed through it until he found what he wanted. There were several non-stops to the United States, a daily to the west coast and one every night to the east. All Boeing 777-200s, capacity of 283 passengers: 48 in Business Class, 235 in coach, and a crew of fifteen.

Two hundred and ninety-eight human vectors breathing the same stale, unfiltered air for fourteen hours uninterrupted, incubating a killer virus in the efficient reproductive machinery of their cells. Nearly three hundred semi-automatic weapons for the rogue Colonel's attack on America.

His finger moved slowly down the neat rows of numbers and stopped.

There it was, the obvious choice.

Flight 004.

Newark.

The New York metropolitan area would be an ideal target. What better way to cripple America than to assault its economic core from Boston to Washington?

Manhattan was still every terrorist's favorite target. But despite its enormous population and symbolic importance, it was a very small island, easy to blockade and relatively simple to protect. Especially after militant Islamic extremists from the Middle East sent their suicide bombers into the Twin Towers on September 11.

Every New York cop had since undergone extensive counter-terrorist training. Special electronic sensors embedded in scanners in each approach lane now secretly guarded every bridge and tunnel into and out of Manhattan. In addition, both New York airports, LaGuardia and JFK, had crack SWAT teams on constant alert around the clock.

But not Newark.

Nearly 50 million passengers transited Newark International Airport each and every year. More than 4 million people a month, 100,000 human vectors every day. Newark was America's third-busiest airport and a critical hub for connecting flights for international travel to the heartland.

What's more, the nucleus of America's rail and ground transportation network knifed straight through the heart of New Jersey. Buses, taxis, airport limos, 18-wheelers, private cars, all sped passengers and cargo to destinations throughout the nation's most densely populated tri-state area via the New Jersey Turnpike.

It was the east coast's own life-sustaining artery: a modern, state-of-the-art, EZ-Pass-equipped, twelve-lane super highway 150 miles long with 28 complicated, pretzel-like interchanges and more than 500 bridges and overpasses impossible to defend.

A giant symbol of the American Empire relentlessly on the move.

Half a *billion* people used the Turnpike every year to commute to and from work, to transport essential goods, to visit friends, to sightsee, to gawk. More than a million human targets *a day* for the Colonel's killer flu.

Col. Fu glanced at his watch. September would be perfect. Just before the *fengpai* made its historic State visit to San Francisco at the end of the month. And a day prior to the anniversary of the very day the American devils had brutally bombed China's Embassy in Belgrade during the audacious NATO raids on Serbia.

Sweet justice.

It was preordained.

◦ **36** ◦

The Jiangxi flu epidemic went from bad to worse as Hong Kong struggled to cope with the worst crisis in its history.

Despite Ellen's advice, the DOH dragged its feet in appointing a single person to brief the media every day. When Amy Wu finally got clearance to name the moon-faced Youngston Yee, it was nearly too late. He was little more than a distance marker on the River Styx.

Two daily newspapers, the South China *Morning Post* and the Hong Kong *Standard*, ran "Man on the Street" features every day. They fanned the flames of panic and hearsay even further.

A Kowloon woman, a devout Christian and retired schoolteacher, stood in tears every morning at the Star Ferry Terminal in Tsim Sha Tsui, a mask over her face and latex gloves on trembling hands, quoting Revelations 6:8: "I saw a pale horse, and behold, his name was Death, and Hell followed him."

The police removed her when health officials closed the ferry and stopped the subway, shutting down all traffic across the harbor.

A young stockbroker from Wan Chai screamed it was fate, bad *feng shui*, the result of greed and uncontrolled economic growth. He leapt to his death from the roof of the Hotel Regent in Kowloon. Two teenaged girls, eyes wide with fear, publicly ripped off their nose rings and lip studs to renounce facial piercing as a mortal sin.

Nervous and trembling, a Sha Tin textile manufacturer and assembler of designer clothes for important European markets cried that the "chicken flu" had destroyed him. His exports plunged when foreigner buyers insisted on a special document, verified and stamped by the DOH, certifying that all goods made in Hong Kong had been disinfected prior to shipment. The new regulation spawned a profitable and active gray market in forged export certificates from Guangdong. China's experienced copyright pirates had found a new outlet for their illegal skills.

Black rumors were as ripe as summer fruit.

The local Chinese believed that Britain had unleashed a terrible curse on Hong Kong to avenge its return to China. Some said the United States was behind it in a crude attempt to force human rights concessions from Beijing.

Tourists had stopped coming, of course, totally afraid of the plague. Inbound flights were empty except for returning residents. The few tourists who ignored public health warnings stayed on Hong Kong Island where there were no confirmed cases.

Airline crews stayed at Chek Lap Kok airport just long enough for their aircraft to refuel and depart. Mechanics, flight service personnel, and baggage handlers alike worked silently in gloves and masks.

Chaos ruled the terminal. Hong Kong residents lucky enough to get British National (Overseas) Passports prior to 1997 queued anxiously for outgoing flights. They had the right, guaranteed by Britain, to reside in the United Kingdom, providing they had valid medical certificates and blood test results confirming they were flu-free.

Massive numbers of Hong Kong police patrolled the terminal armed and masked to maintain order. They installed special metal detectors and X-ray equipment at the airport train station to check all baggage and personal effects. Those without official BNOP papers were turned back.

Others swarmed around ticket counters like termites. They shouted and screamed for exit permits. Those possessing only Hong Kong Certificates of Identity were denied permission to depart.

The US Navy's flagship carrier *Enterprise* steamed into Hong Kong Harbor but every officer and sailor stayed aboard. Foreign container ships offloaded cargo without docking, using old Chinese junks floating on the open water. Stevedores looked like bandits, masked and gloved.

In the New Territories, shops and stores closed because their proprietors were sick or dying. Restaurants took *kung'pao* chicken and Peking duck off their menus. Retail enterprises discriminated not on the basis of race or ethnicity but on compliance with public health regulations.

Bank branches and investment brokers were shut down after a run on the Hong Kong stock market. Trading was suspended when investors flooded brokers with sell orders and the Hang Seng Index plunged to its lowest level since the collapse of Japan's bubble economy more than a decade before.

Violence erupted in Sha Tin like a dormant volcano. In a cruel twist of irony, unmasked bandits held up masked victims who capitulated quickly to avoid exposure or contact. A public health worker became so nervous at the irrational behavior of one unmasked local resident that he shot the man when he refused to wear a mask.

Many tried traditional folk remedies to keep themselves plague-free. Normally a pungent delicacy, thousand-year-old eggs were strung together and worn like necklaces by men and women alike. Some wore garlands of garlic and onions like beads in hopes that the foul stench would ward off the plague.

Others burned candles non-stop because they thought the plague attacked through electric wiring and became virulent only when the lights were switched on.

Deaths mounted beyond the ability of Dr. Yee's small hospital to cope. Its entire ventilation system had been converted to negative pressure with the help of power generators and HEPA filters from the CDC, which also dispatched an extra team of specialists at Ellen's urgent request.

But purifying the air couldn't add more beds.

Folding cots were assembled in the hospital cafeteria and soon lined the corridors and halls as the institution's population more than doubled. With only six slots in its tiny morgue, the hospital had to double-bag fresh cadavers, seal the zippers with tape, disinfect them with sodium hypochlorite, and store them in rented refrigerated containers.

The New Territories morgue was quickly at capacity, too. Sha Tin mortuaries were overwhelmed with funeral demands and turned people away. Hearse drivers heard about the "red plague" in local bars; you didn't die of natural causes, people said, you bled to death. They refused to drive.

Bodies stacked up in the streets like firewood, creating a public health menace all their own. Hong Kong police feared the cadavers. Street cleaners wouldn't touch them. They turned stiff and reeked with the rotten stench of decay and death.

Wearing yellow moon suits and filtered respirators, special workers from the Hong Kong sanitation department combed the streets of Sha Tin in the darkness of night to haul away the cadavers. They drove the familiar red double-decker tourist buses that quickly became known as morgues on wheels.

Health officials issued a temporary order mandating burial by cremation. As devout Buddhists, the Chinese were fortunate. The decision was easily accepted in Hong Kong but would never be tolerated in the West because of the tragic horror of the Holocaust inflicted by Hitler's cruel crematoria in Nazi Germany a half-century before.

In Sha Tin, theatres were shut, public events were cancelled, mass gatherings banned. Religious services, Buddhist and Christian alike, were prohibited. Schools were closed. People were ordered to stay at home and off the streets.

Hong Kong hovered on the edge of panic until Dr. Yee could give the press data from Ellen's latest reports that showed new flu cases finally on the decline.

Hospital admissions began edging down as the massive doses of rimantadine took effect. Patients were able to develop H5N1-specific antibodies that weakened the virus, preventing it from hijacking the reproductive machinery of their cells.

And like all viruses, the avian flu itself had gradually become less virulent. Healthcare workers found that newly infected patients were able to produce antibodies more quickly and without as much medication. Although recent victims got sick, they were no longer dying. Normal human defense mechanisms kicked in.

Ellen's "containment within containment" strategy for Sha Tin had worked. When she studied the map and saw how the Tolo Harbor inlet protected Fo Tan, which sat within Sha Tin like the hole of a doughnut, the strategy suggested itself. She let Amy Wu take credit by proposing it to the DOH. Although constant vigilance was the watchword in the New Territories, only Sha Tin and Fo Tan suffered the extremes.

The Fo Tan wet market, the Burger King, the Wing Lung Department Store, the middle school, and Housing Estate #207 had all been closed and disinfected. Chow Fat, the proprietor of the Fo Tan market, died before he could answer questions about the sick birds, but a routine scan of his receipts showed nothing out of the ordinary.

Special squads from the Department of Agriculture and Fisheries had slaughtered every bird in Fo Tan, which were disinfected and hauled away to distant landfills for burial. Special DAF decontamination teams would eventually destroy every single live bird in Hong Kong.

Homes of confirmed patients were also disinfected. DOH workers wearing the familiar canary moon suits removed contaminated material from adjacent buildings for disposal in double-sealed containers.

Blood samples collected from nearly 10,000 additional cohorts throughout Sha Tin were analyzed for the presence of H5N1. Health officials nearly collapsed in tears of joy when they saw the newest numbers and read the results.

They were safe at last. Hong Kong was finally over the hump.

The chicken plague had been defeated, but at a terrible price.

There were more than 2,000 confirmed cases of H5N1 and more than 700 innocent people dead -- a mortality rate of more than 30%.

The Jiangxi virus was murdering one out of every three of its victims.

◦ **37** ◦

Col. Fu Barxu glanced at his watch when he saw the parallel beams swing into the yard outside. The lab windows were wet with droplets from a light rain that sparkled in the glare of the headlights.

"Your military escort is here," he said.

He turned back and raised a thimbleful of *dàojiu* in a toast to commemorate the Russian's success.

Col. Fu stuffed a sheet of paper with numbers from the adjutant's latest report into his shirt pocket. More than two thousand confirmed cases of the Jiangxi virus and a mortality rate of over 30%. General Min would be thrilled.

Several cans of Lukanov's compressed and aerosolized virus sat locked in a small vault in one corner of the laboratory. Billions of microdroplets of the deadly virus were ready.

Lukanov raised his small cup in a salute to the rogue Colonel.

"Here's to the future," he said.

"And to China," Fu replied.

They emptied the thimbles of rice wine in one swallow. Lukanov winced as he felt the bitter liquid burn his throat.

"I'll get my things."

"Don't dally," Fu yelled after him. "You'll miss your flight to Hainan. It's the last one tonight."

Lo Fengbu sat in his darkened room, fully alert. He watched through the narrow slit as the escort left the van to enter the pressurized doorway while the detection sensors scanned him and his clothing for contaminants.

Without a wristwatch, Lo paced back and forth to emulate the number of steps the escort would need to walk from the van to the entrance, knowing he'd be in the decontamination chamber for at least five minutes.

Lo rolled a thick blanket and spare lab coats into rough shapes and stuffed them under the top cover of his cot as a crude decoy. He had no misconceptions about the efficacy of this old ruse but it could buy him an extra hour or two if he were thought to be sleeping late the next morning.

He reckoned that Colonel Fu would never start the next day as usual. Not on the heels of his dramatic success in Hong Kong.

Barefoot and nearly naked except for his shorts and an undershirt, Lo slipped quietly out a back exit used for disposal of contaminated material that could not be autoclaved in the high-temperature vacuum wash. It led to a lined trench where the toxic material was double-bagged, disinfected, and buried. Any attempt to regain entry to the lab through this doorway would trigger an alarm. Access was restricted to the front decon chamber.

Lo inched his lithe frame toward the front of the building. He cursed the rain until he realized it could be his ally. Rain always enhanced concentration, so the driver would be less likely to notice unexpected sounds.

When he reached the front corner, Lo saw the young PLA private behind the wheel of the mud-scarred vehicle. He was staring out the windshield, hypnotized by the intermittent wipers that slapped back and forth like a metronome.

In a blur, without even glancing at the front chamber that he knew would be empty now, Lo was at the driver's window. His left hand opened the door in one quick motion while his right hand went straight to the private's neck and squeezed.

Lo pressed his thumb like a hammer into the peripheral cervical nerve that would cause temporary paralysis of the upper body. He watched as the driver's body slumped down in his seat, unconscious.

Wasting no time, Lo pulled the limp body out of the car and hoisted it onto his shoulders in a fireman's carry. Dragging it across the short stretch of wet gravel would leave marks. Marks would raise questions. Questions would trigger alarms.

In the semi-sheltered darkness at the far side of the building, Lo swiftly removed the driver's olive uniform with the familiar crimson stripes and pulled it on. It was a size too large. He tugged at the cap, which was a size too small, but it would have to do. He rolled the lifeless body until it was snug against the wall where it would remain through the night and slipped behind the wheel of the idling van to wait.

Lo had conservatively estimated the time he thought it would take the Russian to emerge with the escort. He sat alone, his heart thumping, his eyes fixed on the gate ahead.

In minutes, if all went well, he would be outside again for the first time in more than a year. He could barely restrain his sense of anticipation. He pocketed his eyeglasses and pulled the military cap down over his eyes. Then he slumped against the door by the driver's seat, feigning sleep.

Moments later, Lo heard footsteps. His heart skipped a beat as his pulse quickened.

When the escort tapped on his window to signal help with Lukanov's baggage, Lo didn't budge. He couldn't risk getting out but he didn't mind risking reprimand.

A second tap. Still no response.

Cursing, the escort stepped behind the wet van, opened the rear doors and threw Lukanov's bags in the back. Lo could hear their familiar voices as the two co-conspirators said goodbye.

"Stay as long as you like this time, Professor," the rogue Colonel said. "You deserve it."

"Maybe I stay for good," Lukanov said.

Then he laughed.

"Maybe fall in love."

They both laughed now as the doors slammed shut. Lukanov and the guard climbed in the back seat.

Lo breathed a silent sigh of relief. Boris Lukanov was directly behind him.

The guard reached forward and whacked Lo on the shoulder, cursing his driver for falling asleep.

Bobbing his head, Lo straightened his cap and sat erect. He gunned the accelerator, released the hand brake, and shifted into first gear.

Col. Fu stood by Lukanov's door.

"I fly to Beijing tomorrow," Fu said. "To brief General Min on the next phase. As the Master said, a journey of a thousand miles begins but with a single step."

When Fu shut the Russian's door, Lo didn't hesitate. He stepped on the gas immediately and heard the gravel ricochet in the wheel wells. The van's headlights pierced the damp darkness ahead like twin tunnels as he pulled away.

When he stopped at the exit gate his heart was pounding so hard he was afraid the gate guard would hear it. Staring relentlessly forward, he felt the escort reach over his shoulder with the crumpled pass. Lo took it and gave it to the sentry without looking up.

The sentry glanced at the exit permit, saluted, and stuffed the slip in a small box. He pressed a button and Lo watched as the electrified fence rolled to his right. The red-and-white arm of the horizontal barrier rose to let them through.

"It won't be long now," he thought, his lips tight.

Lo pressed down on the accelerator and shot through the opening into the wet night.

∘ **38** ∘

Ellen Chou flopped down on her bunk bed, weak as a rag doll.

She had worked around the clock without sleep for nearly five days and her eyes burned, ringed with jet-black circles. Her lab coat reeked of sweat and denatured alcohol. She was closer to burnout than she could remember since she started her career as a disease detective.

She asked Amy Wu to call a meeting with Hong Kong's Chief Executive, C. H. Tung. Only a public statement, broadcast by the Governor himself with key health officials at his side, would reassure everyone that Hong Kong was safe. That the government was in full control. That fear and death had been defeated. That panic was in full retreat.

The equally exhausted Amy Wu agreed. She arranged for them to see the Governor after his last meeting that day.

Ellen reviewed her notes as she got ready to brief the Governor.

In barely five days with the H5N1 epidemic, Hong Kong had 2,157 confirmed cases of the killer flu and 759 had died. The mortality rate was a staggering 35.2%.

From a viral subtype of the flu.

It was far worse than the plague of 1918, she thought. Not even close.

She didn't want to think about the frightful implications of a global pandemic but she had no choice. She'd seen the tip of the iceberg in Sha Tin.

They had a ton of work to do in Atlanta to prepare for an infectious epidemic of this magnitude. The nation's infectious disaster plan was incomplete. She would pull no punches in her final report to the CDC's Director. This was no time for internal politics.

After a quick shower, Ellen placed a hurried call to Paul Cerrutti.

Except for cryptic voicemails, they hadn't spoken since the day she left Albuquerque. She knew it was thirteen hours earlier on the east coast and Paul would still be asleep. But his cell phone didn't answer. His outgoing message said he was in Boston so she left a brief message to reassure him she was okay and that the Hong Kong epidemic had been contained.

The black official car cruised silently through the empty streets of Sha Tin like a hearse, past the packed housing estates of Kowloon Tong and into the sparse late-afternoon traffic. They slowed as they entered the Cross-Harbor Tunnel, still closed to private cars, but then picked up speed again as they emerged minutes later on Hong Kong Island.

Ellen noticed the stark contrast between the colorful neon billboards flickering in the semidarkness of dusk and the solemn stares of ordinary people on the street. It wasn't the first time she'd seen this disparity and she knew it wouldn't be the last.

Before long the car began climbing Upper Albert Road toward Government House.

Governor C. H. Tung was a former shipping tycoon who replaced Britain's last emissary, the honorable Christopher Francis Patten, when Hong Kong formally returned to Chinese soverignty on July 1, 1997.

Born on the mainland of China, Tung had moved to Hong Kong with his family in the late 1940s, like countless others from Shanghai and Guangdong who feared the consequences of a Communist takeover in Beijing. Tall and stocky, like a tradesman, he had his graying hair clipped short in a burr cut that accentuated youthful looks despite his advancing years.

Ellen hurriedly checked her profile in a hallway mirror before she entered his office with Amy Wu and two of her colleagues from DOH. She wore the same pearl gray gabardine slacks and navy blouse she had worn on arrival. She'd worked non-stop in the same lab coat and her street clothes had hung unworn in a closet all week.

She wasted no time briefing the Governor and his staff with the latest data. She strongly urged him to address the city in a televised broadcast that would reassure Hong Kong as no other statement could.

The Chief Executive listened intently, his eyes thin slits of concentration. He nodded as she ran through the numbers.

"Until the epidemic peaked," Ellen said quietly, "I feared a full quarantine might be mandatory for Hong Kong. But the evidence shows that this will no longer be necessary. However, it's imperative that your entire live bird population be controlled by stricter regulations. New inspection procedures need to be established at the border crossing in Shenzhen and wooden cages should be banned. Plastic or polyvinyl cages can be disinfected and they're also cheaper, which should please the poultry farmers. We assume the government will make arrangements to compensate the wet markets for their losses."

The Governor made a few notes as she spoke. The blank expression on his face conveyed neither acceptance nor rejection.

"But," Ellen went on, glancing sideways at Amy Wu, "we strongly urge you to impose a full quarantine at Chek Lap Kok airport. Check all travelers before they leave to make sure no one takes this horrible virus with them. And examine all incoming passengers to confirm they are flu-free. If this deadly virus escapes, Hong Kong will not only lose its lucrative tourist business, it will become the curse of the world."

Ellen watched as Tung rose from his leather chair to pick up a briefing folder from his desk. Opening it, he pulled a single sheet from the file and sat down again.

"Forgive me for being so direct," he said, "which as you know is contrary to our tradition. But you also know the seriousness of this situation only too well."

He paused as one of his staff served water to the assembled guests. The antique crystal glasses struck Ellen as bizarre and out of place.

"This is by no means a simple matter," Tung went on. "And not just because of the severe public health problem. Perhaps you are not aware, but there is to be an historic meeting in San Francisco on October 1. Top officials from our government -- President Jiang and a high-ranking State delegation from Beijing -- will sign new trade and human rights agreements with the United States that will put our two nations on a new track for the new century."

He raised the sheet of paper and glanced at it through half-moon tortoise-shell glasses.

"Based on your recommendations," he said, staring at the page, "I believe Beijing will accept the stricter live bird regulations, the border inspections, and the conversion of cages from wood to plastic. For these, there is no argument and no choice."

"And the airport quarantine?" Ellen asked.

She looked nervously across at Amy Wu.

"Beijing will never touch the airport."

Ellen gasped.

"But -- "

"I'm sorry," Tung said, his face drawn. "My hands are tied. I was on the phone with President Jiang at Zhongnanhai just before you arrived. He's adamant. He will agree to any procedure so long as it brings no unfavorable publicity to Hong Kong. The San Francisco accords are too important. Airport quarantine is out."

Ellen turned toward Amy Wu, who stared at the Governor with a mixture of fear and awe. She glanced at the other two officials, who kept their heads down like toy dolls, eyes glued to their notes. She knew that politics and public health often collided at dangerous intersections and she felt like she was in the middle of one right now.

She drew herself upright and tried to keep her voice steady.

"Then please inform Beijing that we have no option but to order quarantine procedures at all foreign airports that accept direct flights from Hong Kong. Protection of the public health is paramount. Until this crisis fully subsides, common sense dictates that we can't be too careful."

Tung peered down at her over the tops of his half-frame glasses.

"You mean, Western common sense," he said.

"No, Governor. I mean unadulterated, everyday-ordinary, plain-vanilla common sense," Ellen said. "Medical science is not political correctness, offering different answers to different constituencies in an effort to keep everyone happy. We have the technology for a blood test that's simple, quick and accurate, and we are using it. The Hong Kong airport should, too, but it's obvious Beijing does not concur."

Tung shook his head.

"I've told you what Beijing is prepared to do."

His voice was stern, like a scolding father.

Undaunted, Ellen opened her file folder and took out a page of notes.

"There's one other important issue China needs to address," she said. "Beijing may choose to ignore this one, too. But at its peril."

"Oh?" Tung said. "What might that be?"

He glanced toward his administrative staff with raised eyebrows. They shrugged their shoulders.

"Our laboratory believes this deadly virus was genetically engineered," she said.

"That's outrageous!"

Tung erupted in a roar. He slammed the file onto his desk.

"If this is true," Ellen continued, holding up one hand, "and a killer flu is being fabricated somewhere in China, the lab site needs to be located and destroyed and the perpetrators apprehended without delay."

The Chief Executive whirled to face his chief of staff, who shook his head vigorously. He had flipped through the entire briefing folder and found no reference to this allegation from the Americans.

Tung leaned back in his leather chair.

"This smells to me like another malicious attempt by the right wing in your country to embarrass China," he said firmly. "It's your cultural imperialism at its worst."

He punched a forefinger on his chair arm for emphasis.

"My country, like yours, is a respected signatory to the 1972 Bioweapons Convention. We would never dishonor that agreement."

Ellen looked him straight in the eye. Her hand shook ever so slightly as she held the fax with Atlanta's findings in one hand.

"Scientific evidence doesn't lie, Governor," she said. "You give me no choice but to present these empirical findings to our people in Washington."

The tall, tired man was silent for a moment as he returned Ellen's gaze. His face was hard as granite.

"I see you are not shy about taking risks, Dr. Chou," he said. "But be very clear about one thing."

"What's that?"

"The Politburo in Beijing will allow nothing to cause China to lose face on the verge of its historic meeting in San Francisco. You may feel free to do whatever you like in your country, but if China is publicly humiliated you and your government will pay the price."

"Forgive me, Governor," she said. "But that's the difference between us. The Chinese always seem willing to risk loss of life as long as they can manage to save face."

Maybe it was the bone-numbing fatigue that put her on edge, but Ellen felt a little chagrined now at having been so pushy with the chief executive. Still, she felt she couldn't back down in the face of Sandy's evidence, and she kept her eyes glued to his.

A staff assistant whispered in Tung's ear. The Governor nodded and stood, casting a glance at his watch.

"I'm sorry," he said. "I have to tape my broadcast with the Commissioner of Health. It will run each quarter-hour on every channel for the next twenty-four hours. The print media will carry the full text on their front pages in the morning."

Ellen stood up, dwarfed by the most powerful man in Hong Kong.

His eyes narrowed as he shook hands with the American visitor.

"I trust you will keep this genetic disclosure confidential," Ellen said quietly.

The Governor nodded.

"Of course," he said.

For the first time, a half-smile creased his face.

"Because I doubt you'd want to lose face, either."

He disappeared through the massive floor-to-ceiling oak doors behind his desk as another aide came to escort Ellen and her team out.

In the car on the way back to Sha Tin, Amy Wu broke the silence.

"Part of me admires the way you stood up to him," she said, her voice unsteady. "That's not something we could ever do, you know, to challenge authority like that. But another part of me is afraid. Hong Kong no longer controls its destiny. We have to obey orders from Beijing now."

"I'm sorry if I embarrassed you," Ellen said softly.

She stared out the side window at the lifeless streets as the car whispered through the canyons of Kowloon. Her face looked strained, almost ghostly.

"My comments at the end were personal, not official. I hope you understand."

"Don't worry about me," Amy Wu said. "You helped us so much. I'm just worried about you."

"Me?" Ellen asked. "Why me?"

"Didn't you notice? The Governor never once said 'thank you.' That's extremely rare in Chinese protocol, as you may know, and conveyed the real depth of his anger. For a foreigner to dispute him in what was practically a public setting -- well, there's no telling what he might do. Or ask Beijing to do."

Ellen closed her eyes as the official car climbed toward the hospital.

"Well, don't worry about me, either," she said. "It's not the first time I've been in hot water."

But she was already dreading her mandatory debrief with LeRoy Harper, the CDC's Director, when she got back to Atlanta.

○ **39** ○

It was normally a two-hour drive to Fuzhou, the capital of Fujian province. But the trip was taking longer tonight because of the rain.

Large, flat drops hammered Lo's windshield like bird dung and the flimsy wipers smeared the murky water across the front glass. Without his glasses, he had to squint. It had been a long time since he'd last driven so he was being cautious. He was also in danger of making Lukanov late.

"Speed it up," said the escort, prodding Lo from the rear. "Faster!"

Lo nodded.

He downshifted and accelerated.

The escort spoke no English and Lukanov knew only a smattering of Chinese, which he had exhausted in the first three minutes of the road trip. The Russian dozed in his seat, unaware of the time.

The thought crossed Lo's mind that he could take advantage of Lukanov's drowsiness and just run the van off the road. Time his jump carefully. Bury the Russian and the guard in a rutted heap of steel and smoldering rubber.

But he'd have to make the rest of his way on foot and risk being discovered. Once knowing his disguise, the PSB thugs would shoot on sight. And not delivering Lukanov to the airport would raise more questions, triggering even more alarms, putting Col. Fu on his case like a bloodhound.

No.

It was safer to press on, stay alert, pass the slower farm vehicles and ox carts that strayed onto the road at night. Traffic was thin but the pink laterite was slick and glistened like wet lipstick in the rain.

As he sped ahead, Lo glanced in the rear-view mirror and saw the guard lean back in his seat, satisfied. He said little to the driver anyway, as a privilege of rank.

Before long Lo saw a chain of lights on the outskirts of the capital city. He picked up the first sign for Sanshan airport, named after the three classic hills of Fuzhou. He turned in the direction of the arrow and curled around a hillside toward a straight stretch in the distance. Over the next hill, he saw the telltale beacon sweep across the horizon.

There was little traffic at the airport at this late hour. Lo slowed to stop at the departure terminal. When the escort got out, he commanded Lo to unload Lukanov's bags. This time if he disobeyed, he would risk detection.

With his cap pulled low over his eyes, he feigned tiredness, stretched, and shuffled lazily to the back of the van. He opened the rear doors and lifted the Russian's heavy bags out.

After setting them down on the pavement, he turned to reenter the van.

"*Zàijiàn*," Lukanov said. One of the few phrases he knew. "Goodbye."

Lo nodded and saluted casually, but as he did so his head naturally came up. The escort had turned his back to pick up Lukanov's luggage, but Lo's eyes met Lukanov's and there was an unmistakable glimmer of recognition.

Without hesitating, Lo jumped back in the vehicle, released the handbrake and floored the accelerator. The rear tires squealed as the van took off.

In the rearview mirror, Lo saw Lukanov gesturing wildly, trying to tell the escort who he'd just seen. But Lo knew the guard's English was as limited as the Russian's Chinese.

The escort pointed to his watch, to remind Lukanov he had no time. His only obligation was to get the Russian on that plane. He knew the van would come back as it always did, so what was the foreigner gabbing about?

When Lo glanced in the mirror one last time, they had vanished inside.

He sped toward the coastal village of Fuqing to ditch the van. He found the deserted, one-lane gravel road that led to the seacoast. Suddenly a front tire exploded on the sharp rocks and he bounced ahead unevenly until his headlights beamed across the sand.

He slowed and stopped and killed the engine.

Working quickly, he tore off the PLA uniform jacket and threw it on the front seat with the military cap. He ripped the vertical crimson stripes off the olive drab trousers and draped them across the steering wheel. He released the handbrake and stepped back as he watched the van roll silently into the water.

It sank without a sound as the dark sea poured in through the half-open windows.

After rubbing sand on his ripped pants to rough up the fabric, he climbed back up the rocky path toward the main road. The rain had slowed to a drizzle but he was still soaked. When he reached the road, he waited.

He thought about searching for a compassionate soul who might shelter him. Someone he could tell about the horror he'd suffered, the horrible Jiangxi plan he had heard Fu describe. Tired and hungry, he argued with himself in the loneliness of a starless night.

No, he decided.

He couldn't risk stopping in Fuzhou. No one in the ancient port city would believe him.

Fuzhou was the first harbor created by the unequal treaties with the West a century and a half before and it was still the southern front against the war of attrition with the traitors in Taiwan. It was a no-man's land, a beacon for all Chinese who wanted to escape, refugees who preferred the hopeful fear of uncertainty to the gnawing fear of repression and death.

No, Lo had to press on, find a ship, any ship that would take him away. Not to Singapore or Jakarta or Kaohsiung, but to America.

To *Meiguó*.

To the Beautiful Country.

To the roots of his poetic inspiration.

There he would never fear arrest or detention. There he would surely find someone to believe his story, someone who could start the cycle of search and destruction of the rogue Colonel's deadly flu factory in Jiangxi. There he would finally be safe.

Before long, he saw the faint beams of a farmer's truck coming slowly toward him. He stepped into the road and waved.

The truck stopped. Lo asked for a ride to the port. The old farmer told him to get in, to say nothing. He would take Lo to the central market and from there he could walk to the docks. He'd done this countless times before. He didn't want to have to lie to the leather-faced PSB goons when they came around asking their ugly questions.

Dockside, Lo bounced from bar to smoke-filled bar looking for tired stevedores nursing their third or fourth *píjiu*, whose minds were floating on beer like their ships at sea, whose tongues would be loose but not lifeless.

He had no money, could buy no one a drink, could offer nothing in exchange for the priceless information he sought. But the dockworkers saw this every day. And they knew, someday, they would try to leave too.

Luckless, his eyes smarting from the thick smoke of countless Red Stars, Lo cruised the tables in the fifth sleazy bar he tried, when a burly barkeep abruptly grabbed his damp shirt by the shoulders and slammed him against a wall.

In defense, Lo held his hands up in front of his face, apologetic, calm.

"Please," he said. "I'll leave."

No fight, no commotion. Nothing to attract attention that someone might remember and report to the PSB the next morning.

But the bartender jerked him around a dark corner, out of sight, into the vacant men's room. Lo gagged at the stench of stale urine and vomit as he hit the floor.

"Try the *Lè Tian Chuán*," the barkeep hissed.

He held a forefinger to his lips.

"I don't know where it's going, and I don't care. But the dockers say it's headed for the west coast of America. Judging from its name, it may take you someplace a lot better than here."

Lo's eyes went wide. He let the muscular barman push him back into the fog-filled bar and shove him out the door.

Few noticed. Few cared. They clamored for more beer.

Lo picked himself up and scurried into the dark, moving anonymously among the dockworkers from ship to ship, dodging the chaotic cranes and forklifts with their big loads, frantically scanning the names on their hulls through the dense fog.

Suddenly he saw it at the far end of the wharf, a small freighter, moored in silence, listing to one side, rusty and wrecked. It looked like it was in for repairs, not headed for a transpacific crossing.

But its rusty, sea-stained name was ominous.

Lè Tian Chuán.

Paradise in Heaven.

Lo swallowed. For the first time, he felt a lump in his throat.

"Never take counsel from your fears," he told himself, and crept aboard.

When he cleared the gangplank, a solitary beam from the night watchman's flashlight caught his face.

"Who are you and what do you want?" the voice asked.

Lo froze. He took a deep breath.

"My name is Wu Kawei," he lied.

His voice was a hoarse whisper.

"Take me to the captain."

"Another stowaway?" the watchman asked.

He shook his head.

"No. No more. We've got a full quota."

"You must," Lo implored. "It's my only chance."

The watchman eyed him for a long minute.

"What the hell, it's only money. Follow me."

They climbed a flight of metal steps to the captain's cabin. The watchman knocked three times and waited.

"What now?" came the slurred response.

"One more," the watchman said, and scurried back down the steps.

When Lo opened the door, he saw the captain leaning on his desk, pointing a cocked revolver at him.

"We're full," said the captain. "Goddam snakeheads already made their drop. Scram."

His eyelids drooped from too much whiskey. Grains of stale rice hung from his stringy beard. His head was unsteady.

"But I have to leave China," Lo said. "I have no other choice."

The captain eyed him warily.

"Another criminal, eh? That's what they all say. What do I care as long as you can front half the fee."

"I'm no criminal," Lo said nervously.

His hands twisted the torn fabric at the sides of his pants.

"I'm ... the sole remaining son in my family. I have to join my older brother in America. For the sake of the family."

The captain stank of stale scotch. He cared less about the reasons than about the money. He eyed Lo cautiously, then uncocked his gun and set it aside.

"Half on departure, half on arrival," he said with a shrug. "Those are the terms."

Thinking quickly, Lo tried to lure the captain with a promise.

"I'm leaving precisely because I have no money," he said. "But my brother has the full amount waiting for you, in dollars, in cash. Everything. When we dock stateside, he'll pay in full, even give you a little extra for your trouble."

The captain had heard all the stories before. But this one seemed different somehow. Maybe it was his resonant voice, the ring of truth, the confidence.

He looked Lo up and down, noticed his wet shirt and torn trousers, saw the genuine look of desperation in his face.

"Hell, what's one more?" the captain said.

Minutes later, he shoved Lo down a ladder into the cramped hold. He slammed the hatch and kicked the bolt into place.

Lo crawled through pitch-black dampness, climbed on top of a damp crate, and waited.

○ **40** ○

Ellen Chou walked smartly from International Arrivals at Los Angeles airport toward her domestic Delta connection. She lugged her overnight bag in one hand and her briefcase in the other. She wore a pair of khaki jeans with a long-sleeve salmon-colored raglan half-collar shirt, her dark hair pinned back by a pair of tortoise-shell berets.

With her official credentials she had cleared customs and immigration without delay, despite enhanced security in the arrivals terminal for flights from Hong Kong. Her public health colleagues hadn't missed a beat.

Glancing up at an overhead clock, she reset her watch. A strong tailwind had pushed the Singapore Airlines overnight non-stop to arrive well ahead of schedule, a frequent bonus on inbound flights from Asia. Ellen had an unexpected gift seldom seen in the information age. Like a rare metal, time was more precious than money.

Her eyelids scraped like sandpaper and her eyes still stung after a dozen hours at 35,000 feet. She knew the irritating signs of jet lag well, when her head nodded like it was detached from her body and her feet dragged as if trapped in leg irons.

So she walked at a brisk pace, inhaling deeply and making her heart rate climb, driving the oxygen faster through her bloodstream and straight to her air-starved brain. When she sniffed the un-mistakable aroma of fresh coffee, she paused at a small stand-up café. After endless days and countless cups of tasteless oolong tea, the expresso was invigorating. When the caffeine kicked in, she felt pumped.

The Delta flight to Atlanta took less than five hours, but the three-hour time change meant she wouldn't get home until late afternoon so she had time to organize her thoughts. Time to prepare for her debrief with LeRoy Harper, the CDC's no-nonsense (and first-ever) African-American Director. Time to sleep uninterrupted in her own bed for the first time in weeks.

Ellen was not looking forward to seeing Harper. Official debriefs were always tense, characterized by second-guesses and 20/20 hindsight. But she had all the data in her briefcase. Not for nothing had she acquired a reputation for being thorough and complete. Anal-retentive behavior always got the most brownie points at CDC.

From the gate, she called Paul to let him know she was back. She found him still in Boston. They spoke without voicemail for the first time since Albuquerque.

"With all the distractions in Mexico, we tracked a pair of terrorist suspects to Montreal," he said.

His own voice was edged with fatigue.

"But you must be bone-tired. Let me guess -- you're not looking forward to your meeting with Harper tomorrow."

"Politics has reared its ugly head," she said.

She told him about the State delegation from Beijing that would be meeting White House officials in San Francisco.

"Since I reported the cloned virus, all of a sudden I've become the house leper. Nobody likes controversy."

"Any new developments from the lab?" he asked.

"No," she said. "Sandy locked in the genetic map, but nobody believes her."

"Well, when can I see you? We owe each other at least a long weekend."

"I wish it could be soon, but if Harper gives me a green light I'll have a lot more work to do. The bioterrorism committee meets next week in Washington, don't forget. And I've got to get the pharmaceutical companies started on a vaccine for this horrible virus."

"Of course," he said, unable to mask his disappointment.

There was a loud click on the line.

"Hold on," he said. "Don't go away."

After a brief pause, he was back on the line.

"Gotta go. GPS just picked up one of our suspects and he's on the move. Call me from Atlanta?"

"Absolutely. And Paul?"

"Yeah."

"Be careful."

"Always."

After takeoff, Ellen went right to work. She pulled a stack of notes from her briefcase and reviewed the Hong Kong data. Three facts slapped her in the face.

One, the mortality rate: 35.2%.

Influenza type A, subtype H5N1, had slaughtered one out of every three people it infected. Normal mortality for the typical winter flu -- type A, subtypes H1N1 or H3N2 -- was less than 2%. Even then, the cause of death was typically a secondary complication related to bacterial infections like pneumonia, never internal hemorrhaging or kidney failure.

Two, the absence of a protective vaccine.

Every January, the FDA's flu committee met in Washington to decide the components of a trivalent vaccine for the coming flu season that would start scarcely nine months later.

The critical decision had to be made by February to give the drug companies time to order chick eggs, culture the virus in their embryos, and manufacture, distribute, and administer the vaccine before the next tidal wave of flu.

But fewer than one in four Americans -- and barely one in three healthcare workers themselves -- opted to get the vaccine.

But H5N1 was an avian virus, so it would kill the chick embryos. This meant the drug companies had to start from scratch, identify a totally new cell substrate as a host for the virus so they could try to culture it. Ellen winced when she thought about how much time that would take. Time they didn't have.

Three, the shocking age range of the dead.

Flu typically attacked the very young and the very old. At the early end of the age spectrum, infants and toddlers had yet to acquire antibodies in sufficient strength to defeat unfamiliar microbes. At the other, seniors had immune systems that were weak from old age and less able to withstand assaults by virulent invaders.

But the tragic majority of those dying from the avian virus, H5N1 -- 85.7%, according to Ellen's numbers -- fell between the ages of 21 and 35. This killer virus had systematically eliminated young, vigorous, active adults.

If it ever got loose, it could go on a rampage and give the 21st century its defining moment.

There was a fourth fact that nagged at her subconscious, too, tugged at her like a bad dream: McDermott's revelation about the genetic reassortant they'd never seen before. A cloned mutant that they strongly suspected had been genetically engineered.

The samples ... all the same ... *right down to the genetic map ...* no variation ... *like Xerox copies ...*

Ellen couldn't shake it from her mind. What could this mean?

She kept thinking about it after she landed and hopped on the airport shuttle to look for her silver-gray Passat. When she was on the freeway heading for Decatur, it came back and mugged her again. It was all she could think about on the drive home.

... identical copies of the same virus ...

If the killer flu had been cloned from the same RNA genome, then there was an underground factory making this deadly virus somewhere in southern China. And if there was a factory, there had to be someone running it. Could Paul help by alerting friends at the CIA? Somehow, they had to make covert inquiries, try to find out what they could, scan some databases, get a satellite pass-by.

Ellen kept struggling with this conundrum all the way back to her small co-op in Decatur, her insulation from the outside world. Her cocoon.

She'd fallen in love with the little apartment the first time she'd set eyes on it, but the landlord had been a died-in-the-wool redneck. He refused to sell it to anyone who wasn't Caucasian. She won that court case, and the apartment, hands-down.

Ellen flicked a switch when she opened the door and entered the spacious living room. The soothing sounds of a Bach harpsichord concerto soaked into her soul.

Two short leather couches flanked a pair of narrow glass doors that opened onto a wide balcony. Row after row of books lined each wall, constant companions, close friends, sources of great pleasure, solace in times of need, with solutions to the mysteries of medical science.

But this was one mystery they weren't going to be able to help her solve.

She tossed her bags on the floor and went into the bedroom to change. She had just enough time for a workout at the local gym. Getting her heart rate up would help loosen her body and tighten her mind.

When she finally flopped into bed that night, she did not sleep uninterrupted.

Another herd of wild zebras chased after her, stampeding through her dreams, trailing huge clouds of mysterious microbes that billowed into the sky, heralds of darkness and death that blocked out the sun and plunged her into a world of total desolation.

∘ **41** ∘

"So tell me about Lo."

General Min paced nervously back and forth across the deep brown carpet in his corner office at PLA Headquarters in Beijing. He was furious with his reckless prodigy for allowing such a careless mistake. His voice had an impatient, demanding tone.

"What about him?" the renegade Colonel replied.

Matter of fact. Rational, not testy.

Col. Fu studied his commanding officer with sharp eyes.

"The Russian's escort called at midnight when the van didn't return," Fu continued. "Unfortunately, he called his CO instead of me so we lost a good six hours. I put the PSB on it as soon as we found the driver's body early the next morning. They've blanketed the stretch between Jiangxi and Fuzhou. To be safe, I ordered a special team to Guangdong in case Lo doubled back. Doubtful, but you never know. We can't be too careful."

"It was not smart to let this happen," said the General. "You should have been more careful, you know that."

"I admit we were distracted by the spectacular results from Hong Kong," Fu said. "But don't forget, we saved precious time by killing two birds with one stone. We don't have to run separate experiments now to test transmission from human to human. We know the aerosolized virus will work perfectly."

"Yes, and now Lo's on the loose. He'll talk to anyone. He'll talk to everyone. The Jiangxi plan may be compromised."

"Let's not overreact, General. As Mao himself often said, Never trust anyone who fights a tiger with his bare hands. Give me someone who is fearful of failure but capable of successful execution."

General Min's hot eyes burned into his subordinate.

"And you are not fearful of failure?" he asked acidly.

"You're asking me if I fear failure? Me? The one Army officer who remained loyal to you, who never shot and killed our own brothers and sisters during the Beijing Massacre in Tiananmen Square? The PLA genius -- your very own -- who bought up undervalued shares of Japanese companies and sold at the market peak to collapse their bubble economy? Russia. Vietnam. Pakistan. Iraq. You and I have a long and proud record together, my friend. A reputation for eliminating foreign adversaries. Our focus is *always* on successful execution, never on failure."

Col. Fu joined his commander at the side of his broad desk.

"Look. Lo may have the wrong ideology, but he's not stupid," he said quietly. "If he talks to *anyone*, the PSB will know who, when and where within 48 hours. Since Lo knows this too, he'll be doubly careful. Especially with his history as a dissident. He's so well known I seriously doubt he'll whisper a word."

"In China, you mean."

Fu stopped. He smiled.

"I anticipated that concern," he said, nodding. "So I contacted the Transport Ministry and got a list of all maritime departures from Fuzhou during the next six days. I could have requested a similar list for Hong Kong but Lo would never risk an area so recently subject to quarantine. Too much security, both in and out."

"So?"

"So there are seven vessels scheduled to depart Fuzhou this week. Four have destinations in Asia -- Kobe, Jakarta, Singapore, Phuket. But they leave much later in the week, which would force Lo to stay longer in Fuzhou, thus risking probable discovery by the PSB. That's a risk I don't think he'd want to take."

"And the other three?"

"One to Birmingham, England; one to Johannesburg; one to Seattle."

"Washington."

"Yes."

"In the United States."

"Precisely."

Neither rogue officer said a word for a full minute.

"And when is that ship supposed to sail?"

Fu smiled again.

"It left last night. I have a full team from the PSB working the Fuzhou waterfront as we speak, to see if they can learn anything."

"Waste of time," said the General.

"I agree," said Fu. "But if I hadn't ordered them to, you would surely have asked me why not."

General Min's lips tightened into a pencil-thin line.

"You know what that means," he said.

"Remember, Lo speaks no English," Fu replied, nodding again. "When he arrives -- if he is in fact on board -- he'll be arrested and detained as an illegal immigrant. It will take the authorities time to locate a translator. And they will ask him all the usual questions."

"But he will be highly agitated. He won't answer the usual questions, he'll want to tell them over and over again in his limited English about Jiangxi, about the mad Colonel Fu, about our killer flu."

"I know."

"So are you thinking what I'm thinking?" the General asked.

He stood and pushed back from his desk.

"I've already spoken with Seattle," Fu said. "If he's on that boat, the Green Dragons will take care of him for us. They are loyal allies."

"They are sometimes an irritating hindrance as well as a necessary evil."

"I told them in no uncertain terms what they could expect if they fail."

"Lean on your little friend there, what's his name?"

"Liu. Eddie Liu."

"Yes. Lean on Liu."

The General turned and walked to a corner window facing the broad, tree-lined avenue of Dongchang'an Jie. The mid-September day was hot and humid. Beijing was wrapped in a thick shroud of late summer smog. Dark clouds massed on the horizon, signaling rain.

From the squat PLA headquarters building in the capital city, he could see straight across Tiananmen Square to the Great Hall of the People and beyond it, to Zhongnanhai. The early-evening crowds were thin, as always under the watchful eye of the feared Public Security Bureau officers who walked incognito among them.

A huge calligraphic poster hung above Tiananmen Gate. It read, "Long Live President Jiang and the People's Republic of China." At that very moment, electronic speakers mounted at each corner of the square began booming the familiar strains of China's national song, "The East is Red."

General Min turned back to face his prodigy.

"What about the American?" he asked.

"The lady doctor? Yes, we hadn't expected that. She isolated Sha Tin and shut down the outbreak very fast."

"How did she do that?"

"She's a very smart woman, apparently. She put a ring around Fo Tan tighter than your sphincter, General. And she even hinted to Governor Tung that the Jiangxi virus had been genetically engineered. What does that tell you?"

The general nodded.

"Like Lo, she is too smart and also dangerous. She must be eliminated."

"Exactly. So I've taken care of that, too. I called our attaché in Washington. He complained bitterly to Russell at the State Department, who spoke with the President's chief of staff. In exchange for a generous contribution to the President's campaign from the China Lobby in untraceable soft money, she is being taken off the case."

"But be ready to intervene more forcefully if she causes any more trouble."

Fu nodded.

"Of course. I've anticipated your concern and am already a step ahead."

◦ **42** ◦

The next morning, Ellen pulled on a pair of lightweight linen slacks and a pastel coral pima cotton crewneck sweater. She arrived early for her meeting with Harper.

She paced his outer office in the new glass tower on Clifton Road, alternately looking at the political pictures on his wall and sipping a mug of institutional coffee.

In little more than half a century, the CDC had mushroomed from a small one-room team fighting malaria in Panama to nearly 7,500 people in twenty modern buildings crammed on a tight campus in Atlanta, battling unknown pathogens all over the world.

Dr. Harper and his executive assistant Marge Kinkaid both had desks fabricated from the dark, mottled hardwood of Africa. Ellen sat in one of the ebony side chairs and gazed at the ebony desk with its ebony in-and-out boxes, ebony stapler, ebony-handled scissors, ebony Scotch tape dispenser, ebony paper clip holder, ebony letter-opener, an ebony-encased battery-operated pencil sharpener. She often wondered if there was any wood left in Kenya after Harper had finished decorating his offices.

LeRoy Harper, the CDC's top gun, was a native Georgian. Following Martin Luther King, who was assassinated on the eve of his high school graduation, Harper led a non-violent civil rights protest in the early 1970s to ban the Confederate flag from the state of Georgia.

It was a long, bitter battle that ended in failure. Harper turned his back on politics after that. He learned the hard way that money moved politics, not the other way around. So he studied medicine at Emory University and joined the CDC after interning at Walter Read Hospital in Washington, specializing in minority health issues.

Harper's rise at CDC had been little short of meteoric.

As a junior member of the Epidemiology Intelligence Service, he joined a special task force dedicated to eliminating smallpox, working with the charismatic D. K. Merriwether. They won that battle, big-time, in 1980.

Then, in collaboration with USAMRIID, he took on the ebola virus and led the charge to upgrade CDC's biosafety containment labs.

Sensitive to issues of skin color and gender, he made damn sure his achievements spoke loudly.

His last assignment before becoming Director brought him full circle back to politics. He headed the National Center for HIV and STD, which hogged more than a third of the CDC's total annual budget of nearly $2.5 billion and a huge staff of 2,000 people. Sexually transmitted diseases, AIDS in particular, hit American minorities like hurricanes punished Florida. By comparison, Ellen's tiny group that battled emerging infectious diseases struggled with fewer than fifty specialists on a shoestring budget of $8 million a year.

Marge Kinkaid's voice pulled her back from the photos.

"He'll see you now," she said.

LeRoy Harper pushed angrily away from his desk as she entered.

"What the hell are you trying to do, Ellen?"

He wasted no time. He waved a manila file folder in the air as he spoke.

"What -- what are you talking about?"

She knew this wouldn't be easy but she'd never expected an ambush.

"I'm trying to do my job, what do you expect?"

Harper slammed the file down on his desk.

"By insulting the Governor of Hong Kong? By ordering their hospital director around like an Army private? And by suggesting they tow barges full of cadavers to Wyoming?"

She swallowed nervously.

"That was just a *joke*. For God's sake, LeRoy, chill. Everybody knows Wyoming gets good money for taking excess garbage from other states. Besides, you know yourself if you don't find a way to loosen up in pressure situations, you'll lose it."

She needed to find a way to take the offensive, fast. Snapping open her briefcase, she whipped out a fistful of papers.

"LeRoy, if you'd just look at my data -- "

He waived her papers aside.

"Nobody ever faults your numbers, Ellie," he interrupted. "But it's the way you go about getting them. How many times do I have to tell you? We have to work with the host governments overseas as a *team*, not like the Lone Ranger."

"Just a cotton-pickin' minute," she said. "I hit the ground running in Albuquerque ten days ago and just now came up for air. When was the last time *you* fought a crisis?"

Harper ignored her question and opened his file.

"I'm telling you, this aggressive streak of yours has to stop," he said as his eyes scanned the folder. "The Hong Kong stuff. Unilaterally disarming some Navajo kid in Taos. That hot tub affair in Montana when they had to call the FBI. And that weird affair in Arkansas which -- "

"That's a low blow and you know it. Everybody *loves* to cite Arkansas when they want to beat me up. How in hades was I supposed to know our next President was going to leap from Little Rock to Washington? But remember, I was the only one who found histoplasmosis -- a fucking *fungus*, for Christ's sake -- and tracked it from a classroom in Pine Bluff to a chicken farm in Jonesboro to a rental truck delivering coal from *Kentucky*. Everybody else ran around screaming tuberculosis at the top of their lungs and it took a midget like me working sub-threshold to pin it down. You call *that* being aggressive? I say it's serving the public, LeRoy, and that's our job."

LeRoy Harper tossed the file onto his ebony desk and slumped into his chair.

"You know as well as I do that deference gets you further than smarts."

His tone was softer now, less cutting.

She lowered herself into one of the ebony side chairs opposite him.

"So how in the world did we get from a killer flu in Hong Kong to corporate survival in a government bureaucracy? We're getting way off track here."

"It's not just Hong Kong," he said.

His eyes were weary, his face drawn.

He reached across and picked up another folder.

"Washington's got me in a straightjacket. The State Department was pissed that you pushed the Governor in Hong Kong, so Russell called the White House. The President's chief of staff started screaming at the Surgeon General and she's now tearing strips off me. They're worried sick about some goddam agreements the Administration needs to sign with a State delegation from Beijing in San Francisco on October first."

"All those people you mentioned are political appointees, Harper," Ellen said. "Is that what this is about? The President's re-election campaign?"

This was the second time in two days that Ellen heard the reference to San Francisco. She thought back to Governor Tung.

"It's not like I have a choice, Ellen. You know we've got a major appropriations bill pending in Congress. I need the White House. Otherwise we can't sell it."

"You mean, sell out."

"That's enough. Listen..."

"No, LeRoy. *You* listen."

Ellen jumped out of her chair and leaned across his desk, eyeball to eyeball with her boss.

"You obviously haven't read the final report I e-mailed before leaving Hong Kong yesterday. We've got a killer virus here -- "

"Which has been contained -- "

"Which has a *huge* mortality rate. Which is killing young adults in the prime of life. Not kids, not old folks. And which -- confirmed by our own people -- has been genetically engineered in China somewhere, somehow, by someone. The states need an urgent advisory from us alerting them to all this. I've got to get some seed money to Wyeth-Ayerst so they can start work on a vaccine. And you know I'm scheduled to brief the bioterrorism committee in Washington next week."

LeRoy Harper rose and sat down on a corner of his desk.

"Ellen," he said, his voice quieter again. "You know we deal with killer bugs all the time. That's what we're all about here."

"Not like this bastard, LeRoy. No way, José."

Her gaze was steady, her tone firm. She'd be damned if she was going to let politics derail this case.

"Look," he said, "I can never ream you out for poor results. Everybody knows your work is first-class. But look at you -- you're a wreck, exhausted. Your patience is paper-thin and your eyes make your face look like a punching bag. You need some time off."

She looked him straight in the eye.

"How can you possibly think about vacation at a time like this? We've got a lethal pathogen here, LeRoy, and an enormous obligation to the public."

"Put Feldman on it," he said, shrugging his shoulders.

"Jonathan? Come on, I'm smack in the middle of it. He's probably still filing reports from New Mexico."

"No, Feldman wrapped up Taos right after you left for Hong Kong. He's rested and ready. Anything comes up while you're away, I'll make sure he's on it."

She shot him a curious glance.

"This smells like a done deal," she said. "In fact, it stinks. You're giving me no choice?"

"Washington's giving me no choice," he said. "They want you off this case, period. Take a week, ten days. Disappear long enough to let me get this budget bill through Congress and the White House off my back."

"But how -- "

"Feldman can handle it, trust me. Brief him before you leave. And let him know where you can be reached, just in case."

Ellen thought for a minute.

She was furious. She'd never been taken off a case for political reasons before. Something wasn't right.

She started to give Harper her stock comment about the low level of talent in politics and advertising but thought better of it and kept her mouth shut. This was clearly no time for wisecracks.

"Three conditions," she said, holding up three fingers.

"Jesus, Ellen. Things are never simple with you, are they? What?"

"First, let me draft the advisory. Put your name or Jonathan's on it, I don't give a damn. But it has to be thorough and it has to be done right away. Second, Wyeth's got to get cracking on a vaccine. And third, promise me I can still brief the BT committee in Washington next week."

LeRoy Harper walked over to a large bay window as he thought about Ellen's demands.

Part of him wanted to say no, he was the CDC Director, damn it, and he'd delegate as he saw fit. He had to listen to Washington. But when he saw the Confederate flag still flying on a flagpole nearby, his blood boiled. The other side of him, the combative side, wanted her to win.

"If I do this," he said cautiously, "you have to promise me something in return."

"Such as?" she asked.

"If you go to Washington, you *present* our case. You don't proselytize."

"You asking me to clip my own wings, LeRoy?"

"No, I'm telling you to cover your ass."

Ellen hesitated for a moment. She knew he was right. She had a tendency to lose support when she pushed too hard. Compromise was never easy in a world dominated by invisible adversaries.

"All right," she said. "Deal. I'll be on my best behavior. Promise."

She stuck out her hand and he shook it.

"Remember, I can't protect you if you step in it again," he said. "When the White House realizes you're in town to brief the Committee, they'll try to sandbag the shit out of you. Just make sure I'm done on the Hill first."

"I will," she said. Then she added, "I'll be careful."

Ellen went back to her windowless office on the basement level of Building 16 to begin drafting her advisory report. It had to be a separate notice, something brief but potent that would get attention, printed and FedEx'd on different color paper. Not just buried on pink sheets in the CDC's *Mortality and Morbidity Weekly Report.*

She gave Feldman copies of her epidemiological data that he could combine with Sandy McDermott's statistical lab analysis so he could start the ball rolling with Wyeth. And she asked him to stick around while she was gone, because you never knew.

Feldman reacted like a kid at Christmas.

As a virologist, he was overjoyed to be on the case. To him, it looked like it might be the Big One. Every epi's dream.

Afterwards, she dialed the number she knew by heart.

"Paul? It's me. When do you figure you might be done with the Montreal case?"

"Ellie! Don't tell me the world's leading workaholic can actually take some time off. You thinking of a real honest-to-God 3-day weekend for a change?"

The sound of his voice was upbeat, reassuring.

"Don't take this the wrong way, Paul, but it's not like I have a choice. I'll tell you why later. How about it, can I pull you away for a short week?"

The reassurance she felt earlier dissipated with his response.

"Now? I don't see how. We're still tracking the two militant Muslims up in Montreal, as I told you. They managed to get a pair of legitimate Canadian passports on the strength of forged baptism certificates since we shut down their birth certificate scam. We can't just walk in and bust them. The Boston office just has a small counter-terrorism team on the case so I don't think I can bail out on such short notice."

Ellen blinked away her tears. She tried a different approach.

"Paul, you know how we always talked about going up to Maine? Well, Camden's practically in your backyard. It's a really short drive from Boston. And it's now the third week of September so it shouldn't be hard to find a room."

"Ellie, listen to yourself. Put yourself in my shoes. Every time I try to pull you away for a weekend, you beg off because of work. This time, it's no different for me."

"Well, this time it's way different for me," she said.

She told him about the fireworks with Harper and the political pressure coming from Washington.

"Somebody in the White House wants me off this case in the worst way, Paul. They've got a high-level meeting with Chinese government officials in San Francisco soon, and as usual they're putting politics first."

There was silence on the other end.

"Paul? You still there?"

"Yeah, I'm just thinking," he said. "This really means a lot to you, doesn't it?"

She bit her lip.

"It's nothing like I've ever experienced before, Paul. I -- I need you."

"All right, look. You go on ahead. Book the Camden Inn, that's a great idea. Let me talk to the agent in charge of the office here. I'll try to come as soon as I can, but it may take me a couple of days to get clear because their counter-terrorism team's really short-handed. You'll owe me big time after, you know that."

"Think carefully about what you want," she said, suppressing a half-smile. "You might just get it."

After she hung up, she made sure she had copies of all the Hong Kong data in her briefcase, locked and ready to go. She checked to make sure her laptop and cell phone were charged and packed.

And she stopped to make a five-minute call to a special number in Washington just before she left.

∘ **43** ∘

The two senior military officers plotted long into the late afternoon. They double-checked and triple-checked their plan.

Finally, General Min stood up behind his desk and stretched.

"Good work," he said. "I'm simply amazed how malleable the Americans are. They have no backbone at all, do they? Quite unlike the Europeans."

Col. Fu nodded as he packed his briefcase.

"Don't forget, we have the advantage of playing Europe like a chessboard. If France won't accede to our demands, we offer a contract to the Germans, who will. If the Italians don't accept our terms but the British do, we give London a green light. Europe may be more time-consuming, yes, but the end result is the always the same. When it comes to America, it is always and only a matter of money."

The general leaned against his desk and rubbed his tired eyes.

"The Americans are really gullible, aren't they? They insist that Beijing stop exporting weapons to their adversaries. So instead of selling missiles to Iraq, we barter them for oil. No cash ever changes hands. And instead of shipping nuclear warheads to Pakistan, we include them as part of our training program at no extra charge. Even when we acquired the Falcon advanced radar system from Israel, they simply gave it to our Air Force for free in exchange for permission to use Gashun Gobi for weapons testing. Our word is our bond: we neither buy nor sell weapons of mass destruction."

Col. Fu eyed his mentor for a long while and smiled.

"I think I've taken the necessary steps to eliminate any further problems," he said. "*Hau?*"

"*Hen hau,*" the general replied. "Very good. You've neutralized the threats from Lo and the lady doctor. Forget them for now. It's important that we not lose focus."

"I agree," said Fu. "The *fengpai* thinks they're ready to ratify the human rights and trade agreements with America. They fly to San Francisco September 29th for the formal signing on October 1st. The Americans picked the site, we picked the date. San Francisco is where China's first immigrants joined the Gold Rush and completed work on their transcontinental railroad. The PLA made it clear to the *fengpai* that the date was not negotiable."

"And the Americans *agreed*?"

"Of course. Because our side had accepted a historical location that symbolized the past oppression of illiterate Chinese immigrants, we made it clear that the Americans should not object to holding the official ceremony on our National Day. Washington has an ugly habit of ignoring cultural protocol when it comes to China."

"Sweet irony."

"Makes my skin tingle," Fu said. "Americans are so unspeakably hypocritical. They conveniently forget that their own laws once barred our people from marrying or owning property or even becoming citizens. They constantly cry freedom and democracy but these cries ring hollow in the shadows of their savage slavery."

"What makes you think they won't get nervous and cancel?"

"On September 29th at dusk, China Airlines flight 004 will land at Newark with a little surprise, an unexpected visitor, an invisible guest. That will be an even sweeter irony. By the time the San Francisco ceremony convenes two days later, Washington will be unavoidably distracted by an infectious epidemic on their east coast. We will be in California and the *fengpai* will be nervous because of the infectious outbreak. Neither they nor the Americans will be in a mood to oppose our demands to weaken the agreements. China's tariff barriers will stay high. There will be no more micro-management of human rights here. And when President Jiang returns to Beijing he will find himself unceremoniously purged. Our loyal troops are ready for the putsch, with you as Jiang's successor and me as their new commander."

General Min frowned.

"And if Washington tries to postpone the signing?"

It was Col. Fu's turn to smile now.

"They wouldn't dare take that risk. Their President has barely a month left in his re-election campaign. His party, which has benefited from our covert contributions to its soft money accounts, would never let him cancel. The Americans desperately need the agreements and will make every concession at the eleventh hour to save them."

The general frowned.

"What next?"

"We can send planeloads of undercover PLA volunteers in mufti to help them fight the public health menace. The Green Dragons can also supply civilian workers. China will look like a hero in the eyes of the world, the selfless poor helping the selfish rich. It will take them years, perhaps a decade, to fully recover. By then China will dominate center stage, not America."

Col. Fu walked slowly over to the general's corner window.

"Afterward," he went on, his voice rising as if addressing the huge square below, "Washington will have no energy to fight us on human rights. The Falun Gong and every other spiritual movement in China can be brought under our control with no further outcry from Washington. The threat from these rebellious splinter groups will be neutralized, the chaos eliminated. And the Americans will either be too distracted or too weak to interfere when we finally attack the renegades in Taipei and recapture Taiwan. The days of America's troublesome interference are over."

The general joined his protégé at the windows.

"The *fengpai* will be out," he said softly, "and China will be ours. We can finally restore the Central Kingdom to its rightful place."

General Min placed a hand on the Colonel's shoulder.

"What about the backup plan?" he asked.

"Surely you don't think -- "

"I think about contingencies all the time and I know you do, too. We didn't expect Lo to disappear and nobody expected the American lady doctor to play the role of magician. So tell me what you have in your hip pocket."

Fu approached the general's conference table and snapped open his briefcase.

"I am totally confident that the Air China vector will succeed," Fu said. "But of course I have a comprehensive backup plan ready for execution."

"And when are you planning to brief me on the fail-safe?"

Col. Fu reached into his briefcase and pulled out a red folder. He flipped open his agenda.

"How about first thing tomorrow morning? Early, say, at dawn."

General Min shook his head.

"I have to brief the *fengpai* in the morning to prepare them for San Francisco," he said. "They're insufferable in the morning. Can you come back in the afternoon?"

Col. Fu made a note and returned the red file to his case. He snapped it shut.

"Tomorrow afternoon then," he said. "I assure you it's more than adequate."

The general pulled out a fat Cuban cigar and puffed it alive in a thick cloud of blue smoke.

"No doubt," he said. "As usual, I expect your work to be flawless."

∘ **44** ∘

"So where are you from?" the young woman asked nervously. "You're not one of us."

Lo Fengbu could see very little in the darkness of the ship's hold. Thin beams of light trickled in from two tiny portholes overhead. The ship's turbines pounded against the hull with a dull whine and the old freighter rolled from side to side with a rocking motion that turned his stomach upside down.

A headache hammered at him like a piston. He was hungry and thirsty and it was hard to hear. The air reeked with the putrid stench of a single makeshift toilet that was shoved into one corner and overflowed with human waste. They were wrapped in a cloud of stale cigarette smoke that forced Lo to breathe in short gasps through his mouth.

"What did you say?" he replied. "I can't hear you."

He sat painfully upright on a small stack of rubber tires, leaning against a rough wooden crate.

She stammered as she raised her voice.

"I ... I said you're not one of us. What's your name?"

"Lo," he said. "Lo Fengbu."

She gasped.

"*You're* Lo Fengbu? But that can't be! He's a famous poet who taunted the PSB beasts in Beijing. He was sentenced to the Shandung *laogai*, everybody knows that. You can't be him."

"But I am," he said.

He spoke about his poetry, his arrest, the prison interrogation, his imprisonment, the circumstances of his release. Not knowing whether he could yet trust this innocent peasant, he said nothing about Col. Fu or the deadly Jiangxi virus.

"What about you?" Lo asked. "Who are you, and from where?"

"My name is Chen Sun," she said with a smile. "My friends and I are from a *lindong renkou* in Hunan province. The floating population."

Lo nodded. He knew about the itinerant groups of homeless and jobless that scavenged for food and scrapped for work all over China. There were nearly 100 million people in these desperate groups now, well outside the safety net of the State, nearly ten percent of China's population ignored by the ideals, platitudes and empty promises of Communism.

These modern-day nomads were not included in any official statistics, not limited to any one province, not part of the socialist worker's paradise. Without residence permits or work units, they tried gamely to stay a step ahead of the PSB. Some rented their bodies. Others sold their lives. Most resigned themselves to a life of despair on the dark side.

"My parents were poor farmers," she said. "There was never work for me at home and they couldn't afford to send me to school. So I wandered around Shaowu looking for something to do. Anything. My father heard about the market for new wives so he put me up for sale. He was desperate."

Lo's headache was getting worse. He stretched his body painfully across the top of the wooden crates.

"So how did you escape?" he asked.

He grimaced with each word.

"My father beat me and dragged me to the auction," she said.

She began to sob.

"It was horrible. I ... I had no choice. A man bought me and took me home. He was very crude and vulgar. He beat me, too, and raped me, then stood by drunk and laughing while his friend raped me and they both got drunk. That same night, I ran away. I found others like me outside the village, men and women alike. We hunted. We begged. But mostly we wanted to escape. We heard about the snakeheads and the Green Dragons, so we came to Fuzhou. That's why we're on this boat."

Lo groaned. He didn't know whether it was simply the hunger that knifed through his stomach or just motion sickness from his time in the hold on rough seas.

"Are you all right?" Chen Sun asked.

"I'm fine," Lo replied, wincing. "Trust me, this ship is truly paradise in heaven compared to the *laogai*. But doesn't the motion make you sick?"

"Not really," she said, shaking her head. "I just drink water and forget about the slop they throw us. You should try it."

"I may have to," Lo said. "Tell me about the Green Dragons."

"The criminal gangs from Fujian?" she asked. "We hear they control crime on the west coast of America. The snakeheads paid the ship's captain a fee to smuggle us in. The agents for the Dragons will pick us up and pay the rest. We're supposed to work for them for a while to pay off our passage."

"Doing what?" Lo asked.

He held folded his arms across his stomach and this helped to ease the cramps. Had to be the sea, he thought. The pain comes and goes, just like the ocean swells.

"You know, sewing clothes, driving cars, working in massage houses," she said. "Or so they say. But it has to be better than Hunan. After I pay off their fee I will save a lot of money and send some to my family through a bearer account. It's anonymous, you know."

Lo nodded.

"I lied," he said. "I told the captain my brother would pay him the full amount when we arrive. Frankly, I was scared. I had to get out of Fuzhou. I would agree to anything."

Lo thought about the reception Chen Sun and her friends would face when they arrived, and suddenly he grew sad. He knew they would have no real jobs. They would become virtual slaves to a criminal gang. Lo would be put to work in an urban sweatshop or employed as a drug runner on the coast. Chen Sun would wind up as a prostitute. If she escaped again, she'd be part of a *lindong renkou* in America, a fish out of sea. Without friends, without relatives, without the comfort of her own culture and language, how could she possibly survive?

"Anything is better than staying in China," she said softly, closer to him now. "There is so much money in America. That is why they call it the beautiful country, you know?"

"Yes, I know."

Just then the hatch opened, letting in a sharp shaft of sunlight that forced them both to shield their eyes.

Lo could see the other stowaways now, a dozen of them, straddled across other crates, waiting, silent. They kept their distance because he was the only one with motion sickness. They thought he brought bad luck, bad *feng shui*.

Several bundles wrapped in burlap came bouncing down.

"Dinner," said Chen Sun.

She collected the parcels, unwrapped them, and distributed leftovers from the galley to others. She offered Lo a small block of dried beef and two pieces of stale bread.

"America may be a land of freedom and opportunity," Lo said, tearing off a thin scrap of bread. "But it is also dangerous for newcomers because only the fittest can survive. There are traps for the unsuspecting. They will try to take advantage of you. You must be careful."

Unable to eat, he tossed the stale loaf aside.

Chen Sun gave him some water and reassured him. She spoke again about how desperate she was to leave. She was confident that the devils she didn't know couldn't possibly be worse than the bastards she did.

Lo was impressed with her spirit. Despite her youthful innocence she had a strong sense of direction. She seemed resilient and unbreakable, like bamboo.

"You're not discouraged at all?" he asked.

She shook her head. Her eyes glowed with hope.

"I have the future," she said. "In America. Why should I be discouraged?"

"Your parents named you well, Chen Sun. You have a bright spirit indeed."

Lo decided he could trust her with the story of his incarceration, the covert laboratory in Jiangxi, Col. Fu's killer flu. He said he would tell the authorities himself when he landed, but he wanted her to know in case anything happened to him. But she should not -- could not, must not -- say anything to the Dragons. After the *laogai*, after Fu, he knew he could survive anything. But he worried about her.

Chen Sun sat down next to him. Leaning down, she kissed him lightly on the forehead.

"You are very brave," she said.

"No, you are the brave one, Chen Sun."

"We thought silence would do more for dissent than noise. For us, Gandhi was the perfect role model."

"Silence can't be heard by the silent," Lo replied. "That's why I chose to express my opposition through poetry."

He turned his head quickly and sneezed, twice, in rapid succession.

Chen Sun smiled.

"Read me one of your poems," she said softly. "I've heard so much about them."

He held her in his arms and whispered a few verses as she lay her head on his chest.

> *We think all the time*
> *We are learning how to win.*
> *But we must eventually learn*
> *That to win is no more*
> *And no less than to lose.*

Their faces were but inches apart, exchanging millions of microdroplets with each breath.

◦ **45** ◦

Ellen zipped up her dark green windbreaker and took Paul's hand as she led the two of them down a rocky peninsula that jutted across Camden harbor.

It had not been easy for him to pull out of Boston, even for a couple of days.   But when they had tracked one of their Islamic suspects to Buffalo and arrested him with a suitcase full of C-4 plastic explosives, the pressure was suddenly off and Paul was able to slip away.   Still, he would have others to thank -- and owe -- when he got back.

It was another glorious September day on the Maine coast.

The bright, early-afternoon sun streamed across the smooth rocks like a spotlight while a stiff, cool breeze whipped the water from the north and turned the late summer day into early fall.   Maples lining the shore glowed with the first hint of color, streaks of yellow and red and gold in a rainbow of silent splendor.

With Paul, she had shared her worries about H5N1, about the genetic cloning of the killer virus, about the horrible way it systematically murdered people.   Whatever happened, she had to make sure the right people knew about her briefing to the bioterrorism committee.   But she refused to play the blame game.   That only led to recriminations, and recriminations turned into doubts, and doubts quickly became fears.   She was adamant about not letting fear dictate her actions.

Ellen spoke with Feldman every morning, helped him finalize the Hong Kong report and deal with endless questions from Wyeth. The drug company reported encouraging results from initial experiments with Madin-Darby canine kidney cells that showed early promise as a reliable substrate for viral replication in the first stage of fabricating an H5N1 vaccine.   Still, it would be months before they had a candidate ready for FDA review and another year before it was even available for trials.

When Ellen phoned Stan Novak at the Institute for Viral Diseases, she asked him repeatedly for news of any unusual outbreaks through his sentinel network of reporting centers in China.

No, he said, nothing from China. They were getting the same response from the IVB in Beijing every day: flu situation normal.

Paul spent hours on the phone with an old friend, Sam Taylor, a colleague who ran the FBI's information systems in Washington. He wanted to check out possible leads to splinter factions in China on the plausible assumption they might be possible conspirators in a rogue bioterrorist initiative.

From his counter-terrorism work, Paul knew that China had its share of government hardliners just like the United States. Rock-hard conservatives who would just as soon pull a trigger as talk to an enemy. Taylor organized a few offline searches in the interagency databases but came up empty-handed. The scans were all consistent on one thing: China was adamant about observing the 1972 Bioweapons Convention, so Paul couldn't unravel a single lead. All the signposts pointed to their usual suspects: militant Islamic extremists in the Middle East. To the Axis of Evil.

So they worked every morning, exercised hard in the afternoon, and made slow, unhurried love at night.

Ellen began to feel more confident about their relationship after several intimate days in Maine. Their time together had also helped Paul open up more. For the first time she saw him more relaxed, less self-conscious, not so focused on the physical side of their intimacy.

And she also felt herself become less domineering, more caring, more accepting of Paul for who he was. She sensed a better balance between the give-and-take of their companionship as a result of their time together.

"Where on God's earth are we going?" he asked as they jogged across the peninsula.

"You'll see," she said. "Just suck in this wonderful air and soak up the beauty. Isn't it gorgeous?"

They headed down a rocky path that unwound like a corkscrew toward the shore and curled back toward the harbor, rising again as it came to a point.

"Some fine villas on this side," he said, puffing.

A row of large and expensive stone bungalows lined the quiet harbor to the north.

"Second and third homes of former dot-com millionaires," she replied.

"Excuse me?"

"You know, the Internet mavens. Winners of the overvalued lottery in Website startups, until their bubble popped. Now they're mostly vacant. The older, traditional New England homes are on the other side. I'll show you, we're almost there."

Soon they were running uphill and emerged onto a plateau of flat granite with an unencumbered view of the open harbor.

Sailboats of all shapes and sizes floated silently on the dark green water, their hulls still in the quiet of the protected cove. White seagulls, fat yet ever hungry, circled above them, their yellow beaks open for business as usual.

Beyond the breakwater, they saw a pair of colorful puffins on the rounded top of a great glacial boulder that was washed by small whitecaps. The native birds preened their black and white feathers with bright orange beaks.

"There," she said, pointing across the inlet. "Now, that's really something."

Paul pulled a pair of long-distance Bureau-issue binoculars from a small backpack, trained them on the far shore, and twirled the lenses into focus.

"Warm and cozy," he said. "Like they belong here."

"They do. The great thing about Camden is that it has an honest history as a real working port, not just a seaside resort for vacationers from Boston and New York. Here, let me see."

She reached up to remove the field glasses from his neck and as she did so, he bent down and kissed her lightly on the lips. She pressed against him and let it linger.

"See what we're missing with you running all over the world?" he asked.

His tone was a mixture of absence and hope.

She didn't say anything but gazed into his deep cerulean eyes. She stood on her toes and kissed him again.

As she refocused the binoculars she said, "You know, these past few days have been wonderful. You were right, Paul. At first, I was resentful -- about being away from my work, I mean. But you've helped me think about how I might be able to get off this treadmill."

He pulled the lenses gently away from her eyes.

"Ellen, do you realize what you're saying? We're in the middle of a potential time bomb here. You know you can't walk away from a killer flu."

"I know," she said. "I'm talking about after. There comes a time when the excitement of the hunt begins to wane and the bureaucratic weight of it all just wears you down."

She handed the binoculars back to him.

"You're not letting Harper get to you, are you?"

"No, not him, he's just symptomatic. But if we're ever going to make our relationship work, one of us has to get centered. You know how much the lure of discovery means to me. Being a disease detective helps me understand what drove guys like Lewis and Clark. Exploration of the unknown, navigating uncharted waters, always working on something *new*."

"So?"

"So maybe I'll stop the circular chase. Put down some roots and start writing or do some research. Or teach. I don't need the constant whiff of jet fuel to get high. And I certainly don't like the bureaucrats constantly clipping my wings."

They sat side by side for a while with an arm around each other. Paul's long arm curled easily around Ellen's waist and found the front zipper on her jacket. Even with a stretch, she could barely reach his far hip pocket.

When the air began to chill, they walked slowly back, talking about the future. Paul asked if she wanted him with her in Washington. He said he'd try to squeeze Boston for some extra leave. Maybe after Washington, she thought aloud. She'd need his help to try and locate the renegade Chinese lab, wherever it was, and apprehend the criminals who were running it.

Long shadows from the sailboats danced across the water when they finally returned to the harbor. The wind had died down but the mid-afternoon air was chilly and almost cold. Ellen shivered slightly and zipped her jacket.

When they got back to the old inn, perched high on a bluff overlooking the harbor, a telephone message waited for Ellen at the front desk.

"Who's it from?" Paul asked as they creaked up the narrow stairs to their 2nd-story corner room.

"Wilson Cutler," Ellen said with a frown. "He's one of the security guards in my office wing at the Center. Maybe there's a FedEx package for me; that's usually why he calls."

Ellen stood at the bay window, looking beyond a cluster of majestic Douglas firs to the flat open ocean as she dialed the number Cutler had left with the desk.

On the third ring, he picked up. She recognized the familiar lilt of his Southern drawl instantly.

"Dr. Chou? Thanks for gettin' back to me. I just took a call from the Coast Guard -- out in Seattle, you know? Seems like one of their cutters intercepted a boatload of illegal immigrants from China and they're all sick as dogs. I thought since you're just back from Hong Kong and all, well, I figured you'd probably want to know."

Ellen's knuckles turned white as she gripped the receiver tightly.

"Who's on the case?" she asked.

"Dr. Harper put Feldman on it," Cutler replied. "I hear he's s'posed to head out there on the first flight tomorrow morning."

"Wilson, don't you dare breathe a word to Harper but we're on our way right now."

∘ **46** ∘

Ellen and Paul had packed and left the hotel in less than half an hour.

Paul drove while Ellen worked the airlines from her cell phone.

"I've got a Southwest non-stop to SeaTac that leaves Portland in less than two hours," she said, cupping a hand over the phone.

Paul's response was immediate and automatic.

"Book it. If we drive all the way back to Boston, we'll miss the last flight from Logan for sure."

Ellen charged the tickets to her own Visa card. She couldn't risk using her CDC card because she knew their internal auditors would flag her account the next day. Travel by division heads was routinely approved by Harper himself. She'd sort it out with him later. He wouldn't want an audit distraction before his testimony on the Hill and neither would she. He needed to think Ellen was still in Maine, but there was no way she could let this latest development go unchecked.

Not when it involved China.

Paul took the phone and called his Boston office, said he had to extend his leave a couple of days. He used up another IOU but he still had a credit balance.

He accelerated and took a little-used logging road west to the Interstate. If he stayed on the old coastal highway, they'd never make Portland in time.

Paul called ahead and they cleared airport security quickly. They ran down the jetway just as the flight was about to close. After takeoff, Ellen scanned the background on Admiral Evans that she had downloaded from the Coast Guard's Website before leaving the hotel.

Harold Evans was a career officer, rose from the Academy right up through the ranks. Previous assignments included Pensacola, Southwest Harbor, San Diego. A mandatory stint at headquarters in Washington, judge advocate corps. Two kids, both grown. Top man in the 13th District the last two years. Another two and a half, figured he could retire. Said he wouldn't live anyplace that wasn't by the water. If he had *his* way, he'd live *on* the water but his devoted wife of thirty-five years said NFW to that. The scanned photo showed a heavy-set man with white hair, honest eyes, a confident face.

She dialed his number and Evans stepped out of a meeting to take her call.

"Atlanta told us to expect a Dr. Feldman tomorrow," he said hesitantly.

His voice had the ring of confusion.

"I'm in the air heading for SeaTac right now, Admiral," Ellen replied.

She gave him their flight number and arrival time.

"Just Commander. But Dr. Harper didn't say anything about your coming."

"Dr. Feldman works for me. Can someone meet us on arrival?"

"Us?"

"Special Agent Cerrutti is with me."

"NSA?"

"FBI."

There was a pause and an exchange of comments on the other end.

"Excuse me, Commander, did you just request a car?"

"Affirmative."

"How far is it from SeaTac to the 13th?"

"Depends on traffic. Maybe an hour, maybe more."

"And how much daylight will you have left today?"

There was a another short pause with background chatter.

"Captain Ferguson will meet you at the gate with a chopper standing by. You'll be here about ten minutes after you land."

Evans said he'd gone through official channels, tried to get Department of Transportation approval to authorize his request for a CDC team since the Coast Guard was under the DOT's bureaucratic umbrella.

"But there was no response from DOT, so I had to call Atlanta directly."

"You did the right thing," Ellen said. "Paperwork delays are routine. Public health comes first."

But she heard echoes of Youngston Yee and Hong Kong.

"What will you need when you get here?" Evans asked.

She ran down a list of protective clothing, decontamination equipment, and special patient transport gear.

Evans balked.

"We don't have that kind of stuff," he said bluntly. "We run sea patrols here, not hazmat rescues."

"This could be the most deadly hazardous material you've ever seen, Commander," she said. "I'll requisition the equipment. A truck will arrive at your gate from Camp Shelton with a container for me. Ask your men to hold it for us."

"Shelton? That's Army."

"Correct. They've got the Early Response team for VII Corps. Region 7, West Coast."

"But it could take them two hours to get here in this traffic."

"Where's the base, exactly?"

"Grays Harbor, Aberdeen. Due west, right on the coast."

She unfolded an area map and found it.

"Shelton will deliver, that's their job.   Tell me about the intercept. When did your men find the ship?"

"Late this morning. Drifting in open water, listing to one side. There was no response to our radio signal and no reaction when we hailed it by bullhorn."

"How many guys on the cutter?"

"Ten. The *Reliance*, standard 82-foot patrol."

"How did they know the freighter was Chinese?"

"English name under Chinese characters on the bow.   We radioed the registry bureau at DOT.   They told us the freighter's registered in Liberia but based in Fuzhou. Small, maybe fifty thousand deadweight. Routine cargo, crates mostly."

"How many stowaways?"

"Thirteen, all in the hold. Plus the captain and two crew."

"Who found them?"

Another pause, another muffled exchange.

"Lieutenant Baker."

"Where is he now?"

"Back on the cutter."

Ellen froze. She told Evans quickly about Hong Kong, about the killer virus they had just tamed, about the potential risk if the boat was infected.

"Baker may have compromised his own crew, Commander. Even if all he did was take one breath of contaminated air in the hold of that freighter. This bug is hot and incredibly infectious. Tell the captain to isolate Baker in his quarters and keep everybody on board until they receive further orders."

"But they're heading back to base right now."

"Then order them to drop anchor offshore. No way they're coming on land. Not yet, anyway. And find me two yellow flags."

"What for?"

"We're going to quarantine that freighter and your cutter along with it."

∘ **47** ∘

When they arrived at SeaTac and deplaned, Captain Wayne Ferguson was waiting for them at the gate. He led them down a security staircase beneath the jetway to a waiting jeep, its yellow lights flashing.

They sped to a side runway and climbed aboard a giant Sikorsky HH-60 Jayhawk. Its single 54-foot rotor was spinning with a muffled roar from twin gas turbines, the hulk of its huge body crouched like a giant bug, ready to spring. They strapped in and lifted off in a light mist.

Through the filtered twilight, Ellen glanced down at the lush green foothills of the Olympic mountains. The gray drizzle pelted them harder as they picked up speed. They flew across the broad expanse of Boeing's massive aircraft production center, acre after acre of arched metal that housed half the commercial jetliners sold in the world, ten percent of America's global exports alone.

She cursed the reduced visibility. It would hinder the rescue but they'd have to adjust. It was always raining in the Pacific Northwest. The dry season there is said to last two days, from July 31 to August 1.

When they touched down at the base in Grays Harbor, Ellen yelled to Captain Ferguson to keep the rotor spinning. They'd lift off again as soon as they had changed clothes and loaded the gear.

Another jeep rushed them to the base gate. As Ellen had predicted, the container from Shelton was there and waiting. So were Commander Evans and his chief medical officer, Dr. Nelson McKee.

Ellen and Evans made the introductions.

The Commander was a bear of a man, much larger than Ellen would have guessed from his file photo. Thick-lensed black-framed glasses set off a chiseled, no-nonsense face. His hand swallowed hers when they shook hands. Water dripped from his face and poured off his yellow slicker.

Two Army aides checked Ellen's ID with a hand-held scanner. As soon as they got confirmation, they quickly unlocked the big steel box and began unloading.

Ellen tossed Paul a bright yellow moon suit and stepped into the container to disrobe and pull hers on.

"I don't know the first thing about bicontainment," he said.

"Well, you're about to learn pretty fast."

Cerrutti stripped and tugged at the bulky rubber costume.

A box came flying out and landed at his feet.

"What the hell's this?" he asked.

"Adult diapers," Ellen said.

Her voice echoed in the steel chamber.

"No bathrooms out there, so you better strap one on before you zip up."

Minutes later, she emerged looking like an oversized canary.

She was holding a roll of black duct tape. She tore off strips and sealed the zippers on Paul's suit and he did the same for her. She stretched a pair of butyl rubber gloves over her surgical latex undergloves and sealed them to her sleeves with tape. Next she did Paul's.

Now completely enclosed, she had to shout through the HEPA-filtered respirator in her facemask.

"We'll work with hand signals once we're on the ship," she shouted to Ferguson. "Make sure your pilot understands. Let's get going."

Ferguson and the Army team loaded the gear.

A pair of bright-red, 5-gallon pump-spray cans of sodium hypochlorite for decontamination. Three cartons of rimantadine anti-viral drugs. Two cartons of IV drip. Extra moon suits and diapers. Two boxes of latex gloves and surgical masks. A half-dozen high-intensity handheld searchlights. Multiple strips of tarp. A pair of ventilation units. A supply of double-layered, zippered, black vinyl body bags.

Finally Paul and Ellen stepped out of the steel container carrying a large, clear plastic enclosure attached to a stretcher. It looked like a transparent coffin. Four circular ports were sewn into each side with clear rubber gloves attached, hanging inward. A battery-operated air vent was punched into one end.

"The hell's that?" Ferguson yelled.

"It's a patient bubble," Ellen shouted back. "Special containment with portable BL-4 protection under negative air. It's the only way to transport highly contagious patients until they can be isolated. You got an isolation ward here?"

Captain Ferguson turned to the chief medical officer.

"One room," McKee yelled, shaking his head and holding up a single digit. "But no negative air."

"Ground-floor, window access?" she asked.

He nodded.

"Then we'll have to improvise."

The rain was coming down harder now. It turned her facemask into a windshield without wipers.

She reached over and grabbed a sheet of canvas.

"Take the tarp. When we find the index case, we'll bring him or her back here and unload from the bubble directly through that window. We can set a vent unit in the window cavity and connect it to a power generator. Cover the whole window and the vent with tarp and then double-seal it with tape so it's airtight. That'll give you negative pressure."

Ellen looked at the darkening sky.

"We've got to get moving. Let's go."

Commander Evans handed her two bright yellow flags as they reboarded the jeep. She gave him a thumbs-up in return.

They motored through the driving rain back to the waiting Jayhawk and transferred the gear, bubble last. The whirling rotors chopped the raindrops into a fine spray.

They lifted off.

"How far out's the ship?" Paul yelled.

"About 30 miles," the pilot yelled back. "But this chopper does 200 knots so it won't take long. Ten, maybe fifteen minutes depending on the wind."

Once they were airborne, Ellen saw a smaller ship moored offshore.

"That the cutter?" she shouted.

"Yep, that's Fat Albert," the pilot said.

"Hover overhead. We've got to drop them a flag. Can you raise the captain?"

The pilot tuned his radio to a dedicated frequency. Ellen relayed instructions for the flag and reminded the captain to keep Lt. Baker isolated. Through the pilot, she asked him about the stowaways and listened to his response on the intercom.

"Baker said all the Chinks stayed away from one guy, young dude, slumped alone in one corner down in the hold. Said it looked bad."

Probably the index case, Ellen thought. They were usually the sickest.

"Tell him thanks," she said. "And the word is Chinese. We'll be back."

Minutes later, they saw the rusted hulk of the old freighter, motionless in the water. It was listing slightly to one side and looked like a dead whale. Lifeless, it rose and fell with the waves, a ferry of death.

Paul and Ellen strapped themselves into the rescue hoist as the pilot hovered overhead.

A gust of wind whipped into the chopper and it groaned like a sick horse.

"You sure this thing's okay?" Ellen shouted.

"No prob," the pilot shouted back. "Just do your job and let me do mine. This baby's the backbone of our rescue ops."

He pressed a lever. Twin bays opened beneath them. Paul and Ellen hung in the air like marionettes as the steel cable dropped them toward the deck while the rain pelted their suits with tiny darts.

Once aboard, they unhooked and yanked on the line. When it snaked back up, one of the flight crew strapped on the bubble.

While Paul waited to secure it, Ellen switched on her searchlight. Her feet slipped on the slick surface as she lurched from step to step. She steadied herself on the bulkhead as she inched forward.

She opened the hatch.

Insulated by her filtered respirator from the foul stench of decay and human waste, she didn't have to whiff the stale air. She knew it reeked of sweat, stale urine, and feces in a putrid incubator of disease.

Ellen played the beam from wall to wall. Only a few heads moved in response. One man sat alone and still in a far corner, just as Lt. Baker had said.

A young woman lay not far away. She raised a limp hand to shield her eyes when Ellen's flashlight caught her face.

Ellen shuffled back to Paul.

"We need the guy in the far corner," she yelled. "Get him up the ladder so we can load him in the bubble. He was barely moving, but it looks like he's still alive."

She helped him steady the plastic coffin as it dropped onto the deck. Holding onto each other for balance, they inched back to the hold.

Ellen leaned in and played her light on the target corner as Paul made his way down the ladder. In a quick motion, he lifted the sick man onto one shoulder in a fireman's carry and began climbing back up.

The hatch was too small for them to exit together. Ellen took the man's arms as Paul pushed from below.

Once he was on deck, Paul scrambled out and they carried him to the bubble. Ellen unzipped one square end, up, across, and down. They placed him inside and Paul zipped it back up. Ellen took a roll of tape from one pocket and tore off long strips which they used to seal the seams. Paul cursed under his breath as the tape got slick in the rain so they had to tape twice to make a double seal.

While they worked, the flight crew lowered the other gear onto the deck in a net-like sling secured to the rescue hoist with four cables.

Paul and Ellen unhooked the cables and clipped them to four steel O-rings at the corners of the bubble. Before they signaled the pilot, Ellen grabbed the big yellow quarantine flag and clambered up a flight of stairs. She fastened it to a signal cord with tape. When she came back down, she pulled a decontamination pump off the sling.

As she pumped the handle to pressurize the red can, she slipped. Her left leg slid under a rusty chain. She looked down and her heart skipped a beat.

There was a small tear in the rubber fabric.

"Tape!" she shouted.

Paul whirled around from the far end of the patient transport.

"What?" he yelled.

"Double-tape this rip," she shouted back. "Quick!"

Cerrutti tore off two strips and sealed the breach in her pants with a big X. He took another long strip and wrapped it completely around her lower calf.

He double-checked the seal, then helped her back up.

They checked the four corners of the bubble. Cerrutti hand-pumped the decon cartridge while Ellen took the hose and sprayed the plastic enclosure. They took turns hosing each other down with the spray.

They gave a thumbs-up to the crew and watched the bubble rise.

"What about the others?" Paul shouted.

"Can't take them to base," she yelled. "Too contagious. We'll need to create a makeshift ward someplace else."

She glanced up. The rescue hoist was on its way back down.

"Check the crew up top while I go back down below. Meet back here in ten."

Ellen grabbed a supply of rimantadine and a handful of hypodermic syringes. Paul climbed the stairs to go above deck.

When they regrouped, they hosed each other down again and strapped into the hoist.

"The captain and his crew are all dead," he said. "You?"

"Five gone, but seven are still alive. I gave the survivors each a double injection but they don't any of them look good."

Up top, they pulled themselves aboard and unhooked as the twin bay doors slammed shut. The pilot pressed the throttle and they lurched forward toward shore.

"Raise the Commander," Ellen shouted. "We need an unused building near the base so we can isolate the others."

Ellen recognized the Admiral's voice as soon as he came on the line.

"Not much around here," he said. "Closest village is Elma, 12 miles inland. They've got an old schoolhouse we sometimes use for special events."

Through the pilot Ellen said, "Contact the state, call the local police, call the village mayor. We absolutely need that school. If you can't get it, don't waste time, call Camp Shelton right away. Ask for Colonel Reed, ER. He'll have a list of abandoned warehouses, shuttered schools and other mothballed buildings. We airlift tonight."

"In the dark?" came the response.

"This chopper's got searchlights, right?"

The wind started blowing harder out of the northeast and the Jayhawk bounced in the air like a small toy. It was going to be a lot rougher when they went back for the others, Ellen thought.

Minutes later they were back at Aberdeen. Ellen asked the pilot to land as close to the improvised isolation unit as he could. He set down in a grassy courtyard adjacent to the building.

McKee and two cadets stood by the side window in bright orange Day-Glo slickers that glistened in the lights. Silver reflector strips glowed on their sleeves. They wore surgical masks and latex gloves.

Ellen and Paul unloaded the bubble and positioned one end against the open window. The two of them climbed through as the cadets held one pair of the stretcher handles, resting the other pair against the sill.

Inside, Ellen unzipped the transparent cover and Paul helped her pull the survivor out of the bubble and onto the waiting bed. Quickly, Ellen went to a sideboard and tore open a pack of IV needles and bags.

She shouted for Paul to toss her a vial of fluid rimantadine. Her fingers felt thick and numb in the rubber gloves as she fumbled to get the plastic cap off the IV needle.

Slowly and carefully, she rubbed the man's forearm with alcohol and tried to find a vein. The layered gloves made it hard for her to feel. She had to squeeze his wrist hard with one hand until she saw a limp vein pulse. When she tried to insert the needle, it missed the vein. The second time she made it. She hung the IV bag on a pole and unclamped the tube.

Paul threw her a box of anti-virals through the open window. She snapped a vial open and upended it into the infusion port on the side of the tube to drip with the IV fluid. Totally insulated, she couldn't use a stethoscope to check his vital signs. But she could see that he was still breathing. She grabbed a blood pressure cuff off the wall. Wrapping it around his arm, she inflated it and took a quick read.

Not good, she thought. But he has a chance.

Ellen climbed back out the window and watched McKee's team install the negative pressure vent. They stayed to monitor the vital signs of the index case.

Satisfied that the isolation ward was sealed tight, she nudged Paul and they ran back to the waiting chopper.

As they reboarded the Jayhawk, Ellen turned to the pilot.

"Raise the Commander for an update on our school."

She had a throbbing headache and her throat was dry from all the shouting. But she knew it would be hours later before she'd get anything to drink.

She sat back down behind the pilot, stretched out and let her bladder soak into the cotton padding around her midsection. That took care of the headache.

"Good news, Dr. Chou."

It was Evans.

"What've you got?"

Her voice was hoarse. She made a mental note to outfit the next generation of moon suits with speech enhancement devices to cancel extraneous noise. Otherwise the ER teams would gradually go mute.

"Elma's mayor was uptight about hosting illegal immigrants," he said, "even in a public health emergency. So we called the Governor's office. They gave us an executive order right away. You're good to go."

"Excellent. Can you send a team over there right away? They have to seal those windows and put a ventilator in place so we've got negative air when we arrive. McKee's crew can show them how."

"Anything else?"

"Yes. Nobody goes into that isolation ward on base unless they're masked and gloved. Tell Dr. McKee to let me know as soon as the patient's conscious. Rusty as my Chinese is, I need to talk to him as soon as possible."

"10-4," barked Evans.

Ellen shot the pilot a thumbs-up.

"She says 'way to go,' Commander. Over and out."

They returned to the freighter and had to make four trips to get the survivors to Elma, even after doubling them up in the bubble. Before they sealed the cadavers in body bags, Ellen took fluid and blood samples for lab testing back in Atlanta.

They zipped, taped, and sprayed the bags, then placed them in the hold pending proper disposal. Working now in near darkness under the chopper's powerful searchlights, they decontaminated their suits, then the hold, finally the deck. The Coast Guard could take it from there. They knew how to deal with abandoned ships.

They made one final drop on the cutter so Ellen could dose Baker and the crew with rimantadine. She took swabs from each of the men and bled them, marking the tubes for testing. She reminded the captain that their supplies had to be continuously airdropped until the cutter could be cleared.

It was nearly midnight -- 3:00am body time -- when they choppered back to base and stripped. As Paul peeled off his respirator and mask, the first whiff of fresh air reinvigorated him. Ellen saw his eyes brighten and felt an adrenalin herself surge as the cool, damp air kissed her face.

After a quick shower and an energy bar, Ellen donned a fresh mask and gloves. She took fluid samples from the index case in the sealed isolation ward. It was orders of magnitude easier now without the moon suit and double gloves.

The young Chinese man was febrile, dehydrated, and delirious. His head rolled back and forth and his lips moved mutely, like a ghost. His eyes opened and closed, flickering at random. Ellen added Demerol to the IV drip so he could rest without pain.

When she had done what she could, she asked Ferguson to drive them to Elma so they could collect fluid samples from the others.

Back at the base lab, she selected a few samples at random, starting with the index case. She took the HP/UP chip-scanner from her case and tested them with the device. One after the other, the LED display glowed with the same response.

A/H5N1.

Her hand was shaking as she disinfected it and put it away.

The same questions swept through her confused and tormented mind.

Why a bathtub freighter?

Why here?

Before collapsing from exhaustion, she and Paul packed the swabs and tubes in ice and Ferguson choppered the insulated package to SeaTac. American Airlines had a milk run through O'Hare that could get the samples to CDC by noon the next day. A flight attendant dead-heading in Atlanta agreed to hand-carry them to McDermott's lab.

Evans had two single rooms prepped for Paul and Ellen in the guest quarters. She called McKee and asked him to be sure to secure the isolation ward.

"Limit access to authorized medical personnel only," she said. "Strict protocol, sign-in, sign-out only with valid ID. Same with Elma. Universal precautions, everybody gloved and masked. No exceptions. You got that?"

"We're on the same wavelength, Dr. Chou," he said. "We know a thing or two about security here."

She looked up as Paul came into her room.

"Now I understand what you had to go through in Hong Kong," he said. "This is spooky."

His voice trailed off. He bent down and kissed her goodnight.

She smiled weakly and stood on tiptoe to kiss him back.

"Paul, something's very wrong," she said as she flopped down on the bed.

She looked up at him, her eyes wide with fatigue and fear.

"This looks exactly like the same killer flu we stopped in Hong Kong. That means one out of three victims will die. But if something big's about to go down, why would a covert terrorist ship a dozen random vectors on a broken-down boat to a remote corner of the sparsely populated Pacific northwest?"

○ **48** ○

After the long day's meeting with his clandestine collaborator, Col. Fu Barxu stepped out of PLA Headquarters into the hot, moist September air. His driver stood at attention next to the renegade Colonel's shiny black S-class Mercedes sedan.

Fu had another important task that evening, a task he had committed himself to after graduating with honors from Dengshen Military Academy so long ago.

Once a year, Col. Fu visited a leading Chinese middle school to interview teachers and preview some of China's most promising students. He had never forgotten Capt. Min's visit to his tiny classroom in Puqi to solicit young recruits for the Army. Fu felt a strong obligation to honor that tradition.

The big car whispered quietly down the broad, tree-lined avenue of Qianmen Daijie toward the district of Xuanwu in Beijing's southern sector. Col. Fu gazed at the long row of narrow bookshops, textile merchants and tiny mom-and-pop restaurants that clogged both sides of the street.

Street peddlers hawked surplus goods from the State factories -- two-tone canvas sneakers, blue cotton trousers, skin-thin T-shirts that failed to pass China's shaky quality control inspections. Flat, cylindrical bricks of coal, ubiquitous in Beijing as fuel for heating and cooking, stood stacked in small pyramids on each corner.

Suddenly, the driver stopped.

There was an altercation in the intersection ahead at Yongdingmen.

Fu watched as two tough, heavy-set Public Security Bureau agents subdued a pair of young protestors. One PSB goon ripped the brush-scrawled signs out of their hands while his partner grabbed an arm and twisted it painfully, throwing the man to his knees on the hard pavement. He whipped a rubber baton out of his belt and whacked the demonstrator repeatedly across the small of his back.

Fu cocked his head and tried to read the hand-painted script.

"Freedom to all Chinese," one read. The other said, "Spirit more powerful than the State."

He shook his head. There had always been isolated opposition to imperial rule throughout China's long history, he thought. Somehow, young people never seemed to learn.

Confucius, the earliest master, had said it best: let the ruler be a ruler and the subject a subject. The State was supreme, whether the Emperor or the Army held power. But with the *fengpai* in charge under the feckless President Jiang, these outbursts were becoming more frequent, more humiliating.

Fu could barely conceal a smile. That would all change soon enough.

Around the next corner, the large multi-story concrete structure of the Nan Ming school loomed into view. The big black sedan pulled up and stopped.

Fu got out of the car and sprang up the steep concrete steps to the entrance where a small reception committee stood waiting. A large bronze memorial to Mao Zedong sat next to the wide front doors.

The school principal stepped forward and bowed.

"The students are ready for your tour, Colonel," he said. "They have spoken of little else all week."

As the principal rose from his bow, Col. Fu saluted him crisply. His dark green dress uniform was adorned with full battle ribbons and stood in stark contrast to the somber gray suits worn by the staff.

"I apologize for being so late," Fu said. "But it's an honor to visit your school. China will always prosper as long as the Army has access to the nation's best students."

The principal led them down the main hall.

Fu glanced into several classrooms and saw teams of students busy washing blackboards, mopping floors, sponging windows, sweeping up the day's collection of trash. He was reassured to see the tradition of student teamwork still strong. He knew it reinforced social cooperation and toughened individual character.

The Nan Ming school was typical of large, urban middle schools, the principal reminded him. With 6,000 students in grades seven, eight, and nine, it had an average class size of 45. Nan Ming was the top school in Beijing South and the number one choice of every parent in that district.

They stepped into a history classroom off the main hall. The teacher, an older woman dressed in standard ash-gray cotton trousers and shapeless jacket, stood next to the blackboard as she watched the guests enter. She fidgeted nervously. Her hands were clasped tightly behind her back so Fu could not see the whites of her knuckles.

Familiar names and dates were scrawled on the board in yellow chalk. Since it was early in the school year, Fu assumed the class would be studying the Zhou and Ch'in dynasties when the solid foundation of China's greatness had been established more than three thousand years before. The hierarchical levels of society. The wisdom of the ruling class. And above all, the country's venerated position as first among equals in the world.

Col. Fu stood ramrod-straight at the head of the class. He looked across the sea of eager faces in the large group. His mind leapt back to Puqi and he saw his own fresh face among them. The students sat forward on the edge of their seats, backs rigid and firm, eyes unblinking, their identical navy-blue uniforms neat and tidy.

Fu took a step back and circled a date on the blackboard.

It was 221 BC.

"Who can tell me the significance of this year?" Fu asked.

Silence filled the room. Not a single chair squeaked in response.

"Anyone?"

A small hand rose slowly in the air, halfway back.

"*Buhau*," Fu said, shaking his head.

The young girl meekly dropped her arm.

"I would like the boys to answer."

Fu patrolled the front row of desks stiffly. No hands shot up.

A small, shy lad in the front row suddenly rose from his desk and stood up, his dark eyes staring straight ahead at the blackboard.

"This date was the end of the Zhou dynasty and the beginning of the Ch'in," he said.

His eyes darted toward the Colonel. He quickly added, "Sir."

Fu walked back across the front row of desks until he approached the boy, whose black hair was clipped uniformly short around his small head.

His gaze was cockeyed. His left eye stared straight at the date on the blackboard while the other skewed right toward the Colonel. When he moved the left eye to watch the Colonel, his right eye darted out the window into the open courtyard.

"Almost," Fu said.

His voice was firm but not hostile.

"You told me what happened in that year but not what the date *signifies*. Think again."

He stood and gazed down at the young boy. Tiny rivets of perspiration broke out on the student's upper forehead.

Suddenly, the young student stomped his right heel onto the floor. He brought his left eye back to the blackboard and flooded the classroom with his eloquence.

"The date signifies, *sir*, the shift in power from the Zhou, who formed China's oldest and longest dynasty and from whom our great nation derived its name -- Zhongguo, the Central Kingdom -- to the Ch'in dynasty, which initiated the vigorous expansion of Chinese authority into central Asia and beyond."

His left eye flitted nervously back at the Colonel again. He blinked twice.

"This date thus signifies, *sir*, the beginning of China's esteemed position at the head of the worldwide family of nations, which come to us not as equals but as tribute-bearers. It marked the beginning of China's destiny as the father of that family."

"*Sir*," he said finally, returning his gaze to the blackboard.

Fu stepped back and spoke in a louder voice to the whole class.

"Could everyone hear?" he asked, gesturing toward the young student.

All their heads nodded in unison.

"Did everyone *understand* it?"

Again, the uniform response.

"This is critical to know, to understand, and to remember," Fu said.

He walked back and forth in front of the class pounding his right fist into his left palm.

"There are those who say that our history began only in 1949 when the Great Helmsman brought unity to our great country again. But we cannot deny three thousand years of rich history, three thousand *long* years of influence from all the great masters -- Confucius, Mencius, Mo Zi -- who planted the seeds of authoritarian greatness in our culture. Who trained us to repel the foreign barbarians. Who taught us that our people should always obey their leaders under the will of heaven. And who laid the groundwork for centuries of proud achievement in art -- masterpieces in painting, in ceramic sculpture, in jade -- achievements never before or since equaled in human history."

Col. Fu paused and scanned the class. Every eye was on him now.

"China's problems with the corrupt Western powers began a century and a half ago. In 1850, China was on center stage. Its Emperors ruled with the Mandate of Heaven, providing a stable political system based on our hierarchical values that we believe govern all mankind. Woman is subservient to man, younger brother to elder, subject to ruler. For thousands of years, the authoritarian principles of Confucius and Mencius took deep root. Nations from all over the world paid homage to our Central Kingdom."

Then, one after another, Col. Fu explained the deadly infections from the West.

Opium. Hong Kong gone, ceded to the British in a humiliating treaty that created a foreign colony on precious Chinese soil for more than a century.

Gunboats. Germany, Great Britain, America, Japan, carving up the Central Kingdom to create selfish spheres of political influence and economic control.

Capitalism. Attempts to replace age-old economic feudalism with an unproven market system as greedy American capitalists drooled over selling oil for the lamps of China.

Democracy. Unrelenting pressure to replace China's resilient authoritarian structure with an electoral system based not on hierarchy and authority but on individual rights and free will.

The Colonel finished with a flourish.

"Our historical greatness notwithstanding, there are those among us who maintain that China is still just another member of the family of nations," he went on.

He smacked his fist into his palm again. His pace accelerated as he glanced at the nervous teacher standing stiffly by the blackboard.

"Just another pawn on the chessboard of conflict with the new imperialists who govern America. But your classmate correctly noted China's proper role as the *father* of the family of nations. That is simultaneously our greatness and our destiny! And that is your challenge for the future, to ensure that our authoritarian heritage remains strong, to enable the Central Kingdom to regain its rightful place in the world. Mark my words, students. A generation from now, you will be making decisions that shake the world as America inevitably declines to the second tier, where Japan is stuck today, a second-rate power in search of its soul. *Think about that.*"

The principal pointed to his watch. Nodding, Col. Fu started for the door but stopped briefly in front of the young student who had answered so crisply.

"What's your name?" he asked.

"Zhang," the boy said.

He stood proudly, his good eye fixed on the blackboard.

"Zhang, is it? You do your homework every night, do you?"

"Yes, sir. Without fail."

"And you obey the wishes of your parents?"

"Of course, sir. At all times."

Fu nodded.

"You will do well, my son, providing you do not stray. Beware the evil temptations of the West."

"Yes, sir. Thank you, sir."

After touring the school, Col. Fu was led up a flight of stairs to an overhanging balcony to watch the closing assembly.

On the ground level below, the Nan Ming school embraced a huge open courtyard of packed sandy clay, three football fields side-to-side in size. The three classes had assembled on the dirt field, their uniforms creating a sea of blue.

Each class leader held a calligraphic poster in China's national colors, yellow ideographs on a crimson background. One read, "the nation is most important." Another, "always take responsibility." The third, "duty for the sake of society."

At the principal's signal, the school band played the national anthem and six thousand hands folded across six thousand hearts as the Nan Ming students sang proudly in one voice. The national flag came down slowly as they sang, all eyes riveted on the familiar red banner.

Col. Fu saluted smartly as the lyrics of the final stanza echoed across the cavernous courtyard. His skin tingled with pride.

The Red in the East raises the Sun,
And gives Birth to the Greatness of China.
Our Humble Leaders work for all the People,
So the Spirit of the Central Kingdom will never die!

∘ **49** ∘

As Paul and Ellen dropped into a deep sleep, Ensign-One Rashid Tompkins worked late in his cramped cubicle at ComCom on the far side of the Coast Guard's Aberdeen base.

He had the night shift and he wasn't at all happy about it, but he kept his head down and did his job. He knew he'd rotate out at the end of the month and he needed another good performance review.

Ensign Tompkins had his eye on a base command some day. He was a rising star and there were no limits any more on how far African-Americans could go in the military. Former Chairman of the Joint Chiefs of Staff General Colin Powell had shown them the way. If he could rise to become Secretary of State, nothing would hold Rashid Tompkins back now.

Every night, Communications Command sent a routine rundown on the 13th District's search and rescue ops to Coast Guard headquarters in Washington, to local law enforcement agencies along the coast, and to the local press. Tonight was no different.

Ensign Tompkins had a frame as thin as carbon paper and a Brillo buzz cut. He took one last look at his brief dispatch, checked it for errors, and punched *Enter*.

He uncrossed his pencil-like legs and reached up to snap off his lamp. He vacated his 5-wheel naugahyde swivel chair and shoved it under his desk. His job was done.

Within minutes, the Seattle *Observer* had a tiny two-sentence, one-paragraph filler ready for their morning edition. It went over their wire to other news services. The *Observer* also stuck it on their Website where it was sucked up instantly by ubiquitous electronic vacuum cleaners called search engines. In nanoseconds, Alta Vista, Infoseek, Yahoo, Google, and sleuth.com all had the microstory in their databases, stored on countless Internet servers powered by IBM, Sun Microsystems, and Dell.

From there it went instantly to multiple UseNets. When thousands of news junkies switched on their browsers the next morning their screens would be buried under an avalanche of news articles, bulletins, and reports. A digital potpourri.

Miles away, in a top-floor penthouse suite in south central Seattle, Eddie Liu paced his plush office. He couldn't sleep. The *Lè*

Tian Chuán was late. Very late. The ship hadn't docked when it was supposed to and there was no word from the waterfront as to why.

The telecomm office said they'd lost radio contact days ago. Eddie's customers were not happy. They had paid good money as a down payment on their new workers and as far as they were concerned, it was all Eddie's fault.

Eddie Liu was the head of the Green Dragons in Seattle. The *tong*. A third-generation Chinese-American, it would be *his* head if he couldn't deliver. His word was worth millions, to his customers on the west coast and to his partners in Fujian.

The Green Dragons were an offshoot of the triads, modern-day criminal mutants of medieval Chinese secret societies that centered on Fujian and Guangdong in southern China. They were heirs to roving bands of 16th century religious fanatics who inspired landless peasants to rebel against corrupt central governments whenever the Emperor lost his mandate of heaven. Today, they made corruption their ally.

The triads shipped massive amounts of money back and forth between overseas Chinese entrepreneurs in Asia and local Chinatown merchants in Vancouver, Seattle, San Francisco, and Los Angeles. The Green Dragons, headquartered in Fujian, dominated the west coast. The Red Dragons, centered in Guangdong, controlled crime in New York and the east.

They had quickly learned a valuable lesson from their thick-headed Italian counterparts in crime: it was so much more profitable to divide and conquer than to fight for total control.

Money and merchandise passed through the hands of countless brothers and sisters, sons and daughters, uncles and aunts. Cash was laundered through cheap restaurants, illicit massage parlors, sleazy tourist traps, fraudulent real estate parcels, subterranean gambling dens, shabby hotels.

Drugs, prostitution, money lending, betting pools, and sweatshop labor all flourished under the Dragons. Drugs and cheap labor came in, cash and cars went out. It was a two-way partnership, forged in hell.

The Dragons on both coasts had reached an accommodation with their local police. The *tong* agreed to keep street crime under control if the cops cut them some slack on their retail business. Occasionally there was even a third-gen on the force who could serve as their eyes and ears downtown, let them know when a bust was coming.

The *tong* knew what the cops didn't: that to keep a capitalist system pure and profitable, you had to allow for the existence of victims of that system, just like a biological organism has to eliminate waste to keep its blood clean.

The Dragons were capitalism's necessary waste, no matter how useless, putrid, or filthy the police thought they were.

So Eddie Liu paced anxiously back and forth, his thin frame moving across the thick carpet in silence. His bald head shined like a naked globe when he passed under the elegant chandelier in his ceiling, making his onion-shaped face appear tight and drawn. He stroked his small pencil moustache with jittery fingers.

It was much too soon to call the pier again. Besides, they were getting irritated with his constant harassment. They said they'd let him know the moment they had any word from the ship.

After all, they said, it was an old hulk. Maybe this was its last trip. Maybe it had only one screw. Maybe the radio was dead.

Maybe I'll be dead, Eddie thought.

He sat down at his desk and flicked on his computer. If he couldn't sleep or call the waterfront, at least he could amuse himself online. The porno sites were hot 24 hours a day. If he was lucky, maybe he'd have another young girl on this ship he could sell for a big bonus to sex-dot-com. He punched in a series of different URLs but his anxiety ate at him like an ulcer.

Yeah, right.

Maybe I'll be dead, he thought again.

The Green Dragons had learned long ago that cash was the loudest language, even in a so-called classless society like China. The Chinese mafia had its paid protectors in Fujian. Police and customs inspectors were caught in the net. Once in, they could never refuse to cooperate for fear of being revealed. The police helped the Dragons build a conduit to the PSB. And the PSB took them to the PLA, all the way to the top.

If a high-ranking general wanted a new S-class Mercedes, the Dragons would target the desired model, steal it without a sound from the parking lot of a suburban shopping mall, pack it in a standard shipping container and truck it to the pier.

For a fat fee, underpaid and overworked American dock hands were all too willing to overlook or misplace or throw out the paperwork when it came time to load the container. Ten days later, the vehicle would be offloaded in the port of Fuzhou and the local network would do the rest.

Late-model, upscale European cars, shrink-wrapped Japanese DVD players, S-VHS video decks, digital sound systems, new-generation antenna receivers, state-of-the-art American desktop PCs -- everything banned for export to China wound up in the hands of China's highest-ranking military and civilian officials.

Whatever they wanted, the Dragons could procure.

For a fee.

In exchange, the Dragons provided key services to their mainland protectors. When official State delegations from Beijing required security in America, the Dragons supplied the personnel. It was a blissful marriage, marred only by infrequent spats. Disagreements were settled with sharp knives or guns with silencers, in the old style, or with potent poisons carefully administered by local doctors on their call list. Doctors whose own sordid backgrounds insured compliance.

Eddie Liu quickly tired of the on-screen sex. His own parlors were much better equipped than these amateur electronic freak shows with their herky-jerky streaming video and blurred bodies.

He punched in his UseNet address and scanned the streaming text to pass the time.

He did a double take when he saw the story.

No doubt about it. The name was unmistakable.

Lè Tian Chuán.

He picked up the phone and auto-dialed Fuzhou immediately. The digital signal passed from the telephone through a software encryption program in his computer called PGP, then up a thin wire to the roof and through a wireless antenna no larger than a coffee saucer. In seconds, the endless stream of scrambled 0s and 1s beamed up to a low earth-orbiting satellite and the LEO bounced it straight to Fuzhou.

An FBI team sat in a brown, unmarked van just around the corner from Eddie Liu. They sipped cold, stale coffee from used Styrofoam cups and cursed again when they heard the signals in their analog headsets.

They called it the Rice Crispies of the new millennium. Instead of snap, crackle and pop, all they could ever hear was a digital buzz, crack and hiss.

∘ **50** ∘

"Fu..., " he mumbled. "Lo ... Colonel ... Jiang ... Sun ... xi ... Fengbu... "

The next morning, Ellen sat in a stiff wooden chair next to Lo Fengbu in the isolation ward.

His vital signs were stronger but he was still delirious and on full IV. She held a clipboard with a yellow pad in her lap, jotting down the sounds he made.

From time to time she tried to ask a question but never got a coherent response. His mumbling in Mandarin was random, without pattern. She was stumped.

Jonathan Feldman had arrived as scheduled on the early morning flight. Ellen put him right to work at Elma tending the other survivors in the makeshift ward at the schoolhouse. He never got over the shock of how much Ellen and Paul had done the previous night. Despite that or maybe because of it, Ellen made one thing patently clear.

"Jonathan, if Harper ever calls, remember I'm not here. You did it with help from the 13th and Camp Shelton. I was in Maine the whole time, in the local loop by phone."

"But -- "

"No buts," she said. "My ass is on the line and you know it."

To Commander Evans she had said, "When you talk to Washington, Feldman gets credit for everything. Keep me invisible."

There was a knock on the door and Paul entered, masked and gloved.

"Any luck?" he asked.

She shook her head.

"Take a look," she said.

She handed him the clipboard.

He scanned the sheet of half-words and disconnected sounds while Ellen took another blood pressure reading and replenished the IV feed.

"Nothing but unrelated gibberish to me," he said. "Even if I could understand a little Chinese, it would still be nonsense."

"I know," she said. "He keeps saying 'fu,' like he's trying to say 'flu.' But that's crazy because that word's *liuxing* in Mandarin.

Maybe there's a connection to Fujian because the ship sailed from Fuzhou."

Ellen took the pad back and looked at it again.

Paul uncapped a Polaroid camera and took several head shots of Lo Fengbu for their files. The young man's eyes winced in pain at each flash.

"Lo," she said. "He keeps saying that over and over, too. Maybe it's his name. Or half a word, I don't know. Could be anything in Chinese, depending on the tone. He looks vaguely familiar but I just can't place the face."

She sighed.

"Let him rest. Let's go see what Jonathan's got."

Evans had a car and driver standing by. It didn't take them long to reach Elma.

Feldman was catnapping, slumped in a wooden chair against the wall when they arrived. Ellen poked him awake.

"Sorry," he said, rubbing his eyes. "Jet lag, you know? Anyway, nothing of substance so far, but check this out. The young woman you found near the index case in the ship's hold keeps muttering something repeatedly."

Ellen followed him to the cot.

She looked down at the young girl. Her face was drawn and pale. Behind the dull, lifeless eyes, Ellen thought she saw a glimmer of brightness, a tunnel of hope.

"Lo...," she mumbled. "Fu ... Fengbu ... Jiangxi ... Lo ..."

Ellen shook her head.

"There it is again," she said. "*Lo* could mean building, could be hug. Could mean trouble."

"Fu...," she muttered. "Fu..."

"The index case has been mouthing the same sounds. But they wouldn't use English to say 'flu'."

Paul stepped forward with one of the Polaroids he had just snapped.

"Wait a second. I have an idea."

He held the snapshot in front of her face.

They saw the girl's eyes widen instantly with a flicker of recognition.

"Lo..." she said.

She smiled faintly.

She tried to raise one hand but was too weak. It fell back limply on the cot.

"There it is again," Paul said. "Lo?"

The young girl nodded feebly.

Paul turned to face Ellen.

"The guy's name has to be Lo," he said. "Repeat some of the other sounds."

Ellen did so. When she came to 'Fengbu,' the girl's eyes brightened again. As she listened to all the other sounds, she either closed her eyes or turned away.

"Fengbu, Fengbu," Ellen muttered.

She circled 'Lo' and 'Fengbu' repeatedly on her yellow pad.

Finally, the coin dropped.

"Wait a minute! Of course, it's Lo Fengbu! How could I have been so dense? If he's for real, then we may have a hot one, Paul."

"How so?"

"Lo Fengbu's a very well-known young dissident," she said excitedly. "He was arrested and sentenced to prison in a famous kangaroo trial a couple of years ago but then he simply disappeared from everybody's radar screen. Beijing said he died of natural causes, but they always say that so you never really know what happened. His family was too frightened to open an official inquiry."

She turned back to the girl.

"What's your name?" she asked softly in Mandarin.

"Chen…," she replied faintly. "Chen… Sun…"

She closed her eyes and drifted off.

Ellen looked up at Paul. Her eyes were moist.

"Chen Sun means bright future," she said.

She leaned down and whispered a few words of solace and encouragement. The young girl's eyes flicked open briefly and she managed a faint smile.

Ellen told Feldman she'd check back after lunch.

"No unauthorized visitors," she reminded him.

"Then tell the base to send over an armed guard," he said. "I can't keep unauthorized visitors out with just a stethoscope."

Paul and Ellen drove back to Aberdeen. She relayed Feldman's request through McKee to Commander Evans. As they walked across to the base mess, Ellen's cell phone trilled.

She fished it out of a side pocket of her lab coat and flipped open the case.

"Ellen? Sandy. What is it with you? Everywhere you go these days, you take a lethal bug with you. I haven't tested all your samples but I've done enough to know it's exactly the same ugly virus you had in Hong Kong. The identical splice job, no doubt about it, right down to the *exact* H5 site on the H1N1 genetic map."

Ellen was quiet for a minute.

"I figured from the readouts last night that we were dealing with the same deadly virus. But why would someone waste their time on a boatload of random immigrants?"

"You think it's a test? See if we're ready?"

"Not likely," Ellen said, shaking her head. "Every country in the world knows the Coast Guard runs constant patrols up and down both coasts now, non-stop. They know September 11 changed everything. But why would a bioterrorist intentionally target a sparsely populated corner of the Pacific Northwest that's relatively isolated, surrounded on three sides by water, and easy to defend? It doesn't make a lot of sense."

"So what do you think?"

She looked up at Paul.

"I don't know. Maybe a mistake, a tragic error, something inadvertent. Or possibly even a decoy. But the more time we spend being distracted by it, the less time we have to focus elsewhere. Test the rest of them, Sandy, then fax us a copy of your results."

As they finished, an orderly rushed into the dining hall, whipping his head from side to side, cupping his hands and shouting Ellen's name.

"Dr. Chou? Dr. Chou!"

She looked up and raised a hand.

The orderly tripped over a chair in his rush to reach her.

"Come quick!" he yelled. "Your patient's in a coma. He may be dying."

Ellen sprinted down the hall, Paul matching her stride for stride. They pulled on their gloves and masks as they ran. She yelled at an orderly to find McKee.

She needed Lo Fengbu to hang on, to get stronger, to tell them more. She whispered a curse. It was always tough to lose the index case early because it gave the disease detectives so many potential clues. But a killer virus like H5N1 had no preference. A human host was a human host.

When they got to the iso ward they signed in quickly with the guard and Ellen rushed straight to Lo. His body was twisted like a pretzel on the bed. His head arched back and his tongue protruded between his teeth, disgorged and blue.

She felt for his pulse while listening through a stethoscope. She propped open an eyelid and saw that his pupils were severely dilated. Strangely, she noticed there was no blood in his mucous.

She shook her head and wheeled around when McKee hustled in. He checked the IV feed to make sure the clamp was open, felt Lo's forehead, held litmus paper under his nostrils.

"Very faint," he said. "He's going fast. You may never learn anything now."

"We've got to save him!" Ellen shouted. "Get me a vial of adrenalin from that shelf behind you."

McKee sprang up and rifled through the boxes of drugs. He found the rubber-capped bottle, snapped it onto a hypodermic and prepped the syringe.

Ellen ripped open Lo's gown and probed the muscles near his heart. She took the needle from McKay, jammed it into Lo's chest and emptied the vial in one smooth motion.

"Digoxin!" McKee yelled. "I'll open a vial and get it going in the IV."

As he did this, she looked over her shoulder at the wall.

"You got a patch?" she asked.

"Right-hand side."

Ellen jumped to the wall shelf and began tossing aside unneeded drugs. Vials tumbled and fell at her feet as she searched for a nitroglycerin transdermal patch.

She found it, ripped off the foil wrapper, peeled away the adhesive backing and slapped it onto Lo's chest directly over his heart. Digoxin would help his heart pump more blood with each beat as the nitro patch relaxed the connecting capillaries. The shot of adrenalin to his system was like a jumper cable to a weak battery.

McKee fitted an oxygen mask snugly around Lo's mouth and nose, squeezing his jaws to retract the protruding tongue. He spun a dial to start the airflow.

Ellen wheeled an EKG monitor to his bed and slapped four leads around his heart while McKee stuck the remaining wires to his chest and stomach. Ellen flipped on the machine.

They watched the numbers on the digital readout, perilously low, fewer than 30 beats a minute. But as the combination of adrenalin and digoxin began to take effect, the digits slowly started rising, beat by beat. When they hit 40 and kept rising, Ellen collapsed into a chair against the wall.

"Out of the woods?" Paul asked.

He stood out of the way by the window.

Ellen nodded.

"Just barely. Somebody's going to have to monitor him non-stop now," she said. "But it looks like he managed to cheat death."

She looked over at McKee.

"I want an armed guard at this door 24/7," she said. "I can tell you from experience that those symptoms had nothing to do with the killer virus."

◦ **51** ◦

While they were fighting to save Lo Fengbu's life, a forest-green metallic late-model Buick Riviera SL sedan purred quietly into an empty space across from the Elma school and stopped.

Two muscular Chinese teenagers got out.

They were dressed in starched, heavy-denim designer jeans and shiny mint-green leather jackets. They wore identical Ray-Ban wraparound shades. Their thick black hair was combed straight back and slick with a viscous No. 7 gel that made it stiff as glue. Seen from a distance, they might have been twins.

One of them approached the Coast Guard sergeant outside the schoolhouse door and engaged him in a friendly manner. He kept the guard distracted while his partner slipped unnoticed around the back.

His questions were polite and friendly.

He'd heard some sick immigrants had been brought in from a broken-down ship to get well.

How sick were they? Would they be here long? It was just possible that one of his cousins might be in there. Did the sergeant have any names? Could he possibly check the list?

The sergeant did his job thoroughly, did it as exactly he was trained.

Standing pole-straight and barely making eye contact, he told the visitor he'd have to go to the base and ask there if he wanted answers to his questions. The sergeant said he wasn't authorized to comment in any way, couldn't give him any information whatsoever.

Sorry.

And no, sir, you may not go inside.

Quarantine.

As the two of them spoke, the other leather-jacketed, slick-haired punk located the ventilator unit in the window cavity on the backside of the building. Opening the vent, he squeezed the contents of a palm-sized plastic bottle into the filter. Pocketing the vial, he emerged around the other corner and walked straight to the Buick without looking back.

Over the guard's shoulder, his partner saw him nod as he got into the car. He thanked the sergeant, said he was sorry to bother him and would contact the base for more information, just as he'd been instructed.

The sergeant watched him slide behind the wheel, start the engine and slowly pull away.

Just as it dawned on him that there were not one but two figures in the car, Feldman slammed through the door, coughing and screaming, his two hands covering both eyes.

He smacked into the sergeant and knocked them both to the ground.

Temporarily blind, Feldman dug frantically into a side pocket of his lab coat and pulled out a small bottle of ampules. When he couldn't immediately unscrew the lid, he smashed it on the sidewalk under his heel and groped through the plastic cartridges.

He found one and snapped it open onto his sleeve, gulping air through the soaked fabric, sucking the fumes deep into his lungs.

"What's the hell's going on?"

"Stay out of there!" Feldman shouted, breathless. "Radio for help. We need filtered respirators. *Now!*"

The sergeant patched through to the base. Feldman could feel the atropine take effect as his muscles relaxed and his air passages cleared. He could gradually sense his eyes start to dilate.

Blinking, he partially opened them again as the stinging sensation slowly subsided. He felt his breath come more easily as his heartbeat returned to normal.

"You gonna tell me what the hell happened in there?" the sergeant asked, holstering his phone.

He glanced at the yellow frame building that looked so peaceful and still.

"Cyanide gas," Feldman said, leaning forward and puffing hard.

His voice was hoarse, his throat dry as sand.

The young virologist broke open a new ampule and soaked his handkerchief now, sucking air through the impregnated cloth.

"Most popular respiratory poison in captivity," he said between gulps. "Freezes the central nervous system so it can't utilize oxygen efficiently. I'm telling you, stay out of that schoolhouse and don't let a soul go in without a HEPA mask. Those poor bastards are gone."

"How in God's name did you -- ?"

"Knee-jerk, just like we're taught," Feldman sighed, hands on both knees now, inhaling deeply. "We carry a mandatory supply of atropine sulfate wherever we go. First time I've ever had to use it."

He looked up at the Sergeant between breaths.

"You got any water in that canteen? I must have inhaled a whole gram of that stuff."

° **52** °

Unaware of the tumult just a few miles away, Ellen turned to McKee and handed him a blood sample she'd just drawn from a vein in Lo's right arm. She patched the pinhole puncture in his arm with a Band-Aid.

"What've you got so far?" she asked.

"Looks pretty routine," he said, studying the computer printout through clear goggles. "X-ray showed a ton of fluid in his lungs, pretty typical for flu virus. But no pneumonia bacteria. The anti-viral medication probably prevented a secondary infection."

He took the fresh blood sample and poured it into small tube containing a clear liquid. After swirling the mixture, he mounted it on a centrifuge. While it spun, he picked up another sheet.

"Anything from the other blood sera?" Ellen asked.

"Not much yet," he said.

Ellen knew what it would show, a long readout of standard blood contents. What she wanted to know is what had caused Lo's convulsions and put him in a coma.

"Toxicology?"

"Nothing out of the ordinary so far."

Suddenly, McKee frowned.

"Uh-oh," he said. "This is pretty strange."

"What?"

"Well, it shows normal trace minerals -- iron, iodine, potassium, zinc -- all in low quantities. No surprise there, since he's undernourished and under siege with a virus, but --"

"But what? Based on what we saw in Hong Kong, the sera ought to confirm renal hemorrhaging, but that wouldn't explain his critical condition today."

"No," said McKee. "That's what I was trying to say. Looks like he had a massive dose of strychnine in his system. Enough poison to kill a dozen rats."

"*What*? Let me see that."

Ellen snatched the sheet out of his hands and scanned the numbers herself.

"This is impossible," she said, breathless.

She showed the page to Paul.

"With the killer flu, his kidneys should have begun to fail."

"But this is no ordinary poison," McKee said.

"What do you mean?"

"Look at the hierarchy of numbers. You see the concentration of furanone dihydro on the top line? That's a primary ingredient in gamma hydroxy butyrate."

He folded the sheet of numbers and placed it on a table nearby.

Ellen looked up at him.

"GHB," she said.

"Exactly."

"But that's been banned by the FDA."

Cerrutti turned to face the Coast Guard medic.

"So what?" Paul said. "You can get it over the Internet, roving dot-com Websites like LoveLife and HealthQuest, no questions asked. It's the #1 date rape drug in captivity, widely sold as a dietary supplement under popular names like Enliven or RenewTrient. We see it all the time at clubs in New York and LA. Stupid kids passed out, half-nude, practically in comas. And some of them never recover."

"What makes it so dangerous," McKee added, "is that there's a fine line between a joy dose and a lethal dose. Somehow some of it got into Lo's IV tube went straight to his central nervous system and almost shut him down. In chemical assays it masquerades as strychnine. Once in a blue moon one of our plebes gets some and tries to be cute until he realizes too late that it's grounds for automatic discharge."

Ellen spun around when she heard a low moan behind her.

She saw Lo's eyelids flutter.

He coughed.

"Oxygen," she said curtly.

McKee replaced the cup over Lo's nose and mouth while Ellen cranked the bed into a more upright position.

His eyes blinked open.

"That's good," she said. "Stay close."

Lo's eyes darted fearfully from McKee to Ellen to Paul. They focused on the IV drip and drifted back to her.

"Where ... am I?" he said faintly.

His spoken Chinese was choppy and slurred.

Ellen told him. For the first time, she felt a ray of hope.

She pulled the chair back next to his bed and sat down.

"The ... ship..."

"It's gone," she said quietly. "Half the stowaways survived. You were one of them."

He closed his eyes and swallowed.

"Chen ... Sun?" he asked.

"She's with the others nearby."

"Thank ... you," he said faintly.

Ellen reached down and took his hand in hers.

"Don't strain yourself," she said. "Can you tell us anything about this terrible virus?"

He lay still and cleared his throat. His breathing was labored and heavy.

"Jiangxi... " he said. "Laboratory... "

Ellen glanced at Paul and made a writing motion with her free hand.

He handed her a notepad.

"Go on," she said. "If you can. We have time."

"Horrible... "

She nodded.

"We know."

She waited, saying nothing.

"Fu... "

There it was again, she thought. Not flu.

"Fu," she repeated.

Lo nodded weakly.

"Fu... Bar..."

His voice trailed off weakly and his head collapsed onto the pillow.

McKee checked his pulse, stared at the EKG monitor, double-checked the IV.

"He's doing okay," he said, "but we shouldn't put him under too much stress."

Suddenly his eyes opened again as he squeezed Ellen's hand.

"Thank ... you," he said again. "Help me ..."

"We will," she said. "Have no fear."

He drifted off.

Ellen gave his hand a final squeeze and folded it across his stomach.

"Well, that's something at least," she said, standing and looking at her notes. "Something about a laboratory in Jiangxi province. We know the virus was genetically cloned, so maybe Lo knows where it was made. And hopefully, by whom."

"He made that reference to 'Fu' again," Paul said.

"I heard that," Ellen said. "It could be another name, or possibly the first half of Fujian. We'll have to wait until he's stronger before we can ask him more."

Cerrutti turned to McKee.

"Who's authorized to access this ward?" he asked.

"Medical staff only," the Coast Guard doctor said, looking up. "Strictly routine. The guard controls the door, checks IDs, collects the signatures on his list every time anyone signs in."

"So let's take a look at that list," Paul said. "You and Ellen are the only two principal investigators. Anybody else ought to stick out like a sunny day in Seattle."

"You think somebody got in who shouldn't?"

"You think a member of your staff gave him GHB by accident?"

"No way."

McKee stepped outside and took the sign-in list from the guard.

The three of them huddled over the clipboard.

Ellen and McKee recognized their signatures immediately. Paul saw his. McKee ticked off the others, one by one, all apparently authorized and all with valid IDs.

"Who the hell's this?"

Cerrutti pointed to a squiggly line.

McKee shrugged.

"No idea."

"You're positive there've been no unauthorized visitors?"

"Yes. I'm telling you, nobody but medical staff's been in here. This room's tighter than the butthole on a rat's ass."

Paul stepped outside the room to question the guard.

They went down the list name-by-name and confirmed that every visitor had presented a valid medical ID before entering.

"And everybody had lab coats, sir. They were all masked and gloved. I made sure of that. Yes, sir. Every single time."

"This is starting to *smell* like a goddam rat's ass," Paul said. "We better check the front gate. If someone unauthorized got in somehow, they'd have to clear there first."

"Shouldn't we call the police?" McKee asked.

His eyes were hollow with fear now.

"That won't be necessary," Cerrutti said. "This is Federal property. The FBI has jurisdiction and I'm the police."

∘ **53** ∘

Colonel Fu Barxu stood erect with his back to the wide windows and eyed his commanding officer. A steady late-September rain hammered the glass.

"You're sure?" Fu asked.

The response from the speakerphone on the General's desk was unmistakable.

"Confirmations from both sites," the echo said. "Absolutely no mistake."

There was a tone of ecstasy in Eddie Liu's voice now, like a broker whose stock had suddenly soared.

"Of course," he said giddily. "I hand-picked the assets myself."

Fu stared at General Min.

The senior renegade leader studied the speakerphone without saying a word, his chin propped thoughtfully on his fingertips. He thought for another minute, then crisply nodded his assent without looking up.

"Stay in your office," Fu ordered. "When the bodies are discovered, there will be questions. A lot of questions. And you're nearly always the first suspect on their list."

"I was here the whole time and I have witnesses who can prove it," Eddie Liu said confidently. "Don't worry about Seattle. I'll take care of things here as always. You can count on it."

"Tell your doctor friend he better take a vacation. Starting now."

Fu's voice was more military-like now. It was another command, not a request.

"And keep those two punks out of sight."

"You do your job," Eddie squeaked. "Let me do mine."

"Don't get cocky," Fu warned. "There's still one more job we need you for."

"Oh?" Liu said. "I thought Lo and the survivors were your only worry."

"This one is considerably more delicate," the Colonel said, his voice smooth as camphor oil. "The lady doctor has intervened once too often. She must be taken out now, not just sidetracked."

"But my sources say she will return to Washington since the others have been eliminated."

"So?"

"So you know the rules. The Green Dragons don't touch anything east of the Mississippi River. If we even piss in it, the Red Dragons will send a team of thugs from New York to remind us in a most unpleasant way. You want another gang war after we've worked long and hard to divide and conquer? Think about your comrades in Guangdong and how they would react. This is a job for the Reds."

"I don't give a damn about them," Fu said sharply. "This is too sensitive. Pick a man you can rely on and get him moving. Do it *now.*"

There was silence on the line. Nobody said a word while Liu mulled over the Colonel's order.

Finally, his tinny tenor voice creaked through the speaker.

"There is one man," he said carefully. "Fan Guo. He's older, more experienced, knows how to use weapons that are silent and leave no trace. He's called the Chameleon because he can blend seamlessly into any background. He should be able to find the lady doctor in Washington and slip out before the Reds even know he was there."

"All the same, make sure he understands she's a dangerous adversary."

"Leave the Chameleon to me," Eddie Liu said. "He's a pro."

"No mistakes, Liu," Fu barked. "You know the drill. No results, no cash. The stakes are much too high this time."

Fu snapped off the connection.

He looked up at the general, his lips a thin line.

"As the Master once said, a good runner leaves no tracks."

The Colonel folded his arms across his broad chest and smiled.

General Min arched an eyebrow.

"And little faith can be put in those whose faith is small," he said with a nod.

He walked to the large windows and closed the drapes, blocking the light from the dull gray sky.

"Let's get on with the briefing," the general said. "You've done all you can for now with Liu. You were about to give me details of the backup plan."

Frowning, Col. Fu snapped the cap off the lens of a large overhead projector and sharpened the focus. He shuffled through a stack of color viewgraphs, hand-picking the ones he wanted General Min to see.

He switched on the projector and bathed the room in a flood of white light.

"First, some basic demographics about America at the dawn of the new century," Fu said. "Their famous baby-boom generation is getting old."

He placed a first slide on the projection glass. A press photo of a crowded shopping mall, available from any mass-market magazine, filled the screen.

"They total 81 million in all," he went on. "The single-largest piece of the American demographic pie. Born between 1946 and 1964, eight and a half million are moving inexorably into middle age every year until 2014, when the last cohorts turn 50. They're mindless knee-jerk consumers, obsessed with nutrition and health."

The next slide was an aerial view of the northern California freeway system near San Jose. Gridlocked cars jammed the spaghetti-like roads bumper-to-bumper in every direction.

It was a digital image from one of China's reconnaissance satellites. Three of them now orbited the earth in low-orbiting trajectories, thanks to technology illegally acquired through their covert network of high-tech spies at sensitive American laboratories like Lawrence Livermore and Los Alamos.

"Americans today worship two gods," Fu said. "Money and time. They spend money like it was water and treat time like it was gold. Two out of three women work, so meal preparation time has dropped from three hours a day to 20 minutes."

General Min shifted uncomfortably in his chair.

"I don't see how this is remotely related to -- "

"Please watch the next slides," Fu interrupted. "If you would, sir," he added.

"Very well. Go on."

Fu removed the aerial image and replaced it with a high-resolution photograph of open terrain. It showed mile after mile of neatly furrowed rows that disappeared into the distant horizon.

"Crops?"

"Just watch," Fu implored. "This is a full-color scan of agricultural land in Salinas, California. This state is America's number one source of food, with farm sales totaling $25 billion a year. Just south of San Francisco, Salinas alone sells $5 billion a year to the aging health-crazed Americans."

He replaced the open scan with a close-up of the terrain. Thousands of small, green spherical bumps protruded from its surface like pimples on skin.

"Iceberg lettuce," the Colonel said. "A very popular food. Per-capita consumption is 50 pounds a year -- a full head of lettuce per person per week. It's also the fastest-selling, thanks to a new American technology called modified atmosphere packaging, which keeps it fresher longer."

Fu overlaid a slide showing a refrigerated container truck being loaded by a small army of olive-skinned Hispanic migrants, shirtless, leather-skinned and sweaty.

"Lettuce heads are automatically picked and wrapped on-site," he continued. "GPS-equipped reefer trucks with wireless terminals ship the lettuce within 48 hours to every superstore in America at a constant temperature of 34~36°. Five retail chains -- Kroger, A&P, Acme, Safeway, and Wal-mart -- control the market, and three salad producers -- FastPack, Green Foods, and Salad Express -- supply them. Self-serve salad bars dominate quick-service restaurants and cafés, already causing 100 million cases of gastrointestinal illness and half a million hospitalizations a year."

Fu's last slide showed a small, single-engine propeller airplane flying at low altitude over the parallel rows of harvestable lettuce. It trailed a cloud of brown smoke.

"I have contacted a crop dusting company in Salinas Valley called Ag Air," Fu said, striding proudly to the screen. "A friendly but extremely naïve young customer service manager by the name of Ted Simmons has agreed to rent me a Turbo Tractor so I can photograph the Monterey coastline by moonlight. Two large cylinders of our aerosolized virus will fit very comfortably under the wings. The Turbo Tractor can cover 9,500 acres in three and a half hours with its fuel capacity of 228 gallons. By flying counterclockwise in concentric circles, I can coat 200,000 tons of iceberg lettuce with the Jiangxi virus. Lettuce that will be in American homes and supermarkets and salad bars in less than two days."

"Wind conditions, weather?" the General asked. "You've checked these critical factors?"

"Of course," Fu replied. "And they work to our advantage. Lukanov's spray absorption is relatively low volume, so we have to avoid air inversions -- a warm layer above cool ground. Otherwise the spray will simply rise in the air and not settle. So the best conditions are pre-dawn, when there is little wind, at an altitude of 200 feet. Late afternoon rains are predicted at the end of this month, which would be even more ideal because the lettuce heads will be slick and more of the microdroplets will stick. For myself, I will have a HEPA-filtered rebreather mask to avoid air drifts during flight."

General Min's face relaxed in a glow of fascination and disbelief. Then just as quickly, he frowned.

"But surely the Americans would never be so gullible as to rent such sensitive equipment to a stranger, let alone a foreigner," he said.

Fu's eyes sparkled.

"For the right price, Americans will sell anything to anybody," he said. "All you need is valid photo identification and a pilot's license. Ag Air even will take a credit card, though I will of course pay cash. And as long as I stay below a thousand feet, a flight plan with their regulatory authorities is not even necessary! Can you imagine? They are so incredibly stupid, even after the mad Muslims bombed New York and Washington."

"But you can never use your own ID. "

"Of course not," Fu agreed.

He handed the General two small documents.

"With his usual efficiency, my covert operative Lt. Kang has fabricated a California driver's license and a replica of my pilot's credentials with the military markings removed. As you see, both photographs bear the unmistakable likeness of Lo Fengbu. Arrangements are being made for you to replace General Li in the official Beijing delegation. With Lo permanently out of the way, I will accompany you wearing one of Lt. Kang's formidable disguises. You inform the *fengpai* that they will release the famous dissident in San Francisco in order to insure the success of the historic agreements. When they in turn tell Washington, and the President releases this information publicly in San Francisco, the American press will fawn over Beijing's conciliatory gesture to human rights."

General Min stood and looked his protégé squarely in the eye.

"My friend, this is brilliant. If the *fengpai* had the power of your imagination, none of this intricate planning would be necessary."

He walked to the windows and drew open the large drapes. The rain had slackened and he saw China's most famous public square begin to fill with the usual traffic of pedestrians, nomadic merchants, and bicyclists. A few half-hearted protestors attempting to hand out leaflets were surrounded and dragged away quickly by the PSB.

"But they don't," Fu said, "Naturally, we want the Newark operation with China-four to be perfect. But you see the advantage of splitting both coasts. This plan enables us to do that."

"Sun Tzu's cardinal rule," the general murmured softly. "Create an uproar in the East so you can strike in the West. Now, what is your next step?"

"Next?" Fu asked.

He collected the viewgraphs and placed them carefully in his briefcase. After snapping it shut, he joined his mentor at the tall windows.

As he gazed out across the huge expanse of Tiananmen Square, he saw himself standing high atop the famous gate to the Forbidden City with Tian Ling proudly by his side, reviewing the PLA troops soon to be under his command. He'd come a long way, from the desolate village of Puqi in Hubei province as a skinny, undernourished farm boy on the brink of disease and despair to the threshold of national leadership as the next commander-in-chief of the world's most powerful Army.

"I fly to Shanghai next," Fu said, his eyes smiling. "Phase Two starts tonight."

∘ **54** ∘

Paul and Ellen hustled out to the front gate with McKee, whose cell phone chirped as they ran. Commander Evans relayed the bad news from Elma.

When Ellen heard, she stopped suddenly. Her eyes narrowed.

"Paul, this is your territory now," she said.

Her face was angry.

"This attack on Lo and the schoolhouse murders were no coincidence. We need some answers, and fast."

Cerrutti nodded, breathing heavily.

"Let's see what we've got here first. Call Feldman, get him back to base."

Sergeant Miller Bates saluted smartly as they entered the gatehouse.

A rotund man with close-cropped auburn hair, Bates had a barn-wide stomach from too much time spent in sedentary assignments. A neatly trimmed toothbrush moustache hid his ample upper lip. He was eager to rotate out of guard duty and get back to Cutter patrol so he could bring his weight back under control.

McKee introduced them. Paul asked for the list of all visitors allowed on base during the past twenty-four hours.

Bates pulled a clipboard off the gatehouse wall.

Cerrutti keyed the base sign-in sheet to the iso ward check-in list line-by-line on the clipboard. They scanned the names for any possible matches.

"Check this out," he said to Ellen, stopping halfway down. "Same squiggle."

Paul turned to McKee.

"You recognize this signature now?" he asked.

Cerrutti made a checkmark by the scrawl.

The base medical officer shook his head.

Cerrutti turned to the guard.

"Sergeant?"

Bates glanced at the name.

"No, sir, I don't. It's been a busy morning. Most of our deliveries hit on Mondays."

He ticked off the entries, line by line, starting straight from the top.

"This one here's Bradford Foods, for the mess. This one's the construction crew for the back quarters. And here, Camp Shelton sent a truck to pick up their gear. Said it had to be inventoried and restocked."

Ellen nodded.

"Then these three guys came back, base staff, all returning from temporary leave over the weekend. This here's Cooper Electric. And Johnson Plumbing. And UPS."

He squinted at the scrawl again and scratched his head.

"I can't make out his name, but I do remember he showed me a valid medical ID."

He paused, then nodded.

"Yeah, he was the one all right. I remember now because all doctors write lousy, you know?"

Ellen jumped when he mentioned a medical ID. She looked again at the scrawls on both lists. They were clearly identical.

"Tell me about your security setup here, Sergeant," Cerrutti said.

The stout man swiveled on his stool and shrugged.

"Tight, sir," he said. "Pretty standard controls now, which became mandatory after September 11. Rolling mirror checks under all vehicles, handbag searches, X-ray scans, metal detection -- "

"Not the routine mechanical stuff, Bates. I'm talking about the new electronic sensors -- imaging devices and remote scans."

"Oh," he said, "you mean the sexy stuff."

Sergeant Bates swiveled his thick midsection in the other direction and punched a keyboard. In seconds a multi-windowed screen emerged on his computer display.

"We got digitals here of every vehicle entering and leaving the base," he said, swinging the monitor toward them. "After those insane suicide bombers attacked and anthrax followed, every military installation in the country went for belts and suspenders. Right above you near the ceiling is a camouflaged camera that's programmed to target the human head so we can get headshots of every visitor. As it scans, it uses object-detection software to recognize the shape."

He angled his head toward the front of the gatehouse.

"A second camera is forward-mounted and triggered by motion-detection. It activates when it senses a vehicle start to pull ahead. It tracks 'em, gets their rear bumper in focus and automatically captures the number plate. Let's see what we got on this guy."

Bates cycled back through the images captured by the system that morning. Paul stood behind Ellen and leaned over her shoulder. McKee looked on from one side.

"Here we go," he said. "There's the Bradford Electric guy. You can see the patch on his cap. And the Army team from Shelton. And now ... your Kodak moment."

As they watched the screen, they saw the crisp image of a middle-aged Caucasian, fully bearded and wearing tinted, thick-lensed glasses with a rain hat pulled down over his forehead.

"Can't tell a whole lot from that," Paul said. "Print me out a copy anyway."

Bates did so, and then activated the number-plate sequences.

"This system uses a Kodak XL-33 imager," he said, scrolling through the license plates that popped up like a sheet of postage stamps on his screen. "Since the vehicles accelerate pretty quick, the camera captures the images in low-bitrate wavelet format, compressed for faster access. Least, that's what the geeks tell me."

Bates matched the stranger's visit to the time sequence and double-clicked on the stamp-like image. It expanded to fill the screen. It was blurry at first but snapped quickly into focus. Wavelets loaded three times as fast as the typical .gif files in JPEG format that slinked down, scan line by scan line, and took forever to load.

The familiar shape of a local license plate filled the whole screen.

"Washington State. VDL-113," Paul said as he jotted it down. "Got it. Thanks."

Cerrutti keyed a number into his cell phone as they walked back inside. He spoke to the Bureau office in Seattle and asked them to run a plate-check through state DMV.

Feldman was back and waiting when they regrouped in the Commander's office. He gave Ellen the details on Elma and told them not to worry about interviewing the schoolhouse survivors. There were none.

Ellen glanced up at Paul.

"What do you think?" she asked.

"With that degree of coordination and timing?" he said. "Got to be related."

Within minutes, the FBI's Seattle branch rang back.

"Name's Alvarez," the voice said. "Eduardo. Caucasian male, age 58. MD, abortion butcher downtown. More citations than a batch of lottery tickets. Arrested and detained but seems to make bail every time, constant pattern. Never indicted, never convicted. Can't pin anything on him."

Paul made notes as they spoke, tucking the phone between his shoulder and left ear as he stood off to one side in the Commander's office.

"Stay put, I'm coming in," he said quietly. "Find me an address for Alvarez and get me the make of his car. And see what you can get on a pair of Chinese punks. The sergeant here will give you a description of one of them. You get anything, fax it out here and call me on my mobile."

Ellen turned to Evans.

"I thought we had an understanding here, Commander," she said. "Somebody break press silence?"

Evans shook his head.

"Not to my knowledge. I've been through the night reports. Strictly routine."

"Mind if I have a look?"

He handed her the dispatch sheet from the previous night. When her eyes caught Rashid's two-sentence release on the rescue, she realized instantly what might have happened.

She glanced back up at the Commander.

"You call this silence, sir?" she asked, pointing out the news summary.

Evans took it and tossed it on his desk.

"This is a military operation, Dr. Chou. We have to follow strict orders here. If I don't submit a daily summary, Washington will nail my ass fast."

"You could have waited to do the rescue report today."

"Not on my watch," he said. "Your operation started at dusk last night, so it had to be captured in yesterday's summary, which Ensign Tompkins cut way short. Besides, what's so important about a boatload of illegal immigrants anyway?"

She cast a nervous glance at Paul.

"We don't know yet. It may have been a sideshow, possibly a decoy. But it makes us think something bigger's about to go down. Lo -- the index case in your isolation ward -- told us about a clandestine flu factory in Jiangxi province in China where we strongly suspect this deadly virus was genetically cloned. You shouldn't have any more trouble now that somebody's taken the poor refugees out, but Lo has *got* to be guarded around the clock."

Commander Evans was unmoved.

"All I know is that the DOT's all over my commanding officer in Washington and he's all over me about this mess. For some reason they go ballistic at any mention of China. They say there's supposed to be a high-level A-team meeting in San Francisco in a few days' time. And you know what? They still haven't given your guy Feldman here official authorization yet."

Ellen winced as she thought back to her own situation in Hong Kong.

"Well, can we just stick to the story we agreed to for Jonathan, Commander? This news summary doesn't exactly elevate my confidence."

For the first time, Evans relaxed.

"Don't worry. They only have to know what, where, how, and when," he said. "They don't have to know who."

"Thank you. By the way, you can radio the *Reliance* and tell them they can take down their yellow flag and come ashore now. When the lab called from Atlanta today, they confirmed that your cutter was clean."

"That's good news," he said, making a note. "I'll notify their families right away."

He put an arm around her shoulders as they stood to leave.

"And don't worry about Feldman, Dr. Chou. We'll make sure Atlanta knows he's the only sailor on deck."

"Commander, I may need to use one of your cars. Can you authorize that?"

Evans propped himself on a corner of his desk and looked up at Cerrutti.

"Bureau use? I don't see why not. I'll ask Bates to notify carpool."

Ellen turned to Paul.

"I'll get my things and you can drop me at the airport. I want to catch the late afternoon flight to Washington if I can. The BT committee meets tomorrow."

"What about Lo?"

She glanced at McKee.

"I'll touch base with you regularly by phone. Let me know when he's more coherent so I can interrogate him further."

She turned back to face Evans as he was hanging up.

"I can't emphasize enough how important it is to keep the isolation ward under 24-hour armed guard, Commander. We desperately need Lo alive. We still need some critical information from him when he's rested and finally able to talk."

"10-4," Evans said. "I will personally guarantee that."

Before leaving, Ellen stopped by the isolation ward to check on Lo Fengbu one last time. When she signed in and entered the room, he was still on forced oxygen. She glanced at the EKG unit and was encouraged when she saw the numbers. His heartbeat was near normal and holding steady.

"What do you think?" she asked.

McKee walked over from the oxygen unit to join her.

"Vital signs look pretty good," he said. "He should pull through okay. I've added more Demerol to his IV solution and inserted a catheter to drain his bladder. Once the GHB is fully out of his system, I think he'll start to perk up. That is, if the virus doesn't take hold again in his weakened condition."

"Keep the rimantadine levels high," Ellen said. "We can't afford to lose him."

"After this security breach, we've got guards with automatic weapons posted outside the door and at each end of the hallway. Nobody will even get close."

"Excellent. I'll call you from Washington tomorrow."

An hour later Paul eased a gray, unmarked Chrysler Cirrus into a temporary parking space in front of the main SeaTac terminal.

"You sure you need to go back?" he asked. "We're starting to make a pretty good team."

"You're right, Paul," she said, collecting her briefcase and carry-on. "But after these new developments, I really have to do the BT briefing. The interagency committee needs to know about this killer virus and Harper's cleared me to speak. Remember, he thinks I'm still in Maine so he'll expect me to be there ahead of time tonight."

She leaned across the front seat to kiss him goodbye.

Paul reached around with his long arms and held her close for a long minute.

"Be careful," he said softly as their lips parted. "After this shit out here, keep an eye on your backside."

"Paul -- "

He placed a finger on her lips.

"Don't worry about me. Like you said, this is my territory now. I'm dealing with scum I can see for a change instead of invisible germs. Call me after you check in and don't forget to recharge your phone while you're in the air."

Ellen blew him a final kiss. As she watched him drive away, he shot her a thumbs-up out the window.

After clearing security, she went straight to the gate, where she was picked out for a random search and pat-down before boarding.

She barely had time for a final five-minute call to Washington before she climbed aboard.

∘ **55** ∘

Colonel Fu Barxu pulled up on the throttle of his pitch-black, single-engine *Jayan* FH-8 military jet and glanced down as the Beijing runway disappeared from view below.

Moments later, he reached his cruising altitude and leveled off at 15,000 feet as he angled the little trainer south toward Shanghai. The cool amber lights of his plasma instrument panel glowed eerily in the clear plastic facemask of his flight helmet.

The clouds had lifted and the sky was clear above the perennial smog that clung to Beijing like a heavy shawl. There was too much light from the big city for him to see the stars, but the air was calm so he estimated he'd arrive at Hongqiao airport in Shanghai well within his filed flight plan of an hour and forty-five minutes.

He traced the steps carefully again in his mind. Nothing predicted success quite like the vision of a flawless rehearsal.

From a subordinate in Shanghai he had obtained a list with the names of the crew who would be staffing China Air 004 to Newark that night. He'd requested detailed dossiers on four of the female flight attendants. Judging from their gender and age, they would be least likely to resist the command of a senior officer in the People's Liberation Army. Particularly when the request was so innocent on the surface. And especially when accompanied by a small envelope with a hefty cash bonus.

Col. Fu had singled out a young woman from Hebei province, a single flight attendant named Yang Rumei. His choice was based not just on gender or age, or the fact that she appeared to be the most attractive of the bunch, or even because she was the daughter of the Mayor of Shanghai and a relative of the ruling Communist elite.

He also had history and geography in mind.

The province of Hebei abuts Beijing to the north. Its northernmost edge borders Mongolia. For centuries it had suffered the cruel attacks of foreign invaders, from historic barbarians like Genghis Khan to modern-day marauders from Japan in the last century. The people of Hebei had long ago stopped resisting. During its history, the Great Wall of China was more often in need of repair in Hebei province than anywhere else on its long perimeter.

Fewer natives of Hebei died if they showed they could be flexible and accommodating.

And that was what Fu wanted. Someone who would *oblige*.

Col. Fu saw the process unfolding in his mind as if he were going through it in real time. Open access to the crew's quarters because of his military credentials. A feigned official request from the PLA to Miss Yang Rumei. The printed certificate signed by General Min that would be placed in her personnel file at China Air, commending her cooperation and support. The explanation by Fu that the PLA's commercial arm needed to test the efficacy of a new Chinese disinfectant in order to win important new contracts with foreign companies.

All for the greater good of China.

As he nudged the throttle to start his descent toward Shanghai, the rogue Colonel smiled.

He knew Miss Yang would be expecting him. He'd taken time to phone her from Beijing, having already spoken with the copilot of Flight 004, Li Guizhou, to make sure the crew was on hand and preparing for departure.

Fu saw the Hongqiao runway lights flicker into view in the distance below. He reached down and pulled a heavy metal case into his lap for one last check.

When he flipped open the lid, he saw that both aerosol cans with the pressurized H5N1 virus were there, exquisitely labeled by his acolyte Lt. Kang, as new as if they had come straight from the factory. Bright red security pins sealed the valves to prevent accidental discharge. Fu closed and locked the case and set it back down.

Constant vigilance, he thought to himself as he feathered the wheels of the light aircraft onto the smooth asphalt runway with a skilled touch.

You can never be too careful.

He taxied forward and parked away from the terminal building but not far from the giant Boeing 777-200 that was being prepped for imminent departure.

The new non-stop Shanghai-Newark run was the crown jewel in China Air's expanding international network and the flagship carrier's flights were consistently full. Its crimson tail with the gold stars of China's national flag sparkled proudly in the white light from the tall columns atop the corners of the terminal building.

The words of the Master echoed in Fu's mind.

Death has been with us since the beginning of time.

He smiled as he crept toward the widebody, the metal case with the deadly virus securely in his grasp.

◦ **56** ◦

Kicking off her hand-sewn tan suede moccasins, Ellen tucked her short legs beneath her slim body and tried to organize her notes on the flight to Washington Monday night. She wore a pair of her favorite stonewashed jeans and a collarless loden-plaid poplin shirt with the sleeves rolled up.

The hazardous sea rescue had added a new twist to her briefing. The fact that the ship was infected with the same killer virus strengthened her hunch that the Early Response teams had to be ready for a possible bioattack from Asia. Not just from the more predictable Middle East.

She closed her eyes and imagined the howls and catcalls she'd get when she dropped *that* bomb.

Her mind raced back to the chaos in Hong Kong. To the hideous mortality rate of the killer flu. To the horrible truth that it attacked and murdered young adults -- not infants, not seniors -- unlike any other subtype of the type-A flu virus. To the undeniable fact, confirmed by Lo Fengbu's painful revelation, that someone was genetically engineering this horrible pathogen somewhere in Jiangxi province in China.

Chemical weapons were immoral and disgusting and ugly enough, she thought. But at least you could fight what you could see and antidotes were readily available. However odious, chemicals and explosives were not infectious, so a larger population was never at risk outside the impact zone. They created a terrible disaster but never an epidemic.

A deadly virus was an invisible weapon that could be used anytime, anywhere, without warning. What was worse, it trapped unsuspecting people as innocent vectors and used them as involuntary collaborators to spread the attack. A weapon only shameless cowards would launch on purpose.

She stiffened as she remembered Harper's sole condition for gaining access to the elite group of Washington policy makers.

Present, but don't proselytize.

She made a marginal note, reminding herself to let the facts speak for themselves, to put her data before them so they could see with their own eyes.

Dr. Ellen Chou, M.D., had a reputation for unassailable data. She was a disease detective. An epi, one of the best. How could they possibly not agree?

With a shiver, Ellen rolled down her sleeves and pulled a blanket out of the overhead bin. Wrapping herself snugly, she knew the answer to that question and it was not pretty. All through her career, she'd consistently produced reams of statistics on every case she solved.

But the dark side to her legendary thoroughness was an inherent conservatism that earned her a different sobriquet. Miss Stubborn, they called her. Uncompromising. Risk-averse. Always ready to cry wolf, to don a mask and gloves at the slightest hint of an unknown bug.

Well, let them be derisive, she said to herself. That was an integral part of the Washington game, refereed by Lucifer. Power represented the only points worth scoring.

Politics was a blood sport that threatened lives in its own violent way, cutting careers short, truncating professional judgment, putting a premium on chicanery and deception. If that was the game they wanted, she'd be ready, despite what Harper said.

But something else nagged at her now, something more critical. Ellen Chou was first and foremost an epidemiologist. A disease detective, one of the finest. So far she had been focusing like a laser on the disease. Now she had to start playing detective.

She flipped to a new page on her yellow pad. Down the left-hand side she scribbled a list of keywords based on what they knew so far about the killer virus. These she labeled the "whats."

Down the right side she wrote a list of short questions based on what they knew about international terrorism, both from Paul's practical knowledge and from her own work through months of ER training. These she labeled the "what-ifs."

Next, she started amplifying the right-hand side.

What if there was a madman in Asia who wanted to see America suffer? A nutcase, a crackpot, a dedicated enemy of capitalism? She scratched a few names with question marks: Malaysia/Mahathir? North Korea/Kim?

What if there was a stealth organization in Asia that patterned its principles on Mideast fanatics?   Japan/Aum Shinrikyo? China/Falun Gong?

What if some unstable splinter states from the former Soviet Union were using China as an unwitting co-conspirator, a camouflage to disguise their own insidious tactics?   Azerbaijan?   Kazakhstan? Tajikistan?

What if one of these rogue states had installed some of their advanced bioweapons technology on Chinese territory, unknown and undiscovered, in the Gobi desert or the foothills of Tibet -- or in a remote sector of Jiangxi province itself?   God knows they had easy access to Russian scientists and equipment, not to mention stockpiles of aerosolized weapons with lethal pathogens ready to launch.

What if the remnants of al Qaeda had drifted into a corner of Jiangxi to fabricate this terrible virus?   Their irrational case against America was no secret.

And what if Hong Kong had been a test, an experiment, to prove the efficacy of this killer virus?   Was the boatload of Chinese immigrants just a distraction?   If so, why was a prominent dissident infected and on board?   Had Lo been the primary target?

Or was something bigger about to go down?   If so, where was it coming from?   And where would the attack occur.

And when.

And how?

She came back to Lo's disclosure of Jiangxi.   At the bottom of the page, she printed the word "China??" in capital letters with double question marks and circled it.   She wrote a single word underneath, circled and underlined.

"*Why*?"

Ellen Chou stacked her notes, clipped them in order, and put them back in her briefcase.

She pulled on a set of headphones and twirled the dial, searching for something upbeat to match the tempo she needed for her talk the next day.   Something persistent, a little stubborn. *Uncompromising.*

She found an old classic by Aretha Franklin and sat back, eyes closed, as she felt the rhythm thump into her soul.

Later, as the flight began its descent into Washington's Reagan airport, Ellen straightened her seatback and stuffed the headset away.

Glancing down, she noticed a copy of *The New York Times* from that morning lying in the seat beside her.

She picked up the front page and scanned the lead stories.

Israel and Palestine were trading insults and exchanging bloody terrorist attacks again as they had for decades, not an inch closer to peace. A new strongman dictator of another banana republic somewhere in Africa was slaughtering the tribe of his just-deposed predecessor, thumbing his nose at the Western governments that had financed his regime.

And a high-level State delegation from China was coming to San Francisco later this week to sign new trade and human rights agreements with Washington. Ellen thought back to Harper's fearful preoccupation with the White House as her eyes focused on one sentence.

The Beijing delegation would arrive in San Francisco Wednesday afternoon for the formal signing ceremony Thursday night.

Was the deadly Jiangxi virus somehow connected to this visit?

Jesus, she thought.

That's only three days away.

∘ **57** ∘

Paul Cerrutti parked the gray, unmarked government-issue Chrysler a block away and around the corner from the skid row address the FBI's Seattle office had given him for Dr. Eduardo Alvarez.

He shut the door and zipped his windbreaker against the damp chill. A thick fog was blowing in from the harbor on top of the ever-present drizzle.

Looking at the dingy shop fronts, Cerrutti knew he was on the dark side of Chinatown. A colleague on the Asian Organized Crime task force had given him the bottom line on the Green Dragons and the local neighborhood.

He walked by a Cantonese restaurant with dusty duck carcasses hanging off-center in the window, their scraggly shapes ghostly pale in the light of a tired red neon light that flickered nearby.

Next-door was a coin laundry. As Paul glanced in, he saw a cluster of young toughs playing poker as they waited, using clothespins as chips and slapping them at a stack of crimpled bills on the Formica sorting table.

Across the street stood a threadbare hotel, the metal Chinese ideographs on its marquis crooked and rusting with age. Its façade was pockmarked with gap-toothed holes where bricks had fallen out, giving way to an arrogant army of urban rats that crawled the wall without fear.

Early in the evening pedestrian traffic was light.

A pair of teenage drug dealers bobbed in and out between parked cars hawking ersatz smokes. Paul stopped and stared when he saw the body piercing on the short guy.

Seven earrings hung from his left ear lobe and five from his right; a pair of eyebrow loops, a nose ring, two cheek studs and a lip rivet dotted his face. If he were to walk nude through a metal detector, Paul thought, he'd light it up.

An older pimp and his young prostitute patrolled the intersection. Prancing on foot-high cork-soled jump-me pumps, she flashed passing cars with a chest as flat as a paper plate and was getting no takers.

Cerrutti turned the corner and spotted the 3-digit number on a doorway diagonally across from the corner. There were no names above the door. A small, hand-stenciled sign read, "By appointment only." He could see light through the opaque glass, so he stepped back inside a dark entryway across the street to wait.

Paul Cerrutti wasn't interested solely in Eduardo Alvarez. He was too far down the food chain to be of much use. Paul had to know who sent him to Aberdeen, and why.

They had more than enough empirical evidence to arrest the man on suspicion of murder. Recent judicial revisions of the Miranda ruling meant he could bring the quack in without hassle. Just to be safe, one of the local agents got a search warrant from a circuit judge so Paul could legally have a look around. Still, Paul thought, this guy's not going to know anything except maybe a useless name or two.

Minutes later, a hatless form wearing a long raincoat emerged through the door and lurked toward the corner. Cerrutti pulled a pair of small Nikon field glasses to his eyes. He couldn't tell from the back whether it was a man or a woman but he knew from its size it wasn't Alvarez.

Cerrutti smiled.

"Looks like the doc's about to have a little unscheduled appointment," he said to himself. He patted his jacket to make sure his Glock 9mm was holstered and ready.

He stepped quickly across the street and through the opaque door.

Cerrutti edged silently down a long dark hallway until he found the office door he was looking for. When he tried the knob, it was locked.

He looked at it and saw immediately that it was a simple tumbler lock. From his left coat pocket, he removed a set of steel spikes on a small ring. Eyeing the knob, he selected a nail-like tool, slipped it silently in the slot and rotated it counter-clockwise.

The door lock snapped open. Cerrutti pocketed the tools and turned the knob.

When he heard the hinges creak, he stopped. He knew the doctor might sense an unexpected visitor now. He tiptoed quickly through the reception room, past the lukewarm pot of stale coffee, past the plate of half-eaten raised-glaze doughnuts, past the stack of month-old magazines, past the ancient IBM Selectric on the scarred wooden desktop.

The veneer door to Alvarez's office was locked too. As Paul moved forward, he knew he had no time to pick another lock so he unholstered his gun and rammed a shoulder through the paper-thin door. It gave instantly.

As he slammed into the room, Alvarez was sitting in the window sill with his back turned, ready to leap. Cerrutti leapt forward, grabbed him by the shoulders and jerked him back.

Alvarez's fingers scraped splinters from the window frame as he tumbled backwards into the room. He cringed, closed his eyes and raised both hands over his head.

"Don't hit me!" he screamed. "I told Eddie I was leaving! They'll never find me. Swear to God!"

Cerrutti holstered his gun. The doctor's face was a perfect match to the digital image they'd captured at Aberdeen.

"Guess what, doc?" he said. "You've just been found."

Alvarez opened his fearful eyes in time to watch Paul slip a pair of Bureau cuffs around his shaking wrists.

○ **58** ○

Ellen had pulled away from the airport terminal in a Yellow Cab on the last leg of her trip when she heard her cell phone chirp.

The late September air was dense and muggy. To her, Washington was just another small-time Southern town, its parochialism permanently trapped in a claustrophobic layer of thick humidity. All that seemed to be missing were the broad verandahs, the mint juleps, and the ubiquitous Spanish moss that clung to trees in the South like cobwebs.

She extracted her phone and flipped it open as the cab accelerated.

"Ellie, it's me," Paul said. "I got Alvarez just as he was about to skip for Mexico. A real bottom-feeder, in way over his head. Melted like hot wax, said he didn't know why Lo had to be taken out. He was just obeying orders because he said if he didn't, he knew he'd be dead himself anyway. So he crossed his fingers and hoped he could skid by on this job, too. But they hadn't counted on the Coast Guard having a new image-capture system."

"So who sent him out there?" Ellen asked.

The taxi skirted Arlington and turned to cross the Potomac.

"Guy's name is Liu, apparently. Eddie Liu. Our boys in Seattle knew him well; he's the head of the Chinese mafia, the *tong*. Must have been pretty important, coming straight from the top. So I paid Liu a visit along with a little backup from downtown. Arrogant bastard, squat-shape, pencil moustache, acts like a pint-sized Hitler. Denied everything, of course, said he had an iron-clad alibi and several witnesses to back him up. I said bullshit; we had Alvarez behind bars. He didn't believe me until we let the two morons talk, felon to felon."

"So what'd he say?"

"I told him if he'd give us the pair who gassed the school we'd try to plea bargain the judge. But he had to give up some key names in China too because our guys knew he wasn't acting on his own. They gave me chapter and verse on all his crap here. But he was adamant, said no way, told us to go to hell. I said, Fine. You clam up, we'll shut down every massage parlor and gambling joint and illegal sweatshop in Chinatown and arrest every single Chinese suspect in our files.

Straight by the book, no more tit for tat. Goddam Dragons want a taste of hell? We'll put 'em out of business and stick their crummy little crime world up for grabs and they can slug it out for themselves on the streets with their competition."

Ellen grabbed the roof bar as the taxi swerved sharply around Washington Circle and sped down K Street.

"Paul, please tell me you didn't resort to -- "

"Relax, Ellen. You've been seeing too many B-grade movies. Anyway, he starts sweating, says he wants a lawyer. I said *after* he gives us some names. He says, what about Miranda? I said it's not like that anymore. So he sits there with a pair of huge Feds hunkered over him and grabs a pad off his desk. He jots down three names and I stuff the sheet in my pocket. As the Seattle team takes him downtown I take a look at the note. Get this, Ellie -- at the bottom of the page was an impression, you know, an indentation left from what he'd written earlier on the previous page? So I took a soft lead pencil and made a rubbing over the marks. It's all in Chinese so I'll have to fax it to you. Where you staying?"

"The DuPont," Ellen said.

She dug out the fax number.

"I'm practically there. Fax it as soon as you can and I'll take a look."

"He printed a couple of other names in block letters," Paul went on. "I'm heading for SeaTac now, booked on the redeye tonight. I'll get Sam Taylor to run these names through our database in the morning and try to run some matches in the CIA's system too. Call me when you get the Chinese characters. If it's from Liu's pad, I'm willing to bet it's not an escort service."

"Will do."

The taxi pulled into the circular drive in front of the DuPont Hotel and Ellen paid the driver.

"We'll talk tomorrow morning," he said. "When are you done with the big shots?"

Ellen frowned.

"Not soon enough," she said. "Probably not until mid-day."

She got out of the cab and stood by the revolving door with her bags at her feet.

"Call me as soon as you or Sam learn anything. This could give us another hook to the killer virus in Jiangxi. Eddie Liu wouldn't just whack a half-dozen anonymous immigrants sight-unseen, because they were probably critical to him as sweatshop labor. He had to have been following orders. This adds a new dimension to my briefing tomorrow. I don't care what Harper says, I'm taking the gloves off."

Paul's fax was waiting for her at the front desk after she'd waded through a long line to check in.

She tore open the envelope and studied the crisp, laser-jet page excitedly as she rode the elevator up to her room on the 8th floor.

After she let herself in, she sat down quickly at the small desk and called him right back. He was in the unmarked Chrysler on his way to SeaTac.

"Paul?" Ellen said when she heard him pick up. "The character reads 'Fu,' the same name Lo may have been trying to give us. That ideograph is crystal-clear. The other two are given names but less legible. Could be Baixi, Baixu, Barji, something like that."

Paul pulled over and stopped the car.

He asked her to spell each one phonetically so he could jot them down.

"Thanks, Ellie," he said. "I'll call Sam from the gate before I take off. Good luck tomorrow."

As she lay back on her bed, she stared at the name. Her heart quickened as she thought about Lo Fengbu and what else he might be able to tell them. If and when he recovered.

Ellen was as excited as a child on Christmas Eve. She couldn't sleep.

She was ready.

∘ **59** ∘

First officer Yang Rumei twisted the Pierre Cardin lipstick tube shut and tucked it into her shoulder bag. She rubbed her lips together to smooth the scarlet paste and made one last check in the mirror. She preened a loose tuft of hair back into place behind one ear and pulled down on the sides of her jacket.

She looked fine, she told herself.

Two more round-trips to America and she'd have enough mileage to qualify for promotion. The unexpected bonus from that nice Colonel would come in handy, too, she thought. Perhaps a little present for her sister this time from one of those fine Manhattan boutiques on Fifth Avenue.

She unhooked the door to the lavatory, parked her handbag in an overhead bin and passed down the left side of the aircraft to make a final seatbelt check.

Next she came back up the opposite side, in the precise way the helpful Colonel had instructed her to spray the dual cylinders of disinfectant. This will be pretty easy, she thought. There's still lots of time before the captain pushes back from the gate.

Yang Rumei joined a male colleague at the bulkhead between business class and coach. They went through the usual routines -- demonstrating the oxygen masks, pointing out the emergency exits, reminding the passengers how to strap on and inflate the life vests.

First officer Yang put the demonstration gear away and stepped behind the bulkhead.

She pulled one of the aerosol cans out of an overhead bin, snapped off the red security ring and tossed it in a trashcan.

Retracing her steps, she walked slowly up and down the cabin holding the can above her head, pressing her right index finger on the undersized button and spraying a cloud of fine mist in tight semi-circles across the rows of occupied seats.

When she finished in the main cabin, she repeated the process in Business Class until the aerosol was depleted.

One can should be enough, she thought. We'll save the second one for the return flight. She threw the empty cylinder into the trash and made sure the other container was securely tucked away in an overhead bin.

Yang Rumei sat down in her jump seat in Business Class and checked the manifest.

"Full house again," she said to her companion.

Two hundred and eighty-three passengers.   Forty-eight in business class, 235 in coach.   Fifteen crewmembers brought the total to nearly 300.

And all of them would be traveling for more than fourteen hours in a confined space, non-stop, crammed together like livestock, inhaling and exhaling millions of unfiltered microdroplets of the same stale air.

○ **60** ○

Early the next morning, Ellen decided to take the Metro instead of a cab from DuPont Circle to Farrugut North so she could stretch her tired legs. She wore a navy linen pants suit with a silk blouse in antique white.

The interagency committee was meeting on the third floor of a typical limestone office building at the corner of 16th and H Streets near Lafayette Square.

As she sat in the subway, she thought how simple it would be to release a lethal pathogen in an urban underground tunnel and infect the thousands of people who used the subway every day.

Innocent morning commuters sat absorbed in their own individual worlds, reading their newspapers, listening to CD players, talking on cell phones. But Ellen knew that the subways were a critical vector and one of many strategic targets the ER teams had clearly in their sights. If anything happened in New York, or San Francisco, or Washington, they'd be ready to respond in minutes.

Ellen stepped out onto the platform at Farrugut North and edged forward with the rush-hour crowd toward the distant escalator that would take her upstairs to Lafayette Square at the intersection of 16th and K.

Commuters were eerily silent and as self-absorbed on the platform as on the train.

Civil servants had their heads buried in the *Washington Post*. A pair of young lovers held hands and stared into each other's eyes. Lobbyists in custom-tailored suits arrived from their Virginia and Maryland suburbs and headed for Gucci gulch. Somewhere behind her a boom box blared.

As Ellen neared the moving stairs, a hand suddenly came from behind and snapped onto her left arm like a vice.

"Don't make a sound," the voice said.

"Who--?"

"I said, don't make a sound. Just ease back and stay close."

As they inched back through the crowd, Ellen tried turning her head to get a glimpse of her captor. But the man they call the

Chameleon only squeezed her arm harder, causing her to neck to stiffen.

When she tried to jerk free, Fan Guo jabbed her left kidney sharply with the outstretched fingers of his right hand and her legs suddenly turned to rubber.

"That's for starters," he said. "Edge forward now. That's right, look straight ahead and smile. We'll take the elevator at the other end of the platform."

Ellen closed her eyes briefly and moved forward as the crowd thinned. Her left arm went numb. When she tried to wiggle her fingers, she felt nothing.

She glanced left and right without turning her head and hoped someone, anyone, would see the fear in her eyes and call for help. But nobody caught her glance. Why would they even bother, she thought. It was rush hour. People still scanned their morning papers or gabbed into cell phones or punched plastic styluses at the screens of their Palm Pilots.

"Press the up button," Fan commanded when they reached the elevator doors. "If anyone looks this way, keep smiling. We'll just be a typical hard-working Chinese couple having a quiet squabble on our way to work."

The wait for the elevator wasn't more than a minute but it seemed like a week to Ellen. She was running out of ideas. Perhaps if she could stick out a leg and trip someone getting off, cause them to bump into this strange man who terrified her and held her captive. Her heart pounded like a drum and she could feel her left hand start to throb.

Fan Guo pulled her to one side as the elevator creaked into place. The doors opened slowly and they had to wait for an old woman in a wheelchair to roll herself out. But the floor of the car had stopped a half-inch below the platform so she couldn't move the wheels.

The lady looked up at Ellen.

"Would you mind?" she asked.

Ellen was paralyzed in place, stiff as a statue.

She started to say something when another man moved quickly in front of them and reached forward with one arm to pull the woman out.

"Why, thank you, young man," she said, and rolled forward.

When she looked back to thank him again, she screamed.

She noticed that the good Samaritan was Chinese, too. He had just slipped a shiny four-inch stiletto silently into the side of the Chameleon's neck and shoved Ellen into the elevator as Fan's grip slipped away from her arm.

"Get out of here *now!*" he hissed at her in fluent Mandarin. "Don't ask questions, don't look back. This doesn't concern you."

He reached quickly inside the car, punched the door-close button with his free hand and jumped back as the doors slid shut.

Ellen pressed her hands against the glass and watched in horror through the rising cage as her rescuer knelt down and twisted the knife in the Chameleon's neck.

By the time the car reached the top level, the assassin had disappeared anonymously into the morning crowd. He shot a cuff and glanced at his watch. Just another Beltway commuter late for work.

The dense crowd continued to surge across the platform, unaware and unimpeded. Too many urban tragedies resulted from strangers helping strangers, and this knowledge prevented others from stopping.

Another pair of trains stopped and emptied their passengers into the throng. A young woman slipped on the surging pool of blood near the elevator. As she backed away from the dead man, eyes wide, she punched 911 on her cell phone, turned, and moved quickly away.

Ellen was still shaking as she stepped out of the elevator and walked on wobbly legs across Lafayette Square. She eyed a small coffee shop on the corner and headed straight for the ladies' room. When she emerged minutes later, she looked composed on the outside but felt full of terror inside.

On the threshold of her briefing, a new question nagged her. Was someone trying to keep her off the podium? And what did he mean, *this doesn't concern you?*

She ordered a double expresso and downed it in a single swallow.

○ **61** ○

David (Skip) Salomon, 47, Senior Marketing Officer for AT&T International, sat with his wife, Bitsy, 42, on China Air 004 in Business Class, Row 15, Seats A and B, directly across from First Officer Yang Rumei who was belted into her jump seat.

Theirs was an exit row, which Salomon had expressly requested so he could stretch his pole-like legs during the flight. At six-feet-nine, he was forever in pain on airline trips, even when he didn't have to coil his limbs like a pretzel in coach. Years of varsity basketball at the University of Maryland had put a lifetime's worth of wear-and-tear on his knees.

But his joints were the least of his worries today.

"This is the last time I ever fly China Airlines," he said, curling his long arms around his stomach again. "They'll hear from our chairman when I get to the office tomorrow and e-mail him about this horrible flight. I don't give a damn how many contracts may be at stake, life's too short."

Skip Salomon had single-handedly put AT&T on the map in China.

He shuttled back and forth between New Jersey and Beijing or Shanghai every other month, schmoozing the slick government bureaucrats, countering strong bids from his monopolistic, government-owned European competitors, making sure the Japanese didn't have an unfair advantage simply because they were strategically closer and could fly to meetings on short notice, like he used to do when he traveled to Denver.

"Well, I told you not to eat the shrimp," his wife said.

She dipped a washcloth in a glass of ice water, squeezed it, and laid it across his forehead.

"I took one look at those diseased shellfish and never even touched the plastic lids. It's not the airline, you know, it's their food caterers in Shanghai. You've told me many times before that these flights have a reputation for airsickness. Even United and Northwest, remember?"

He didn't want to remember but gave a reluctant nod as he lurched forward in his seat. The dry heaves had started again.

Bitsy Salomon jerked her feet quickly out of the way. Her wrinkle-free Bergdorf-Goodman linen khakis were already flecked with spots from her husband's earlier projectiles. Shivering slightly, she unrolled the top of her cinnamon-colored cotton turtleneck up her neck for warmth and locked an arm in his.

The line of passengers waiting to use the lavatory seemed to be permanent, she noticed. Every time someone opened the door, the rotten stench of sour food and vomit penetrated the cabin.

A man across the aisle sat with a blanket over his head. The couple sitting behind her was moaning worse than her own husband and giving flight attendants fits every time they passed by.

Complaints throughout Business Class were growing more hostile as the passengers got sicker. Bitsy reprimanded herself for not having told others near her about the shrimp, but Skip was forever on her case about making idle conversation with strangers.

"Still, it was a fascinating trip," she said, turning back to him and trying to put the cabin bedlam out of her mind. "Thanks again for taking me to Pudong. The old waterfront was really spruced up, wasn't it, despite all the smog. I can't believe Shanghai is so polluted. It's as bad Cairo or Mexico City. How do the Chinese manage to breathe with the air that bad? And the water in the harbor was so thick with garbage it reminded me of those stories you used to tell when you covered Africa. But our hosts seemed genuinely pleased that the wives could join this time. That was nice."

Her husband reached up and pressed the washcloth against his head. He leaned back and closed his walnut-brown eyes.

"At least, we got the deal," he said with a sigh. "I'll be damned if I'm going to let the corrupt Japanese bribe their way into that market and eat our lunch again. But if I have to go through this much pain to close the next one, I may not live to tell about it."

Bitsy Salomon reached across and tamped down his thread-thin auburn hair. It was speckled with gray and glistened with pearls of sweat in the cold cabin.

"Just think of the wonderful bargains we got," she said. "Such incredible artwork! Can't you just see those beautiful Guilin landscapes in our living room right between those windows behind the sectional leather couch."

"Christ, Bitsy, how the hell can you think about decorating the house at a time like this? Don't you even feel sick at all?"

"Try to breathe more rhythmically," she said with a smile, "and put this all out of your mind. We'll be on the ground before you know it and Star Limo will be there to take us back to Basking Ridge. I'll call Dr. Starkey first thing in the morning and get some of those industrial-strength painkillers for your stomach.   You know they usually do the trick."

She glanced at his face, saw his breathing become more regular, and gave him a gentle tug of reassurance. She knew he'd be okay after they got home. Sometimes it took a couple of days but he always recovered. If it wasn't the airline food, it was the water.

Bitsy Salomon recalled the first time her husband had come home from China feeling like this. He had bought what he thought was bottled mineral water on a street corner in Hangzhou, the scenic resort city near Shanghai. It turned out to be nothing more than untreated tap water sold by enterprising teen-agers in shiny shrink-wrapped bottles at a fancy price.

Just then a young Chinese boy no older than six or seven came running up the aisle from coach, strings of vomit dangling from his chin, screaming uncontrollably.

His mother was a pace or two behind, arms outstretched, her eyes clouded with fear. With a single motion, she swept him up into her arms and quickly turned and disappeared back behind the curtain.

The child's fulsome wailing only made Skip Salomon's condition worse.

"Why can't they simply seal off the main cabin?" he said to no one in particular. "If it's not the goddam kids, it's their idiot parents screaming at the flight attendants. I swear, China may think it's a civilized country with Confucius and two thousand continuous years of all that historical stuff, but the way its people behave is another -- "

Salomon heaved forward again and retched. He looked up at his wife.

"How in the world can you sit there so calmly?" he asked, his face drained. "This plane is headed straight to hell and you're as serene as the day our first child was born. Don't you feel *anything*?"

"Just a little sore throat," she said. "I'm sure it's probably the dry air at this altitude. The co-pilot told us he had to get above 45,000 feet to clear the turbulence, remember? So close your eyes and lie back, it's only another hour or so. We just passed over Chicago."

Bitsy Salomon leaned forward in her seat.

"Could you check again?" she asked Yang Rumei.

Her voice was sterner now.

"My husband really does need an extra blanket."

○ **62** ○

Ellen walked across Lafayette Square toward the squat gray stone building and took the elevator up to the 3rd floor. She took a series of deep breaths and exhaled slowly.

As she stepped out of the car, her cell phone trilled. Couldn't be Paul, she thought, glancing at her watch. She flipped open the lid.

"Ellen? LeRoy Harper."

"Dr. Harper!"

She edged down the third-floor corridor and pulled into a vacant corner.

"I'm about to brief the committee. Where are you?"

"Still in Washington," he said.

His voice was scratchy and hoarse. He sounded depressed. His tone implied defeat.

"What happened?" she asked. "You sound terrible."

"They screwed us, Ellen. Major double-cross. I've been stuffed in a room with White House creeps for the past 18 hours. They promised to back us on our big budget bill but they pulled the rug out from under me and left the CDC hanging in the wind. They just wanted to be sure we stayed clean on China."

Ellen kept quiet about the subway mugging as she let his revelation sink in. Her heart was still pounding.

"So what are you going to do next?" she asked.

"Nothing I can do," he said. "It's out of my hands now. Budget's dead."

"You're not coming over?"

"I'm sending Gupta. Go for it, Ellen, push hard. You're officially back on the case. Give 'em everything you've got."

"Took the words right out my mouth, LeRoy."

She felt more determined than ever. Still, she said nothing about Lo Fengbu or Jiangxi for now. She'd let Feldman take credit for that breakthrough since Harper had sent him to Oregon, not her.

She pocketed her cell phone and moved back down the corridor.

The conference room was packed and buzzing when she entered.

Ellen found her nametag on a side table and moved among the big crowd, greeting familiar faces and introducing herself to those she hadn't met. This was not a process she enjoyed. To her, it was individuals seeking selfish personal advantage that drove the frenetic pace of information-age networking. But for disease detectives, it was collaborative effort that produced results.

The Executive Branch was well represented with a cast of high-ranking specialists. The Departments of State, Energy, Justice, Defense, Transportation, Health and Human Services, Treasury, had Assistant Secretaries or deputies present. All the intelligence agencies were there –- FBI, CIA, NSA, DIA, INR, Defense Counter-Intelligence –- some in uniform with a rainbow array of medals, most not. There was a large contingent from the Federal Emergency Management Agency –- FEMA –- the household name that made national headlines with every natural disaster. And the Office of Homeland Security, the new kid on the block, was trying its best not to get lost in the shuffle.

Justice sent specialists from its Criminal Division, the National Security Division, the Criminal Investigative Division, International Terrorism Operations, the National Domestic Preparedness Office, Domestic Terrorism and Counterterrorism Planning, a Domestic Emergency Support Team, and a Computer Investigation and Infrastructure Threat Assessment Task Force. Belts and suspenders all the way.

Energy sent three, from Nonproliferation and National Security, Emergency Management and Defense, and NEST. State had high-level suits from the Bureau of Consular Affairs, the Bureau of Diplomatic Security and the Coordinator for Counterterrorism, in addition to a Foreign Emergency Support Team.

Not to be outdone, Treasury was there in abundance, too, with specialists from the Office of Foreign Assets Control, the Secret Service, Customs, and ATF. DOD had reps from the Joint Chiefs of Staff, the Office of the Secretary, the Threat Reduction Agency, Military Support, National Commission on Terrorism, Central Command, Special Ops Command, the Army, the Navy, the Air Force, the Marine Corps, the National Guard Reserves, the Naval Medical Research Institute, USAMRIID, TEU, CBDCOM, CBIRF, and Special Operations Low-Intensity Conflict. Space permitting, they would have sent more.

The FAA was there, and the NIH, and the CDC, of course (she saw Rakesh Gupta and gave him a nervous wave), and the Office of Emergency Preparedness, and Emergency Response, and the

Metropolitan Medical Strike Team, and the Environmental Protection Agency (which had lobbied to add yet another name to the burgeoning list, this time from its Office of Solid Waste and Emergency Response), as well as an official from Chemical Emergency Preparedness and Prevention.

Washington's infamous alphabet soup was alive and well, thick and getting thicker.

In all, more than a hundred risk-averse bureaucrats representing more than forty Federal agencies from every conceivable department of the Executive Branch were jammed into the cramped conference room.

Every chair was taken.

Everybody wanted a piece of the action on counter-terrorism now. They all had to play, to be there for the Big One, to push and shove and trip and elbow others out of the way so they could jostle for their own precious Fifteen Minutes.

It was typical of Washington, Ellen thought. Nobody ever ceded primary responsibility to anybody else, until and unless something went wrong. Then every finger would point in the opposite direction.

The only problem was that when a real crisis broke, incident command had to be unified. There would be no time for turf wars or their ubiquitous interagency bickering. As she made her way toward her chair, a single thought cycled through her mind.

When the shit hits the fan, only one person can stand up and take charge.

And she thought she knew who that person had to be.

She glanced at the Agenda and saw that her brief was scheduled nearly halfway through the session. That meant she'd be up just before lunch. Speakers were given ten minutes -- five to present, five for questions. It was unrealistically tight but it had to be if they were to finish in a day.

When her time came, she noticed that attention had already begun to lag. People were dozing off, chattering into cell phones, whispering to neighbors. She'd have to be blunt and to the point.

When her name was announced she took a deep breath, put the subway terror out of her mind, and walked up to the podium. Harper's call putting her officially back on the case gave her renewed confidence.

Ellen gave them point-blank data from the recent epidemic in Hong Kong. She cited the abnormal H5N1 subtype, its shocking mortality rate of 35.2%, the morbid fact that the killer virus appeared to be an engineered clone, a man-made genetic monster that attacked and slaughtered young adults.

And then she dropped the bomb.

She gave the Beltway tribe the first hint that something unexpected, something big, could hit America from China, not from the Middle East.

She walked them step by step through the hazardous sea rescue in the Pacific Northwest barely two days before and heard audible gasps from the few who were paying attention.

Innocent immigrants murdered with cyanide gas after the rescue operation. A prominent Chinese dissident on life support, barely hanging on, who revealed a critical link to Jiangxi province. And without naming names, the FBI's work in tracing the Green Dragon connection to China.

This was all news and it was totally unexpected and it set them off.

Cell phones snapped shut. The buzz of idle conversation went silent. Half-closed eyes popped open, alert now and wide awake. The hum of the air conditioning system became audible for the first time.

The next few minutes exploded. Angry denials erupted and isolated snickering accompanied ad-hominem derision as the conference room rang with putdowns of Ellen's hypothesis.

"You should stick to medicine, Dr. Chou, and leave politics to the experts."

State Department big shot, Ellen recalled, and swallowed hard.

Kevin Phillips, heavy-set, linebacker build, buzz cut, brush moustache, tasseled loafers, expensive suit. His syrupy Virginia voice was marinated in Ivy League arrogance.

"You better keep your cotton-pickin' hands off China," Phillips went on. "The President is about to sign a pair of historic agreements Thursday with the highest-ranking delegation ever to visit the United States from Beijing."

Ellen stood her ground.

"As sure as I'm standing here today, Phillips, and based on what I've just been through, China could well attack us before some crackpot in Baghdad does."

"You don't know what the hell you're talking about."

Ellen spun toward the voice and saw Leo Smolinski, CIA.

Built like a fireplug with bone-white shoulder-length hair that framed a leather face, he sported cowboy boots, a wrinkled tropical suit and an attitude. Not a nice bone in his body, she remembered from previous encounters.

"If you had access to intel reports from our assets in Pakistan, Iraq and Afghanistan, you'd know why we target the Middle East. Militant Islamic extremists like Osama bin Laden and renegade Arab leaders like Madrasa Khaddar are on a holy war against this country. Every detention and arrest we make confirms this. Portable nukes and chemical explosives are our primary concern here, not germs. You're way off base with China. If anything goes down, we'll know when and where long before it does. And I'm telling you, it won't be from the Far East."

Ellen was unyielding.

"You want names, Leo? I'll have some for you by the end of the day."

Sally Spencer slapped her next. They had tangled often before.

"I agree that incident command has to be unified," she said. "But make no mistake, Dr. Chou. FEMA will take charge, nobody else."

Ellen shook her head.

"With all due respect," she said, jabbing the podium, "there's not a single one of you who knows first-hand the horror of infectious disasters like the deadly virus we just put down in Hong Kong."

Her voice was firm, not angry. Matter-of-fact, without confrontation.

"Sorry, but FEMA is the master of disasters," Spencer went on. "When emergencies hit, FEMA gives the orders. Train wrecks, bus accidents, hurricanes, tornadoes, floods -- you name it, we run the show."

Ellen stacked her notes on the podium.

"All self-contained events," she fired back. "Two, maybe three days max. Tragedy, then containment. Call the local police and fire, sift through debris, dish out Federal funds. But when a bioterrorist attacks and all your victims are suddenly contagious, they'll infect your front-line workers in a heartbeat and spread death faster than you can say FEMA. You won't have a prayer of a chance."

She prepared to step down when another adversary blindsided her.

"You couldn't be more wrong about China."

It was Phillips' boss at State, Deputy Secretary Brian Russell. Smug, overconfident, always a 10-pound chip on his shoulder.

"If you make any more public comments prior to San Francisco, the White House will have no alternative but to retaliate in the most direct way possible. You know what that means."

Ellen stiffened visibly. She thought immediately of Harper.

"Are you threatening me, Mr. Russell?"

"It's a warning, Dr. Chou. Not a threat. China is this country's most important political ally in the war on terrorism now. These new agreements are critical to our bilateral future."

Her eyes narrowed.

"Mark my words," she said.

Her voice was stern as her eyes scanned the stunned crowd.

"We ignore China at our peril. You know we can't separate terrorism from politics and no country is ever an ally forever. This boatload of illegal immigrants is either a tragic accident, or -- "

"Or what?"

Russell strode several paces into the aisle.

"Or a deliberate diversion from an attack that could hit this country without warning at any time, possibly even to torpedo your own precious agreements. In the vacuum created by the end of the cold war, there's been no end to cultural conflict with the United States around the world. Islam's fight with Christianity may pale in comparison to the coming battle between Chinese authoritarianism and American democracy. Make no mistake, China is the most dominant power in Asia today, not the United States."

With that, she stepped down. She gathered her things as an anonymous staffer tried gaveling the crowd back to order. As always, Washington's elite had begun to bicker among themselves like dysfunctional children.

Ellen slipped quietly through a side door to her right. She didn't see Russell nod to his left.

She shook her head as she thought about the patchwork quilt of political tradeoffs she knew always had to be made in Washington. Maybe they worked in the timeless, give-and-take, horse-trading world of Congressional politicians who had to seek compromise in order to find common ground on issues that were irrelevant in the real world. But trade-offs never worked in a hands-on crisis. Sally Spencer at FEMA was typical.

Ellen had a few close allies at the agencies, especially FBI and Defense. She respected their professionalism and felt confident in their take-charge, no-nonsense approach. She would backchannel with them later.

Things got done, solutions got wired, pipe got laid in private between individuals. That's how real decisions were made, never in public and certainly not in an unwieldy group of feuding bureaucrats. They'll plow the same soil all afternoon and never get anywhere.

She walked out of the building and was standing by the curb ready to hail a cab when she felt another painful grip on her arm.

"A taxi won't be necessary, Dr. Chou. You've caused enough trouble for one day. Come with us, please."

She jumped and spun around. She recognized the ghostly shoulder-length hair at once.

"I'm not following you, Leo," she said. "What in the world are you talking about?"

She jerked her arm free this time.

"Leave me alone. I've got other people I need to see."

"We don't think so," Smolinski said. "Not today."

She started into the street and raised her arm to flag a passing taxi but stopped when she saw the snub-nosed Sig Sauer he was holding just under the flap of his jacket.

∘ **63** ∘

Co-pilot Li Guizhou knew something was terribly wrong as China Air 004 held steady high over Lake Erie, just north of Cleveland.

The whole planeload was sick. Chaos ruled the main cabin. His flight attendants had exhausted their meager supply of airsickness bags and the stale stench of vomit was penetrating even the cockpit.

Li Guizhou had a pounding headache, too, though for him it was nothing worse than usual. His sinus cavities always got tight at high altitude but the congestion normally went away after he landed. Except for the constant coughing and sneezing this time. That was far from normal.

At 43, Li Guizhou was one of China Air's most promising young pilots.

He hailed from Xi'an, home of China's famous life-sized terracotta soldiers. At 16, he had organized a typical teenage rural gang that spent its creative time ripping off foreign tourists who came to see the age-old subterranean treasures. Poor, undereducated, and facing a bleak future like all illiterate Chinese peasants, Li and his sidekicks targeted travelers with fanny packs because they knew that's where the rich foreigners kept their valuables. Upscale tour groups from Japan and the United States were especially vulnerable, typically unsuspecting and particularly profitable.

Li and his gang stole only travelers' checks, cash and credit cards. They knew the fearless toughs from the Public Security Bureau would hammer them like hell if they swiped foreign passports. That was a State crime punishable by death. But the PSB goons and the hotel managers also got their cut from Li so they could turn a blind eye.

Unless he became too successful.

When he started flaunting his fraudulent riches by wearing DKNY designer jeans and Ralph Lauren sunglasses that he bought from gray-market smugglers with his new wealth, they swept in and picked him up. He'd made the mistake of being more powerful than they on their own turf.

The PSB had its own scam going with the tourists. They accused foreigners of fabricating their own thefts so they could fraudulently claim the insurance losses when they returned home. The PSB also fined the confused travelers for breaking Chinese law.

Li was arrested and detained and threatened with a long prison term in the Shaanxi *laogai*.

But he recanted, to demonstrate his loyalty to the State. In exchange for leniency, he cooperated with the PSB and turned in his gang mates. The State gave him a rare second chance.

Li joined a State-sanctioned spiritual movement, became reborn in the Socialist faith and went to commercial aviation school. After flying safely with China Northeast for several years, he qualified for transfer to China Air, passed their comprehensive entry examinations and advanced swiftly to join the international cockpit team. For the past five years, his record with China's premier airline had been practically flawless.

But this time, Li sensed, things were different. The whole cabin was ill.

He knew it wasn't just food poisoning again. They often had problems with the caterers in Shanghai, it was true. Quality control was not yet up to world-class standards and foul shellfish occasionally made their way into the airline's dinner salads. But it was always just a handful of cases, never a full cabin and never limited just to China Air.

No, this was clearly something more serious.

He glanced across at the pilot, who as usual benefited from his superior rank by sleeping during the home stretch of the flight. Li nudged him once, twice. There was no response. Li could smell the alcohol on his breath when he exhaled. Near retirement, the old man always drank too much *shiaoshin* but Li thought nothing of it until he saw the crimson froth bubbling on his lips.

Miss Yang Rumei sat in her jump seat with her arms folded across her small chest, clutching her pocketbook. Like most of the passengers she was nauseous with a throbbing headache and fever. Shivering, she reached up and tried to adjust the thermostat one more time. If it was so hot in the cabin, why was she so cold? She pulled the midnight blue blanket tightly around her shoulders.

The young flight attendant settled back, tightened her seat belt and closed her eyes.

She'd done everything she could for the passengers and her crew, especially the nice American couple sitting opposite her. But the blankets were gone now. All the lavatories overflowed with half-digested food and reeked of the disgusting odor of vomit. No matter how hard she tried, she couldn't put the constant crying of small children and the endless moans of their parents out of her mind.

It had to be food poisoning again, she thought. Just had to be.

She tried harder to think about the expensive souvenir she would buy for her sister in Manhattan after she landed. Surely there would be some medicine in New York that would make her feel better. America had the best of everything.

Co-pilot Li Guizhou swallowed hard.

Despite the bi-weekly classes that he attended without fail, his English was still halting. Should he radio the tower and tell them they had a planeload of sick passengers? He thought twice about how that would look on his record and told himself no. The ground crew could deal with this after he got the aircraft safely on the ground. His primary responsibility was to fly the plane, protect the safety of his passengers, and get them to their destination. He was just doing his job.

Halfway across the state of Pennsylvania he radioed Newark to confirm his position. China Air 004 was on schedule and could soon begin its descent. It would not be long now. The young co-pilot could hardly wait to hand this nightmare over to the ground crew and get some medication for his pounding headache.

Li Guizhou sneezed again, but he couldn't see the pink microdroplets splatter against his instrument panel in the darkness.

∘ **64** ∘

Ellen identified the colonial elegance of the Hay Adams as soon as the unmarked Jeep SUV with the smoked windows parked under the ornate canopy. Minutes later, Smolinski nudged her out of the antique elevator and into Suite 512. His gun was hidden in a jacket pocket now.

Inside, she recognized the buzz cut and shoebrush moustache of Kevin Phillips instantly. He sat on a broad satin settee with another woman, someone whose picture she had seen in the papers, someone she had never met. But she remembered Catherine Brewster's name when Phillips stood to introduce them.

Cathy Brewster was the chief White House trade negotiator with China. Stylish and sophisticated, she was as brilliant as she was beautiful, a point not lost on a President who made sure she was a regular at his private dinners.

Brewster's family had a long pedigree in Washington politics going back to Theodore Roosevelt. With a degree in international law from Harvard, she had become a powerful and rising star in the Republican party.

Phillips told Ellen to sit down.

"I can't apologize for my boss," he said, massaging his moustache with a thumb and forefinger. "But I don't think you realize the seriousness of our situation."

"This is total nonsense, Phillips," she snapped. "Would you mind telling me exactly what you think you're doing?"

"Ask yourself the same question," he replied bluntly. "You stepped way over the line today and we just want to make sure you don't do it again."

"I can't believe this is happening," Ellen fired back, jerking her shoulder out from under Smolinski's claw-like grip. "You think you can get away with this? I suppose you were behind that incident on the subway platform this morning, too."

Smolinski and Phillips glanced at each other with confused looks.

"We don't know what you're talking about," he said. "We just want to keep you under wraps for a while until the China delegation arrives tomorrow and the President's signature is safely on those documents the next day."

Ellen glanced across at Catherine Brewster.

Long, auburn hair caressed her smooth, tanned shoulders. She bent forward to extinguish a cigarette, exposing firm, ample breasts beneath a low-cut beige silk blouse. She wore a short burgundy gabardine skirt with side slits and a pair of dark brown open-toed leather pumps.

"So she's a glorified babysitter?" Ellen said.

She tried to force a smile.

"Isn't this just a little absurd?"

"Not in the least. Harper warned you well in advance not to touch China. We got him to send you packing on a forced leave of absence. But no, you had to go to Seattle anyway, and then you said a hell of a lot more than you should have this morning."

"All in the national interest," she reminded him firmly.

"We'll decide what's in the national interest," he said. "Not a bunch of disease detectives in Atlanta."

"You cut Harper off at the knees."

"And we'll do the same to you in a heartbeat."

"So loyalty is the litmus test now?"

"What else is there?"

Ellen folded her arms defiantly across her chest.

"You guys are in way over your heads," she said, "We've got to do something about this deadly virus —"

"The next election's all that matters right now," Brewster interrupted, lighting another cigarette. "It's barely a month away. China's key because the President's campaign is lagging and he needs a big bump from the polls. He wants to keep the White House in the worst way. It's pretty simple."

"So I'm what, a prisoner in your cage?"

Brewster exhaled, shaking her head.

"No, a houseguest," she said. "I'm here to make it interesting for you, Ellen. May I call you Ellen?"

Leo Smolinski stepped between them.

"Tell us about your boyfriend. Where is he now?"

Ellen looked up at the CIA operative. The floor lamp illuminated his ghostly hair from behind, turning it into a sinister halo that framed a pink and unforgiving face.

"He's a big boy," she said, backing away. "He can take care of himself."

"Fine, don't tell us. We'll find him. We know how to make our friends at the Bureau -- how should I say, cooperate."

"You *bastard* -- "

"Fine, play dumb," Smolinski sneered. "Where's the dissident?"

"Screw you."

"He's here illegally. Tell us where and we'll keep him in protective custody."

"Yeah, right. I believe that like I believe I'm an honored houseguest."

Smolinski turned to Phillips.

"We're wasting our time with this bitch. I'll get one of our Seattle assets to transfer custody. The Chink has to be at the Coast Guard base anyway, based on her presentation this morning."

"You can't -- "

"Can't what?" Smolinski barked.

He whirled and slapped Ellen across her face with the back of his hand. He shoved her hard into a wing chair opposite the windows.

"Leo, that's enough," Phillips broke in.

He turned to Ellen.

"I hope you understand how serious this situation is. Smolinski has fixed the door lock so it's accessible only from the outside on instructions from Brewster. Stay put and don't cause any more trouble. I think you'll find the amenities at the Hay Adams more than sufficient."

Snatching Ellen's case away from the chair, he fished into it and retrieved her cell phone. He tossed it to Brewster.

"No calls."

Phillips disappeared through the door, Smolinski trailing.

Ellen heard the lock snap shut.

She rose, walked to the floor-length window and pulled aside the sheer curtain. She saw that the room was on the backside of the hotel so it would be fruitless to signal for help. The alleyway below was deserted and the room was too high up to be seen anyway.

"So," Cathy Brewster said. "I'm hungry."

She strolled over to the imitation Louis XIV desk and picked up a leather-bound room service menu.

"What looks good for lunch?"

∘ **65** ∘

"Got em!"

Paul Cerrutti sat hunched over a computer keyboard punching in the Chinese names one by one. His flight from SeaTac had been delayed by weather and he hadn't reached the Bureau until noon. Ellen had said she expected to be done by lunchtime, but he worried that she hadn't called and wasn't picking up when he called her either. Frowning, he focused on the screen in front of him.

Two of the names from Eddie Liu gave them very little but enough to know they weren't central to Ellen's problem. Both were in the FBI database, two low-level criminals working out of Fujian.

"What'd you find?" Taylor asked.

"One of these scumbags is a corrupt Customs inspector by the name of Gu Danzhang," Paul said, reading from the amber display. "He's the first point of contact at the port in Fuzhou where containers of stolen S-class Mercedes and 740iL BMWs arrive from the west coast. Gu clears the containers, stamps the papers with an official chop and collects a fee when agents claim them for his high-profile customers in Beijing and Shanghai."

Sam Taylor rolled his swivel chair across the linoleum floor so he could read over Paul's shoulder.

"The other guy is a Fuzhou waterfront gang boss named Kung Bao. More pond scum."

Paul studied his face on the monitor and saw the scars that symbolized his badge of belonging.

Kung had risen through the calloused ranks of tough dockworkers and joined the triad when he saw how much he could make in a very short time compared to the long hours he was putting in for the trifle he got from the State in the name of the Socialist workers' paradise. Kung organized the pickups when the freighters docked and was the principal conduit to Gu.

Before Paul tried any of the remaining names he called Ellen's number again. Still no answer.

Something was wrong. Wherever she was, whatever she did, she'd always pick up even if just to reschedule the call. This time, nothing but voicemail.

Something had happened.

Frowning again, Paul input the name "Fu" several times. He tried all the first names Ellen had given him and a few additional permutations.

Nothing.

So he turned to his friend.

Sam Taylor headed the Bureau's exploding electronic data retrieval system, a system that had grown in significance and size ever since the audacious events of 9/11.

He and Paul had spoken every day when Paul and Ellen were in Maine. Taylor was a graduate of Carnegie Mellon and survived the same pressure-packed training program with Paul at Quantico as a college graduate two decades earlier. He wore rimless granny glasses and a black T-shirt with neon yellow digital lettering in Latin across the front that read, "Vini, Vidi, Velcro."

I came, I saw, I stuck around.

"Try Langley next," Paul said. "Check the CIA's database and test the Fu surname with a full range of forenames, see what you can find. We got dick here."

As the nation's top law enforcement agency, the FBI had jurisdiction for criminal prosecution in all domestic cases. The CIA covered everything foreign except for crimes committed on American property overseas, like terrorist bombings of American embassies or military bases, where the FBI had primary authority. But like everything else, even when terrorism was involved, turf issues invariably intervened.

So the CIA, the FBI, and ATF -- Alcohol, Tobacco, and Firearms at Treasury -- constantly fought with the Office of Homeland Security over who had access to what information in what priority with the result that all of them wound up duplicating data in massively expanding Federal databases that any reasonably quick teenager with peach fuzz and a nose ring could crack.

Taylor tried each of the half-dozen CIA mainframes with his authorized access code but kept getting the same cryptic response.

Invalid password. Access denied.

A frown creased his face.

"This is nuts," he said. "There's no access at all. Zip."

Sam called the Agency and spoke to his counterpart in another windowless basement cubicle.

"Systems are supposed to be down for maintenance," he said. "No idea when they'll be back up.   Maybe tomorrow, maybe Thursday. Give it another try then."

While Taylor was talking to Langley, Paul scanned the Polaroid of Lo Fengbu into a Bureau computer and initiated a file search using an object-based coding option. The FBI also had direct access to backup files from State.

Minutes later a confirmed match came back. At least they had Lo pegged.

Sam Taylor hung up, shaking his head.

Looking Cerrutti in the eye, he said, "Paul, something stinks pretty bad here. CIA's got redundant systems up the kazoo in Langley just like we do over here and they back up everything at least twice, too. No fucking way they're down for maintenance."

"So when do you think can you get in?"

"Can't. No time soon anyway. Seems like they don't want us poking around in their data right now.   It's a smokescreen.   We occasionally do the same to them. You know, the pecker principle."

Paul thought for a long minute.

He glanced at his watch and then back at Sam.

"You think you could manage to hack into a couple of computers in Beijing for me?"

○ **66** ○

Ellen was getting really pissed now.

She was angry with Phillips, furious that her own government would stoop so low, worried about Paul.

She wanted to call and warn him about Smolinski but Cathy Brewster wouldn't let her near a phone. She also had to call Commander Evans and warn him to strengthen security even further for Lo Fengbu. But she was trapped and going nowhere fast. She felt stuck in quicksand and her face showed her discontent.

She paced back and forth in front of the large window, alternately slapping at the curtains and glancing at the vacant alleyway in the off-chance she might see a passerby.

When Ellen heard her own phone ring again she stood stock-still. She figured it would be Paul again and she knew he'd be worried too. After a half-dozen chirps, the ringing stopped and voicemail kicked in.

Brewster emerged from the adjoining bathroom wiping her hands on a royal blue monogrammed terrycloth towel. She ignored the phone but caught Ellen's eye.

"Come on, Ellen, loosen up," she said. "This isn't going to hurt. It doesn't get any more important than this. Play your cards right, you just might enhance your career."

Ellen frowned as she stepped back from the window and approached her captor.

"I beg your pardon?" she snapped. "My career is out there, not in here, and it's sinking like a lead weight. This country's facing a potential disaster. You think you can just thumb your nose at the law and keep me prisoner?"

"Whatever it takes to get the President reelected," Brewster said.

Her tone was serious, almost scolding.

"You're a major liability to us right now and I have a reputation for neutralizing liabilities."

The lithe White House aide smiled and sat down on the settee.

She put an arm around the back of the couch and patted it, inviting Ellen to join her. When she crossed her legs, she exposed a long stretch of smooth, chocolate-brown thigh.

Nervously, Ellen sat down next to her on the couch.

"Look, it's like this," Brewster said, her voice softer. "I have A-list access to the President. I spend a lot of time with him, especially now that these China agreements are imminent. A word or two from me could open a lot of doors for you if you cooperate."

Cathy Brewster reached across and laid a manicured hand on Ellen's shoulder.

Ellen shivered. She began to see where this was going and she was not amused. But she saw the faint glimmer of an opening, the proverbial eye of a needle.

"What do you mean, cooperate?" she asked.

She leaned back coyly.

"Just sitting idly by, all cooped up, doing nothing in the face of a potential national crisis, waiting here helplessly with my hands tied behind my back?"

"That's not exactly what I meant," Cathy said. "You want to keep moving up, don't you? Well, maybe I can help."

Ellen leaned forward.

"Help? How?"

"Oh, in lots of ways. You'd be surprised, after we get to know each other a little better."

When Ellen crossed her legs, her foot brushed Cathy's knee.

"You have a pair of advanced degrees from a couple of first-class schools," Cathy said. "As do I. So the prospects of some heavy-duty networking come to mind."

Ellen tilted her head.

"Such as?"

"Such as Washington. I think you'd like it here. Work with me and I can get you anything you want in the Executive Branch. How about Health and Human Services?"

"Work with you? In what way, exactly?"

Cathy inched closer to Ellen and one by one, slowly unfastened the top two buttons on her own silk blouse, exposing firm breasts in a one-piece, black-lace Calvin Klein bra.

"You're an attractive woman," she said. "I'm an attractive woman. Doesn't that suggest something?"

"I thought you preferred men," Ellen said.

Her tone was softer now too.

"Powerful men."

Brewster smiled.

"I love people of power," she said. "Of every persuasion. Because they know how to cooperate."

Nodding slowly, Ellen leaned in closer. Her hand brushed Cathy's left breast.

"You mean, cooperate like this?"

She felt the nipple harden beneath her light touch.

"Exactly," Cathy said.

She shivered.

Brewster reached down between Ellen's legs and stroked her thigh.

"Is this what life is like in the White House?" Ellen whispered, her lips inches away from Cathy's.

"This is what life is like, period."

Cathy pressed her lips to Ellen's and felt a smooth arm reach around her neck.

As their bodies embraced, Cathy moaned as Ellen spread her legs in a widening V. Brewster's hand massaged a thigh.

"Oh, Cathy... "

"Resistance is futile," Brewster said softly.

Ellen feathered Cathy's lips with her tongue and as Cathy pressed against her she let her lips part. Cathy thrust her tongue deep into Ellen's mouth, pulling her closer.

Ellen sensed her opening and snatched it with confidence.

She bit down hard on Cathy's tongue and felt her sharp front teeth penetrate the upper and lower surfaces of the soft muscle. The reaction was instantaneous.

Brewster screamed.

She leapt back, pulling both hands over her mouth.

An instant later, she collapsed writhing onto the floor. Blood drained through her fingers, down her neck, onto her generous breasts, staining the sheer fabric of her lace bra and forming a dark pool on the antique beige carpet.

"You *bitch*..." she shrieked, but her badly swollen tongue muffled the words.

In one motion, Ellen leaped around her stunned body and grabbed the hotel telephone.

She punched zero.

Reception answered instantly.

"Emergency, Room 512!" she said breathlessly.   "Puncture wound, blood. Send a doctor immediately!"

She hung up.

Ellen found her cell phone and pocketed it. Grabbing her case, she ran quickly to the door. She stood quietly to one side and held a finger up to her mouth.

"Don't worry about your tongue," she said under her breath. "As a physician, I can assure you it will heal quite quickly, assuming you keep your mouth shut."

She heard the lock unsnap outside.

As soon as the door opened and a pair of familiar white EMS lab coats rushed into the room, she disappeared outside in a blur and locked the door behind her.

Ellen ignored the elevator and took the stairwell down to the basement two steps at a time. She emerged through a service entrance into the back alleyway alone.

Within minutes she was in a cab heading for Georgetown.

She whipped out her phone and punched in Paul's number. He picked up on the first ring.

"Ellen! I've been worried sick. What -- ?"

She interrupted him.

"Paul, listen up. There's no time for details. Drop everything. Get a cab and meet me in Georgetown right away."

She gave him an address.

"But – "

"I'll explain when you get there. Now get moving!"

Next she rang the Coast Guard in Aberdeen and got Commander Evans on the line.

"You need to double the guard in the isolation ward and keep Lo Fengbu out of harm's way," she said. "Around the clock."

She gave him a shorthand version of her day in Washington.

"We'll triple it," Evans said.   "And keep McKee there with him."

∘ **67** ∘

Co-pilot Li Guizhou listened nervously to the radio signals from Newark.

He lowered his back wing flaps to increase drag and dropped another five thousand feet to the designated holding altitude. Perspiration streamed down his face in small rivers. He was trying to guide the widebody jet safely down without being distracted by the persistent chaos behind the cockpit door.

The mob of adult passengers was angry now, and scared. They demanded immediate assistance. Raising havoc in the main cabin, they threatened lawsuits. They said China Airlines would never again fly into U. S. airspace. But it was the screaming children who worried Li the most. He knew something was horribly wrong.

Li's hand shook uncontrollably as he reached to push down on the throttle. He sighed with relief as he felt the airspeed drop. He coughed -- once, twice, three times. Then he sneezed again. If he could just hold on until they got to the gate.

He wiped his nose on his sleeve because there were no tissues left. There were no paper towels, no airsickness bags, no plastic cups, no blankets, nothing.

Newark ATC picked him up and squawked their code into his headset. One of the controllers asked about the clamor in the background, all that noise coming from the cabin.

"Yo, China-four. Everything all right up there?

Li Guizhou acknowledged in the affirmative.

He could begin to make out the parallel runway lights now, with the huge heavy-duty dockside cranes of Port Elizabeth illuminated in the distance, familiar shapes that reminded him of the giant Trojan horses of ancient Greece he'd studied so long ago in school.

Then he leaned back in his leather seat and relaxed.

They were landing him south-to-north today, which he knew would work to his advantage.

Because as soon as China-four touched down he could slam on the brakes, kick in the reverse thrust and taxi straight to Gate 57 at Terminal B.

◦ **68** ◦

When Ellen saw the intersection of Wisconsin Avenue and O Street, she told the taxi to pull over and stop. For her own protection she got out and went the rest of the way on foot, zigzagging across the street every fifty feet.

She was about a hundred yards short of her ultimate destination when she stepped quickly into a coffee bar. She declined a menu three times as she glanced furtively outside the plate glass window to make sure she wasn't being followed.

She scrambled back outside and scurried up O Street until she saw the brownstone she knew so well. She took the stairs two at a time.

The door opened as soon as she reached the stoop.

Ellen ran past the aide and jumped into the waiting arms of Lieutenant General John J. Wilcox. She threw her small arms around his broad shoulders and squeezed him tight.

"You don't know how glad I am to see you, Uncle Jake."

She squeezed him harder and wouldn't let go.

The General held her in his arms as he had done so often when she was young.

Smiling down at her, he said, "Ellie, if you don't unhook your arms, I'll have to call a specialist to fix my neck."

She unwrapped herself from his solid frame and looked up into his face. His hair was soft and ash-gray but still full. He wore a pair of half-frame tortoise-shell reading glasses that accentuated his height.

"Sit down, Jake," she said. "We've got to talk and we may not have much time. This case keeps getting more dangerous and unpredictable by the hour."

Lieutenant General John J. (Jake) Wilson was a three-star general in a city where it took at least a two-star to get anything done. He had earned his spot in the sun in 1990 during the Gulf War against Iraq as Chief of Staff to Stormin' Norman Schwarzkopf, helping to craft the strategic battle plan that won so decisively for the West.

Whenever Gen. Schwarzkopf gave his public briefings or convened a news conference, Brigadier General Wilson was never visible. He was always off to one side or standing behind a curtain but his scripted words were always audible out front.

When Chairman of the Joint Chiefs Colin Powell retired from active duty in 1996 and the popular Schwarzkopf followed him, Wilcox was promoted to Major General and sent to NATO as deputy to General Wesley Clark, who commanded the European strike force against the Serbs in Kosovo three short years later.

As he had proven in the past, Maj. Gen. Wilcox was an invisible if invaluable aide to Clark and created the brains behind a covert information assault on Belgrade.

It was Jake Wilcox who commandeered a group of computer experts at the Pentagon. Their secret and successful invasion of enemy databases secured access to the Serbs' advance war plans, enabling NATO allies to destroy strategic enemy targets with their advanced, object-tracking, computer-guided weapons.

At the dawn of the new century, Wilcox returned to Washington and was promoted again, this time to a full three stars. The Joint Chiefs of Staff gave him supreme command of CBDCOM, the U. S. Army's Chemical and Biological Defense Command headquartered at DOD. CBD had prime responsibility in case of a terrorist attack, regardless of where the enemy was based or what weapons were used.

In the world of Washington acronyms it was once known as NBC, which lumped Nuclear together with Biological and Chemical. The Pentagon created CBD so they could maintain a separate and distinct command for nukes as special weapons of mass destruction.

Two decades earlier, Colonel Jake Wilson had been stationed at Fort Randolph in San Antonio when his wife Lucy collapsed with a heart attack. When she was hospitalized at the base, the Army doctors urgently recommended a specialist. The closest and best cardiologist in Texas was Dr. William Hartley in Dallas. He flew to Randolph immediately and completed a complicated 3-hour surgical bypass procedure that successfully defibrillated her heart and restored its pace to normal.

Having saved Lucy's life, Bill Hartley became an intimate friend of the General's and Ellen had a new aunt and uncle who took her into their lives. Wilcox could never forget what Ellen's father had done for them. Since they were unable for other medical reasons to bear children, there was nothing they couldn't and didn't do for Ellen.

Ellen cut straight to the bottom line for Jake. She gave him chapter and verse from that morning's briefing, Harper's clearance putting her officially back on the case, and details of her bizarre encounters both on the Farrugut North platform and at the Hay Adams hotel. Since neither of them had eaten, the general buzzed an aide and ordered sandwiches.

As they waited, Gen. Wilcox said, "You know, Ellie, I thought about what you said when you called previously from Atlanta and again last night from Seattle. I spoke off the record with our attaché in the White House. The situation doesn't look good."

"Tell me about it," she said. "It's getting really absurd. The White House wonks keep hammering me and until this morning they had successfully pressured Harper into muzzling me, too. Can the China agreements be so critical that the President would risk an infectious epidemic in our own country just to get them?"

Jake Wilcox removed his half-frames and stared at the floor.

"Political expediency is always ugly," he said, his voice soft. "Especially when it concerns the White House. You know my feelings about politics."

"But what do your people at the Pentagon say?"

"Not much. There seems to be no solid basis to your hunch about China. We've gone through back channels all the way to the top of the PLA in Beijing. It took time to locate General Li because he's ill himself and recuperating in Tianjin. But he adamantly denies any involvement of the PLA in bioweapons and I believe him."

"But the data!" Ellen interjected. "Atlanta has proof that the killer virus was genetically cloned and Lo Fengbu has told us that the covert flu factory's in Jiangxi province."

"I realize that, Ellie, but --"

The front doorbell rang, interrupting them.

"I'll get it," she said, jumping to her feet. "That's probably Paul."

When she let him in, they embraced and the two men shook hands as the general's aide emerged with a tray of food.

"So what the hell was going on when you couldn't pick up?" Cerrutti asked.

She gave him a crisp synopsis and watched as his eyes widened with each detail.

Paul Cerrutti thought for a long minute.

"Dollars to doughnuts that subway incident was related to Eddie Liu," he said. "Now that he's in custody, we should be able to find out pretty easily."

"But what did the second man mean when he said it didn't concern me?" she asked. "He spoke fluent Mandarin."

Cerrutti shrugged his shoulders.

"We may never know," he said. "But it wouldn't surprise me if they were from rival gangs. We barely understand the Byzantine rules by which the Dragons live. The main thing is you're safe, and what happened today almost trumps what I got for you."

He told them about Taylor's unsuccessful efforts to access the CIA database. But Sam had hit pay dirt when he hacked into Chinese government computers in Beijing. He had cracked the PSB database and those of the PLA and the Ministry of Foreign Affairs. The only ones triple firewall-protected were in the Politburo and the Central Committee.

"But how --?"

"It was easier than Sam expected," Paul said, pacing now on the General's carpet. "We know the Chinese government is scared to death about their people having access to computers outside China. So they spend all their time trying to prevent them from getting out. University profs, intellectuals, entrepreneurs, they're all harassed by random searches and late-night visits by the PSB. They also have to register their passwords so the police can track them whenever they're online. The cops monitor foreign databases and websites around the clock. But they're so paranoid about their own people getting out that they have virtually no defense against anyone from the outside getting in."

Ellen sat forward on the edge of her chair.

"So what did Sam find?"

"We already had the data on two low-level scum-suckers from our own computer system. They were just discards. But once Sam hacked through to Beijing, he ran multiple searches for Fu with all your forename combinations. Turns out there was a Fu Baixi but he's just a meaningless junior clerk at the Foreign Ministry. And a Fu Baixu who's a low-level functionary in the Wuhan branch of the PSB. There was no Fu Barji."

He stopped pacing and looked at them both.

"But there *was* a Fu Barxu," he said, reading from his notes. "Career PLA, top guy. Graduated 20 years ago from Dengshen

Military Academy with highest honors. Highly decorated during the border disputes with Russia and Vietnam. Special assignments to Pakistan and Iraq. Rose to the rank of Colonel. Had a covert assignment in Shanghai during the early 90's because the data said only 'Temporary Leave, Internal Priority.' "

"That's it?" Jake Wilcox said, frowning. "That's not much to go on, Paul. We put our best people on special assignment all the time -- covert, need-to-know access only."

"Yeah, but get this," Paul went on. "He drops off the database completely about two years ago. Then it's totally dark, nothing but a single three-letter alphanumeric acronym, M21. Nothing since. No new assignments, no awards, no promotions, nothing. Does a top officer and rising star in the People's Liberation Army suddenly just disappear into the ether? I don't think so."

The room was silent for a moment. They could hear the loud ticks of a tall grandfather clock that stood against a far wall in the alcove.

Ellen snapped her fingers.

"Jake, can you get a copy of the Beijing delegate list so we can see who's coming to San Francisco on Thursday?"

"I've already taken care of that," Paul said. "Sam's working on it as we speak. He's trying to get into the White House database this afternoon."

"No need for him to risk that," the General said. "I can call one of my guys at the Pentagon and get a copy."

Turning to Ellen, he said, "You think this Colonel Fu may be on that list?"

"I don't know," she said. "But it wouldn't surprise me if he were. At this point, nothing would. Jake, if this were the other way around and the President was on an important state visit to Beijing, wouldn't he take key military aides along?"

Wilcox stared at the carpet, stroking his chin.

"Of course, he would," the General said, nodding. "That's SOP. I assume the Chinese will do the same and bring General Li if he's well enough to travel. But they wouldn't include lower-ranking officers like colonels and neither would we."

"But if you saw something like this in your own database, wouldn't you say the guy doesn't want anybody in his government to know what he's up to?"

"Except for his commanding officer. A Colonel would never act on his own."

Paul snapped his fingers.

"Ellie, Atlanta says the killer virus was genetically mapped, deliberately cloned. And Lo confirmed the source as Jiangxi. I have an idea. General, can you get me a piece of paper?"

Jake Wilcox went to a desk in one corner and pulled out a yellow pad.

"Here's China," Paul said, drawing a large oval on the pad. "And Hong Kong's down here, with Fuzhou here. If my geography's any good, the province of Jiangxi should be about here. Right smack in the middle of -- what did you call it?"

"The flu epicenter."

He sketched a smaller circle at the bottom inside the larger one.

"Where are you taking this, Paul?" Ellen asked.

"Watch. So Fu drops off their radar screen. I'm thinking, if we did something like this why would we do it? To mask a secret operation, pure and simple, right? So maybe we have another piece of the puzzle. If Atlanta knows the killer virus has been manufactured and Lo has pinpointed Jiangxi, let's find the goddam factory. Maybe we'll find this Colonel Fu there, too."

"But I've got Stan Novak's daily reports from IVD and they confirm there's no unusual flu activity in China's regional reporting centers."

"Not from any *legitimate* sources," Paul said. "But we're looking for something secret and illegal. This operation may be completely independent of the PLA, with Fu working under deep cover."

"You're talking coup, Paul?" Ellen asked.

"Exactly. Maybe Fu and his commanding officer have something covert up their sleeves."

He turned to Wilcox.

"Jake, it takes a three-star to authorize an unscheduled satellite scan. Let's point one of your birds at southern China and take a look. You have that high-resolution imager, the -- "

"Chronos-II," Wilcox said, nodding.

He shot a glance at his watch.

"I'll call O'Flaherty right away."

Ellen shook her head.

"But the weather's notorious there this time of year," she said, frowning. "Thick clouds, constant rain, humidity like a thick blanket. You'll never see anything."

The General smiled.

"Chronos has 1-meter resolution, Ellie," he said. "Weather's not a limitation anymore. This digital camera is ten times more powerful than SPOT-4 or Radarsat. You can read the fine print on a postage stamp from up there."

Wilcox picked up the phone. He called the National Reconnaissance Office and gave NRO a crisp, two-sentence command.

Ellen thought for a minute. She got up and paced in front of the big clock.

"Jake, there's got to be somebody in the President's inner circle who will listen to reason. Surely they're not all knee-jerk political junkies over there. Who can you turn to when you want the straight stuff?"

The general leaned back in his swivel chair and stared at the ceiling.

"If I wanted the unvarnished truth or needed to get something straight to the President with no spin," he said, "I'd call Henry Warshevsky. He's on loan from the National Security Agency and has served presidents of both parties. Everybody likes him because he's non-partisan and his NSA credentials are squeaky-clean. Plus he's got a built-in bullshit detector that makes him invaluable."

Ellen walked forward and put a hand on her uncle's shoulder.

"Then I think you ought to give him a call," she said. "We're going to need a little help on the inside because the President shouldn't go into Thursday's meeting naked."

Suddenly an ear-piercing alarm rang. An amber light began flashing on the general's office wall.

Wilcox reached across and pressed a button.

"Yeah."

A speakerphone squawked to life.

"General Wilcox, sir? CBD Ops here. Early Bird, sir. Repeat, Early Bird."

"*Jesus*! Where?"

"EWR, sir. Terminal B, Gate 57."

Jake Wilcox flicked off the speaker and shouted to his aide.

Seconds later, the three of them were out the door.

∘ **69** ∘

Tuesday, September 29.
5:23pm.
Rush hour in New Jersey.

Master Sergeant Michael (Big Mike) McGuire stood outside the motor pool at the 15th Tactical Support Division of I-Corps, First Army, CBDCOM, in Edison, pumping a clenched fist up and down while the sharp scream of his whistle pierced the air.

"Let's get these chariots *moving!*" he yelled. "This is no drill."

The long olive drab convoy accelerated onto U. S. Route 1, heading north toward Newark. A line of jeeps was in front, red lights flashing. One peeled off at each of the seventeen intersections between Edison and the airport, shutting down cross traffic so the huge chain of humvees, personnel carriers, fuel trucks, communications trailers, explosive containment vehicles, tow trucks, light arms haulers, medical units, food trucks, water tanks, and container carriers stuffed with decon gear, transparent patient bubbles, yellow moon suits, double-density body bags, power generators, construction equipment, ventilator units, HEPA-respirators, tarp and tape could proceed at full speed, nose-to-butt and unimpeded, until they reached their target destinations.

These were the First Army's Early Responders, the sharply honed 2,585 men and women of the crack ER team of the 15th TSD, CBDCOM. They wore canary yellow caps with mirrored initials [ЯE] stitched in block letters above the bills in black, and canary-colored rubberized protective jackets with the same logo over the left breast and in giant jet-black capitals on their backs.

Their names were sewn over the right breast below a symbol that signified their specialty.

A telephone handset for communications. Skull and crossbones for decontamination. Red cross for medic.

And stenciled on the sides of every land vehicle and chopper was the 15th's motto:

Target Perfection, Hit Excellence.

This was their call. This was what they were trained for. Every single one of them down to the greenest private knew exactly where to go and precisely what to do.

And tucked in a zippered shoulder pocket, each and every one of them had the most current version of the HP/UP analyzer chip for positive diagnosis of microbe specificity. Theirs was a generation ahead of the device Ellen Chou had used in Hong Kong.

It was the new prototype with a small, disposable latex-rubber cup that fit over the mouth. A simple exhalation of breath could now confirm the presence of a suspect virus. Collecting and testing sample fluids with delays of even a few minutes was no longer necessary.

A row of ten MH-53J Screaming Apache helicopters loaded up and lifted off in a cloud of debris from the tarmac directly behind Big Mike McGuire. They thundered overhead, rose in sequence, and arched up single-file to follow and eventually overtake the convoy above Route 1.

They carried the initial wave of frontline enforcement troops, communications specialists, and emergency medics who would be first on the scene to plug the tunnels, stop the trains, and block exits 13, 13A, and 14 on the New Jersey Turnpike until every incoming traveler could be checked and cleared. Each twin-engine, heavy-lift Apache carried 35 men and women and 2 tons of advance gear.

Colonel Frank Murphy sat in a forward chopper with the CBDCOM incident command team.

He spoke non-stop over a wireless radio using digital encryption on a dedicated frequency of 2.783 GHz, punching through a sequence of autodial numbers that connected him instantly to every police force, fire department, and emergency medical team in Essex County, New Jersey's third most populous but most densely packed urban center. They in turn would put the four neighboring counties -- Hudson, Passaic, Morris, and Union -- on standby alert.

When Murphy gave the simple two-word command code, everybody kicked instantly into gear. For Newark, it was Early Bird. For Los Angeles, Sun Set. For Chicago, High Rise. Each of the 15 ER units across the country had its own instantly recognizable command code.

As Murphy's chopper screamed toward the airport access road, the Colonel could see the first civilian teams already arriving on the scene. Newark police had begun to barricade the airport exits; no one could now get out.

Horns blared, a torrent of unambiguous New Jersey curses filled the air and tempers flared as angry drivers craned their necks, honking and shouting at the cars ahead of them. Fights erupted at the tollgates until the 15th's crowd control specialists arrived and settled the disputes with authoritarian quickness.

There was no explanation given, none needed. The bullhorns said it all.

"Emergency! The airport is now closed. Shut down your engines."

Col. Murphy and his 3-man command team set down in front of Terminal B and jogged across the linoleum floor of the arrivals section on the lower level. Their boots echoed off the hard surface as they ran toward the special office reserved for CBDCOM located between Customs and Immigration.

They could see the stunned faces of confused passengers watching as the canary-jacketed Army team hustled through the crowd. People stared at ceiling speakers, transfixed by the repeated message.

"This is an emergency. The airport is closed. Step aside and make way for the yellow jackets. Repeat: make way for the yellow jackets."

As Col. Murphy began outfitting his command post, the first tow trucks and humvees carrying Captain Damon Carter and his conversion crew arrived at the multi-story AAPCO Parking Garage directly across from the airport entrance on Route 22.

The cavernous structure had a capacity of 1,053 cars. On Tuesday, September 29, just before 6:00pm Eastern time, there were 681 vehicles parked in the stalls. Vehicles belonging to passengers who were just departing or would soon return.

Tow trucks smacked through the barrier gates, roared up the garage incline and spiraled up to the roof on the 7th floor. Hook under the rear axel, jack it up, take off. One by one, the tow trucks followed each other like links in a giant chain, empty up the ramp and dragging cars behind them as they came back down.

Each and every one of the 681 sedans and SUVs, late-model luxury models and ancient wrecks, vans and light trucks, 4x4s and suburban station wagons were coming out to be stored in a specially marked asphalt lot behind the Anheuser-Busch brewery not a hundred yards away. Never let it be said that Budweiser wasn't brewed in the national interest.

When the tow trucks had emptied the top levels, Captain Carter's installation crew was right behind them with their special gear. Their yellow jackets glistened in the overhead lights as they installed a bank of water tanks along one side of the roof. Perpendicular to those, they set up a supply center and stocked it with medical supplies from the trucks.

Stethoscopes, blood pressure cuffs, gauze, breathing tubes, rimantadine anti-viral drugs, hypodermic syringes, IV feeds, surgical masks, latex gloves, disposable nursing gowns. Full loads up the ramp, empty trucks down. The drivers knew exactly where to go and precisely what to offload next.

Starting with miniature, hand-held battery-powered jackhammers on the 6th floor, a conversion team went from stall to parking stall smacking I-bolts into the floor and ceiling directly along each of the parallel yellow lines. Their platoon partners moved in sync right behind them, stringing heavy-gauge high-tension wire through the bolts and clipping tarpaulin curtains to the wire.

Other supply trucks roared up to the 6th floor to begin offloading convertible beds that another ER team quickly unfolded and set in place. Two legs of each bed were 0.625" shorter along one side to allow for the 6.973° slope of the parking ramp so the bed surfaces would be flat.

At one end, another team set portable toilets in place directly beneath the rooftop water supply. Next to them came the portable shower stalls and washbasins.

Directly underneath, identical teams converted the 5th floor. And others worked the 4th floor directly beneath them, floor by floor down to ground level.

Simultaneously, a team of rope climbers began rappelling from the rooftop, smacking I-bolts into the side of the building and pulling tarps into place.

To their right, teammates snapped sections of polyurethane water pipe vertically into position with outlets at each floor to supply the portable showers and washbasins. To their left, others installed powerful HEPA-filtered ventilating units at each level, wrapping them in duct tape and sealing their sides to the tarp. Below them, a rack of refrigerated container trucks angle-parked on the ground level, ready to take on body bags as a temporary morgue.

Captain Damon Carter stood at the garage entrance as the last truck roared out. He looked at his watch. Forty-seven minutes, 15

seconds.   Not bad, he thought.   Their target: 50 minutes to convert
AAPCO's 7-story, 1,053-car parking garage into a fully functional,
state-of-the-art, negative-pressure, makeshift hospital ready for triage
and quarantine.

On the roof, a soldier hammered a temporary pole into place
and ran up a yellow flag.

Downstairs at the entrance another member of the 15th TSD
hand-stenciled three distinct symbols in black ink on a large metal sign
with a canary yellow background illuminated by a powerful spotlight.

A/H5N1.

35.2%.

Q.

As Capt. Carter flashed a thumbs-up for the converted garage,
Lt. Gen. Jake Wilcox was on the radiophone with Col. Murphy.   His
UH-1 Skyhawk light-lift command helicopter settled like a huge
butterfly onto the asphalt outside Terminal B.

Turning to Paul and Ellen, he cupped a hand over the phone.

"This is it for you guys," the General said.   "I have to run this
show from Edison.   You need anything, talk to Murph."

The CDC detective and the FBI agent jumped out of the
chopper, jackets and caps in place.   Ellen pulled a HEPA-respirator
into place over her face.   Cerrutti steadied her with an arm around her
shoulder as the helicopter lifted off again in a wash of air.

"I'm going in with Murphy," Paul shouted.   "You heading for
the gate?"

Ellen nodded.

"I know where to find you," she yelled back.

They held onto their caps and watched as the single-engine
Curtis workhorse hammered into the air above them, veered sharply
and disappeared to the south.

As he ascended, Jake Wilcox could see the 15th TSD team living
up to its motto.

Traffic was at a standstill around the perimeter of the airport.
No vehicles went in or out.   Trucks, buses, taxis, private cars, delivery
vans all stood stock-still, frozen in time.   In the distance Wilcox saw
flashing red lights at the nearby Turnpike exits, where the 15th medic
teams had stopped every vehicle to check whether their occupants had
deplaned from China Air 004 or had come into contact with anyone
who had.   They were testing everyone with the HP/UP breathalyzer
chip.

As he swung around to look west, he saw roadblocks in place on I-78 and I-280 where another TSD team performed the same function. Exit traffic on Route 1, directly beneath him, was still under control of the forward jeeps. Just ahead, a NewsChopper 4 helicopter angled toward the airport control tower. Wilcox nudged his pilot to intercept.

The pilot fired two quick warning bursts from a 7.62mm minigun and they watched as the intruder rose and veered away. The general would catch hell for that later but this was serious business: total press blackout until he gave the word.

Next he radioed Washington on the same dedicated frequency to check the status of his Executive Order. He'd jumped rank on the Commander of New Jersey's National Guard and he needed those orders from the Pentagon. The Governor would be furious as soon as he heard the news that Essex County had been placed under martial law without his advance approval and concurrence. But there was no other way. With an infectious disaster potentially putting millions of American citizens in harm's way, only one person could take charge.

Wilcox acknowledged the report and radioed out.

The White House had approved the Order and faxed a copy to the Governor's office in Trenton as well as to the National Guard. The General had been a little devious when he made his request to the Pentagon. He'd accurately cited the deadly virus and the planeload of infected passengers but he had intentionally omitted the fact that it was a China Airlines flight. He was counting on the shock effect when the President saw the eye-opening two-word Early Bird command code, and he'd been right.

Three-star Lt. Gen. John J. (Jake) Wilson now ruled Essex County.

∘ **70** ∘

Ellen bounded up the stairs from the tarmac to Gate 57. Despite her identical gear, the yellow-jacketed guard unshouldered his automatic weapon when he saw her coming.

Orders were orders. He was taking no chances.

Ellen unzipped her jacket and fished out a plastic Motorola RF/ID card that hung on a small chain around her neck. Smaller and thinner than a credit card, it contained a measly 512 bits of digital data that identified her, her authority, and her function in a national emergency.

When she waved it over her head, a tiny wireless transmitter embedded in the card beamed a constant stream of her personal data via radio frequency to a dedicated desktop in Col. Murphy's incident command post a level below. His computer processed the bits instantly and unlocked the door, letting her in. As soon as she went through she heard the lock reset immediately with a loud click.

She ran down the corridor to Gate 57 and saw a young African-American public health inspector, masked and gloved, standing inside the windows that had been cordoned off with black-and-yellow crime scene tape. She knew they were on negative air because she had to tap on the window above a ventilator unit that had been set and taped into the cracked glass below.

Ellen froze when she saw the scene in front of her.

It was Hong Kong all over again. She knew she wouldn't need her microanalyzer because the telltale signs of the killer virus were unmistakable.

The cramped space was jammed with sick travelers, sneezing, coughing, throwing up. Strings of bloodstained mucous hung from their mouths like rotten spaghetti as empty stomachs spewed out sparse remains. Some adults sat slumped against a wall in soiled clothing, dazed, as they tried to comfort crying children. Others lay on the carpet, oxygen masks fixed to vomit-smeared faces. Still others stood weakly in line berating the China Air ground crew who were trying in vain to cope with a totally alien situation. Behind gauze masks, their tired, drawn faces and confused looks said they weren't succeeding.

This was no drill.

This was real.

Ellen entered the holding area.

"Shawna," the African-American public health officer said, extending a hand until she realized they were both gloved. "Shawna Alexander. Good to see you, Dr. Chou."

She read Ellen's name off her jacket.

"What've you got here, Shawna?"

They had to shout over the pandemonium.

ER medics moved from patient to patient, tagging them for triage in the method they knew so well. Black tags symbolized no hope; these people were gone, beyond help. They needed a body bag. Red tags meant urgent and immediate assistance; they got priority attention for transfer to the temporary hospital. Green tags signified the walking wounded, people with no signs of infection who could be left unattended but quarantined while the ER medics continued to triage the others.

"It's ugly," the young inspector said, scanning a clipboard in her hand. "China-four had a full house -- 283 passengers, 15 crew. Pilot never alerted the tower so it was a huge mess from the get-go. To make matters worse, they landed at the same time as four other jumbos from overseas -- Lufthansa from Frankfurt, BA from London, Air France from Paris, Continental from Tokyo. More than two thousand travelers have turned international arrivals into massive gridlock. Fortunately, most of them are still down in immigration or baggage claim so we can keep them from getting out."

"Have you checked all the names against the China-four manifest?"

"Yeah, but-- " Shawna Alexander said, shaking her head.

"But what?"

"By the time I got here more than a dozen had already pushed their way past the airline staff. I have their names here. We're trying to track them down now."

Downstairs in international arrivals, Bitsy Salomon handed two passports to Immigration and Naturalization Service officer Wayne Luciano, who sat in a small standard-issue cubicle behind a gray Formica counter. One passport was hers, one was her husband's.

Skip Salomon stood behind her and leaned on the Plexiglas window that separated incoming travelers from INS officials. Holding his stomach, he coughed at his shoulder and winced at the pain

Behind him, the long lines of returning citizens stretched beyond the snake-like stanchions into the corridor beyond. The terminal's AC system was down so the air was stale and still.

"Please don't lean on the glass, sir," inspector Luciano said politely without looking up.

He scanned their passports into his computer and watched as the screen processed the data. Finally, he looked up and smiled.

"Sounds like a bad cold you got there, Mr. Salomon. You must be pretty glad to be back."

"You don't know the half of it," Skip Salomon said hoarsely. "Whole goddam airplane was puking except for my wife."

"Lots of bad Chinese food up there, eh?" the passport officer said. "Never touch the stuff myself, even down here on terra firma if you know what I mean. All that MSG, you know? Whole bunch of you folks coming through sick today, apparently."

The screen cleared and released the Salomons' passports.

"Welcome home," Wayne Luciano said again, and smiled as he pushed the passports back toward Bitsy on the counter.

They nodded as they wheeled their carry-ons by Inspector Luciano's Formica counter toward the escalator that would take them past baggage carousel #4 one level down, through customs to the Star Limo driver they knew would be waiting two levels below.

Upstairs, Ellen grabbed the passenger list and glanced at the circled names.

She froze.

Seventeen sick people had gone through baggage claim, coughing and sneezing on others. They had cleared customs, handed their infected passports to immigration officers, hailed cabs, taken buses, rented cars, met friends on arrival, maybe walked straight across to the Airport Marriott and put another entire building at risk.

"Who's working it?" she yelled.

"Murphy's team, downstairs."

Ellen nodded and reached for the door. She stepped aside as an Army team came in bearing a patient bubble. They loaded another red tag, zipped up the bubble, and rushed out. Another bubble was right behind it, and another behind that in an endless column of transparent coffins.

Confident the medics had the gate under control, Ellen went to find Paul at Murphy's command post.

Snapping off her respirator mask, Ellen bounded down the stairs toward the basement level command post. When she tried to push through the door, it wouldn't budge. Something heavy but pliable blocked it. She stepped back and lunged at it with all of her 95 pounds.

The door gave way to a cascade of floodlights, camera crews, and hand-held microphones. Seeing her canary jacket and cap with the embossed logo, a TV broadcaster jostled through the crowd and stuffed a microphone in her face.

"FoxFive here. What's the latest, ma'am?" the interviewer asked.

Ellen's eyes narrowed.

"You know there's only one authorized source here," she shouted above the noise. "That's the incident commander, Colonel Frank Murphy."

Another Fox newscaster stuck her microphone through the thicket of jostling arms and smacked Ellen in the head.

"Rumor has it that terrorists have taken over the airport," she said. "Can you confirm this?"

"Get over to the Marriott," Ellen yelled. "They'll brief you there."

She shoved the microphones aside and knifed through the crowd.

More shouts followed her as she pushed through the jungle of bodies. When she got to the command room she pulled out her wireless card and waved it at the door. When it opened she shoved her way through.

Inside, perspiring visibly and breathless, she saw Murphy on the phone. Paul Cerrutti had a clipboard in one hand.

Turning to Paul, she said, "Can you tell me how those guys got down here?"

"One of their choppers was on the roof before we arrived," he said. "They were jamming the hallway as we came down."

"Then throw them a bone and radio for an armed escort to get them out of here," she said. "And do it right away. We'll never get anything done otherwise."

"First things first," Paul said, nodding. "Murph is working the list of passengers who slipped through, talking to the Newark cops right now."

As soon as the Colonel saw she was there, he finished and hung up.

In seconds, they crafted a cryptic statement for the press. Paul told Murphy about Ellen's briefing and the two attempted kidnappings in Washington. The China connection was too sensitive, Ellen argued. They had to turn this into a practice drill for the press. A simulation. If the full truth came out, the White House would have all their heads.

They called Edison. Wilcox concurred.

Before stepping out into the hallway, Murphy ordered a platoon down on the double. Moments later when the door opened and a Lieutenant stuck his head in, Murphy stepped out.

He announced the simulated exercise and said the platoon would escort them to the Marriott where they could listen to an official statement and hear regular updates. He disappeared back inside. There was an explosion of shouts and questions. The hallway went quiet as the horde of reporters was forced out.

"What's the sit-rep on the passengers?" Ellen asked.

"As usual, a little of this, a little of that," Murphy said. "Thank God only seventeen got out. Head count upstairs confirms 266 passengers and all the crew accounted for. My guys've been working the phones and found one family through their limo service, on its way home to HoHoKus. Another couple was in a Yellow Cab heading for Penn Station in New York. We ordered both drivers to stop and wait. If they're infected, the ER teams will bring them right back to the converted hospital for treatment and observation."

"So far, so good," Ellen said. "What about the others?"

Murphy shook his head.

"The remaining eleven either had their own transportation here at the airport or were met by friends. Because the DOT requires all American citizens to fill out a pre-departure form overseas before boarding, China Air had emergency contacts on file for all of them. I've dispatched two-man teams to each of their homes. We'll get them, don't worry."

He took the clipboard from Paul.

"One couple from Morristown, a family of three from Bridgewater, a quartet of singles in Manhattan, and an AT&T exec and his wife from Basking Ridge. We learned that this pair has a Star Limo waiting for them downstairs. They must have gotten trapped in the big INS queue so a team of yellow jackets is on its way to intercept.

The others don't know it yet but within the hour we'll be aware of every inch they took getting home, who they talked to, whom they met, where they stopped. Our guys are on it."

Ellen glanced at her watch and did a double take. It was nearly midnight.

A call came in from Captain Carter at the makeshift hospital.

As of 11:41pm, 281 passengers and crew had been admitted from China Air 004, 87 of them in body bags that had been black-tagged and placed in the refrigerated containers pending notification of next of kin. The hospital staff was frantically triaging the reds.

In addition, the ER team confirmed 227 other civilians, not from China-four but from the airport ground crew and support staff, all admitted to the upper levels with green tags. They were quarantined under strict security and being heavily dosed with rimantadine.

Ellen did the math quickly in her head. Thirty percent dead, one out of three.

The Jiangxi virus was still killing, and fast.

She turned to the Colonel.

"You've got things under control here," she said. "I'm going to check out the plane."

The door opened as she was about to leave.

"Took the words right out of my mouth, ma'am," the voice said.

He turned to Murphy.

"We'll take it from here."

The tall interloper had the letters FEMA stitched in red on his black cap. Joe Klemmer's stringy salt-and-pepper hair was pulled back in a ponytail, revealing a pale face pockmarked with the remnants of childhood chickenpox.

"Goddam it, Klemmer," Murphy said. "How many times do I have to tell you it doesn't work that way? Get the hell back upstairs and tell your people to stand by."

"Bullshit, Colonel," said Klemmer. "We're in charge now. We've got the legal specialists to deal with the airline and psychologists to work with the survivors to help them through the crisis. Plus the numbers crunchers to start figuring out how much this is going to cost the taxpayers."

Murphy jabbed an index finger in Klemmer's chest.

"Klemmer, tell your goddam people to back off. No way these people are ready for ambulance chasers and shrinks."

He grabbed the radiophone and punched in a single digit.

"General? FEMA's on our ass again. Here's Klemmer."

He tossed the handset to the man with the pony tail.

Joe Klemmer's face turned pale as a winter sky as he listened to Jake Wilcox. Ellen couldn't make out the words but she recognized her uncle's familiar voice thundering on the other end. Her father always said that Jake had ice water in his veins and balls like bricks.

Klemmer handed the receiver stiffly back to Murphy.

"We'll see each other again, Colonel," Klemmer said, spitting the words out. "And next time it won't be a goddam practice drill."

He went out the door and slammed it shut.

When Ellen got upstairs, the gate area had thinned as the 15th TSD medics had transferred the remaining passengers to the makeshift hospital nearby. Only canary jackets were left to deal with the aftermath.

Tugging her respirator mask back on, she ducked under the black-and-yellow barrier tape through the overlapped tarp by the negative air vent and went down the jetway toward the big jet.

A dozen yellow jackets were busy at work on the interior, collecting samples from clothing, blankets, vomited food, plastic drinking cups, personal effects. They made surface scrapings from the walls, lavatories, seatbacks, tray tables, overhead bins. Even though masked, Ellen knew how rancid the odor was inside. The cabin was a cylinder of death.

She saw a yellow-jacketed soldier spraying the inside of the fuselage with an aerosol can. He was not using the standard red decon tank that should have been strapped to his back. A cloud of dust-like particles followed him as he sprayed.

"Stop it!" she yelled at him through the respirator. "What do you think you're doing?"

She ran over to him and chopped at his arm. The can fell to the floor.

"Decon, ma'am," he said, surprised.

He straightened up.

"SOP, right?"

"Absolutely not," Ellen said. "Where's your sodium hypochlorite?"

"Portables are on the way," he said, jerking a thumb over his shoulder. "I found this in the meantime."

Stepping around him, she reached down and picked it up.

When she saw the plain black lettering on the white paper label, she realized instantly how the cabin had become contaminated. It was a scenario they had practiced themselves countless times.

"Just thank God you're wearing a respirator, soldier," she said. "Now get those decon tanks down here."

Ellen took the can but she couldn't dispose of it because the entire contents of the fuselage were contaminated and the can was medically hot. As she started to exit the cabin, another team arrived with the recognizable red tanks. She motioned to one of them to follow her.

She ran through the jetway and set up a temporary decon shower just inside the gate area in negative air. First she sprayed the can at her hand-held chip and watched the red LED indicator glow H5N1. Next they sprayed her jacket, gloves, rubber trousers, boots. Together they sprayed the chip and the aerosol container.

Holding the dripping can, she ran downstairs to the colonel's command post.

"Get me a bag, a box, anything I can pack this in," she said as she stormed through the door.

Murphy and Cerrutti stared at her, their faces haggard and drawn. When she told them what she was holding, one of Murphy's aides pulled an evidence bag out of his backpack.

"USAMRIID's closest," she said. "Chopper this down to Fort Detrick in Maryland along with the cabin surface scrapings right away. Label the packet toxic and mark it 'BL-3.' We need to know the substrate that's keeping this virus alive."

As the aide wrapped and packaged the aerosol can, the phone buzzed.

It was Wilcox.

"Jake, anything from the satellite scan yet?" Ellen asked.

"No, not yet," he said. "But I've got the delegate list from Beijing and we're faxing it over now. General Li must still be indisposed because it looks like Lt. General Min Taibao is taking his place. I've tangled with him before on weapons inspections and he's as hard-ass as they come. But check this out, Ellie. That dissident Lo Fengbu who's at Aberdeen is on the list too."

Ellen held the receiver in one hand and watched as the laser printer whirred and a single sheet emerged.

She grabbed it from the tray.

Her eyes narrowed when she saw the name that was now second-nature to her.

"But that's absurd, Uncle Jake. I personally spoke with him in the isolation ward two days ago and Paul's already confirmed his ID in the FBI database. He's recuperating under armed guard around the clock as we speak."

"Dime for a dollar the Lo on that list is your Colonel Fu, Ellie. Leave Newark to us. You and Paul get out to San Francisco. I'll call Warshevsky to alert the President and let VII Corps know you're coming."

○ **71** ○

Because China's capital city was a full 13 hours ahead of the East Coast, it was already mid-afternoon on Wednesday, September 30, when Colonel Fu Barxu called General Min.

They were preparing to depart for Beijing International Airport to join the official State delegation prior to boarding a specially equipped China Air Force jet that would ferry them non-stop to San Francisco that night.

The general had completed packing when he took Fu's call.

"What do you hear?" he asked. "The East Coast of America should be sheer chaos by now."

"Martial law in New Jersey," the rogue colonel said.

His voice rang with quiet excitement.

"China-four is down. Just confirmed by our attaché in Washington, who spoke with our contact at the Pentagon. But they have no details yet because of a press blackout."

Min managed a half-smile.

"Given the known rate of infection," he said, "the Americans could be coping with this disaster for months, maybe years."

"The Jiangxi virus is very hot," said Fu excitedly, "and the Russian's freeze-dried substrate can keep it alive for days, even on inert surfaces. The mortality rate will be nothing like they have ever seen."

"Still," Min said, "you will take no chances."

"Correct," Fu nodded. "The two large canisters are ready for California. Our official delegation won't be subject to baggage inspection at customs so there's no chance of their being detected. The single-engine plane is confirmed and I will be in Salinas by midnight tomorrow, ready to spray pre-dawn."

"I'll call our consulate in San Francisco from the official plane as we approach. They'll have more details, if not from Washington then certainly from the American news broadcasts. With their mindless addiction to violence, Americans love nothing more than high drama on their television news. As they put it, if it bleeds, it leads."

"Good," Fu said. "By the time we arrive, they'll be in total disarray. You keep me with you under guard as the disguised Lo Fengbu at all times. When the *fengpai* meets with the Americans the next day, we'll be ready to move. The core troops are in place?"

"All of them."

"*Hau.* Very good. I daresay you won't recognize the disguise when you pick me up. Lt. Kang has done a brilliant job, as usual."

"You choose your people well, my friend. You always have."

"It's a pity General Li cannot make the trip."

"Yes, I hear the flu season started unusually early in Tianjin this year."

∘ **72** ∘

Decontaminated and cleared for departure, Ellen and Paul waited on the rooftop helipad of Terminal B in Newark, watching the light-lift chopper from Edison lower into place. In the steady drizzle, backwash from the rotors wrapped them in a cloud of mist. They boarded and lifted off.

Ellen felt she was in a time warp with the airport eerily calm and quiet at 2:30 in the morning. Nothing was visible in the rooftop lights now but CBDCOM's yellow jackets, as if construction workers were putting the finishing touches on a brand new building.

They had left their personal gear on the general's Skyhawk when they landed from Washington so they'd shower and change in Edison before heading south to Philadelphia. It would be several days at the earliest before Newark could reopen.

Jake Wilcox had advised Ellen against taking a space-available military jet from Washington to avoid the unnecessary confusion when an unscheduled Army aircraft with civilian passengers sought clearance to land in the Bay Area so close to the arrival of both Air Force One and the official delegation from Beijing.

So the general's staff had booked them on the earliest commercial flight out of Philly Wednesday morning, scheduled to arrive San Francisco early afternoon local time.

The big Skyhawk stood by, ready to chopper south as soon as they changed. Before they left, Ellen hugged her adopted uncle and reminded him they wanted an update as soon as he had any images from Chronos-II.

He told her his team at I-Corps was working it and he'd call when he had word. He also said he'd speak with Warshevsky before the Washington delegation departed, to alert him to the likelihood of a diplomatic snag because of the doctored delegate list from Beijing.

Warshevsky had been in meetings all night and hadn't returned the general's call. Given the President's desperate re-election bid, they knew the China-four incident would have to be handled in the most delicate way possible.

In fresh clothes but tired bodies, Ellen and Paul arrived at Philadelphia International in ample time, only to learn that ATC had delayed all outbound flights because of the chaos in Newark.

Nearby airports like La Guardia, JFK, Pittsburgh, and Philly were taking the diverted flights, giving regional air traffic control fits and causing a jigsaw realignment of departures. But this was standard procedure after 9/11. No questions asked, no complaints.

To make matters worse, the American Airlines 757 widebody lost its place in the outbound queue after a maintenance crew had flagged a pair of worn brake pads that had to be replaced before the jet could be given clearance to leave. Ellen groaned when they learned the new departure time: eleven a.m.

While Paul hustled them a pair of muffins and some coffee, Ellen punched in the number of the Army's Medical Research Institute for Infectious Diseases. She wanted to make sure they had received the aerosol container and swab samples from the plagued flight.

USAMRIID confirmed their arrival. Capt. Jane Malloy was in the BL-3 lab analyzing them as they spoke. They patched her through to a wall-mounted speakerphone in the lab.

"No, no results on the substrate yet," she said. "We're starting to test the cabin samples now. Need another couple of hours before I can give you anything definite."

Ellen gave Malloy her cell phone number and said they'd probably be airborne but to call as soon as she could.

They scanned the Beijing guest list again while they waited.

Ellen recognized the powerful names that had become so familiar to her over the years: President Jiang Zemin. Premier Zhu Rongji. Foreign Minister Qi Xien. Minister of Commerce and Industry Zhang Yuan. Minster of Electronics and Information Wu Shiang. Even Lieutenant General Min Taibao as the delegation's senior military representative.

And there, buried in the middle of the list between the senior ministers and their lower-level aides, was the name that scared her to death.

Lo Fengbu.

Ellen noticed that the delegation was booked to stay at the Pacific Club under tight security.

Wonderful, she thought.

It was a great irony because she knew the famous club had always been a bastion of racism. Caucasians only, very exclusive, a long reputation as one of the most prejudiced private clubs in America. Not a single, hardworking Chinese -- whether immigrant or naturalized citizen -- had ever been allowed in except as an itinerant dishwasher in the kitchen or as a janitor to mop the floors.

Meanwhile, Paul knew the Bureau wouldn't give much credence to a field agent calling with news of a *possible* double agent *possibly* being smuggled aboard a China Air Force jet *possibly* bearing a lethal bioweapon with the most senior official delegation ever to visit the United States from Beijing.

They needed hard evidence. The hi-res satellite images. An undeniable link to Fu.

The Chronos-II had to give them *something*.

Ellen called Atlanta and asked McDermott to cover Malloy at USAMRIID while they were en route. Paul called Sam Taylor at the Bureau to see if he had heard anything from the Pentagon on the satellite scan. Negative.

Ellen called Jake again.

"Any word from Chronos-II?"

"Negative. Nothing yet."

"Warshevsky?"

"No."

They rang off.

She glanced at her watch. She snapped her fingers and quickly punched in Aberdeen. Once she had the Commander's office, they patched her straight through to McKee.

"How's our famous patient?" Ellen asked.

"Condition stable," the Coast Guard doctor replied. "He's still not too verbal but his vital signs look pretty good."

"I need to speak with him as soon as you think he's able," Ellen said. "He's the only one who can answer some critical questions. Try increasing his caloric intake. I'll call you back after we're airborne."

When he asked McKee about security, he said they now had Lo triple-guarded 24/7 and were scrambling all communications to and from the base.

Since she was officially back on the case, she called LeRoy Harper to say she was heading for San Francisco.

She told him about Lo Fengbu, and the Jiangxi connection and the bizarre incidents in Washington. He already had a direct report from Newark on China-four and asked her to call if she needed anything when she got to California.

It was nearly noon by the time they took off.

An hour later, Ellen's cell phone jarred her awake. She'd been dreaming of a granite coast and bright sun and clean air that she could breathe without the worry or weight of a filtered respirator.

It was USAMRIID. Capt. Jane Malloy.

"Ellen? This is some pretty weird stuff you sent us. Never seen anything quite like it."

Ellen stretched a stiff arm over her head as she blinked sleep from tired eyes.

"No doubt about the virus. Avian, right?"

"Yes, it's definitely H5N1. That part was easy. I'm talking about the substrate."

She sat up now, eyes wide.

"What do you mean?"

"Well, it's a freeze-dried substance, which we expected in an aerosol, otherwise the virus would just float away in the air and dissipate. But the base ingredient really threw us a curve. You're not going to believe this, but it's some kind of grain dust. Microscopic particles of corn or wheat. Really tiny, less than 3 microns in size."

Ellen's eyes darted back and forth in front of her.

"So the virus has a temporary host?"

"Precisely. It's not just an airborne weapon -- "

"But designed to stick to physical surfaces and infect at touch."

"Exactly. You say this stuff came off a flight from China, but the only folks we're aware of who can fabricate intermediate host particles this small are the Russians."

Ellen sat bolt upright in her seat. That brought them full circle, from China back to Moscow. Her mind raced in a dozen different directions at once.

"Thanks, Jane. Call me if you learn anything else."

She snapped the phone shut and quickly relayed the gist to Paul.

"Shameless cowards," she hissed.

Ellen could feel her heart thumping.

"This is doubly cruel," she said. "It's airborne so it attacks through the nose and throat. And it adheres to inert objects, infecting people from whatever they touch. Those poor passengers on China

Air. Not only did they breathe it, it was on everything they handled. Whoever cloned this killer virus did it perfectly."

She stared briefly out the window at the shapeless sky. They flew above a layer of angry rain clouds but below a cover of gray nimbus as thin as flannel.

"Paul, listen. Fu may be bringing the virus to San Francisco so he can hit both coasts. With diplomatic immunity there'll be no baggage search. But he must have something else in mind this time because the Bay Area is a peninsula surrounded on three sides by water. Like Manhattan, it's too easy to quarantine and just shut down. We've got to figure out what he's going to do!"

When they passed into Colorado airspace, flight attendants began cruising the aisle with carts of airline food. Food that had become increasingly cheap and convenient for every commercial carrier: dry cereal vacuum-packed in small plastic cups, fruit-flavored yogurt, bags of pretzels and chips, day-old fruit. Anything and everything to cut costs in an era of competitive airline deregulation.

Ellen looked up at a tiny, pre-packaged meal, hermetically sealed in cellophane on a petite plastic tray. She waved it aside.

Paul took a tray and asked for an extra salad.

"You know you'll be hungry before we land," he said.

"Hunger's the last thing on my mind, Paul."

She pulled out her cell phone and jabbed angrily at the buttons.

"Who're you calling?" he asked.

"McKee. See if Lo can tell us anything more."

When she heard McKee's familiar voice, she said, "Is our patient awake? I really need to ask him a few more questions."

"Hold on, let me see," McKee said. "He perked up after I doubled the ratio of glucose in his IV but he's still a little weak."

There was a short pause until she heard the weak patter of Mandarin on the line.

"Dr. Chou?" the feeble voice said. "I can't ... begin to thank you enough ..."

"We'll have plenty of time for that soon, Mr. Lo," she said excitedly. "But it's urgent that we know more about this deadly virus. Is there anything else you can tell us?"

There was another long pause as she listened. Her eyes darted back and forth and widened as Lo told her about the genetic cloning, about the Russian virologist, about Fu's intended disguise, about the crop dusting plan and the lettuce.

When she heard his voice falter, she broke in.

"Don't strain yourself," she said. "You've helped enormously. The Coast Guard will keep you safe and I will see you soon."

"*Nuoyàn?*" he asked.

"Promise," she said. "May I speak to Dr. McKee again?"

When he came back on the line, she said, "Remember, nobody goes near that room, even if they say they're from Washington. Lo's a vital witness to corroborate what we have to do next."

"When Evans says the room's secure, it's secure," he assured her. "Don't worry."

She put her phone away as Paul stripped the clear cellophane cover off the top of his miniscule salad. The crisp green lettuce sparkled like jade in the cabin lights. Ellen could hear the familiar snap and crunch as the person sitting to her right began eating.

"What'd he say?" Paul asked as he took a bite.

"Incredible," she said, her voice a whisper.

Grabbing the seat back in front of her, she stood up abruptly and looked around.

Virtually every passenger was chomping away on the cheapest, most popular, most readily available vegetable in America. She saw every salad as a potential bioweapon now, their innocent leaves coated with invisible microdroplets of the deadly virus.

"*Absolutely incredible!*" she cried under her breath.

"What?" he said between chews.

"*Lettuce!*" she said, grabbing his sleeve. "Lo confirmed the source of the killer virus and said they had a Russian named Lukanov who cloned it. He also gave us the rough location of the lab, which is in southern Jiangxi. The final phase of Fu's attack is underway. He's planning to dust lettuce fields in Salinas tonight."

She sat back down.

"Remember Oregon, five years ago, when the Bhagwan Cult infected salad bars in Portland by spiking all the dressing with salmonella bacteria? Well, this time it's not the salad dressing but the lettuce itself. And the largest lettuce-growing area in the world is in Salinas County."

She picked up her cell phone again and punched in another number.

"There are only two ways to broadcast an aerosol," she said, cupping the handset. "Line source from a moving object, like a crop duster or a helicopter. And point source, from a single location like a spray can or a windmill. During training we learned how our own government did it prior to signing the 1972 Bioweapons Agreement."

Paul pulled the airphone from between the seats in front of him.

"So who're we calling now?" he asked.

"4-1-1, information for area code 408. We need the numbers for every crop dusting and ag spray service in and around Salinas. We'll check them against hardcopy after we land."

A flight attendant interrupted, reminding all passengers to switch off their cell phones, computers, and electronic devices until the aircraft was on the ground and safely at the gate. Paul kept his airphone engaged and had connected with an operator when the pilot made another announcement to an orchestra of groans in the main cabin.

Strong headwinds had further delayed their arrival and the tower informed the cockpit that an angry mob of anti-Chinese demonstrators was clogging ground access into and out of San Francisco Airport. ATC had assigned all incoming commercial flights to a predetermined holding pattern until a priority military aircraft had arrived from the Far East.

American from Philly was currently number nine in line for landing at SFO.

° **73** °

As the gleaming white China Air Force jet with the crimson tail neared the rocky coastline of California, the turquoise ocean stretched out below like a giant swimming pool.

General Min Taibao phoned an attaché at the Chinese consulate in San Francisco and asked for a routine summary of the latest American news so he could brief the Beijing delegation prior to arrival.

He pulled a notepad from his breast pocket and unfastened a jet-black Mont Blanc pen as the consular attaché read him the news from a typical day in America.

Another incident of high school violence, he scribbled, this time in Chicago. Four teenagers killed, 21 wounded, by a local student depressed with his low grades.

A trio of militant Islamic terrorists had been arrested the day before as they attempted to cross into the United States from Vancouver. The trunk of their car was filled with plastic bags of urea and timed explosive devices.

A speedboat with a dozen dead Colombian cocaine smugglers on board was found adrift in the Gulf of Mexico near Mobile Bay, Alabama. More than a ton of drugs was recovered but no survivors.

"The east coast, what about the east coast?" Gen. Min hissed. "Anything from New York or New Jersey?

His voice showed the slightest hint of irritation.

"Not much," came the reply. "There was an isolated incident in northern New Jersey late yesterday, just a few seconds on the morning newscast today and a filler in the *Chronicle*. The American authorities announced another routine anti-terrorism practice drill at Newark Airport but gave no details. Situation normal."

The general's jaw dropped.

Routine practice drill? Situation normal?

He turned to Colonel Fu sitting next to him and wrote a cryptic note so as not to be overheard.

"Newark in question. Backup plan critical now. You go tonight for sure."

Fu frowned as he read the message. His mind churned as he rehearsed the precise scenario he would soon have to execute in detail.

When the seatbelt light chimed on, the cabin was quiet. After the pilot touched down, the large aircraft whispered to a stop.

The Chinese delegation deplaned and Fu glanced up at a bank of monitors on the wall. All the incoming flights from Newark blinked steadily with the same message.

Delayed.

Fu frowned again. Perhaps the authorities were still insisting on a press blackout. That's what we would do. Maybe the Jiangxi virus was loose after all.

He shook his head. Never mind. He was ready for the final phase.

A special contingent of the Secret Service met China's incoming flight. They escorted the official delegation to a fleet of American cars that had been arranged for their use by General Motors. GM was in the midst of delicate negotiations with Beijing for expansion of its huge assembly plant in Tianjin and needed to make a special impression on this important group of visitors.

The designated route, the Secret Service spokeswoman explained, was being kept secret due to the unexpected crowd of protesting demonstrators. Police estimated the mob at close to 50,000 people, she said. The White House had sent an emissary to ask the Beijing delegates not to take the demonstration seriously. The protestors were merely exercising their rights of free assembly and free speech, guaranteed by the Bill of Rights. The safety of the distinguished visitors was assured.

General Min slipped into the front seat of a metallic silver Buick Park Avenue sedan with charcoal-gray leather upholstery, as Fu in the disguise of Lo Fengbu climbed in the back. They drove single-file on the elevated ramp leading away from the VIP lounge and could see the massed throng on the arrival level below, shouting slogans and waving signs.

"Let the Chinese People Go! Stop Prison Labor Now!"

"Non-Tariff Barriers Unfair. China Exploits Women!"

"Shanghai Software Pirates, Go Home!"

The caravan accelerated when a small group of angry demonstrators recognized some of the occupants and pelted the cars with gravel flung by slingshot.

General Min turned around and caught the expression on Colonel Fu's face. He was thinking the same thing as he whispered into the back.

"We would never tolerate such chaos in Beijing."

Tall, colonial palms stood like sentries around the emerald-green perimeter of the elegant Pacific Club downtown. The convoy of late-model cars snaked through the circular driveway and deposited its guests under a canvas canopy dressed with the crimson and yellow bunting of China's national colors.

White House aides met each car and escorted the distinguished guests inside.

Fu and Min rode up the gilt elevator with a Secret Service escort, arguing in Mandarin about what happened at Newark.

"Wait until we're in the room," the General hissed.

"What for?" Fu asked. "These people can't understand us."

The three men walked down a corridor to Room 303. They saw one armed security guard posted at the elevator and another in a chair outside each room.

Two Chinese-American bellhops suddenly materialized bearing their luggage from the service elevator around the corner.

They were festooned in the Club's familiar maroon uniform, crisp starched jackets with three ash-gray stripes on each cuff, stiff white trousers, and an oversized pillbox cap, recognizable in San Francisco for more than a century as a symbol of privilege and exclusivity for the city's rich and successful Caucasian business elite.

"So how do you plan to get past those guards?" Min barked when they were safely in the room. "Did you think about *that* when you made this plan?"

Fu frowned.

"Stay calm and listen to me," he said. "This is what we're going to do."

◦ 74 ◦

It was nearly dusk when Ellen and Paul emerged through the American Airlines jetway. The Chinese delegation was being whisked away by their Secret Service escorts at the opposite end of the terminal as they made their way down the long concourse.

Inside the building the San Francisco police were posting large blue-and-yellow signs everywhere, announcing that access to the Bay Area Rapid Transit system would be sealed at 6:00pm. BART would be shut tight for 24 hours until six o'clock the next day for seasonal maintenance.

Paul knew immediately that Jake Wilcox had gotten through to VII Corps. There might be commuter chaos tomorrow but at least the subway system would be safe until the Chinese left. He glanced up at the arrival monitors, saw the flight delays from Newark and assumed the airport was still closed.

The crowd of demonstrators had begun to disperse from the airport entrance, forced away by a ring of mounted police in riot gear who lobbed tear gas and shot pepper spray at the rowdy mob. A burly task force of SWAT specialists with gas masks and riot shields ran through the crowd, splitting them into harmless splinter groups and separating them from their leaders. Obstinate and unruly picketers were handcuffed and thrown into waiting paddy wagons.

Microdroplets from the pungent pepper gas had been caught in the terminal's circulation system, which was not HEPA-filtered, and knifed through the lobby air. Passengers walked with handkerchiefs clamped to their mouths or dabbing their eyes. Small children walked behind their parents, eyes shut, temporarily blind and crying. Tears streamed down their cheeks.

"Come on," Ellen said, blinking away the sting. "We've got to get busy."

Since the airport exit was still blocked they hurried into the American Airlines AAdvantage lounge nearby.

"I have three numbers," she said, coughing. "You?"

"Two. Both helicopter services."

She pulled the Salinas County Yellow Pages from an overhead shelf.

One by one, they itemized the local ag spray services, eliminating San Francisco, San Jose, and other distant airports because they were too far from Salinas and would force Fu to waste too much fuel before reaching his target.

Helicopter Applications. AgRotors. York Aviation. Aerial Applicators. AgAir.

Like telemarketers, they spent the next hour talking to each of the aerial services.

Did they have any reservations for that evening? Any planes booked for individual flights? Any special services ordered? Any requests for special equipment?

One by one the answers came back negative.

No flights were booked for Wednesday night. No requests for special equipment that day. No orders for special services. Like a well-rehearsed chorus, they all said the summer spraying season was practically over and demand was virtually nil.

Besides, Paul learned, the copter services were both non-starters. Helicopter Applications told him that they permitted only their own pilots to fly; it was too dangerous otherwise, insurance premiums were prohibitive. AgRotors said both their machines were temporarily out of service for maintenance.

"What about charters?" Paul asked Ellen between calls.

"Fu would be smart enough to arrange something like that," she said. "But he'd need special nozzles under the wings and I doubt he could bring the heavy equipment from Beijing, even under diplomatic immunity. I suspect he'll have more aerosol canisters like the one we found in Newark, only larger."

"What if he's decided to use a point-source attack?"

She thought for a minute but shook her head.

"Too unpredictable," she said. "Look at Hong Kong and Newark. Precise targets, well planned, well executed. If Lo's right he'll try to infect a specific area."

She punched in another number.

"I'm calling Jake," she said. "We need help getting out of here."

It didn't take VII Corps long to respond.

After lift-off, Ellen reached Wilcox again on the dedicated frequency of his Skyhawk radiophone. She and Paul both wore helmets with a built-in wireless headset and microphone that filtered out the noise of the single rotor overhead as a light-lift Dolphin chopper sped them toward Camp Presidio.

"It's nearly midnight for you now," Ellen said. "What's the status at Newark? All the airport monitors here indicated delays."

"Terminals A and C actually reopened late this afternoon," the General said. "But it will take a few more days before air traffic returns to normal. We're keeping Terminal B and the hospital garage quarantined."

"There was nothing on broadcast news during our flight," Paul said.

"Good. That means the press blackout is still working. Practice drills are never that exciting for the media, but we'll probably have to lift the blackout tomorrow. Pressure's getting too intense."

Ellen told him about the aerial spray threat, Lo's knowledge of lettuce as the strategic target, their calls to the local ag companies and crop dusters, the negative results.

Paul gazed out the transparent cockpit at the sparkling lights of the peninsula below. The night was cloudless, cool and clear. The first few puffs of fog had begun to spiral up the towers of the Golden Gate bridge like balls of cotton.

He interrupted Ellen with a sudden question.

"General, when's the optimum time to do a line-source laydown?"

There was a momentary pause. The rhythmic thump of the rotor broke the silence.

"Early morning," Wilcox said. "Well before dawn, to avoid inversions. With even a light layer of warm air above the ground, the stuff won't settle but rises instead. That's also when you have less wind. More than five knots, it will just blow back in your face. Either way, you defeat your purpose so you always line-source pre-dawn."

Paul looked across at Ellen as he spoke to Jake.

"If Fu's flying himself, he'll go after midnight tomorrow morning. So we've got to call the three ag services back right away because we only asked about flights going out tonight and they took us literally."

Jake's response was stiff.

"Fu disappeared from the Chinese computers because he didn't want anyone in his government to know what he was doing. You guys could be in real danger. If Fu's planning a line-source laydown, he's probably armed and may not be alone."

○ 75 ○

When Colonel Fu rang for room service, they said it might take a while because the carts had to be inspected carefully both before and after leaving the kitchen. Security was tight. Standard procedure for visiting foreign delegations.

You can't be too careful, they reminded him. It was for his own good.

Forty-five minutes later, a maroon-clad bellhop shuffled out of the service elevator rolling a squeaky cart in front of him. A starched white tablecloth was draped over the sides. On top sat two bell-shaped sterling silver food warmers.

The Secret Service guard in front of Room 303 stopped the cart, raised the food covers and slipped a slice of bacon from one plate. As he chewed it, he checked under both tablecloth flaps. Done, he nodded and waved the cart by.

The bellhop pressed the gold-plated doorbell. An instant later the door opened.

When the cart pushed through, General Min grabbed it and pulled it quickly to one side. As the bellhop struggled to stay with it, Colonel Fu stepped out from behind the door and hit him with a stiff chop across the carotid artery at the side of his neck. Before he hit the floor, the general caught him under the arms to cushion the fall.

Dazed, the bellhop struggled until Fu sliced him again and he passed out. Min and Fu pulled his uniform off and bound his arms tightly behind his back. After gagging him with a hand towel, they stuffed him in a closet.

Colonel Fu swore under his breath.

The bellhop was Hispanic, not Chinese.

Now he had to hope that the Secret Service guards in the hall would be half-asleep and not notice the switch.

General Min told him to get going.

"Here are the keys to the American car," he said. "The driver carelessly left them above the visor."

Colonel Fu shook his head.

"Put them back," he said. "They'll have the official cars watched too closely after that demonstration at the airport today. It's too risky."

Snapping the maroon jacket shut, he pulled on the pillbox and tucked the elastic band under his chin.

"So how do you expect to -- "

"With this," Fu interrupted.

He held up a small identification card, the product of Lt. Kang's expert craft. It was the precise replica of a California driver's license.

"Remember, AgAir can't rent the plane without a photo ID," he said, tying his shoes. "And a car rental agency requires a valid driver's license. There is a company called Avis with a branch office two blocks away."

Fu held up a map and quickly stuffed it under his jacket. He rolled the two large canisters of aerosol spray in a large bath towel and placed them on the shelf under the cart. The folds in the starched tablecloth hid them completely.

He exchanged a smart salute with his commanding officer.

When he emerged from the room, he wheeled the empty cart lazily into the hall and kept his head down. He hurriedly flipped the silver food covers over. The Secret Service guard outside opened one eye and waved him by. The guard by the service elevator was fast asleep.

After an agonizing wait, Fu disappeared down the elevator, through the kitchen and out the door.

◦ **76** ◦

When Paul and Ellen reached Camp Presidio at the foot of Golden Gate Bridge, Jake Wilcox had radioed ahead and had a small office waiting for them. They were out of the light-lift Dolphin and on the phones in a heartbeat.

Ellen called York Aviation and Aerial Applicators while Paul tried AgAir.

Bingo.

Paul got through on the third call.

Customer service specialist Ted Simmons confirmed the job.

Technically, Simmons said, it wasn't tonight, it was Thursday morning, October 1st. Different month, different day, see? That's why it hadn't come up in our computer. Yup. One a.m. liftoff. Hell, no, he didn't say anything about spraying. Said he was going to take some aerial photos for a friend. Yeah, that's right. Name's Lo.

"Good night for it, too," Simmons said in a friendly voice. "Just had a little rain about an hour ago so the landscape will be shining real pretty in this clear sky. And with the Turbo Tractor's big fuel tank, he could be up there a good two-three hours."

Paul hung up.

He had the AgAir address and their GPS locator.

Ellen called Jake back and got clearance for a chopper to fly them to Salinas.

She looked at her watch.

It was nearly midnight. It would take them at least a half-hour. They had to hurry.

"Warshevsky got back to me late this afternoon," Jake said. "I gave him the full story, from Lo to the Air China tragedy at Newark. He's rushing to San Francisco himself tonight and has requested an urgent debrief for the President."

"I hope you didn't tell him where we've got Lo stashed."

"Negative. Warshevsky knows me well enough to realize that when I say I've got something, I have it."

"Good. Anything from Chronos-II?"

"Hang on," he said.

There was a short pause.

"The Pentagon's just sent up some satellite images by courier. I'll fax them out."

Paul gave him Sam Taylor's home number in Washington and asked him to get copies down to Taylor on the double.

Ellen glanced quickly at the satellite photos as they peeled out of the fax machine. She frowned at the crisp images of what looked like farm trucks, then folded and stuffed them in a jacket pocket as they ran out the door to the waiting Dolphin.

They threw an assortment of decon gear, respirator masks, double-sided bags, tarp and duct tape into the back of the light-lift chopper, just in case. As they lifted off, the short-range Dolphin groaned briefly under the extra load but angled forward and sped south.

Ellen took the faxed pages out of her jacket pocket and handed them to Paul

She wondered what help a collection of high-resolution color images of unfamiliar Chinese landscape and anonymous farm vehicles could possibly be to them now.

∘ 77 ∘

AgAir's conscientious customer service agent Ted Simmons loved the quiet hours of the night shift. It was the only time he could drive to and from an office in California without suffering the mind-numbing traffic, noise, and exhaust that polluted the state's clogged freeways.

He'd tried the Silicon Valley routine but wherever he worked and whatever he did, it was always the same: up at four a.m. for a two-hour drive bumper-to-bumper one-way on congested roads from a modest apartment he could barely afford in a state that prided itself on a non-stop real estate boom.

Every new start-up and IPO seemed to have multiple stock options and gave him some of their worthless paper as a bonus every year, but what good was that if you had no time to spend it? He held onto the options anyway and used them as placemats in his cramped kitchenette. Who knew? Someday they might actually be worth something.

Since he was already driving to the office and coming home in the dark, he figured, why not work nights? The AgAir hangar was situated less than a half-hour from his undersized apartment and he wouldn't have to fight the rush-hour maniacs who suffered from overblown greed and knee-jerk road rage. And his outstanding performance reflected his positive spirit.

After his first year of on-time execution without a single day lost to sickness or unexcused absence, AgAir gave him a framed certificate as Employee of the Year and a generous raise. He didn't use the award as a placemat this time but hung it proudly on the wall of his tiny living room for all his friends to see.

Colonel Fu Barxu eyed the AgAir customer service agent nervously as he pocketed the forged pilot's license and phony California ID. He'd left the pillbox cap and the spray canisters in the rental car, so when Ted Simmons had noticed his maroon uniform he naturally asked if he had a Chinese customer who was celebrating that night.

Fu shrugged his shoulders.

"You could say that."

"You're paying cash, right, Mr. Lo?" Simmons asked.

He reached down and snapped the fan-fold invoice off the printer.

"Yes, in advance," Fu said.

He reached into a pocket and withdrew an envelope.

"Remember, you got to stay below a thousand feet or the FAA will give my boss hell about visual flight rules."

Fu's eyes narrowed as he looked up.

"You said no VFR."

"*If* you stay low."

"Two hundred feet low enough?"

"Works for me. But where's your camera? I thought you were taking the Tractor up for pictures."

Fu paused.

"It's in the car."

He peeled off a sheaf of bills and handed them across the counter.

Simmons counted them twice and tore off a receipt.

As Fu turned to leave, the conscientious customer service agent smiled.

"Oh, I almost forgot," he said. "A friend of yours rang a little earlier, said he was just calling to confirm your flight."

His tone was casual, a by-the-way recollection.

Fu stopped and spun around.

Without saying another word, he whipped out a tiny Tokarev pistol and fired one 7.62mm slug right between Ted Simmons's proud blue eyes.

○ **78** ○

As they bounced in the choppy air over the endless agricultural land above Salinas, Paul gazed down at the broad expanse of slick terrain that glistened in the moonlight after the evening rain. It looked like a moonscape in the silken light, acre after acre rippling with colorless lettuce heads.

Soon they could see the AgAir landing field lights and the Dolphin angled down. Ellen jabbed Paul with her elbow.

"There's someone! Under the wing of that plane. See?"

Paul craned his neck and saw a lone figure stooped under the wing of a Sawyer single-engine Turbo Tractor in the soft glow of the parallel runway lights.

Colonel Fu looked up and froze when he heard the unmistakable thwock of a helicopter rotor. Kneeling, he took aim and fired two quick shots from the Tokarev.

One bullet nicked the Dolphin's rotor. The chopper pilot pulled away in an evasive maneuver and throttled out to gain altitude.

Fu quickly scrambled aboard the Turbo Tractor, pulled on his rebreather mask, revved the propeller and taxied full-throttle down the runway with the canopy open. As the chopper tried to hover behind him, he peered over his shoulder and fired again.

One slug glanced off the olive fuselage, the other punched a hole in the Plexiglas cockpit. The pilot put one hand on the trigger button of his machine gun and arched around to bring Fu's plane into target range.

"Don't!" Ellen shouted. "It's too dangerous! You may detonate the virus if you hit either one of those canisters."

She climbed into the storage area behind Paul. Seconds later, she emerged with a sheet of heavy tarpaulin and rebuckled her seatbelt.

"Come at him again from the back," she yelled. "Then swoop down."

Paul reached forward for the tarp.

"Get back," he said. "Let me do it."

"No, you use that," she said.

She pointed overhead and he unsnapped a .30 caliber rifle with a telescopic sight.

"If you get a clear shot, take him out."

The Dolphin circled back and trailed the Turbo Tractor as it jockeyed into takeoff position. They could hear the familiar high-pitched whine of a propeller as the small single-engine plane powered up for takeoff.

When the crop duster began moving down the runway, the Dolphin dropped down quickly from above and pulled even with it. Paul yanked hard on his seatbelt to tighten it and kicked back the Plexiglas door. He pumped a cartridge into the chamber of the high-powered rifle and brought the gun butt to his shoulder.

Just as the Turbo Tractor was about to lift off, the chopper cut sharply across the nose of the small plane. Ellen leaned out and dropped the heavy tarp onto the spinning propeller.

The Dolphin veered up and away as the propeller caught the tarpaulin and tore it to shreds. It jammed the blade and flipped the light plane onto its back as if it had hit a deep pothole on the runway. The three of them watched as it scraped to a stop in a shower of sparks.

Upside down, Fu quickly unbuckled his seatbelt and scrambled out from under the plane. Momentarily dazed, he crouched on one knee, took aim, and began firing again.

The chopper pilot dropped abruptly and rocked the helicopter from side to side in a diversionary tactic to avoid being hit. He gained altitude and leveled off to give Cerrutti a stationary target.

Colonel Fu paused to reload.

As Fu pulled out a spare clip and snapped it into his Tokarev pistol, Paul closed one eye, stared through the magnifying scope of the rifle with the other, exhaled slowly and fired two crisp shots through the starched neck of the Pacific Club's maroon jacket with the ash-gray chevrons on each sleeve.

When he saw Colonel Fu slump to the ground, the Dolphin pilot looped back and down to land a safe distance away. Paul leaped from the chopper and went to his knees, rifle ready. Ellen unbuckled but stayed aboard. They all stared at the motionless form in the distance as the pilot shut down the rotor.

Paul rose slowly and with every ounce of caution he'd been taught to use, he approached the upside-down Turbo Tractor in a crouch. He counted silently to thirty. When he saw no movement he rose and started toward the plane again.

"Paul!" Ellen screamed.

Suddenly a hand reached toward one of the upended canisters.

As Fu tried to twist the cylinder loose, Paul Cerrutti pulled the rifle to his shoulder and emptied the chamber of the semi-automatic into the Colonel's chest.

Fu Barxu crumpled lifeless to the tarmac.

Quickly, Ellen ran to the flipped propeller plane. She detached the two heavy canisters from what was now the topside of the wings and carried them gingerly, one-by-one, to the waiting Dolphin where she sealed them in a double-sided black plastic body bag for decontamination later.

She walked slowly back to the Turbo Tractor and looked down at the dead military officer, nudging him with her foot. His body rolled over and lay face-up.

She unfastened his facemask and gasped when she saw the unmistakable likeness of Lo Fengbu. It was a face sculpted in soft plastic with features nearly identical to those of the famous dissident whose life she had saved just days before.

Reaching down, she tugged on the plastic skin until the disguise tore loose, revealing the sinister face of Colonel Fu. Ellen looked away as she pulled a section of the torn tarp over his upper torso to cover his body.

Paul was on the phone to the Salinas police. When they confirmed they were on their way, he pulled out his 9mm Glock and ran to the hangar. As soon as he saw the solitary body in a crimson pool behind the wooden counter, he holstered the pistol. There was nothing more anyone could do there.

Back outside Paul helped the pilot load the Colonel's dead body into another heavy-duty bag and into the helicopter as the red-and-blue flashing lights of a Salinas patrol car appeared on the runway. Paul identified himself and told the local cops what they'd find inside.

Ellen and Paul climbed into the chopper as the pilot restarted the rotor. When it lifted and began heading north, Ellen radioed Jake Wilcox.

"You were right," she said into the wireless headset. "He was armed, and you said he might not be alone. We're heading for the Pacific Club now. Can you find out what room they gave General Min and get a small team to meet us there? This isn't over yet."

"Will do," Jake said. "I'll arrange a platoon from the Presidio and call Warshevsky. You don't want the Secret Service firing at you when you arrive."

When she switched off, Paul raised Sam Taylor in Washington.

"Slam dunk this time, Paul," Taylor said. "Nobody ever firewalls a DMV computer, anywhere in the world. The plate numbers for those vehicles in the Chronos-II scans belong to Chinese Army trucks, assigned to your Colonel Fu. GPS coordinates put the location squarely in southern Jiangxi province."

A half-hour later, knowing where to go, four heavily armed soldiers from VII Corps raced up the stairs toward Room 303. The platoon leader fired a burst into the door lock and quickly stepped aside as two enlisted men fell to the floor, bodies down, guns up.

General Min Taibao was ready and waiting, his pistol held waist-high as soon as he heard the commotion outside. The unmistakable sound of a helicopter rotor had alerted him that something had gone terribly wrong with his protégé's plan.

But he hadn't expected the first two intruders to crawl forward on the floor, so he fired chest-high in the dark. His shots flew left and right, some smacking into the wall, some flying through the open door.

The American M-15 automatics chattered and a quick burst hit Min in the left arm and shoulder. A standard issue flash-and-bang flare sailed through the doorway and exploded in the room.

Min was momentarily stunned, frozen in the bright light and sprawled across a chair, too weak to retaliate. One of the soldiers trained his weapon on the Chinese general while the other disarmed him and flicked the room lights on.

A Sergeant spoke hurriedly into a handset. Room 303 was secure.

Moments later, President Jiang Zemin appeared in the doorway in a maroon bathrobe and slippers, surrounded by security guards. It was 2:23 in the morning.

He started toward the General but the guards held him back.

"Traitor," Jiang hissed. "You can never inherit power by stealing the mandate of heaven."

"You and the pathetic *fengpai* are the real traitors," Min said weakly. "You have dishonored the nation's mandate and are unfit to govern."

"The Chinese people will determine that," Jiang said. "Not a criminal in our armed forces. You will reveal the others in Beijing behind this outrage."

"Rubbish. You know you can never put wrapping paper around a burning fire. You have no idea how fast our country is changing. Because of you, our traditional values are in danger of being lost."

President Jiang stiffened.

"China will never revert to the chaos of its past. We face different challenges now."

The Presidio team took General Min into custody. Through a headset, the platoon leader radioed for a medic and stretcher.

With Paul at her side, Ellen emerged from behind the cordon of guards in animated discussion with one of the President's aides as his security guards escorted the Chinese leader back into the hallway.

Turning to the President, his aide quickly explained Ellen's work in Hong Kong and Newark.

President Jiang was wide-awake now, his dark eyes like small moons as he listened.

"It seems China may forever be in your debt, young lady," Jiang Zemin said softly.

"Forever is a long time, Mr. President," Ellen said with a slight bow. "Our two cultures must find a way to avoid conflict and coexist peacefully. Otherwise, we risk the terrible tragedy of another cold war with all its negative consequences."

Paul handed her the satellite images.

"These are high-resolution photos of the Colonel's secret bioweapons factory in Jiangxi province," she said. "Lo Fengbu has confirmed that this covert laboratory is the source of the killer virus. It must be destroyed. Mr. Lo also told us that the Jiangxi virus was genetically engineered for China by a Russian scientist named Boris Lukanov. If others were involved, possibly also Russian, they must be apprehended as well."

President Jiang stared at the digital images for a long minute. Then he muttered a string of rapid-fire Mandarin to his aide, who disappeared with a shuffle down the hall.

"We have a stubborn faction of extremists in China that makes my job very difficult," he said. "General Li is still recuperating in Tianjin, but his staff will give your authorities whatever help they need."

"Thank you, Mr. President," Ellen said quietly. "But China is not alone. You know we have our share of extremists in this country, too."

The head of China's Politburo and the diminutive American disease detective stood face to face, their somber eyes inches apart.

"Perhaps," he said. "But I venture to say that no one in your military would ever commit such a brazen and cowardly act. Throughout our history, undying devotion to provincial and regional alliances has made national unity difficult and visionary leadership practically impossible. This is China's past and future nightmare."

"Yes, but I'm afraid more conflict between major civilizations is inevitable in this century," Ellen said. "Including yours and mine. Not even mature democracies know how to change human nature."

President Jiang smiled.

"The Master once wrote, there are three things required of good government. Sufficient food, sufficient weapons and -- "

"The trust of the people," Ellen said, completing the ancient adage. "It's a challenge for every government, not just for China."

Fascinated now, the senior leader shuffled closer to her.

"So tell me, Dr. Chou," he whispered. "Where do you have the dissident, our Lo Fengbu?"

Ellen paused briefly before responding. She glanced up at Paul.

"We may be able to give you that information providing we have firm assurances from your government -- in writing -- that China will agree to his request for asylum in this country after he recovers."

The President of China blinked.

He wasn't prepared for such an ultimatum from an American, least of all from a woman. But his sense of obligation and protocol took precedence.

"I will discuss this with your President later today," he said. "I trust we may be able to execute the necessary papers during our meeting."

She stepped back as the aging Chinese leader bowed briefly and padded toward the elevator, flanked by his security guards.

As he stepped into the car, a short, heavy-set pear-faced man in a dark gray serge suit stepped out, followed by a man Ellen recognized instantly as Department of State Deputy Secretary Brian Russell.

Ellen nervously wiped her sweaty palms on her jeans and stiffened as she prepared for another high-level altercation.

The stout White House advisor approached Ellen and Paul.

"Henry Warshevsky," he said, introducing himself.

They shook hands.

The NSA specialist had a broad forehead that tapered to a narrow chin. He had a bald pate with thick, close-cropped curly black hair on each side of his head that gave him a deceptively Amish look. But a resonant voice dispelled any doubts of softness.

"The President has asked me to convey his gratitude and appreciation to you, Dr. Chou," he said. "He was not aware that others so close to him had stepped over the line and asks that you accept his personal apology by attending our State dinner tomorrow -- tonight, rather -- as his guest of honor."

Humiliated, Russell stood to Warshevsky's rear, hands behind his back and head down, like a student caught cheating on a final exam.

"Thank you, Dr. Warshevsky. Coming from you, I have no doubt his invitation is sincere."

She cast a quick glance at Russell.

"But I'm sure my presence would be an embarrassment to others on his team. I'm also pretty sure I haven't heard the last of this from them, either. They may be even more upset when they learn about what happened here tonight."

"You have my personal assurance that this incident will go no further," Warshevsky said. "I've already discussed it in detail with General Wilcox, who concurs."

"Then please tell the President that I'm very honored," she said, meeting his glance head-on. "But I also hope he'll understand and accept my decision to decline."

There was a long silence. Warshevsky had not anticipated a turn-down.

"Well, the President will be sorry to hear that," he said. "And personally, I am too. But the general has ordered a full debrief of this affair at the White House next week and I insist that you be present at the President's behest."

"Of course," she said. "And I think it would be wise to include LeRoy Harper, given the budget beating the CDC took on the Hill this week. The Center's going to need a little help."

"Consider it done."

They shook hands again and the two Washington officials departed.

Paul pulled Ellen to him and she collapsed, exhausted, in his arms.

"I'm proud of what you said, Ellie.   But you ought to be thinking about your career."

She looked up at him and smiled as she wrapped her arms around his neck.

"I am," she said.   "But I have a promise to keep first, don't forget."

They disappeared down the hall, past the remaining soldiers, and into the elevator.

○ Epilogue ○

Chinese New Year's fell on a Friday the following February, when the sun sat low and squat in a clear blue sky above Manhattan. It was a bitter cold day, calm and still.

Wisps of steam curled lazily from the rooftops of tall office buildings and high-rise apartment towers, drifting into the quiet air. Traffic in Chinatown stalled as a colorful chain of costumed children snaked its way through the crowded streets in the guise of a huge dragon under the chatter and smoke of exploding firecrackers.

Inside, insulated from the clamor outdoors, Ellen sat next to Lo Fengbu around a small table in a private dining room at the Golden Orchid, a modest family-run Hunan restaurant at the south end of Mott Street. They drained small thimbles of *dàojiu* in a toast to the Year of the Tiger.

She pushed a plateful of spicy *mabo* tofu toward him and grinned when he raised his arms in defense.

"Enough!" he laughed. "More would be too much."

The table overflowed with a potpourri of familiar delicacies: deep-fried *gyozu*, *mujiu* pork, chili-pepper chicken with almonds, steamed *bao* stuffed with shrimp, braised carp with mushrooms and bamboo, stir-fried crabmeat with snow peas and eggplant, *bokchoi* cabbage in oyster sauce, barbecued spareribs, steamed rice.

A trio of incense sticks smoldered at the center of table, giving off the perfumed aroma of joss.

Their friends joined the next toast as another round of rice wine went down. Paul flanked Ellen, and Jonathan Feldman sat across from them. Sandy McDermott was there, and Sam Taylor, and Jane Malloy from USAMRIID, in mufti.

They shouted *Happy New Year* in various versions of broken Mandarin as a young waiter with a tiger's tail pinned to the rear of his starched jacket cleared the table. He laughed, shaking his head.

"My life has changed so much," Lo said, nodding deferentially to Ellen. "Six months ago, I was a captive with no future. After convalescing in the fall, I now have work and a place to belong, thanks to you. But I miss Chen Sun terribly. She still lives in my heart."

"She was a bright spirit for all of us," Ellen said. "And we will argue about who should thank whom for the rest of our lives. New York University is a good home for you. Your place is in the city."

Lo Fengbu smiled as he refilled her small cup.

"Your contacts were most helpful," he said. "I worry about Beijing since I can't go back, though I'm confident my parents can live without worry since the Jiangxi case received so much notoriety. They will be safe. But this wasn't the first time the Army has threatened China's leaders and I fear it won't be the last. The curse of our past always seems to haunt our future."

"May we hope good fortune comes to China," Ellen said.

She raised her glass in Lo's honor.

"As it has come to you."

McDermott downed a final thimbleful of wine and slapped the tiny glass upside down on the table.

She was done.

"Come on, Ellie," she said. "Tell us you're not actually serious about leaving. You can't be."

Ellen draped an arm around Paul's shoulders.

"But I am," she said. "My biological clock is ticking, so I'm either going to teach or do research now. One way or the other, I plan to stick around one place for a while."

She gave Paul a squeeze.

"And stay out of airplanes for good."

The End

Selected Glossary & Acronyms

Jiangxi   Province in southern China (pronounced *John-zee*).
Guangdong   Province in southern China (*Gwang-dong*).
Ellen Chou   The CDC's crack disease detective (*Ellen Joe*).
Fu Barxu   Ellen's adversary; a rogue Colonel in the PLA (*Fu Bar-zhu*).

fengpai   "Wind faction" in Chinese politics (*fung-pie*).
laogai   Chinese prison/labor camps (*laow-guy*).
guanxi   Network of personal contacts (*gwan-zhi*).

snakeheads   covert entrepreneurs who smuggle illegal immigrants
                  out of China, for a substantial fee, in U. S. dollars

CDC   Centers for Disease Control and Prevention
FBI   Federal Bureau of Investigation
CIA   Central Intelligence Agency
USAMRIID   United States Army Medical Research Institute for
                  Infectious Diseases, Fort Detrick, Maryland

ELISA   Enzyme-Linked Immuno-Sorbent Assay
PCR   Polymerase Chain Reaction
EM   Electron Microscope
BT   Bioterrorism

DAF   Department of Agriculture & Fisheries, Hong Kong
DOH   Department of Health
PLA   People's Liberation Army of China
PSB   Public Security Bureau, China's national police

NSA   National Security Agency
ER   Early Response; Emergency Room
URI   Upper Respiratory Infection

Hemagglutinin A glycoprotein in the form of a microscopic "spike"
               that clings to the surface of a virus; acts like radar and
               finds a site where the virus can attach to a host cell to
               initiate infection and reproduction. The "H" spike.

Neuraminidase The "N" spike; a glycoprotein resembling a tiny
               sledgehammer that coats a slimy substance on the
               external surface of a host cell to facilitate the release of
               millions of mature viruses after reproduction.

About the Author

Steven Schlossstein is a well-known author, international strategist and business executive, with extensive experience in the Far East and European business and financial markets. Since 1982, as founder and CEO of SBS Associates, Inc., he has designed, negotiated, and implemented numerous strategic assignments for American corporations in the Far East. From 1969 to 1982, Mr. Schlossstein was with J. P. Morgan & Co. of New York, with assignments in New York, Hong Kong, Tokyo, and Düsseldorf. From 1980 to 1982, as vice president of Morgan's East Asia merger and acquisition unit, he achieved some of the first acquisitions by Japanese firms in the American market at that time. He has also lived and worked in Singapore and Paris.

The Jiangxi Virus is Mr. Schlossstein's sixth book. He wrote the highly acclaimed *The End of the American Century* and *Trade War* ("Greed, Power, and Industrial Policy on Opposite Sides of the Pacific"), an American Library Association "Best Business Book" of 1984 and a best seller in the Japanese edition. He has written two previous novels dealing with the business environment and social change in Japan: *Kensei* ("The Sword Master," 1983), a best seller in the Avon paperback edition, and *Yakuza* ("The Japanese Godfather," 1990). He also wrote *Asia's New Little Dragons* ("The Dynamic Emergence of Indonesia, Thailand, and Malaysia," 1992), a provocative account of Southeast Asia's rise to economic power.

He has two more novels forthcoming: a cyberspace thriller and dark comedy set in New York City that deals with the Russian Mafia and Internet fraud titled *crime.com* (spring 2003), and *Belleville*, a tongue-in-cheek look at the impact of the aging process on America's baby boomers (2005). His columns and articles have appeared in *The Los Angeles Times*, *The Dallas Morning News*, *The Trenton Times*, *Business Tokyo*, and *International Economy*. He has been profiled in *Fortune* magazine and *The New York Times*. A frequent public speaker, he is represented by Keppler Associates of Washington, D. C., and as an author by Phenix & Phenix Literary Publicists of Austin, Texas.

Born in Houston and reared in Dallas, Mr. Schlossstein received his B.A. in history and philosophy from Austin College in 1963; he was its distinguished alumnus in 1990. He has a Master's degree in Japanese history from the University of Hawaii and a business degree from the Business School of Columbia University in New York. He speaks and reads fluent Japanese, French, and German, and lives and works in Princeton, New Jersey, with his wife and their two adopted Korean children. He plays competitive tennis on a regular basis, swims, and has been known to strike an occasional golf ball if temporarily bereft of reason or if no one is around to watch.